The
Ealing Hippies

A Trip through the Swinging 60s

David Gale

DAVID GALE

ISBN: 9798713325374

This book was previously published as The Life and Times of Eric Grimes, © 2016

Author's Note

Had it not been for the Peter Sellers film, I may have titled the book *Being There*. This was my primary goal: to transport the reader back to a magical time when in our alleged naivety, all things seemed possible. The upshot of this spiritual liberation was an explosion of unbridled creativity, the reverberations of which can be felt to this day.

Central to the book is Eric's *coming-of-age* story, set against the backdrop of the sixties decade. The writer in me wanted to evoke the atmosphere of that time. Through the prism of the hippie dream, the politician and the environmentalist insisted upon voicing a few timely reminders. Shrugging and pointing out the obvious, the historian and the thrill-seeker agreed that the work should be laced with a sprinkling of sex, drugs and music. After all, this was the sixties.

Except for the old house on Hanger Hill, the places in Ealing and central London exist, or did in the sixties. The hotel on Eel Pie Island was real, as were the Hyde Park concerts, Kensington Market, etc.

I know, because I was there.

Contents

	AUTHOR'S NOTE	1
1	JANUARY 1969	5
2	THE JAZZMEN	6
3	SKEGNESS	18
4	ZIMMY	36
5	UP ON THE ROOF	49
6	ONE FOOT ON THE PLATFORM	64
7	REG	77
8	THE QUARTET AND THE BARBERSHOP	81
9	THE QUEEN OF THE SUBURBS	94
10	THE PICNIC AND THE POET	107
11	HELP!	117
12	AUTUMN LEAVES	128
13	RAPIER 33	143
14	GRANNY TAKES A TRIP	158
15	BOBBY, MARTIN AND GEOFF	166

16	EVERY COLOUR THERE IS	180
17	THE EALING HIPPIES	196
18	FLOWER POWER	214
19	THE SUMMER OF LOVE	232
20	THE RED SWING	249
21	RAINBOW	273
22	THE CHALK MAN	288
23	HAPPINESS STAN	303
24	A SAUCERFUL OF SECRETS	315
25	THIS WAS WINTER 1960	329
26	THE MIDNIGHT LAMP	343
27	THE LULU SHOW	348
28	THE BEGINNING OF THE END	353
29	THE SUMMER OF '69	364
30	THE ISLE OF WIGHT	379
31	NO CAKES PLEASE	392
32	TEN TO MIDNIGHT	405

1

January 1969

Eric knew he was dreaming. The angel above the coffee table may not have seemed entirely strange, but flying up there with him certainly was. It was good, though – really good.

Paul sat at a harpsichord dressed in his blue Sgt Pepper gear. A box of easy-mix plaster stood on the keyboard.

It's getting better by the second, Eric thought, smiling at the angel who was no longer there. Waking, sleeping, dreaming; this was all three at once. Maybe it was what the Beatles did in India. *Make something happen!*

It was a gloomy January morning, but Eric painted a blue summer sky. Colours flowed from his brush. The record shop by Ealing Broadway Station displayed four LP covers. One was round; that had to be the Small Faces. The tiny paint dots depicting the other three albums were slapdash attempts at Sgt Pepper, Disraeli Gears and Axis: Bold as Love. *Close enough, the colours are about right,* thought Eric.

The dream was still fresh in his mind, and he could have chosen any number of images, so why settle on something so ordinary? Eric had his reasons. And he had visualised the scene from outside himself, making it anything but ordinary for him. Pattie would have called it astral projection.

The zebra crossing was done, and the perspective looked okay. All that remained to be painted were the figures. This was the tricky part. Pretty Pattie appeared gawky, and her arm looked like a cup handle. *I'll fix her later,* Eric told himself, though he never did.

'Oh!'

Eric jumped.

'I see you put me in my orange dress.'

The artist turned, smiling at the young woman behind his chair. 'It's the dress you were wearing in my dream.'

2

The Jazzmen

1960

Bill Grimes cussed under his breath as for the third time that Saturday morning, the greasy spanner slipped from his grasp and fell clattering through the engine.

'I'll get it, Dad!' young Eric offered enthusiastically.

'Mind your head.'

'Okay,' murmured the eight-year-old boy, straining as he stretched beneath the old Standard 10. 'Got it!' he called, inching the spanner towards him with his fingertips and banging his cranium on the chassis.

An hour later, the dark-blue Standard was purring like a contented kitten.

'Done,' declared Bill. He stepped back, standing next to his son on the garden path and admiring the outmoded car with its old-fashioned sweeping wings. 'You don't see many like that on the road nowadays. Not with yellow wheels, anyway.'

Reg the postman laughed when he saw the yellow-painted hubcaps, but Bill thought they looked grand. So did Eric.

The two mechanics looked down, drawn by a movement on the path. An uncommonly large iridescent beetle was making its way up the crazy-paving towards the open front door. They stared at the armoured insect noting its rapid progress and unwavering direction.

'Better step on it,' suggested Bill.

'Me?'

'You've got your Wellingtons on. We don't want it in the house, do we?'

The fair-haired boy eyed the advancing beetle, reluctantly contemplating his father's proposal. In a few seconds, the would-be intruder would reach the threshold.

'Go on!' urged Bill.

Eric brought the sole of his rubber welly down on the giant insect. The beetle's brittle wing-covers fractured, the loud *crunch* shocking even his father. The boy recoiled, stumbling back into his dad's arms. His wide eyes fixed on the dead insect's broken body, its creamy-yellow innards spattered grotesquely on the path.

That lunchtime, Eric managed his chips and baked beans, but the fried egg remained untouched. A brief look from Bill was sufficient to dispel his wife's query before it escaped her lips.

William and Mary Grimes were small in height and stature, though it would be several years before young Eric would fully appreciate the fact. In the eight-year-old's eyes, his dad, though prematurely balding and marginally blind, was the man who knew everything and could fix anything.

When Mary inherited the terraced house in West Ealing from her grandmother, Bill set to work on their new home, epitomising the DIY attitude of the time. Victorian was out, and the Atomic Age was in. Ornate fireplaces were removed, to be replaced by electric heating appliances. Worktops, once bare wood, were overlaid with modern Formica. Plastic appeared on kitchen shelves where previously had stood china and glass. Soon every door in the house had an opaque glass panel inserted to illuminate the Edwardian interior.

Eric spent many hours at his father's side, watching and learning.

'How do you know that?' the curious boy would ask.

'Because I'm clever', his dad would answer, affirming Eric's belief in his mentor.

'Might as well forget it!' the lad said when confronted by a seemingly impossible task.

'Where there's a will there's a way', the father replied, proceeding to demonstrate that there was indeed a way.

Mary Ann Grimes, nee: Mary Ann Winton-Jones, prided herself in her domestic role as wife and mother. When he pictured her in those times, Eric saw his mother wearing a sky-blue chiffon headscarf tied neatly beneath her chin, her dark-brown hair accentuating a pale English complexion. Mary had long been a keen tennis player, known for her infamous spin serve, and she had won many competitions at the local sports club in Hanwell. Sitting on the grass at his father's feet, young Eric often found himself watching from the sideline during the women's matches. Mary regularly brought out a tin of Duraglit to polish her bounty of silver trophies, though they were never on display. Bill believed his wife to be blessed with perfect humility.

Eric amassed sunny memories of trips to central London with his mum during school holidays. Together they would travel on the tube from Northfield Station to destinations in the city. Occasionally they would use a *Red Rover*, an all-day combined bus and tube ticket provided by London Transport for outings such as these. Wonderful, colourful days were spent visiting historic landmarks, shops and buildings. South Kensington, with its fabulous Victorian museums, was a favourite stop. The Natural History and Science museums would feature prominently in Eric's future recollections. The boy and his mother saw the Tower of London, Trafalgar Square, the Houses of Parliament, Buckingham Palace, and walked together by the Thames and through Hyde Park. Eric climbed the Monument's steps in Pudding Lane, and scaled a ladder to the gold ball's interior at the very top of Saint Paul's Cathedral. A packed lunch saw them through the day. Cheese and tomato sandwiches made with white bread seemed to taste better by the waters of the Serpentine. The swans enjoyed them, too. Eric came to love London. The capital was less populated in those times, and he had an excellent guide. In later years, these outings with his mother would feature prominently among Eric's most treasured memories.

With the family car up and running, the Saturday afternoon shopping trip to West Ealing could go ahead as planned. Sunlight broke through the ceiling of grey clouds as Eric assumed his place on the back seat. He half-turned, giving the nodding dog on the rear shelf a tap on the head. Eric produced a handkerchief, blew his nose and farted. His father gave the boy a blank look as he reversed out of the front garden. 'Beans,' his wife said quietly to the windscreen.

Bill parked the old Standard in Canberra Road, less than a hundred yards from the high street. The big shops: Woolworths, British Home Stores, Marks & Spencer's, were just a minute's walk from the car. In 1960, convenient parking was often possible, even on a Saturday.

Turning left at Burton's tailors, the Grimes family entered the busy main road, and Bill reached down, taking his son's hand.

'Da-ad,' whined the squirming boy, 'I'm eight years old!'

'He's eight years old,' echoed Mary, smiling despairingly at her husband.

Bill released the boy's small hand. 'All right, but don't go running off.'

The high street was crowded with Saturday afternoon shoppers, many comprising similar family groups to their own. The first stop was Shelshear's hardware shop. Bill selected a plastic bag containing six tap washers, handing over one shilling and sixpence to the brown-coated assistant.

'One-and-six for half-a-dozen bloody washers!' grumbled Bill.

'Thruppence each,' Mary replied quick as a flash. 'They've got to make a profit. *And don't swear,*' she whispered.

Next was *Marks & Sparks*, pure-white St Michael underwear for all the family. Mary never considered purchasing any other brand. The boys maintained a respectable distance while mother perused the knicker selection. Frustratingly for Eric and his dad, the underwear shopping was extended due to a brief downpour. The family had dressed for rain, though Eric's soiled Wellington's stood back at home in the porch.

Nearly an hour later, having walked the entire length and both sides of the high street, the three shoppers sat together in Joe Lyons' coffee shop. Mary's red polythene shopping basket was full. Bill munched a current bun while Eric slurped room temperature Coca-Cola through two straws.

'Light bulb,' said Mary, holding her pale-green coffee mug between her fingertips and staring into nowhere through the spiralling steam. 'Let's pop to Woolies before we go.'

Eric groaned, then his face lit up, 'Can we look at the toys?'

'He's been very goo –'

'Yes, we can look,' interrupted Mary, 'but we're not buying any toys today.'

At the back end of Woolworths, Bill glanced at his watch. It was nearly 5:15; the store would be closing soon. He watched his wife patiently absorbing Eric's boyish enthusiasm. First, the Meccano kits had caught his attention, then the Hornby train sets. Now their son stood anchored to a glass display case, riveted by a line-up of Dinky cars. Bill wouldn't mind one or two of those himself. It was just as well Mary was in charge, or impulse may get the better of him. Bill picked up a box from the counter he had been leaning on. The picture showed a shallow square dish with straps attached. The top half of the glass was tinted blue, and the bottom half emerald-green. Colour television! Now *that* was interesting...

The late-autumn nights were drawing in and yellow light from the closing shops spilt onto the wet pavement. As the customers filed out of Woolworths, Mary squatted in front of her son. Licking the corner of her handkerchief, she wiped a smudge from his cheek.

'Ee-ew,' protested the boy, screwing up his face and gazing at the tailoring shop across the street.

'You know what they say,' said his dad. 'Cleanliness is next to godliness.'

'That's what they say,' affirmed his mother.

Eric saw two tall men dancing like monkeys in the office above Burton's and assumed the prancing silhouettes to be the *they* that his parents were referring to.

Twenty minutes later, the family were back at home watching Dixon of Dock Green on the nine-inch television in the corner of the living room.

1963

Following his demob at the end of World War II, Bill Grimes found work at a factory in Perivale, manufacturing grindstones. The job was mundane, but Bill, a socialist at heart, was able to find reward in even the most menial task.

At the start of 1963, news of the factory's imminent closure saw Bill facing redundancy. In keeping with the spirit of the time, efforts were made by the failing company to find alternative employment for their staff. So it was that Bill, Mary and Eric found themselves driving north up the recently completed M1 to the new town of Welling Garden City. Recoiling at the concrete town, Mary voiced her opinion unequivocally. The family would be staying in Ealing.

*

In an alcove next to the fireplace, a highly polished long wooden box stood on skinny conical legs: the then ubiquitous radiogram. The radio received occasional use, but Eric played the hell out of the record deck. In recent years, he had shared an interest in Cliff Richard's music with his mother. Mary liked Cliff, but Eric was more taken by his backing group, the Shadows: in particular, the sound and style of the electric guitar.

Although he still played the records regularly, Cliff and the Shadows had begun to pale. A new group had emerged from Liverpool who went by the unusual name of the Beatles.

On a crisp winter morning in February 1963, Eric had accompanied his mother on a shopping trip to West Ealing. He was eleven years old and no longer required to remain at her side, so when he found himself in British Home Stores, Eric chose to wander off. Although the large store sold mostly clothing, it had a record department that provided music for the shoppers. The records being played were the usual mix of Frank Ifield, Cliff, *Island of Dreams* by the Springfields. And then... A stunning sound that Eric had never heard before came shooting across the sock counter, literally stopping him in his tracks. The song was *Please Please Me* by the Beatles. Eric stood rooted to the spot. There was electric energy in the sound: searing vocal harmonies that seemed to slice through the air, hitting him between the ears and connecting with something at the very heart of his being. From that moment, Eric was a Beatles fanatic; their music and influence would reverberate throughout his life.

*

A confirmed bachelor, Reg Proctor filled his days busily maintaining two separate jobs. Rising at the crack of dawn, the fifty-two-year-old ex-serviceman spent his mornings delivering the Royal Mail and passing the time of day with the locals. The tall postman boasted a salt-and-pepper thatch which stuck out like straw from beneath his GPO hat. Below his beaky nose, Reg sported a bushy moustache to match. Residents often heard the postman's tuneful whistling prior to a rattle in the letterbox.

Though generally a gregarious man, when asked about his second job, Reg would become secretive. *'Government',* he would say, winking and tapping the side of his nose with a long bony forefinger. What Reg got up to in the afternoons, no one seemed to know. Nor did they really care.

It was springtime in the suburbs; buds were bursting, and the sun was shining. Reg cycled happily along Mattock Lane on his way home for lunch after finishing his morning rounds. That sunny day he took a detour, wheeling his trusty old bike through Walpole Park, where he bumped into Mrs Hampton by the duck pond. For the third time in as many hours, the postman spoke at great length about the numerous times he had chatted to Dusty Springfield.

Guiding his bike through the park gates, Reg remounted. He barely registered the metallic *click* as he pushed down on the pedals. Approaching King Edward's, the postman whistled a jazzy rendition of *Island of Dreams*, blissfully unaware that he would shortly be visiting the hospital's casualty department.

Eric rounded the corner by St John's Church in time to witness the bizarre accident. Reg shouted (something like) 'Ee-yurrr!' as the welded repair on the crossbar failed. The handlebars twisted right, while the saddle twisted left. The postman watched as the kerb leapt up and hit him, his hat bouncing and rolling across the pavement.

Eric reached the prostrate postman at the same time as two passing nurses. Lending extra drama to the story that Reg would recount many times in his local pub, a couple of porters arrived to stretcher him into Casualty.

'I'll get my dad to pick up your bike,' Eric told the horizontal postman as they carried him past the boy.

*

For the past couple of years, and to his parents' dismay, Eric had been completely vegetarian, meaning school dinners were a thing of the past. At home every weekday lunchtime, the boy would find ten or fifteen minutes to play his guitar.

The budding musician had a moment ago discovered the mystical melancholic beauty of the E Minor chord: an easy one to play, and a tantalising departure from the three or four majors he had memorised, if not yet mastered.

Eric played the E Minor repeatedly, juxtaposing it alongside the G, C and D that he already knew. The new chord added emotional depth, recalling a seminal moment years before when he had stood in a dark hallway, listening at his Uncle Bob's door. Bob owned a portable record player, and one song regularly emanated from his room: *Freight Train* by the Chas McDevitt Skiffle Group. As the old folk song ingrained itself in Eric's young mind, he conjured images of a train speeding through a stormy night, magically powered by the song's driving rhythmical accompaniment.

Eric glanced up at the gold carriage clock on the mantelpiece: 12:24. He would spend another six minutes with Burt Weedon's *Play in a Day* guitar tutorial before cycling back for the afternoon lessons. He was secretly proud to be the first in his class to ride his bicycle to school.

All Eric's parents seemed to talk about nowadays was work and money, specifically, the lack of either. Entering the living room, the boy was relieved to find them no longer rooted in discussion but settled in front of the TV watching Bonanza. That Friday, an advertisement appeared in the Ealing Gazette:

HANDYMAN AVAILABLE
Competent, skilled tradesman.
All offers of work considered.
Competitive rates.
Bill Grimes - Telephone: EAL 8***

Unaccountably, Eric felt a little strange when he saw his family's telephone number in the local paper. Bill instructed that when he answered the phone, Eric should give the number, *Ealing 8****, and try to be extra polite if the call was from a customer. Mary copied out the advert on blank postcards and paid for them to be displayed on local newsagents' noticeboards.

'What if nobody calls?' Eric asked unhelpfully.

'If at first, you don't succeed, try, try again,' answered his dad.

'That's what they say,' said Mary.

The following Monday lunchtime, Bill rode the postman's refurbished bicycle through the leafy backstreets of West Ealing, enjoying the warm hazy sunshine. Intending to replace the mangled frame, Bill had visited the refuse dump by the Grand Union Canal. Atop the highest mountain of Ealing's consumer cast-offs, Bill spied the skeletal remains of a similarly sized bicycle to the postman's crippled machine.

'Stone the crows!' Reg exclaimed, staring excitedly at his rejuvenated warhorse.

Standing in the shadow of the hedge outside the postman's house, Bill watched the beaming cyclist draw circles up and down Leighton

Road. Reg rang the bell, chuckling happily. He had forgotten all about his nagging head injury. The grateful man nearly shook Bill's arm off.

When Reg reached for his wallet, Bill waved his hand dismissively. 'You know what they say; *that's what friends are for.*'

'That's what they say,' smiled the postman.

If Reg had known about Bill's redundancy, he would have been more insistent about the money. Slipping a Louis Armstrong single into his saddlebag, the postman bid Bill a cheerful *goodbye* and cycled towards the high street to begin his afternoon job.

*

Eric reclined beside his mother, watching the six o'clock news. 70,000 protesters had arrived in London, having marched from Aldermaston to demonstrate against the proliferation of nuclear weapons. Eric's parents had acquired the new television via *hire purchase* when Bill had enjoyed full employment. They referred to the HP agreement as the *never-never*, but Bill said if his business didn't get going soon, they would have to call it the *never-ever*.

Over the next few weeks, Bill Grimes found himself clearing Else Winkerman's garden of the rusty car parts her estranged husband had left behind. He also installed a cat-flap for Mr and Mrs Pinkerton (and Smokey). A promising call came through offering a sizable painting and decorating job, but disappointingly the work never materialised.

Eric was sometimes joined in the front room by a couple of school friends who lived on the next road. Paul and his younger brother Tony had been Eric's mates since infant school. The three boys amused themselves with a selection of board games, *Risk* being the current favourite. Eric had borrowed the game from Paul and replicated it, painting a world map on a giant rectangle of hardboard and using tiny Airfix toy soldiers as playing pieces. He reckoned it was better than the original. It was certainly a good deal larger, and the plastic soldiers – English, German and Japanese – added a further dimension. Another game they dreamed up involved climbing around the front room without touching the floor. The furniture, fireplace and windowsill were easy enough to negotiate, but clambering over the open door was challenging. Gangly young Tony came a cropper on more than one occasion.

Mary told her son that if he needed the electric fire on, he should limit it to one bar. The greedy elements devoured a lot of power.

Times were tough in the Grimes household.

Eric had not needed to heat the front room recently: it was springtime, and the weather was lovely. That Saturday morning, he decided to walk to the shops to look at the Beatles' first album. There was no way Eric could raise the thirty-odd shillings to buy the LP, but he would be able to read the notes on the back cover. Maybe if he smiled sweetly and asked nicely, the girl at British Home Stores would play a track or two.

Crossing the Northfield Avenue by the post office, Eric glanced up at the bright yellow sun. Turning away and blinking, he watched purple and black motes float across his vision and considered how different the world now looked compared to the monochrome landscape of a few months earlier. The winter of 1962-63 was the longest and coldest Eric had lived through. Temperatures hit lows not experienced in England since 1740; rivers froze, water pipes burst, and a deep carpet of snow caused disruption across the country. Naturally, the kids loved it. The mother of all snowball fights took place near the Forester pub. Mums knitted balaclavas. The walk to school – sometimes through thick freezing fog – became a fantastic adventure, as piles of snow accumulated along the roadsides, forming frozen mountains for the children to climb. The British media called it *the Big Freeze*.

Approaching British Home Stores, Eric looked up at the office above Burton's tailors, remembering the cold touch of his mother's wet handkerchief as she wiped his eight-year-old cheek.

The department store was crowded with Saturday shoppers. The Beatles' new single, *From Me to You*, was playing as Eric made his way to the racks of LPs. The walk had been worthwhile if only to hear the group's latest release. Finding the B's, Eric pulled a copy of the *Please Please Me* LP out of the record bin. He flipped it over and began reading the liner notes. Eric was halfway through the blurb when he became aware of someone looking over his shoulder. A tall dark-skinned man stepped forward, standing next to the boy. He nodded his brown fedora towards the LP in Eric's hands,

'They're goo-od,' said the stranger, affecting an American drawl. 'But take a tip, get hip, and take a trip with the re-al de-al.'

Eric did not understand all the words, but got the general idea.

A wide grin spread across the tall man's face revealing an impressive array of dazzling white teeth. He held up an album in front of the boy. *'The Bird,'* he announced in a loud elongated whisper.

Eric read the name on the cover, *Charlie Parker*, and wondered what birds had to do with the price of haddock.

Feeling a tap on his shoulder, Eric turned around. 'Hello Reg,' the boy said brightly, relieved by the timely appearance of the postman.

Ten minutes later, Eric crossed the high street and walked a few paces down Canberra Road. He stood back, staring curiously at the glossy red door recessed in the wall by Burton's tailors. Eric had passed the corner shop many times, but although the side-entrance stood in plain view, he had never noticed it before. The boy knocked three times on the bright red door, then rang the bell twice, as per the postman's instructions.

Eric heard footsteps descending wooden stairs, then the red door swung inwards.

'Yee-hee!' exclaimed Reg, a big wrinkly smile lighting his face. 'Come in,' he said, standing back and motioning over his shoulder with his thumb. 'The boss is at a meeting in Hartlepool.'

Eric vaguely recalled Hartlepool, picturing it as the place with the big tower and the lights along the seafront. He followed the postman up the stairs. When they approached the landing, Eric heard jazz music coming from the room ahead.

Reg waved his hand at the empty desks, 'Just me and Sid in the office today.'

The tall, dark-skinned man with the brown fedora sat next to a Dansette record player by the front window. Sid grinned, tapping the tabletop to the infectious rhythm of Dave Brubeck's *Take Five*,

'Good t' see ya, kid!' said the cat with the hat and the dubious American accent. 'How do you do, and welcome to HQ,' he rhymed, handing the boy a gold-edged business card: *Sidney Mars DJ to the Stars*.

Eric looked around the upstairs office. Paperwork lay strewn across the desktops alongside hulking old-fashioned typewriters and bottles of scotch and American bourbon. A paper-tray labelled *IN, OUT* and *SHAKE IT ALL ABOUT* sat beside a watercooler. On one of the walls, a noticeboard bore scraps of paper with scribbled phrases like: *The wife's always right, Time goes past and kids grow fast*, and *Gibbons don't do algebra*. Below the office in the high street, the Saturday shoppers milled like busy ants in the afternoon sunshine, oblivious to the goings-on at the mysterious enterprise above Burton's.

Reg placed his hand on Eric's back, gently guiding the boy towards a partitioned room at the end of the office. Through the open doorway, Eric saw a huge grey-metal instrument panel standing from floor to ceiling, almost entirely covering one wall. The machine boasted a plethora of switches, dials, sliders, meters and lights, some blinking intermittently. Exposed rows of large glass valves glowed hot yellow-orange, more reminiscent of the Colossus at Bletchley Park than a contemporary design from the sixties. A 1930s-style microphone that looked as if it belonged in a BBC museum stood on a desk in front of the apparatus.

At the postman's invitation, Eric sat at the desk facing the big grey transmitter.

*

Time passed, and spring turned to summer. When 1963 reached its seasonal zenith, so too did the sun shine over the Grimes household. The telephone in the hallway now rang regularly with offers of local work that Bill found satisfying as well as financially rewarding. Mary enrolled at the nearby tennis club opposite Lammas Park, quickly landing another silver trophy to add to her veiled collection.

In the front room, Eric leaned over his acoustic guitar and lifted the stylus to track one, *I Saw Her Standing There*. Sitting back, he confidently fingered the E7 chord that began the song.

One, two, three, four...

On the other side of town, an old soldier and his wife stood in a puddle of water, eying a leaking pipe.

'What on earth are we going to do?' asked the woman.

Major Pertwee leaned on his stick, staring at the fractured plumbing, 'Well, you know what they say...'

The elderly couple turned to one another, smiling. The timbre of their voices sounded uncannily like that of an eleven-year-old boy as in unison they chimed, *'Bill Grimes can fix anything!'*

3

Skegness

Laying back in the warm bathwater, Eric flicked a clinging drip from the cold tap with his big toe. This was where he did his best thinking. For the umpteenth time, he tried to make sense of what had happened on that spring Saturday in West Ealing:

Eric sat at the desk, staring blankly at the huge transmitter.

'Just say it loud and clear,' Reg instructed. 'Three, two, one...' A red light blinked on and a yellow sign illuminated above the door: ON AIR.

'Bill Grimes can fix anything,' Eric said into the microphone, watching the meter flutter into the red.

The postman flipped the switch back to the *off* position. 'Nicely done,' he said, smiling at the bewildered youngster.

As Eric turned to leave, Sid rose from his seat next to the record player,

'One little chore before you head out the door,' rhymed the tall, dark displaced American.

Eric looked at Reg, who was smoking a Senior Service with one arm resting on the watercooler. The postman nodded.

Sid pointed to a pile of jazz LPs on one of the desks, 'Put your left hand there and prepare to swear.'

The boy placed his palm on the glossy cover of Miles Davis's *Kind of Blue*.

'Now raise your right hand and say after me,' instructed Sid. 'I do solemnly swear.'

'I do solemnly swear,' echoed Eric, holding his hand above his head as if in response to a question from his schoolteacher.

'I ain't gonna tell nobody.'

'I ain't gonna tell nobody.'

''Bout the shit I seen in this here office.'

Eric stifled a snigger, "Bout the shit I seen in this here office.'

Eric had kept his promise, though he was not entirely sure what it was that he was not telling anyone about. Another drip formed beneath the bath tap.

'Have you drowned in there?' Eric's dad called up the stairs. 'The wrestling's on; Mick McManus and Jackie Pallo.'

'Coming,' replied Eric. Stepping out of the lukewarm water, he watched the yellow plastic duck swim circles around the gurgling plug-hole.

*

The council had decided that it was not in keeping with the times to lock up the swings on Sundays.

'They'll be letting the shops open on the Sabbath next,' Mrs Harris told Reg.

'I'm sure you're right,' replied the postman, though he doubted the old collection box shaker would be around long enough to see it happen. *They'll do it eventually, though*, he thought. Reg had already seen the signs. The sale of foodstuffs was permitted on Sundays, and one enterprising vendor had come up with the idea of selling carrots for thirty pounds each and giving away a free wardrobe with every purchase.

A crimson sun was sinking over Lammas Park's gates, painting purple and orange streaks across the sky. In the play area, three boys sat in a row swinging gently.

'Talos,' said Paul, the chains bending as he leant back.

Eric looked over the head of Paul's nine-year-old brother, 'You're right, but I wouldn't have remembered.'

Staring straight ahead, Tony attempted to change the subject. 'Eric, in *From Russia with Love*, when –'

Paul laughed loudly, a full and hearty burst that belied his age. 'Tony's been wetting his bed ever since we saw that film.'

'I have not!' the nine-year-old retorted angrily.

Paul ran a hand through his heavy black hair, 'Then how come Mum has to sit with you every night till you go to sleep?'

Tony stared at his grubby white plimsolls, tapping his feet agitatedly on the tarmac.

Accompanied by Paul and Tony, 1963 was the year in which Eric went to the cinema for the first time without parental supervision: a milestone moment. *Jason and the Argonauts* was a Hollywood telling of the ancient Greek tale featuring an animated bronze statue (Talos), a talking figurehead, and sword-wielding skeletons, all set against blue Technicolor skies and given an eerie orchestral accompaniment. The film had left a lasting impression, particularly on young Tony. He fearfully imagined the fifty-foot-tall statue stomping through the back gardens on a malevolent quest to wrest him from his bed.

Paul glanced at his Timex imitation diving watch. 'We'd better get going, Mum'll shout.'

Mum was certainly capable of shouting. A motorcycle accident had wrenched her husband out of the picture when Tony was still in his first year, leaving Julia to raise the two boys single-handed.

Julia Ramsey was a notably young mum, slight and pretty, with an unconventional bohemian spirit rarely encountered in her generation. When inspiration struck, Julia painted, her work betraying unspoken dreams of a return to her family's wealthy past: a dwindling prosperity she had only glimpsed. Nonetheless, she retained the vestiges of an upper-middle-class elocution and carried herself with the poise and grace of a ballerina. Paul had inherited his mother's jet-black hair and high cheekbones. Tony exhibited traces of his father's dark-brown hair and had acquired his gangly frame. Whilst all three shared a tendency towards leanness, Tony was the odd one out, continually being re-minded at school that his arms and legs were too long. Both brothers thought the world of their mother.

The sunset cast three long shadows on the pavement of Northfield Avenue.

'When we grow up, I think we should be train robbers,' mused Paul. 'I don't fancy the idea of work much, and one good haul should do the trick.'

August 1963 had seen the daring heist that came to be known in Britain as *the Great Train Robbery*. The audacious railway hold-up had netted the thieves more than two-and-a-half million pounds and was currently all over the news.

'What if we get caught?'

Paul cuffed his younger brother playfully across the head, 'I'm not *serious*, Tony!'

'Got any jokes?' asked Eric.

Tony always seemed to have one stored away. Paul had inherited their mother's good looks and sharp intellect, but humour was the younger boy's special gift.

'A bloke runs out of petrol in the middle of nowhere. A friendly bee buzzes up and says, *"Don't worry, I'll get me mates"*. Two minutes later, a swarm of bees flies out of the petrol tank. The man tries his car, and it starts straight away. *"What did you put in my petrol tank?"* asks the bloke. And the bee says, *"Bee Pee".'*

The nine-year-old smiled as the two older boys burst into laughter. Ninety per cent of it was in the delivery. Tony secretly cherished his innate comedic ability; it was his forte, his niche.

As they approached the side road where the two brothers lived, Tony turned to their friend,

'Eric, in From Russia With Love... When that lady's dancing and shaking her hips really fast... Do her clothes fall off?'

Tony had seen a trailer for the James Bond film, which featured a gipsy girl belly-dancing in a skimpy costume. Eric had seen the film at the Odeon with his dad.

'Yeah,' replied Eric. 'All her clothes come right off, and you can see everything.'

Tony's jaw dropped, his eyes widening like saucers.

Eric was not in the habit of telling fibs, but on this occasion, he could not resist. It occurred to him that if Paul had not been with them, he would have provided Tony with a truthful account of the scene. Paul grinned conspiratorially at Eric as they went their separate ways.

The two brothers upped their pace.

Though twilight was turning to darkness, there were no lights on in the small terraced house. 'Let me do the talking, okay?' Paul pushed his shiny new key into the lock.

In the rear living room, Julia Ramsey was curled up in an armchair bathed in the light from the TV. Tony hung back as Paul addressed their mother,

'I'm sorry we're late in, Mum. It was my faul –'

'Shush!' interrupted Julia, her eyes not leaving the screen. 'Sit down, both of you.'

The brothers joined their mother in front of the television. A huge crowd listened in silence as a heavyset black American man delivered the address that would cement his place in history. Martin Luther King Junior's *I Have a Dream* speech would touch the hearts of millions, irrespective of colour or creed.

Paul watched a tear roll down his mother's cheek.

*

Following his one-man business's miraculous upturn, Bill Grimes had replaced their ageing car with a brand-new A35 van. The little green Austin had already taken them to Devon. Window-stickers with seaside names proclaimed the van's short history. The M1 had opened in 1959, but there were no other motorways, and journey times were long, especially on trips between London and the West Country. The Grimes's collected Green Shield Stamps at garages along the way and listened to the radio.

Eric enjoyed the family holidays, though having reached the ripe old age of eleven-and-a-half, he began to experience a yearning for independence. Bill and Mary had noted the changes in their son: small signs of a developing maturity.

The family headed north to Butlin's in Skegness. Eric's mother recalled how in previous years, the boy had sat behind them singing *der-der-der* electric guitar along with Shadows instrumentals on the car radio. This time he was quiet, lost in thought. No longer did he endlessly repeat the impatient child's question, *When we gonna get there?* Instead, Eric consulted the Esso map, following their progress up the A52 as they neared the east coast holiday camp. Mary smiled inwardly; she felt proud of their son and for once allowed herself and Bill some credit for his upbringing. Eric's friends Paul and Tony were nice boys too, though their uncommonly young mother seemed a little strange. Arty types were a mystery to Mary, and Julia Ramsey fell firmly into that category. Still, as Bill was fond of pointing out, *it's easy to criticise.*

From his seat in the back of the van, Eric dreamily watched the fields go by. The close harmonies of Peter, Paul and Mary's *Blowin' in the Wind* etched images of white doves and deserted shorelines in his mind. He was now only partially present in the van, drifting between the song's lyrical collage and a memory from his junior school play-ground.

The games master had been detained unexpectedly, and the football period cancelled. Deprived of a teacher, a crowd of boys gathered to watch the girls play netball. The lads' keen attention had little to do with the match, but as fate decreed, just when they had begun to develop an interest in the girls, it would soon be time to start life at an all-boys school.

Billy Butlin had opened his first holiday camp at Skegness in 1936. Despite cynical comparisons to World War II prisoner-of-war camps, his vision became a great success. As they drove through the main entrance, Bill whistled the theme tune from *The Great Escape*. Eric scanned the boundary fence but saw no signs of machinegun posts, armed guards or barbed wire.

'The Donkey Derby will begin in ten minutes next to the boating lake,' a cheerful voice announced over the camp's Tannoy system. Eric woke with a start. He had been awake late into the night fiddling with his radio, trying to hang on to the weak signal from Radio Luxemburg. The BBC had no dedicated pop station in 1963, and the kind of music Eric liked was often hard to find. One exception was *Pick of the Pops*, the BBC's chart rundown, which had aired for many years. Current host Alan Freeman had replaced David Jacobs in September 1961 and the show had settled into a regular 4pm Sunday slot in January 1962. Aside from this precious concession, the BBC shunned the growing pop culture, obstinate to change, digging-in its heels, and sticking with safe formatting like *Housewives' Choice, Family Favourites, Sing Something Simple,* and on weekdays (twice daily) *Music While You Work*. Still, in-between the orchestras, big bands and novelty records, a few modern pop songs were beginning to find their way onto the airwaves.

Eric appeared, rubbing his eyes.

'Oh, you decided to join us then,' said Bill. 'You missed the Donkey Derby.'

'I know... I heard.'

'At least they've stopped the *Good morning campers* wake-up call,' said Mary. 'You'd have loved that!'

Bill smiled, 'They dropped it around the same time as the Knobbly Knees Contest.'

Leaving their small wooden chalet, which Bill christened *the Shed*, the family spent much of their first day at Butlin's exploring. The large holiday camp had plenty to offer. The penny arcade captured Eric's attention, as did the rocket ride. Mary spotted the tennis courts, and Bill made a mental note to visit the snooker room. An Alpine-style chairlift afforded aerial views from above the park.

By the second day, Eric felt confident enough to stroll around the camp by himself. The boy's parents stood on the chalet's tiny wooden veranda, watching his slight diminishing figure walking away into the distance.

'Our little boy's growing up,' observed Mary.

Bill put an arm around his wife's shoulders, 'Well, you know what they say... *Time goes past, and kids grow fast.*'

'That's what they say,' replied Mary.

Entering the games room, Eric bumped into an exiting Redcoat.

'There are a few kids your age inside,' chirped the smiling woman.

'Thanks,' replied Eric, vaguely objecting to being referred to as a *kid*.

The games room was empty, apart from two boys and a blonde girl playing table tennis – her versus them. The Searchers' *Sweets for My Sweet* played through the speaker system. Casually running his fingertips along the cushion of a half-size billiard table, Eric made his way towards the three *kids*. The nearest boy's attempted smash sent the ping-pong ball glancing off the edge of his bat and arcing through the air in Eric's direction. The ball clicked once on the floor, bouncing up in front of him. Eric caught it cleanly with one hand. The girl spun around, her flying blonde hair shimmering in a slow-motion blur. Eric looked into the eyes of the prettiest girl he had ever seen and instantly fell head-over-heels in love.

Aeons passed until the girl broke the spell, 'Can we have our ball back please, mister?'

The world started again. Eric tossed the ball back. Her eyes never leaving his, the dream-girl caught it with her left hand. She pointed to the top of the Coke machine where the handle of a bat stuck out, 'I could do with some help against these two.'

Eric had played table tennis at home on the extended dining table, and having assessed their opponents, he felt confident. With a little practice, ping-pong turned out to be easier on a bigger table, and the new partnership proved a formidable pairing, at least compared to the opposition. They proceeded to win three straight games.

Checking her watch, the blonde placed her bat on the table. 'I've gotta go. Same time tomorrow?' The girl smiled at Eric, ignoring the other two boys.

Eric watched her walk out through the double doors and realised he had not asked her name.

That evening, the Grimes family dined at one of the campsite's restaurants, where Eric sampled the aesthetic delights of crinkle-cut chips. Bill and Mary exchanged glances as their son pushed his food around his plate. Eric was preoccupied, presumably by something that had happened while he was out on his own.

'Your dinner looks like a battlefield,' observed his dad. 'Don't you like it?'

'I'm not very hungry.'

Following the subdued meal, Bill took it upon himself to liven things up. 'Right,' he said, rubbing his hands and turning to his son. 'Fancy a go on the dodgems?'

Eric's eyes lit up.

The sombre mood lifted in a flash, and the family left the restaurant chattering happily.

The music was loud: *Runaway* by Del Shannon. It seemed made for the fairground atmosphere; some records just are. Eric headed for an orange car, his dad for a green one. Standing beneath the rows of chasing coloured bulbs, Mary watched, smiling from the side.

'Keep your hands inside the car at all times,' warned the operator. He turned the music up a notch. A claxon signalled the start of the ride.

Eric pushed down on the foot pedal, and the car jerked forward. There was a sharp smell, something like burning rubber and motor oil; the electrical connection fizzed and sparked above his head. Del Shannon sang in his strong falsetto voice as the gleaming metal cars circled the arena, *mostly* in an anticlockwise direction.

'This way round!' Bill shouted, watching his son's car meander aimlessly towards the middle.

Thump! Eric jerked forward as he collided head-on with another wayward vehicle. He looked into the big blue eyes of a dark-haired girl. When Eric smiled, the girl's shocked expression changed instantly to mirror his.

The father took the wheel of his daughter's pink dodgem.

'Sorry!' called Eric.

'My fault.' The girl leaned out, grinning at the boy.

'Your arm!' shouted Eric.

The girl pulled back in the nick of time as another car slammed into hers. *Thank you*, she mouthed, flashing her big blue eyes.

'Can we go on the rockets?' Eric asked, licking his lips and wiping sugary pink candyfloss from his cheek. He had been longing to try the ride from the moment he saw it but had not wanted to appear too eager.

As they approached the *Sky Rockets*, Eric saw a Redcoat sitting at a desk in a small white deco-style building with a *Staff Only* sign on the door. The man spoke into the microphone, and his announcement was amplified through the Tannoy loudspeakers around the camp,

'Ladies and gentlemen, boys and girls; don't miss tonight's cabaret featuring the king of comedy, Eddie Ray, at eight o'clock in the Starlight Room.'

'Never heard of him,' said Bill.

'He's the king of comedy,' Mary replied sarcastically.

'Never heard of him,' Eric said, smiling at his dad.

Metallic clanking sounded beneath their feet as the two astronauts rounded the circular metal walkway, homing in on a vacant rocket. Bill placed his hand on the blue-and-white two-seater cockpit, 'You get in first.'

Eric did as he was instructed, then his father climbed in next to him.

'Centrifugal force,' explained Bill. 'It's better if you're on the inside.'

When the ride began to spin, Eric understood. As the small capsule gathered speed, he found himself being pushed uncomfortably against his father. Faster now: the fairground streaked past in a colourful blur. Eric squashed heavily against his dad.

'I don't like this!' said the boy.

'Take it up.'

'How?'

'Pull that.'

Eric drew the lever back. There was a hiss as compressed air was released, and the rocket rose into the air. Higher and higher they soared, nearing the capsule's maximum elevation. Eric released the lever.

'Better?' asked Bill.

'Much better,' his son replied uncertainly, picturing what it might be like if, due to mechanical negligence, the rocket should become detached from the ride.

Leaving the fairground behind, they made their way back between the gaily painted chalets.

'Shall we go out for a drive tomorrow?' suggested Bill. 'If we leave early, we could take a stroll up the beach, then maybe look at some of Lincolnshire.'

'Lovely,' said Mary. 'We could walk along the pier.'

The couple looked down at their son.

'Um, could we go in the afternoon?' Eric asked delicately. 'I have to be... I arranged to meet some friends at eleven.'

'Oh, all right then.' Bill was not accustomed to being overruled by their son, but his surprise was superseded by a respect for the growing boy.

Later, when Eric said *goodnight,* his mother stopped him, 'Wait, you'd better have this. Don't lose it.'

Walking along the narrow corridor to his room, Eric felt an inch or two taller. He had never before been entrusted with a key.

The following morning, Eric strolled into the games room at eleven on the dot. One of the boys was already there, receiving a predictable beating from the pretty blonde. Her smash sent the ball pinging off the corner of the table.

'My game,' said the girl.

'Nice shot,' said Eric.

The girl flashed her stunning smile, and Eric melted on the spot.

'Grab a bat,' said the blonde. 'I could do with some competition.'

'I'm Eric,' he said, taking a bat from the top of the Coke machine.

'Carolyn,' replied the girl.

This time the competitors were evenly matched. As the game progressed, Eric began to feel that he had the edge skill-wise, but the lovely blonde was so determined to contest every shot, she ended up winning 21-18.

'Play again?' asked Carolyn.

Feeling superfluous, the other boy got up to leave, then the doors swung open, and a dark-haired girl walked in. Eric recognised her immediately from the dodgem ride the previous night.

'Any good at table tennis?' the exiting boy asked the new arrival. 'These two fancy each other, but I'm free.'

Tiny prickles ran up Eric's neck.

Carolyn joined Eric at his end of the table. 'Okay, us two against you two,' said the blonde.

Blondie and Grimes wiped the floor with their opponents, easily winning two games in a row.

'Shall we switch partners?' suggested Eric.

The girl with the big blue eyes smiled across the net.

'No, let's stay as we are,' Carolyn said, lightly rubbing Eric's back.

Surprising himself, Eric reciprocated, running his hand around the blonde's narrow waist.

Stunned by his first affectionate encounter with a real live girl – and a gorgeous one at that – Eric's game went to pieces. He hit the ball into the net, bounced it off the strip-light, and twice swung his bat at thin air. With the game poised at 10-10, Eric's backhand flick saw the ball cannon off a radiator and disappear behind the Coke machine.

'Oops!' exclaimed Eric, 'I *pinged* when I should have *ponged*.'

The blue-eyed girl burst out laughing, then stopped when she saw Carolyn glaring frustratedly at her partner.

Eric pulled himself together and they maintained their unbeaten run, winning the game 21-13.

Billy J. Kramer's *Bad to Me* played as the four new friends stood in a circle sipping Cokes.

'Same time tomorrow, everyone?' asked Carolyn.

'I'll come if I can,' replied Susan, the blue-eyed girl.

'Me too,' said the younger boy whose name no one had bothered to ascertain.

'And me, if I can,' said Eric. 'I nearly didn't make it here today. My parents had plans to go sightseeing.'

'Okay,' said Carolyn. 'But if you can't come tomorrow, I'm in the *Junior Miss Butlin's* competition on Thursday afternoon, so I hope you'll all be there to cheer me on.'

A Redcoat walked onto the stage as the Grimes's sat down near the back of the crowded Starlight Room. When the compere reached for the microphone, a squeal of feedback deafened a family sitting in front of the speakers.

'Ladies and gentlemen, boys and girls, Butlin's are proud to present tonight's star act. Please give a warm holiday-welcome to, *Rocky Beach and the Pebbles!*'

'*Rocky Beach and the Pebbles?*' queried Bill. 'I've heard some daft names, but...'

'Never heard of them,' Eric said, leaning forward and smiling at his parents.

His mother laughed.

The curtains opened behind the departing Redcoat, and the four-man group commenced their opening number, *I'll Never Get Over You*, a recent hit for Johnny Kidd and the Pirates.

'Oh, they're so loud!' complained Mary.

Grimacing, Bill nodded to his wife.

Ignoring his parents, Eric stared at the group, mesmerised by his first exposure to live pop music. From his seat at the back of the room, he could just make out the guitarist's chords: A, E, A, E, D...

A crowd of dancers assembled in front of the stage, jigging and shaking to the bouncy beat. The group began their second song, *How Do You Do It?* a number one for Gerry and the Pacemakers earlier that year.

This one's in the key of A as well, thought Eric, though the guitarist was playing barre chords, and the changes were too fast for him to follow.

Some tables had emptied next to the dance floor, vacated by the dancers or by holidaymakers like Eric's parents with an aversion to loud pop music.

'Dad,' Eric turned to his father. 'Is it okay if I go down the front?'

Eric selected a seat on the right side of the room, directly in front of the guitarist. From the young musician's perspective, the group sounded even better close-up. He peered up between the shimmying dancers, focusing on the guitarist's left hand; *Twist and Shout:* D, G...

Eric felt a tap on his shoulder.

We'll be in the bar, mouthed Bill, pointing towards the double doors at the back of the room.

Eric nodded, giving his dad a thumbs up. Bill walked back to re-join his wife. Eric felt another tap. Expecting to see his father, Eric looked into the big blue eyes of a smiling Susan.

'Dance?' she shouted above the loud music.

Eric wanted to say *no*, then *yes*, then... He found himself on his feet, following the dark-haired girl who was making for a space on the other side of the dance floor. A moment later, he was dancing with her to *Twist and Shout*. Or was it someone else jigging around in front of the girl?

Grinning, Susan leant towards Eric, 'I love the Beatles.'

His face lit up, 'Me too!'

Immediately their dancing improved tenfold.

When the first set finished with the surf-inspired instrumental *Wipe Out*, Eric and Susan made their way back to the table for a well-earned rest. A red-coated disc jockey took over during the group's break, opening with Freddy and the Dreamers' *I'm Telling You Now*. The dance floor emptied, apart from two young boys playing slow-motion football with a purple balloon.

'Are you here with your parents?' Eric asked Susan.

'Yes, they're in the bar.'

'Mine too.'

Eric watched the twelve-year-old girl pick at the corner of a beer mat.

'I'm upset with my dad,' confided Susan.

'Why?'

Her blue eyes focused on Eric, 'He's entered me in that stupid *Junior Miss Butlin's* competition, the one that Carolyn's in on Thursday.'

'Mm,' said Eric.

Two bottles of Coca-Cola landed on the table in front of them.

'Oh, thanks, Dad.' Eric felt his cheeks flush.

Bill gestured towards the double doors, 'You know where we are.' He smiled and headed back to the bar.

'And now,' the Redcoat DJ announced, in a tone befitting a royal proclamation, 'and remember you heard it here first. The Beatles' brand-new single, *She Loves You!*'

Susan and Eric gaped at one another wide-eyed.

(Drum intro...)

'Come on,' Susan said excitedly. 'Let's be the first!'

Leaping out of her seat, the girl grabbed Eric's hand and pulled him onto the dance floor. The couple were quickly joined by other dancers, and within twenty seconds, the floor was packed solid.

But they had been the first.

The following morning, Eric ambled towards the games room, reflecting on the previous day's events. It had begun with a hug, well, a touch, from a beautiful blonde. Then he had seen a live pop group, experiencing the sweet sting of a real electric guitar up close. He had danced with a pretty girl, and to cap it all off, had then been treated to a preview of the Beatles' fantastic new single, *She Loves You*. More than any other, the record seemed to encapsulate the excitement and energy inherent in his favourite group.

Pushing open the doors, Eric heard the soft *plop-plop-plopping* of a ping-pong ball bouncing on a rubber-pimpled bat. Carolyn stood alone by the table, counting out loud, 'Sixty-three, sixty-four, sixty-five...'

'Hello,' Eric said brightly.

'I didn't think you were coming,' replied the girl. 'Sixty... Oh.'

'Sorry.'

Carolyn plucked the ball from the air and smiled, 'Looks like it's just me and you today.'

The doors swung open and Susan walked into the room, 'Hello, how's everybody?'

'Fab,' replied Eric, happy to see his dance partner, but at the same time regretting the loss of his chance to be alone with Carolyn.

The blonde turned to Eric, 'Shall we play first?'

The three took turns watching. Carolyn won all her games except one (against Eric), twice beating Susan 21-2.

'I'd better get going,' said Eric. 'We're off out again this afternoon.'

'Yeah, me too,' said Susan.

'Are you both coming to the *Miss Butlin's* competition tomorrow?' Carolyn enquired, perhaps mistakenly omitting the *Junior* prefix.

Susan's head dropped.

Eric broke the uncomfortable silence, 'Susan's in it, too.'

Carolyn burst out laughing, '*You're* in it?'

Susan continued to look down, 'My dad...'

Eric finished her sentence, 'Her dad entered her in the competition.'

'*Why?*' Carolyn asked, giggling insensitively.

Susan raised her head. Her big blue eyes brimmed with tears. She began to say something, then turned and marched briskly out of the room, leaving the sprung double doors swinging on their hinges.

Eric felt torn. He looked at the pretty blonde but found no words. Then he ran out after Susan.

A smattering of rain pervaded the bracing sea breeze. Mary's chiffon headscarf flapped as she and Bill walked arm in arm along the deserted sandy beach. 'He's gone quiet again.'

Bill held his Macintosh closed around his neck. 'Women problems, I expect.' Half-smiling, Bill narrowed his eyes against the weather. He watched his son wandering pensively by the waters' edge.

Spinning around and walking backwards, Eric looked at the trail of wet shoeprints he had left behind him in the sand. Yesterday had been such a great day, especially the evening. Although he had only heard the song once, *She Loves You* had stuck in his head. He relived those few magical moments he and Susan had shared: the only couple on the dance floor, dancing to the brand-new Beatles record.

'Come on. Let's be the first!'

Then they were surrounded by dancers. The atmosphere in front of the stage was electric, but there was only Susan, the girl with the big blue eyes, those beautiful blue eyes now filled with tears.

Eric stood looking at the grey North Sea, his hands pushed deep into his duffel-coat pockets. White foam curled around his shoes.

The green A35 van drove in through Butlin's main gate at 5:45 that Wednesday afternoon. The weather had deteriorated, leaving the family little option but to cut their outing short. After a dash through the rain, they entered the chalet damp and dishevelled. Still wearing his dripping duffel coat, Eric disappeared into his caravan-style bedroom. He fumbled through the pockets of the two jackets he had brought with him, hoping luck would be on his side.

'Yes!' He held the gold-edged business card up in front of him: *Sidney Mars DJ to the Stars*. The card carried an Ealing phone number.

When Eric emerged from his bedroom, Bill and Mary were in theirs, changing into dry clothes.

'Mum, Dad, I'm just popping out for a minute. I've got my key.'

'Where are you going?' called Mary. 'It's pouring!'

Eric had already vanished into the rain.

A sunny summer Thursday saw Butlin's back in full swing. Yesterday's raincoats remained on their hangers as holidaymakers emerged from their chalets into the sunshine, made especially enticing by the contrast to the previous day.

Eric slept late again, having lain awake pondering his plan. Mary had signed-up for a tennis competition that afternoon, and he would be free to move around the camp as necessary. His luck was holding so far, but the tricky part was still to come.

At 2:30, Eric made his way to the open-air swimming pool where the beauty competition was to take place. Rows of folding chairs had been set out in front of a temporary stage, above which hung a yellow banner with red lettering: *Junior Miss Butlin's 1963*. A long table with four chairs was positioned at a right-angle to the platform.

Eric watched from the patio of a nearby cafeteria. The seats filled steadily. By 2:50, there was standing room only.

Sunlight glinted off his gold neck-chain as the Mayor of Skegness appeared, followed by a smartly dressed woman and two men in suits and ties. Eric's pulse quickened as the four judges took their seats at the table. *Okay, they're all here... Go!*

Peering across the tennis courts, Bill shaded his eyes. *Where's he off to in such a hurry?* Bill watched his son dodging and diving between the strolling holidaymakers.

Eric felt a bead of perspiration run down his face as he jogged past the painted wooden chalets. He could see the *Sky Rockets* ride over the arched rooftops, its shiny steel capsules set against a bright blue sky. He rehearsed the line in his head for the hundredth time, *Quick! There's a little girl over by the dodgems and she's hurt herself!* Easy. What could go wrong?

Coming to a dead stop, Eric stared at the small white deco building that housed the Tannoy system's microphone. He wiped his wet brow with his wrist. As he had anticipated, the side door with the *Staff Only* sign was shut.

Don't think about it, just do it, Eric told himself. *Quick! There's a little girl over by the dodgems and she's hurt herself!*

Anaesthetised, he stepped forward and knocked on the door.

He waited. There was no answer.

Eric knocked harder, hurting his knuckles. He tried the handle, but the door was locked. Walking around to the window, he peered inside. The little room was empty. *What could go wrong?* There was a smaller window at the back that was latched-open a few inches.

Feeling like a criminal, Eric walked casually around to the rear. Squeezing between the high bordering hedge and the back of the small building, he edged towards the window. Privet poked his back, and a money spider ran up his arm. The window opened easily, and he scrambled through headfirst, landing in a heap on the floor.

Kneeling on the linoleum, Eric pulled the business card from his pocket, then reached up and snatched the phone from the desk.

The telephone in Ealing rang twice.

'Sidney Mars, DJ to the stars,' answered the familiar American voice.

'Sid, it's Eric. Are you ready? We've got to be really quick!'

Eric held the telephone earpiece close to the microphone. No sound was audible through the camp's Tannoy system. A passing Welsh Corgi twitched oddly.

Walking back to the chalet, Eric held out his hand and watched it tremble uncontrollably. He remembered Paul's idea and decided he was definitely not cut-out to be a great train robber. Using the key that his mother had given him, he opened the chalet door and made straight for the shower.

By the time Eric reached the swimming pool, the beauty competition was nearly over. He caught sight of Carolyn's blonde mane among the group of young contestants who had gathered behind the judges. Susan was not among them. Eric wondered if she had backed out at the last minute, then spotted her sitting between her parents.

A Redcoat walked to the microphone holding a folded sheet of paper. 'Ladies and gentlemen, boys and girls; thank you for your patience. The judges have made their unanimous decision. It gives me great pleasure to announce the winner of this year's *Junior Miss Butlin's* competition. And the winner is...' The Redcoat unfolded the paper and elatedly announced the winner to the expectant crowd: 'Miss Susan Smith!'

Susan sat bolt-upright. Applause erupted as her parents leaned-in to congratulate their dumbfounded daughter. Eric saw a flailing mop of blonde hair swiftly disappearing past the café.

Susan drifted across the stage in her long blue evening dress with the look of a semiconscious sleepwalker. Edging through the crowd, Eric watched from behind the last row of chairs as the mayor shook Susan's hand and presented her with the winner's trophy.

'Just say *thank you*,' the mayor whispered, guiding the befuddled girl to the microphone.

'Thank you,' Susan said in a quiet voice, more to the stage than to the applauding onlookers. Then a wide smile lit her face. 'Oh, hi Eric!' she called, raising her hand high and waving to the grinning boy.

The mayor leaned over to the Redcoat at his side, 'Well, you know what they say...' Affecting an American accent, the mayor enunciated the words that lay waiting in the minds of everyone at the camp, 'Blue eyes win the prize.'

'That's what they say,' agreed the Redcoat.

The following Saturday morning, the little green van drove out of Butlin's main entrance for the last time. Before they left the chalet, Mary had packed her runner-up medal safely in one of the suitcases. She was quietly pleased; there was no disgrace in losing to an ex-pro. Eric felt inside his jacket pocket and pulled out the beer mat on which Susan had written her address and telephone number. The sweetness of her farewell kiss remained emblazoned on his lips.

When they joined the M1 at Leicester, Eric's thoughts turned to home. Shortly, he would begin his first term at a senior school. Hopefully, the rumours of head flushing's in the school toilets would turn out to be unfounded gossip.

4

Zimmy

The psychological jolt that accompanies graduation to a senior school came as a surprise. Pupils in the fifth and sixth years appeared to Eric as young men, the evident reality of that approaching horizon contributing to the strangeness of his new environment. In years to come, he would compare these days to the culture shock often experienced when visiting a foreign country for the first time. For good Darwinian reasons, senses became acutely attuned, implanting the seeds for déjà vu responses to mundane stimuli such as the smell of the school janitor's floor cleaner.

Mr Styles, the boys' imperious new form teacher, had left the room, leaving the class to write-out copies of the timetable he had chalked on the blackboard. Eric and Paul sat at adjoining desks by the window.

'Well, *he's* a right bastard, isn't he,' whispered Paul.

Eric looked stoically at his friend, 'I'd heard they were strict here.'

Paul had been expected to progress to the grammar school, but Eric's high marks in the Eleven Plus exam were a protractor's width short of miraculous. Naturally, Bill and Mary had been thrilled to bits. While he was pleased to find himself at a desk next to his best friend, Eric worried that the elevated standards would prove too much for him.

Re-entering the classroom with practised stealth, Mr Styles moved silently between the rows of desks. *Skrrrrrrik.* Eric unrolled another four-inch strip of Sellotape and proceeded to affix it to his cardboard timetable, partially overlapping the previous piece.

'Planning on going swimming with it, are you, boy?' enquired a brusque voice from above Eric's head.

Thirty twelve year old boys burst into laughter. Eric looked up into the crabby face of his new form master. With his desperately unfashionable Adolph Hitler moustache and long chin, the bony old man was a dead ringer for the teacher from the Beano's *Bash Street Kids*. Eric groped for a witty reply but managed only an impersonation of a human beetroot.

During the morning break, Paul and Eric stood in the playground admiring the red-brick Victorian architecture that surrounded them on three sides. While much of Ealing had been constructed utilising yellowy-brown London clay, the reddish hues bestowed the grammar school with an air of nineteenth-century grandeur.

'I reckon these walls could tell a few tales,' remarked Paul.

'It's a little daunting,' said Eric, using a word he had picked up from his friend's mother.

'The building or the school work?'

'Both.'

There was a brief silence as, like prisoners coming to terms with a jail sentence, the two boys contemplated the prospect of spending the next five or six years at the school.

Paul changed the subject. 'Ever heard of a singer called Bob Dylan?'

Eric shook his head.

Omitting the Sellotape incident, Eric told his parents about his first day at the new school, then tucked into his beans on toast at the living-room table. Yesterday's *Sunday Mirror* lay in front of him, its headline proffering another snippet of juicy gossip. Good-time-girl Christine Keeler's involvement in the *Profumo Affair* had rocked the foundations of Harold MacMillan's Tory government. The paper had earlier that year changed its name from the *Sunday Pictorial*. Still, the smutty editorial line remained, titles like *How to Spot a Homo*, laying the foundations for a blitz of journalistic sleaze. Prince Phillip was not referenced in the Keeler article.

Leaving his mum and dad watching *The Rag Trade*, Eric strolled around the block to the Ramsey's. The adjoining alleyway was Eric's preferred route, but heavy rainfall had turned the back way into a quagmire.

'Come in, my friend,' Paul said in his best cultured accent. Flashing a silly grin, he ushered Eric past him with a flourish.

'Front room?'

'Yep. Mum and Tony are in the back watching *Panorama*.'

'Tony's watching Richard Dimbleby?'

'Yeah, I banned him from the front room tonight. I wanted us to have a bit of peace while I play you the record.'

Flopping onto the leather sofa opposite the fireplace, Eric looked around the room. Although he had visited the house countless times, the layout still intrigued him, it being identical to the home he had just left, except reversed like a mirror image. Even the radiogram occupied the same spot in one of the alcoves next to the fireplace. The decor, however, was quite different. This house had not been subjected to the ravages of the DIY boom, and most of the Edwardian period features remained. A matt-black iron fireplace with flower-patterned glazed tiles framed the small hearth, though a portable electric fire now heated the room.

Eric had always felt comfortable at the Ramsey residence. Although the rooms were noticeably dusty and the paintwork discoloured and chipped, the old-fashioned furnishings lent an air of cosiness to the home the two brothers shared with their mother.

'What's his name, again?' asked Eric.

'Bob Dylan. He's a folk singer.'

A folk singer?

'It's Mum's LP,' Paul said, reading his friend's expression.

Paul removed the record and handed Eric the cover. The brown-and-blue hued photograph showed the singer in a snowy city street, walking arm-in-arm with his smiling longhaired girlfriend.

The Freewheelin' Bob Dylan.

Paul lowered the stylus onto the spinning black disc and closed the lid of the radiogram. Eric recognised the first song, though not this version; he had heard *Blowin' in the Wind* by Peter, Paul and Mary in the van on the way to Skegness. He looked over at his friend, sitting in the leather armchair next to the electric fire.

'Keep an open mind,' said Paul. Standing up, he drew the green velvet curtains and turned off the light.

The music sounded stark, just an acoustic guitar with a few bars of mouth organ tossed in lazily between the verses. The singer's voice was unrefined, but he was speaking the words as much as singing them. The lyrics painted vivid pictures, every line conveying a different image, all at once surprising, shocking, confusing and beautiful. Eric saw himself as the small boy standing outside his uncle's door, listening spellbound as Nancy Whisky's *Freight Train* carried him through a rain-lashed night, its insistent rhythm propelling the speeding locomotive along shimmering steel tracks. The child could *see* the train, feel the rain, hear the tremendous steaming engine roaring through the storm.

Dylan was the same, but with a twist. And times a hundred.

*

As the weeks passed, Eric settled into life at the old grammar school. He and Paul became acquainted with their classmates, and friendships formed, creating factions within the larger group. At their previous school, lessons had been conducted mainly within one location, but here pupils moved between dedicated classrooms. Every desk in the science lab boasted a Bunsen burner. The art room was set up with a circle of easels and presided over by the eccentric Mr Gale, whose crumpled clothing and uncombed hair earned him the name *Scarecrow*. An upright piano sat on a low stage in the music room next to *Mojo's* desk. Eric was disappointed to learn that the music teacher's tastes were bound up in standard classical pieces and spine-tinglingly insipid light opera. In common with most of the teachers, the headmaster, Mr Hunt, also had a long-established nickname: in his case, one that rhymed easily with his own.

The early morning air blew cold on Eric's face. He flipped down a gear.

"'Ello!' Paul drew alongside Eric, matching the speed of his bicycle.

'I was beginning to think you weren't coming,' said Eric.

'I didn't want to get out of bed,' replied Paul. 'Our house is bloody freezing.'

Eric smiled, 'It's only October. Wait till the cold really kicks in.' His mind went back to the previous winter, *the Big Freeze*.

On winter mornings, before central heating was commonplace, getting out of a toasty warm bed required steely determination. A cold hot-water bottle hit the floor, and a nose appeared from beneath the covers breathing clouds of frozen air. Searching eyes landed on a pile of clothes, sometimes followed by a muttered verbal countdown: *'Three... two... one... Nah, five minutes more.'* Watching the clock, waiting until the latest possible moment, the bedcovers were thrown back, signalling a frantic dash to get dressed.

'I take it you saw *Ready Steady Go!* on Friday,' Paul said, as they cycled past Lammas Park.

'Yup, never miss it.'

'They were great, weren't they. Do you think they were miming?'

'Definitely,' answered Eric. 'It sounded too much like the records. And you could tell Ringo wasn't really playing. I'm *pretty* sure, anyway.'

ITV's new pop programme *Ready Steady Go!* had first broadcast two months earlier at the beginning of August. Opening with Tony's current favourite, *Wipe Out*, the teen-oriented music show aired every Friday evening – *The weekend starts here!* On the fourth of October 1963, the Beatles made their first appearance on RSG, miming *Twist and Shout, I'll Get You,* and *She Loves You.*

'We'd better get a move on.' Paul rose from his saddle, urging his bicycle forward.

Eric sighed, 'Yeah, I'd hate to miss the hymns.'

The following Wednesday evening, Eric dialled the Ramsey's number. He recognised the continuous tone that told him that Mrs Ramsey had failed to pay the phone bill again.

'Mum, could you lock the back door behind me, I'm popping over to see Paul and Tony.'

'All right,' Mary replied, finishing the washing-up. 'Don't be too late; you've got school tomorrow.'

The daylight was nearly gone when Eric made his way through the adjoining alley, avoiding a cluster of overhanging brambles. He reached over the Ramsey's back gate, unlatching the bolt as he had done many times before. Entering the rear garden, Eric picked his way through the long grass and overrun flowerbeds. A light came on, and Julia Ramsey walked into the living room wrapped in a blue bath towel. The young woman smiled, acknowledging the boy at her kitchen door. Eric heard the sound of bolts being drawn, and the back door opened.

'Hello, Eric.' Julia's wet black hair straggled her shoulders.

Eric stepped into the kitchen and stood aside as his friends' mother relocked the door. 'Are Paul and Tony here?' he asked awkwardly.

'No, it's Wednesday... cubs and scouts.'

Eric felt a growing sense of embarrassment.

Julia smiled reassuringly, 'It's all right, Eric. Make yourself at home in the front while I put something on.'

Passing through the hallway, Eric entered the dark front room. Standing in the orange glow of the electric fire, he looked through the half-open door and watched his friends' mother walking up the stairs.

A minute later, Julia returned wearing a red Japanese robe. The knee-length kimono suited her well.

'Would you like a cup of coffee?' Julia asked the lad on the sofa.

'Yes please, thank you,' Eric replied politely.

'Milk and two sugars?'

'Please, yes, thank you,' repeated the boy. He had never been offered coffee before in his life.

The green velvet curtains were drawn, cosily shutting out the world. Eric stared dreamily at the glowing elements on the Belling electric fire, the only source of light in the shadowy front room.

'There you are,' Julia said kindly, handing Eric the drink. She settled in the armchair beside the fire. 'Paul tells me your guitar playing's improving.'

'Yes – no, well, I can only play chords really... But I'm getting better.'

Julia nodded. 'Do you *love* playing?'

'Yes, I... Well, I love music, so... Actually, I can't imagine *not* playing.'

'Then stick with it, Eric. Not everyone is fortunate enough to find a passion in life.' Julia regarded the boy, 'To be blessed with an affinity for the arts is a precious thing. I hope you'll treasure it.'

Eric listened, captivated by Julia's sincerity and her words, considered and heartfelt. With her delicate features and willowy frame, he envisioned the young woman as a wise and beautiful fairy queen from a Disney film he had seen. Her green eyes looked over,

'I hear you're rather taken with my Bob Dylan record. What do you like about it?'

Eric answered right away, 'The pictures.'

Julia smiled. 'Shall we listen to it together?'

Eric nodded.

'An art-school friend of mine moved to New York.' Julia raised the lid of the radiogram. 'She heard Bob Dylan singing in a coffee house and sent me his record. Apparently, he's the talk of the town.'

Sinking into the comfortable old sofa, Eric let the music wash over him. He and Paul had played the LP many times over the preceding weeks, and it got better with every listening. He closed his eyes, and Dylan's elusive pictorial poetry filled his receptive young mind. No words passed between the listeners, and in what seemed like a twinkling of time, side two neared its end.

Half-opening his eyes, Eric focused dreamily on the embroidered Japanese figures, pagodas, and bridges on Julia's shimmery red robe. Animated by his unshackled imagination, the kimono-clad geishas appeared to float among the maple trees and wooden arches, drifting like ghosts across the shadowy silken folds. Julia had slipped down in the comfortable leather chair; she lay still and quiet. Was she sleeping? He didn't think so, though her eyes were closed, and she breathed gently, her slender feminine outline rising and falling beneath the shiny crimson kimono to which it gave form. Eric's gaze traversed her body, settling on her slim pale legs, made orange by the fire glow.

'Perhaps it's time you got going,' Julia said softly, smiling at the boy. 'You've got school in the morning.'

Eric lay awake for a long time that night, staring into the darkness of his small bedroom. His fertile imagination fired by the heavily charged atmosphere of the evening, he closed his eyes and watched as vivid cinematic images flashed by in his minds-eye: images of Julia Ramsey. Sliding down the bed, Eric drew the blankets over his head.

*

Taking his accustomed second lunch hour, Sid closed the glossy red door behind him, strolled past the suited mannequins in Burton's side window, then skipped across West Ealing high street into British Home Stores. Studying the track listing on Sonny Rollins' *Our Man in Jazz,* he felt a prod in the small of his back. A lad stepped forward and nodded at Sonny Rollins,

'He's goo-od,' said the boy, affecting an American drawl. 'But take a tip, get hip, and take a trip with the *new* song and dance man.' Eric held up an album presenting the cover to Sid. *'Zimmy,'* he announced in the most resonant whisper his unbroken voice could muster.

Sid read the name on the sleeve, Bob Dylan, and wondered who the hell *Zimmy* was.

When Eric showed the *Freewheelin' Bob Dylan* cover to Sid, he did not for one moment expect the jazz-loving man to take him seriously, but he did just that. Unbeknown to the boy, Sid left British Home Stores with *Freewheelin'* tucked under his arm, along with four pairs of white socks and a yellow-and-black Rupert Bear scarf.

That evening, Sid flopped into his favourite chair in his flat above the Golden Fish shop in Hanwell, and listened to the record. Around 2am he awoke from a dream in which he was being chased across Tower Bridge by a pair of burly gangsters wielding sawn-off snooker cues. Sid poured two fingers of Jim Beam, then played the LP a second time.

For weeks on end, *Freewheelin'* remained on the turntable waiting for its owner to return home from work and play it again. And again. By the third week, Sid knew most of the words by heart, and there were plenty of them. The more Sid played it, the more confident he became. Little by little, conjecture turned to full-blown conviction. He had gazed into the crystal and seen the future, heard its call. When the mist cleared, Sid saw the door of opportunity looming tall before him. There was a whole pile of money behind it, and you could *bet your bottom dollar* that the boy held the key.

*

On the fourth of November 1963, the Beatles played a short set at the Prince of Wales Theatre in London. Addressing the audience at that year's Royal Variety Performance, John Lennon requested that those in the cheap seats clap their hands while the rest shake their jewellery.

Sid sat at his desk by the office window, staring down at the busy high street below. He had maintained this vigil for the past two-and-a-half weeks, watching shoppers file in and out of British Home Stores. Reg had lied to him about not knowing Eric's address; Sid was sure of it. How could the postman, of all people, not know something like that?

The radio was on quietly. America's President Kennedy had been shot while waving from a limousine in Dallas, Texas. Handsome and charismatic, Kennedy personified the country's upbeat mood. He had handled the *Cuban Missile Crisis* and championed the *Space Race*. Media worldwide reported the assassination with an intensity unmatched before or since. The BBC's *That Was The Week That Was* went so far as to dedicate a non-satirical edition to the late president.

Where were you when President Kennedy was shot?

Eric was at home watching Ready Steady Go! and reading an article about the Beatles' new record. *With the Beatles*, the group's second LP, was released on the 22nd of November 1963, the same day as the Dallas assassination.

While Sid gazed down at the high street, a white-coated man worked on the transmitter in the back room. A fat old lady with lilac hair and a flowery pink apron pushed a mop around the office floor. Mavis, the middle-aged receptionist, sat by the radio, filing her long red fingernails.

Ignoring the pile of paperwork on his desk, Sid listened to the radio with tears in his eyes. Though he had migrated to England at six, Sid regarded the US as his spiritual home. *'Bein' displaced ain't no disgrace',* he had told Reg. When the postman posed the obvious question, Sid said he believed his work to be too important to justify repatriation. Reg raised an eyebrow but let the matter lie.

An American radio reporter described how President Kennedy's limp body was cradled in his wife Jacqueline's arms as the couple were driven to Parkland Hospital.

Sid rubbed his eyes. At 1pm on a Saturday afternoon, West Ealing high street was always busy, but when he spotted the dark-grey duffel coat, he knew his patience had paid off.

Jumping up from his desk, Sid grabbed his coat and hat, toppling the spindly wooden stand as he skidded on the wet floor. 'Be right back,' he called to no one in particular.

Tapping an unfiltered Senior Service on the back of the pack, Reg eyed Sid thoughtfully.

A queue had formed in the record department at British Home Stores. Eric noted that every customer held a copy of *With the Beatles.* The group's popularity had soared, their meteoric rise to fame showing no signs of abating. The *Fab Four* now found themselves empowered, and their second LP cover was an early example. The black-and-white picture of their half-shadowed faces presented a marked contrast to the inartistic snapshot hastily taken for their first long-player.

Eric would be twelve years old on the 31st of December. *With the Beatles* would surely arrive then, if not on the 25th. And both Christmas and his birthday were only a few weeks away. He felt a familiar tap on his shoulder. 'Hello, Sid.' Eric continued to read the notes on the back of *With the Beatles.*

'Hi there kid, thought I saw ya, an' I did.'

Eric turned around, mildly relieved that it *was* Sid who had tapped him on the shoulder.

'Got some time to spend with your very good friend?' rhymed Sid.

'Sure,' answered Eric, saying the only word he could pronounce in an American accent.

A short time later, Eric found himself in Sid's pink-and-white Hillman Minx as the battered old car rattled up the Uxbridge Road entering Ealing Broadway.

Sid pointed across Eric's chest towards Bentalls, 'Dusty Springfield used to work in that there store.'

Eric looked at the big department store, watching a window dresser slot an arm onto a half-naked mannequin. He wondered if Dusty's arms came off, too. Bentalls' display department had been busy in recent weeks and the windows glittered with red, green and gold Christmas decorations. The high street was teaming with shoppers, filling the pavements and crossing between the slow-moving cars.

Pulling up at the traffic lights, Sid leaned over the steering wheel, looking up the road to their left. He nodded in the direction of Ealing Broadway Station, 'Ever heard of the Ealing Club?'

Eric shook his head.

'Up there in a basement under the bakers' shop. Used to be Ealing Jazz Club, but it's more blues these days. Them *Rollin' Stones* got started down there.'

Although he was familiar with the word, Eric did not know what blues was, only that it referred to some kind of musical style, like jazz or classical. But he did know who the Rolling Stones were. The previous evening, the group had been on Ready Steady Go! miming to their first hit, *I Wanna Be Your Man*. Seeing Mick Jagger and co on television for the first time, Eric's mother exclaimed, *'Oh! They're not wearing ties!'* As the Stones launched into their new single, across the Atlantic in Dallas, a sniper aligned his sights on the waving US president.

Sid and Eric exited the Mall reaching Ealing Common. The Minx sputtered and farted, belching black smoke from its rusty tailpipe to the annoyance of a following motorcyclist.

'Bobby Zimmerman,' said Sid.

Eric turned to the driver, 'You've heard him?'

'Oh yeah. Picked up that twelve-inch vinyl you had in your hands at the Home Stores. Bin freewheelin' ever since.'

Sid proceeded to provide his passenger with an enthusiastic review of the Bob Dylan record. His monologue continued as they passed through Acton. When the Hillman drove coughing and spluttering alongside Shepherd's Bush Green, Sid was still talking about Bob. Curiously, somewhere between Notting Hill and Kensington Gardens, Eric noticed that Sid's American accent had begun to slip, revealing tell-tale traces of Cockney brogue. By the time they reached Hyde Park, the dialects had reversed, and Eric found himself listening to a voice that sounded more like Henry Cooper than Henry Fonda.

As they crossed into Oxford Street, a taxicab swerved in front of the Hillman. Sid mounted the pavement, narrowly avoiding a smartly dressed woman being led by two standard poodles. The pedestrians scattered, some seeing their lives flash before them, others distraught at the prospect of losing theirs beneath the wheels of a rusty old pink-and-white Hillman Minx.

'Goddammit!' exclaimed Sid, his American accent returning to enhance the expletive. In the Minx's rear-view mirror, he observed the wheezing crowd, their life-threatening predicament having switched from maniacal car-death to carbon monoxide asphyxiation.

Taking advantage of the distraction, Eric slipped in the question he had wanted to ask for the past twenty-five minutes, 'By the way Sid, where are we going?'

'Soho,' replied the driver. 'We're nearly there.'

Eric had once visited Piccadilly Circus with his mum. Today there were young people sitting below Eros and crowds thronging the pavements. They parked in a nearby backroad.

Sid brushed shoulders with a shuffling vagrant as he pointed across Shaftsbury Avenue. 'Ronnie Scott's place is right over there. Best jazz club in town – an' the competition is killin' me.'

'The competition?' Eric gazed around at the bustling city street with its world-famous theatres and colourful illuminated advertisements.

'You'll see in a minute,' Sid replied evasively. 'This way, kid.'

Eric followed as the man turned off the busy thoroughfare into a narrow side road. Now they were in an altogether different world. The crowds had evaporated, the confined streets and pedestrian alleyways inhabited mostly by solitary men and shady-looking individuals, some of far-eastern origin. They passed tiny bookshops, dark and dusty, and small restaurants serving exotic cuisine from diverse corners of the globe. The boy winced at the sight of featherless ducks hanging limp and lifeless in one of the shop windows.

'You don't like Chinese food?'

'I don't eat meat,' replied Eric.

'Why the hell not?'

'Well, when I realised that what was on my dinner plate was once an animal in a field, I –'

'This is it,' interrupted Sid. He stopped in front of a high terraced building with black metal railings along the front.

Eric saw a handwritten sign in a doorway that read, *Model First Floor*. He looked up at the old three-story house, 'Why are there red light-bulbs in the windows?'

'Not up there, down *there*.' Sid pointed through the railings to a descending flight of steps.

Eric grasped the spiked metal tips and peered down between the bars. Below him was a black door. Above it, an unlit blue neon sign read, *Club de Nuit*.

'Welcome to my nightclub!' Sid said excitedly, his keys jingling in his hand as he trotted down the steps.

The empty club was far smaller than Eric had pictured it to be. The walls and ceiling had been painted matt black. The converted basement had a stage at the far end, large enough to accommodate four performers at a squeeze. Tables were scattered around the floor, and a coffee-house booth-seat sat in a corner next to the door.

While Sid stood behind the bar pouring two glasses of Pepsi, Eric sat stiffly at one of the tables, acutely aware that he was a long way from home.

The nightclub owner handed the boy a cola and drew out a chair.

'Thanks.' Eric sipped his drink, stifling a sneeze as the carbonated bubbles went up his nose.

'That Dylan record,' began Sid.

Eric prepared himself for another half-hour soliloquy on the magical wonders of Bob.

'It kinda got me thinkin'.' Sid paused.

It occurred to Eric that he was about to learn the reason for his Saturday afternoon visit to London's West End.

'Now stay with me; this sorta comes in two parts,' began Sid. 'So, here's the first part.'

Eric listened, pretty sure that he would be doing so for some time.

'The times are changing,' Sid stated, misquoting the title of Bob's forthcoming single. 'The jazz scene ain't what it was, an' I bin thinkin' 'bout headin' in a new direction, musically speakin', here at the club.'

'Good idea,' Eric said, feeling pleased to have contributed to the conversation.

A broad smile spread across Sid's face. Eric was again impressed by the man's splendid white teeth.

'Glad you think so!' said Sid. 'Now here's part two... Part two is *you*.'

'*Me?*'

'Yep.'

'Sid, I'm a *twelve-year-old kid!* Well, nearly. What can *I* do?'

'More than you know,' the man replied mysteriously. 'Fact is, you got your finger on the pulse. All I'm askin' is for a little guidance, a little pointin' in the right direction, tha's all.'

Eric breathed a quiet sigh of relief. The request sounded simple enough. Perhaps he could write a list of his favourite groups and drop it through Burton's letterbox, then Sid could book the groups at his club. Eric looked around. He doubted that the Beatles would agree to play at the tiny venue. Maybe Sid could ask Johnny Kidd and the Pirates. Eric realised that Sid had been watching him. 'Okay,' said the youngster. 'No problem.'

Sid jumped out of his chair, grinning and clapping his hands like he had just won the football pools. Placing his palms on the table, he leaned in close to Eric, 'Boy, you may not know it yet, but you got *Grandmama's Gift*.'

Eric did not know it, nor did he really want to ask.

Peering past the net curtains, Mary watched Eric step out of the battered Hillman. It had been dark for nearly an hour, and the boy's mother was relieved to see her son safely home, though somewhat puzzled by the means of his arrival.

A short distance up the road, the Minx barked a noisy farewell and chugged off into the night.

Ten minutes later, the family settled down to watch *An Unearthly Child*, the first-ever episode of Doctor Who.

5

Up on the Roof

1964

When Top of the Pops first aired on New Year's Day, 1964, Eric and Paul watched it together. Presenter Alan Freeman and a serpentine ex-wrestler with bleached blond hair introduced performances by, among others, the Rolling Stones, *I Wanna Be Your Man*, Dusty Springfield, *I Only Want to Be with You*, the Hollies, *Stay*, Gene Pitney, *24 Hours from Tulsa* and the Dave Clark Five, *Glad All Over*. The show closed with the current number one, the Beatles', *I Wanna Hold Your Hand*.

1964 began cold and misty, the reclusive sun remaining hidden behind a veil of grey for most of January. When the boys returned to school following the Christmas break, their classmates' main topic was the BBC's new music programme. The merits of the featured groups, singers and songs were discussed in detail, and sales charts scrutinised like football league tables on a Sunday morning. Showcasing the latest music and the blossoming fashion scene, Top of the Pops, alongside ITV's Ready Steady Go! opened the door to a glittering world offering wonderful enticements: music and girls!

Eric and Paul enjoyed a boost within the classroom hierarchy, their musical knowledge increasing kudos and serving to instigate new friendships. Paul's enthusiasm for pop music was now almost on a par with that of his best friend.

*

Reg slipped into the room at the back of the office. Placing an envelope on the desk, he lit a Senior Service and sat facing the transmitter. He stared at the unopened letter. A veteran of the Royal Mail, the postman had immediately noticed the Hartlepool postmark, the ink cancellation having endowed Her Majesty with an unfortunate curly moustache.

Reg opened the envelope. Enclosed was a memo and a one-way rail ticket from Kings Cross to Hartlepool. Grimacing, the postman read the letter.

Mr R. Proctor,

Please find enclosed one travel ticket,
Government Issue: 21.16 – 25.15.21.18.19

Arrangements have been made with Her Majesty's Royal Mail, confirming your extended leave of absence, effective immediately.

The duration of your stay in Hartlepool remains undetermined.

Sincerely,
B. Turing

MoD2 CLASSIFIED

Tossing the memorandum onto the desk, Reg picked up the railway ticket and checked the date, 'Tomorrow, 8am, at King's bloody Cross. *Tomorrow*. Bollocks!'
    The door opened, 'How ya doin', there's coffee brewin'.'
    Reg flapped the letter, 'There may be more than coffee brewing.'
    Sid's face dropped, 'Head Office?'
    'Yep,' the postman replied through gritted teeth. 'Looks like our fun and games with this here machine may be over, mate.'
    For three seconds, the two men looked worriedly at one another.
    'Nah,' said Sid. 'There's no way they coulda known. Prob'ly they're gonna put you on some bullshit trainin' course. Coffee?'
    'Tea, please.' Reg leaned his chair back on two legs and scratched his ear.

*

Having made his last stand in Western Australia, Tony had settled into his mother's chair next to the fireplace. The younger boy was now idly gazing through the misted living-room window into the overgrown back garden. It was cold outside and raining heavily.
    Eric pointed to the yellow Risk territory currently occupied by two of Paul's red armies. 'Alaska.'

'You'll ask her what?' asked Paul.

'Three dice from Kamchatka on Alaska.'

The two boys rolled.

'Six and a three.'

'Four and a three, uno apiece.' Paul removed an army, then twisting in his chair, took aim, and flicked the plastic game-piece at his brother.

'Oi!' exclaimed the younger sibling as the well-aimed red army ricocheted off his forehead and fell clicking on the tiled hearth. 'You'll lose all the pieces if you keep doing that.'

'So what? It's my game.'

'And again.' Eric rolled three dice along the heavily scratched tabletop. 'Four.'

Paul threw, 'Two.'

Leaving one behind on the Russian peninsula, Eric shifted thirty-six black armies across the Bering Strait, securing the far-flung US territory beyond reasonable doubt. It was all over bar the gloating. 'Give up?'

'No chance.' Paul fanned three Risk cards studying them intently. 'With this set, that's forty-something armies.'

Tony peered over his brother's shoulder, 'Two cannons and an 'orse.'

Paul threw the cards face-up onto the game-board (two cannons and an 'orse) and chased his brother out of the room. Sitting alone at the dining table, Eric heard two sets of footsteps thud noisily up the stairs. Seconds later, muffled shouts and banging sounded from somewhere above his head.

Eric joined Paul on the upstairs landing.

'He's locked himself in,' Paul said, furiously rattling the handle on the toilet door.

Two cannons and an 'orse!' Tony taunted from inside the small toilet.

The daylight was fading. The three boys sat talking in the front room.

'Where's your mum?' enquired Eric.

'At Uncle Jack's,' replied Paul. 'He lives in one of those great big houses round the back of Ealing Broadway.'

'Must be worth a few bob.'

'The house is, no doubt, but Mum said Uncle Jack's not so rich anymore. His ex-wife had expensive tastes.'

'Can we talk about something else?' mumbled Tony.

Paul half-smiled. 'We went there once, and the place gave Tony the creeps. I can see why. It's big and old and –'

'It's *haunted*,' interrupted Tony. 'It is!'

'Brilliant!' Eric exclaimed, sensing an adventure. 'Let's go and visit Uncle Jack!'

'I dunno,' Paul answered doubtfully. 'He's getting on a bit, and he's not our *real* uncle. We're related, but... he's something like our *distant* uncle or whatever it is. Twice removed and once round the houses.'

Tony frowned, 'Well, *I'm* not going.'

Picking up on Paul's dismissal of an opportunity to rib his little brother, Eric let the subject drop.

'The light's nearly gone,' observed Paul. 'Hide-and-seek in the dark!'

'Yeah, great!' responded Eric.

Spooked by the preceding conversation, Tony was less than enthusiastic, but bravado prevailed, and the ten-year-old agreed. The three boys split up and ran around the house, closing all the curtains and turning off the lights. They gathered in the downstairs hallway.

'Right, I'll seek first,' said Paul, adopting his customary role of games organiser. 'If you get back to the front door before I catch you, you're *not* the seeker in the next game. Okay?'

The two boys nodded; they had played the game many times in and around the local alleyways and backstreets.

Paul switched off the hall light, plunging the house into darkness. He spun around, facing the front door. 'I'll count to twenty. Ready? *Go!*'

Tony crept up the stairs. He knew which creaky steps to avoid. Gambling on a short-distance dash, Eric went into the front room and hid behind the sofa's far end.

Paul issued the time-honoured warning: 'Coming, ready or not!'

Listening for his friend's footsteps in the hall, Eric held his breath. Another moment and he would make his move.

Then the accident happened. Tony scampered along the upstairs landing, reaching the top of the stairway as the front door opened and Julia Ramsey stepped into the hall. Distracted by the appearance of his mother, Tony missed his footing and fell head-over-heels down the stairs.

'Oh!' Julia dropped her open handbag, its contents spilling across the carpet.

The kitchen light clicked on, followed by the one in the hall. Julia crouched over the gangly heap at the bottom of the stairs that was Tony.

The youngster looked up into the faces of his mother and the two older boys. 'I'm fine,' he said, then burst into tears.

Julia sighed, 'Oh Tony, it's always *you*.'

Eric looked away, his gaze landing on Julia's open handbag. Pushed down into the bottom of the bag was a white tennis skirt.

Paul helped his shaken younger brother to his feet.

'Um, perhaps I should get going,' Eric said, trying to sound casual.

'All right, Eric,' replied Julia.

When Eric arrived home, Bill and Mary were watching *Opportunity Knocks*, closely monitoring the all-important Clapometer. Hughie Green minced effeminately towards the camera, brandishing his long microphone.

'Hello Son, had a good afternoon?' inquired Bill.

'Yes, thanks, Dad. I won at Risk. I'm going up to get changed; it's pouring with rain.'

'Cats or dogs?'

'Both.' Eric turned to leave the room.

'Uh, Eric,' his mother called. 'Reg the postman knocked on the door asking for you.'

'Reg? Did he say what he wanted?'

'No, he just asked if you were in.'

Having changed into dry clothes, Eric helped himself to a sizable slab of Battenberg from the kitchen. Then he shut himself in the front room, switched on the electric fire, and picked up his acoustic guitar.

*

The following Saturday, the dull winter weather cheered up a little. Wrapped up snuggly against the January chill, Eric peddled his bicycle up Seaford Road, heading for Burton's. In his duffle-coat pocket was the list of pop groups and singers he had compiled for Sid. The man had been happy to help Eric when he called from Skegness, and the least he could do was return the favour. He thought of Susan and last summer's holiday romance when he had experienced his first kiss – his *only* romantic kiss to date. Susan had written her address on a beer mat which Eric had kept in his wardrobe. Maybe he should...

When he turned into Leeland Terrace, Eric heard the deep guttural growl of motorcycle engines. A hundred yards ahead, fifteen or twenty leather-clad rockers sat astride Triumph's, Norton's and BSA's, on and around the forecourt of Bill Bunn's motorcycle shop. To describe the cyclist as scared would be an overstatement; *wary* would be nearer the mark. A detour was called for, and Eric made a quick right turn, his revised route taking him towards the high street. As he rounded the corner by the Salvation Army hall, a spotty young rocker with greased-back James Dean hair shouted, 'Get off and milk it!'

Eric's stomach somersaulted. He stared straight ahead, focusing on the main road. A full-throttled lawnmower was approaching fast from behind. Eric glanced back in time to see the pillion passenger on a white Vespa scooter giving the young rocker a vigorous two-fingered salute. *'Greaser!'* Eric heard the two mods laughing as they sped past him. Seconds later, he was surrounded by black leather and gleaming metal machinery. The thunderous noise was deafening; the road seemed to rumble. Then they were gone. The air smelled of petrol.

Eric had stopped in the middle of the small side road. Gathering his senses, he looked over at the street vendors to his right.

'Okay, mate?' called a middle-aged man in a flat cap. Retrieving a bunch of bananas from the road, the vendor brushed them off and placed them back on his barrow. 'Feel like World War Two just landed on yer 'ead?'

Eric nodded.

The barrow-man chuckled and turned back to his stall. *''Nanas, 'nanas, luvly yella b'nanas,'* he chanted into the crisp winter air, his voice oscillating like a police siren.

A low sun had appeared from behind its grey hiding place, bathing West Ealing in thin yellow light. Dismounting, Eric pushed his bicycle to the roadside and watched two fluffy kittens play-fighting in the pet shop window. Across the street, the workmen's greasy-spoon café was full of women with shopping bags.

The boy wheeled his bike along the crowded pavement. The office was only a couple of blocks away, and he preferred not to cycle on the congested main road. Eric manoeuvred between the pedestrians, once catching a pedal on a wicker two-wheeler basket.

Leaning his bike against the wall next to Burton's, Eric pulled out the list of pop groups and singers he had written out for Sid. Posting it through the letterbox, he felt a tinge of unease. The atmosphere at Sid's club had been surreal and unsettling. Eric suspected the American wanted something more from him. And what had the man meant by *Grandmama's Gift?*

*

'Let's take a detour through Walpole Park,' suggested Paul.

They had an hour to kill before the film started, and Eric and Tony agreed. Crossing Culmington Road by the post box, the three boys entered the park through the tall green gates and followed the winding path. Beneath a featureless grey sky, the park appeared drained of colour, its floral displays and leafy abundance awaiting spring.

Paul slid a banknote from his pocket and handed it to Eric. 'Ever seen one of these?'

'Ten pounds! Is it real?'

'Yeah, they came out a week ago, twenty-first of February.'

'Is it yours?' asked Eric.

'I wish! Mum said to bring her the change.'

'It's great when Mum goes to Uncle Jack's,' said Tony. 'She usually flashes the cash.'

'Yeah,' replied his brother. 'She probably doesn't trust us in the house.'

'Hang on a minute.' Tony disappeared into the bushes that backed on to Ealing Studios.

Paul sighed, 'Couldn't you wait till we get to the cinema?'

Tony reappeared, proudly holding a white plastic football.

'Well spotted!' smiled Eric.

Impervious to the cold, the boys removed their coats, setting up makeshift goalposts on the damp grass.

'Three and in,' said Paul.

Players rarely wanted to be the goalkeeper. One exception was Ron Hillman, a lad in Eric and Paul's class. Known throughout the school as *Marmalade*, the ginger-haired boy had recently earned himself a Blue Peter badge for appearing on the children's TV programme with his prizewinning ginger cat, Martin. Colour television was still a few years away.

A grey mist was settling upon Walpole Park.

Paul slammed another screamer past his younger brother, who was all arms and legs in goal.

'That's three,' said Tony. 'Your turn to be 'keeper.'

Paul checked his replica diving watch, 'The film starts in ten minutes; we'd better get going.'

Glancing at his own wristwatch, Eric noted that the film was due to begin in *twenty* minutes. As an only child, Eric regarded the relationship between the two brothers as something beyond his comprehension. Still, it irked him when he used this as an excuse to withhold moral judgment.

A fog was descending when the three boys entered Barnes Pickle, the curiously named pedestrian walkway that ran alongside the ABC cinema in Ealing Broadway.

'What shall we do with the ball?' asked Eric.

Paul turned to his brother, 'We can't take it in with us.'

'Why not?' protested Tony.

'Cos they won't *let* us, you ear'ole!' replied Paul. 'How about if we stash it up there?'

The boys looked up at the low flat roof above the cinema's toilets. On the other side of the fence, a fixed metal ladder provided access for the football's subsequent retrieval.

'Give it here,' Paul said, taking the ball from his brother. Adopting the stance of a Harlem Globetrotter, Paul threw the plastic ball up onto the roof of the extension where it settled against the cinema's high main wall.

Their eyes adjusting to the darkness, the boys selected seats in the downstairs back row. This was the afternoon matinée; courting couples would occupy these seats in a few hours. The house lights dimmed, and the big red curtains parted. (Fanfare) Pearl & Dean present: a man informing the audience that *now* is the time for Lyons ice cream; a cheeky woodpecker asking if anyone is feeling *peckish* and suggesting a hotdog from the foyer for a shilling; two heavily made-up young women brushing their shimmering hair to show that Bristow's Star Spray leaves hair *lanolin soft* because it contains Bristow's *special* lanolin. Short clips followed, advertising the local wood yard and the tropical-fish shop on Springbridge Road. When the Babycham Bambi thing bounced across the screen, Eric's mind began to wander...

For a short period, *Saturday morning pictures* had been a weekly routine. The children's cinema show was sometimes reminiscent of a Gunsmoke saloon bar brawl. A Warner Brothers cartoon was followed by an old black-and-white serialised western: galloping cowboys were the young audience's cue to liven things by stamping their feet as rapidly and as noisily as possible. From that point on, Saturday morning pictures was a free-for-all. At the end of the show, there was a stampede to exit the theatre. For one such occasion, Eric hatched a plan to *accidentally* trip and fall in front of the outrushing crowd. Unfortunately, the ill-conceived stunt worked too well: Eric tripped and fell to the floor, the following kids went down like dominoes, and the three boys found themselves beneath a squirming pile of children.

An item on the Pathé newsreel brought Eric back to the present. Actor Peter Sellers and actress Britt Ekland had married after having known one another for ten days. Eric thought blonde Britt was gorgeous and wondered how an ordinary-looking bloke like Sellers could end up with a stunning young woman like her.

'That's what fame gets you,' whispered Paul.

Next up, to Eric and Paul's delight, was a segment featuring the Liverpool pop acts that had risen to prominence over the last twelve months. Arriving under the collective banner of the *Mersey Beat*, most of the performers were contracted to Beatles manager Brian Epstein, himself a Liverpudlian. The Beatles, Billy J. Kramer and the Dakotas, and Gerry and the Pacemakers were followed by Epstein's latest protégé, Cilla Black. The newsreel showed film footage of Liverpool's *Cavern Club* where the Beatles had kick-started their career, and Pricilla White had worked as a cloakroom attendant. Cilla's epic *Anyone who had a Heart* had recently knocked *Needles and Pins* off the number-one spot, the latter by another Liverpool act, the Searchers.

'I love the guitars on this,' Eric said, as a snippet of *Needles and Pins* played through the cinema's speaker system.

Paul nodded. He had learned a lot about music from his enthusiastic friend and now listened to it in a very different way from most people he knew. Or so he believed.

The Pathé editor had saved the best till last, ending the segment with the *Fab Four*. News had filtered through from the United States about the Beatles' record-breaking television appearance on the Ed Sullivan Show. Viewing figures that night exceeded seventy-three million, an astonishing statistic. Perhaps after JFK's assassination, the

US needed some cheering up, and the Beatles' timing was spot-on. Americans – to that point unreceptive to foreign influence – had taken the Beatles to their hearts. The group waved to an enormous crowd of screaming girls from the mobile stairway of a BOAC airliner.

'We had 'em first,' Paul whispered, noisily pulling open a packet of Butterkist toffee-coated popcorn. 'Why do they make these bags so loud?'

Tony glanced sideways at his brother, 'To cover the noise of your farts.'

A trailer for *633 Squadron* showed clips of *the Winged Legend of World War II* bombing German soldiers. A rousing musical score added drama and excitement to the explosive footage.

The featured picture was nearly two-and-a-half hours long, and the ABC showed no B film that week. The big red curtains closed, then reopened, and the screen widened, elevating anticipation for the upcoming presentation, *Zulu*.

'I'll be Mister Hook,' Paul said, as the soldiers were introduced.

'I'll be him,' said Eric, choosing Michael Caine's character.

Tony elected to be a horse: arguably a better choice, as most of the red-coated British soldiers would not live long enough to see their names scroll up on the final credits.

Although colour film had been around for decades, only in recent years had it become the norm. Keen to exploit the potential of luscious colour on cinema's increasingly widening screens, filmmakers selected wild and wonderful locations, shooting panoramic footage of exotic landscapes and brightly dressed actors set against boundless blue skies. Zulu was one of those.

Oblivious to the reprehensible moral circumstances under which the Zulu Wars were fought, audiences patriotically cheered on the lads in red, backing the imperialist invaders against all the odds. A few hours later, Julia Ramsey would make the very same point to the three boys, succinctly expressing her views on empirical expansionism,

'*Huh, well, we had no business being there in the first place*'.

It was dark when Eric, Paul and Tony left the ABC, and so foggy, the town hall across the road had all but disappeared. Stepping out of the cinema's neon light, the boys turned left into Barnes Pickle. Their footfalls sounded dull in the old walled walkway, the echoes muted by murky grey water-vapour suspended in the air around them. Haloed yellow streetlamps showed the way.

'Don't forget the football,' said Tony, his breath freezing.

The boys looked up at the high cinema, its flat roof barely visible in the fog. The white ball was partially discernible on the low toilet roof.

'All right,' replied his brother. 'I'll get it.'

Paul clambered over the wooden fence, jumping down to the corner of the car park. Eric followed his friend, lending moral support and not wanting to miss out. The black metal ladder was cold and wet but stable and easy to climb. The two boys stood on the flat toilet roof, looking down at Tony in the alley below. Paul picked up the football from beside the cinema wall,

'Here, hold this,' he whispered to Eric.

The next roof was accessed by a second ladder, which Paul quickly scaled. 'Throw the ball up,' he called in a hushed voice.

Eric tossed the football up to his friend and climbed the ladder to the second level. A third ladder, this one much taller, led up the side of the main building. Eric and Paul grinned at one another nervously. Paul hurled the football up onto the roof. Moments later, the two boys stood atop the cinema, looking down at the fuzzy yellow streetlamps below.

Paul placed the football near the edge of the roof and stepped back. Taking a short run-up, he booted the ball hard into the night.

From the alley below, Tony watched the white plastic football arc through the fog then disappear into someone's back garden. Up on the roof, Paul clenched his fists, cheered silently, and waved his arms in the air.

Descending the ladders, Eric made a promise to himself. In future, he would be more considerate towards young Tony, even if it meant his coming between the two brothers. It was a promise he would struggle to keep.

*

On the twenty-eighth of March 1964, Britain's first pirate radio station, *Radio Caroline*, began broadcasting from its North Sea mooring off the coast of Felixstowe. BBC radio now had some much-needed competition, and pop music finally had its own station. There were grumblings from the British power base, though a far greater outcry would have ensued had the public become aware of the transmissions emanating from West Ealing. Even the Prime Minister, Alec Douglas Home, remained uninformed of the machine's existence.

Home from school one Wednesday lunchtime, Eric shut himself in the front room and sat down for his usual fifteen minutes of guitar playing. Slotted between the strings of his acoustic was an envelope bearing his name and address. Eric was surprised to see the letter. Birthdays aside, he rarely received anything through the post.

At the top of the headed paper was the address of a hospital in Hartlepool. Below it was a short handwritten message:

> *Eric,*
> *Important - stay away from Soho.*
> *Reg*

Eric stared at the note. The message had been written neatly in blue biro, but the signature resembled the unpractised scrawl of a five-year-old.

*

Enjoying the Easter break, Eric and his dad relaxed in front of the TV, watching Steve Zodiac zoom across the universe in *Fireball XL5*. Transcending age barriers, though to a lesser extent, gender tastes, the space-age puppet show had been popular for the past couple of years. Filmed in *Supermarionation* in a large shed in Slough, the programme featured a catchy theme song and plenty of explosions.

'That's a real hand,' Bill said, studying a close-up, as Steve Zodiac switched the spacecraft into overdrive. Steve's female companion, Venus, vibrated in her seat.

The homely smell of roast dinner wafted through from the kitchen, making the Bank Holiday Monday feel like a Sunday. Eric would have everything except the meat and the gravy, preferring to drench his dinner in a speckled puddle of mint sauce. Mary had prepared a trifle for pudding, garnishing her creation with lashings of Dream Topping and a sprinkling of Hundreds and Thousands.

Dinner had that misty-windows warm cosy feeling that only close families experience. 'Thanks, Mum, that was lovely.' Eric would always remember the lesson in etiquette he had learned from his father: '*Did you enjoy your dinner? Then tell your mum*'.

Eric looked down at the newspaper laying beside him on the sofa. The Daily Mirror headline read, '*WILD ONES' INVADE SEASIDE - 97 ARRESTS, Scooter gangs 'beat up' Clacton*. Finding the main article, Eric saw a photograph of a young rocker wielding a broken deckchair above his head. It was the leather-clad hooligan who had shouted to him as he rode past the Salvation Army hall on his bike, inviting him to *get off and milk it*.

Holding his acoustic guitar upside-down, Eric slid the instrument into its bag. A tortoiseshell plectrum and a set of sparkly plastic pitch-pipes were already in his duffel-coat pocket. 'See you later,' he called down the hallway.

'Wrap up warm!' Mary called back.

Stepping into the covered porch, Eric shut the front door behind him and raised his hood. The weather that Easter Monday afternoon was unseasonably chilly, and there was rain in the air. The boy lowered his head against the wind as he walked around the block.

When Paul opened the front door, Eric did a double-take. His friend was wearing a black polo-neck jumper and pointed Chelsea boots. Even without seeing the red tag on the back pocket, Eric could tell that the jeans were genuine Levi's. Completing his new look, Paul had combed his thick black hair forward. As anyone seeing him at the time would have agreed, he looked like a young Beatle.

'You look terrific!' smiled Eric, walking past his friend into the hallway.

'Oh, ta,' Paul said sheepishly.

Eric leant his guitar against the bannister and hooked his damp coat over the handrail. 'What's that whirring?'

Paul ushered his friend into the front room.

Tony sat cross-legged on the carpet. He too was wearing new jeans, and his plimsolls had been replaced by Converse baseball boots. Laid out in front of him was a Scalextric race track, set up in a figure eight.

'Blimey!' exclaimed Eric.

The slot car racing set was the most desirable boys toy on the market.

Tony grinned up at Eric, 'Wanna race?'

Paul drew a grid in red biro. The boys would race one-another five times, the number of laps increasing as the Grand Prix progressed.

Paul was Jim Clark, Eric, Graham Hill, and Tony, Blinky Wilkinson. Tony's driver's full name was Blinky Broomstick-Up-The-Arse Wilkinson, but Paul insisted there was not enough room on the paper.

An hour-and-a-half later, with the hand-controllers almost too hot to hold, Jim Clark took the champagne. Second was Blinky Broomstick-Up-The-Arse Wilkinson, and last by a considerable distance came Graham Hill. Eric didn't mind; the two brothers had already had lots of practice. Winning was never especially important to him. Where games were concerned, Eric would try his best, but it mattered little if he won or lost.

'Right, are you still up for this?' asked Paul.

'Of course,' answered Eric. 'It's an acoustic, right?'

'Upstairs,' said Paul.

Sitting on the end of Paul's bed, Eric blew a low E on his pitch-pipes. Paul's new acoustic guitar was great. The strings were closer to the fretboard than those on his own guitar, and the tone was deep and rich. Paul watched as Eric finished the tuning and strummed an E chord,

'Sounds fab,' said the guitarist. Picking the highest string, he then struck it again while fingering the twelfth fret. He repeated this on the lowest string. 'The intonation is great, too... It's nicely in tune.'

'What do you mean?' asked Paul.

'I'm playing the same note on the same string, but an octave higher,' explained Eric. 'I'm comparing the pitch of the octave. If the guitar's in good shape, it'll sound in tune.' Eric repeated the exercise. 'Can you hear that it's the same note but higher? That's called an octave.'

Paul nodded. His first guitar lesson had begun.

Fishing inside his guitar bag, Eric produced his well-thumbed copy of Bert Weedon's guitar tutorial, *Play in a Day*. 'You can have this,' he said, handing Paul the book. 'I don't need it anymore. Forget about the music notes; just look at the chords.'

The lesson continued, and Eric showed his friend how to hold the guitar. He told Paul to lean forward over the instrument and not to let the guitar slide down flat on his lap. It was not long before the beginner strummed his first chord, the easily fingered E Minor.

Ten minutes later, Paul complained that his fingertips hurt.

'Okay,' said Eric, 'we'll leave it there for today. Here's my best piece of advice: leave the guitar *out* of its bag – a bit of dust won't hurt. Pick it up whenever you've got a few minutes. And be patient; it seems impossible at first, but you'll soon get going.'

The two boys headed back downstairs, joining Tony in the front room. It was time for the second Grand Prix of the day. Eric watched Paul drawing out the grid. He thought his friend looked fab in his new clothes.

6

One Foot on the Platform

Eric found himself spending more and more time at the Ramsey house. Paul helped him with the challenging grammar school homework, and Eric continued to teach Paul the guitar. Conscious of the promise he had made to himself halfway down the ABC cinema wall, Eric grew closer to Tony. Some moments stay with you, the heightened sensibility of a particular realisation defining a part of who you are. When feeling the tug of his undisclosed commitment, Eric would visualise the swirling grey fog and feel the cold metal ladder on his palms.

For Julia, the increasing presence of her sons' friend was welcome. In the absence of a companion, the young mother immersed herself in the three boys' lives, her role fluctuating between matriarch, big sister, confederate and friend. In Eric, Julia saw far more than a well-mannered young man. She believed that within him dwelt the spirit of a kindred soul, the soul of an artist.

Springtime 1964 arrived dragging its feet. Eventually though, a dull, wet April gave way to fine weather with the turning of the month. And so it was that on a bright and sunny May morning, Eric, Paul and Tony found themselves standing on the open platform at the back of a 55 bus. Paul reached up and pressed the Request button, signalling to the driver that someone wanted to get off at the next stop. Gripping the plastic-wrapped pole, Tony leaned out from the platform at full stretch. The spring air blew bracingly on his face as the red double-decker Routemaster sped along Popes Lane towards Acton. A large dark-brown hand reached out from behind the boy, grabbing him firmly by the shoulder and hauling him back into the bus,

'Watchoo tryin' to doo, knack your 'ead off on a treee?' the bus conductor inquired coolly in a thick West Indian accent.

As the bus pulled in by the pond opposite Gunnersbury Park, the three boys jumped off. Only old people and children waited for the vehicle to fully stop.

"Old tight please,' the conductor called to the passengers.

Everyone liked Gunnersbury Park with its boating lake, museum, and cafeteria. Sprinkled with neo-gothic follies and hiding mysterious nooks and crannies, the park had a tangible history.

On the agenda today was a round of pitch and putt, the first golf outing of the year.

Placing his ham sandwich to one side, the fat attendant slid the golf clubs across the counter. The tickets doubled as scorecards.

'Have you got a pencil, please?' asked Paul.

'Shixpensh,' replied the fat council employee, spraying soggy white breadcrumbs in the boy's face. He slapped a pencil on the counter, then took another bite of his sandwich.

Paul had intended to ask for some tees but changed his mind. And forking out a further ninepensh for a penshil sharpener was out of the question.

'The red or the white course?' asked Paul.

'Let's play the red,' suggested Eric. 'It's got more trees and stuff.'

Paul and Eric stood leaning on their clubs by the apron of the first green. Tony's almighty opening swing had made perfect contact with the sweet-spot on the head of his seven-iron, and the ball had gone sailing out of the course towards the cafeteria. Fortunately, no one was waiting behind them on the tee.

'I read that the Beatles had the top five places in the American charts,' Paul said conversationally.

'And nine of the top ten in Canada,' added Eric. 'Beatlemania seems to be taking over the world.'

'It'll never happen again,' said Paul. 'Not like this, anyway.'

'Why not?'

'No pop group has ever conquered the world before,' explained Paul. 'And there can only be one first time.'

Eric suspected he was hearing Julia Ramsey talking.

When Tony returned with his ball, he began his round with a personal *worst* for the par-three hole, notching up a disappointing eleven. Annoyed by his disastrous start, the youngster took nine hits on the second, to Eric and Paul's four each.

Try as it might, the sunny day did nothing to dispel Tony's prickly humour. An ability to maintain a cool head is an asset to a golfer of any age, but this aspect of the game was absent in the irate ten-year-old's psyche. By the fourth hole, Tony was ready to blow.

'Bollocks!' he shouted, as his attempted chip onto the green saw the ball pass high over the pole, clear the boundary railings, then bounce off a tarmac footpath into some bushes. Tony petulantly swung his seven-iron at a silver birch tree, whipping the shaft violently across the flaking white trunk. Bark flew into the air, then there was silence.

Tony stared at the bent club in his hand. Then as if the iron had suddenly become red-hot, he flung it to the ground.

Three pairs of eyes fixed on the L-shaped golf club.

Tony's older brother was the first to react. Paul picked up the mangled seven-iron and tossed it into a holly bush. 'Right, I don't think anyone saw. Let's dump our clubs and leg-it over the railings.'

Taking a detour to avoid being seen by the fat man in the hut, the boys headed up the slope to the mansion house, now a handsome-cab museum.

'Hang on a minute.' Paul stopped beneath a tree. Reaching into the pocket of his jeans, he produced a ten-pack of Park Drive's. He showed the two boys the three remaining cigarettes.

Tony smiled for the first time in over an hour. 'One each?'

'Uno apiece.' Paul rattled the box of matches he had borrowed from the kitchen. He looked at Eric, 'I got the fags from Ron Hillman.'

The ginger-haired goalkeeper was legendary for once lighting-up between the posts during an inter-school match.

'Where shall we go?' asked Eric. 'It's too open here.'

The three boys knew Gunnersbury Park well. Choosing their route to avoid the frequented areas – and the fat man in the golf hut – they passed through overgrown walkways and along narrow paths, heading for the boating lake's secluded edge. On the far bank stood one of the follies. Two pillars fronted the neo-classical building, which resembled a Mediterranean temple.

Shards of yellow sunlight shone down among the trees as they approached the back of the old folly. It was quiet here. Although they were close to the cafeteria and the putting green, few people ventured to this out-of-the-way place near the edge of the park. Through the bushes, Eric could see brightly painted rowing boats and white swans on the sparkling lake. Beneath an overhanging rhododendron bush, a family of mallards preened by the waters' edge.

Descending the slope, the three boys gathered beneath the Temple. Discarded beer bottles, crisp packets and chocolate wrappers littered the dirt floor. There was a faint odour of urine.

Puckering his lips, Tony failed to blow a smoke ring.

'Like it?' Paul asked, turning to his friend.

'Yeah... I dunno really... Yeah, it's good,' replied Eric. He took another puff.

The Park Drive was Eric's first cigarette. It appeared to have no taste, but the burning tobacco's distinctive smell would never seem so strong to him as it did that day beneath the Temple. His brain added the aroma to its growing list of déjà vu triggers.

'What's going on down there?'

The three boys looked up the slope. A middle-aged man with dark Brylcreemed hair stood looking down at them, his hands pushed into the pockets of his grey raincoat. Eric and Tony held their cigarettes behind their backs.

'Are you boys smoking?' called the man. He walked down the slope. His thick greasy hair almost touching the low ceiling, the stranger stood uncomfortably close. His face looked like wax.

'What?' was all Paul managed to say.

'My friend is a policeman,' said the man.

Tony dropped his cigarette.

'A lot of young lads have been arrested for smoking down here,' the man continued. 'But I won't tell the police if you'll do something for me.'

Grabbing Tony's arm, Paul marched his brother up the slope. Eric followed half a step behind.

'What about the police?' Tony asked as they walked briskly towards the main gate.

'No police... He's bent... A queer,' replied Paul.

Eric flicked his cigarette stub and saw it spark against a tree.

Tony looked up at his brother, 'You can let go of my arm now.'

*

A red sun hung low over the horizon when Eric left the Ramsey house carrying his guitar. Julia had been explaining the Civil Rights Act. The young woman's impassioned description of the racism in the Deep South and the atrocities committed by the *Ku Klux Klan* had held the two older boys' attention. Tony preferred to practice his Subbuteo skills on the dining table.

The talk ended when Julia went to watch something on BBC2. The UK's third TV channel had begun broadcasting on the twenty-first of April, a day late, due to a fire at Battersea Power Station. The new channel's focus on art, drama and culture resulted in Julia's selective viewing virtually doubling.

'BBC Two could never happen in America,' she told the two boys. 'It's important that we hang on to our precious little sliver of socialism. Like it or not, television is hugely influential, and we must keep our standards up, even at the expense of appealing to a minority audience.'

Most of this went over the boys' heads, especially the part about socialism, but the merits and pitfalls of differing political systems would be a topic for another day.

Eric mulled over Julia's words. Turning the corner with the last rays of sunshine at his back, he watched the long shadow of a boy carrying a guitar walk before him.

'Hello,' Eric called from the hallway.

The theme song from Rawhide drifted through from the back. Entering the front room, Eric unzipped his guitar bag and pulled out the instrument.

'What's this about, Eric?'

The boy recognised the letter in his father's hand. 'What's what about?' Eric asked, playing for time.

Bill read aloud, *Important, stay away from Soho.* And it's signed *Reg.*' Bill looked sternly at his son, 'Is this Reg the postman?'

'That's *my* letter,' protested Eric. 'It's priv –'

'Never mind that, your mother was putting your socks away, and she found – What the bloody hell does this *mean*? Don't lie to me, Eric.'

Bill swore: not good.

'I'm not sure what it means,' Eric replied half-truthfully. 'Reg has a friend – I met him in British Home Stores – and he owns a club in Soho. That's what it must be about.'

'All right. And why would this friend of Reg's want you to go there?'

'I've no idea,' lied Eric.

'Is this the man who brought you home in the Hillman Minx?'

Eric paused. 'Yes.'

Bill stared at his son, processing the information. Well, you stay away from this... *friend*. All right?'

Eric nodded.

His father dropped the letter on the chair and turned to leave the room, 'And it's about time you had a bloody haircut!'

The front-room door shut with a bang.

*

Early in July, Eric, Paul, and Tony saw the Beatles' first cinema release, *A Hard Day's Night* at the Northfield Odeon. Filmed in black-and-white, the story followed a few fictional days in the life of the group. Beatlemania having reached fever-pitch, the cinema was packed, and the audience full of girls. The film was great, and the soundtrack sensational. One of the Odeon's exit doors opened from the outside, and Eric and Paul saw A Hard Day's Night three times that week.

Paul's guitar playing had been improving, thanks to his scholarly determination and Eric's patient tuition. A leap occurred when the boys learned the chords to the current number-one, *The House of the Rising Sun*. Recorded by Geordie group, the Animals, the record was a groundbreaker in many respects. Timed at an unprecedented four minutes and twenty-nine seconds, the old folk song told the story of a poor girl driven to work as a prostitute in a brothel in New Orleans. The well-constructed organ solo played by Alan Price lasted a whole verse. The hit proved that a controversial song, once the province of a select minority, could now be seen as mainstream. Dylan was right: the times were changing and fast.

*

Adding another window sticker to the van, that summer, the Grimes family holidayed at St Ives. The picturesque fishing village on the north coast of Cornwall was a far cry from Butlin's. Attracted by its unspoilt beauty and consistent daylight, artists flocked there like pilgrims, immortalising St Ives and making it one of the most painted places in England.

Bill's one-man business had flourished, and he and Mary rented a cottage overlooking the bay. The Cornish Weather Wizard sent down blazing sunshine, turning up the heat to a blistering eighty-two degrees.

From an upstairs window halfway up the tree-topped hill, the family looked down at the sandy-coloured rooftops. Winding cobbled streets fell away towards a sparkling blue sea.

'I've never been so happy,' Mary said dreamily, taking her husband's hand.

Eric saw tears welling in his father's eyes.

In the days that followed, they soaked up the sunshine and breathed fresh sea air. Strolling leisurely along the promenade, they ate creamy Cornish ice cream and watched weathered fishermen tend their nets. A brazen white seagull swooped between Eric's parents, snatching a tuna fish sandwich from Mary's hand. Circling gulls cawed mockingly, laughing in admiration at the audacious theft.

July being the height of the tourist season, St Ives was filled with a colourful mix of people. Boldly dressed holidaymakers mingled among the locals who, despite the annual imposition, were courteous, if begrudgingly friendly; a lucrative trade came curtsey of the bankrolled visitors. Less welcomed by the villagers were the scruffy beatniks: itinerant bohemians with a rebellious artistic bent. The antithesis of the mods and rockers, the beats rejected violent behaviour in favour of intellectual pursuits such as jazz and folk music, poetry, literature, and antimaterialism. The group kept mainly to themselves, surfacing when living requirements necessitated they dip a reluctant grubby toe in the capitalist pond.

Leaving his parents sunbathing in the garden, Eric wandered down the hill. Soon he was lost in the Cornish magic of the tangled narrow streets. He passed a rustic public house and pictured salty old seadogs and shipwrecked smugglers swigging from pewter noggins beneath the low beamed ceiling. Following shaded cobbled pathways, Eric walked through cool enclosed alleys with whitewashed walls. He squinted as a tall dazzling rectangle appeared in front of him. Between the centuries-old buildings, the lanes unexpectedly gave way to a vast expanse of blue.

Along the promenade, tourists lingered by the harbour wall or sat chatting in tea shops. Men in khaki shorts took colour photographs of suntanned women in floral dresses. Brown children made sandcastles and splashed happily in the water, their watchful parents recalling childhood memories of their own.

Eric turned left along the seafront. The short pier, with its small unmanned lighthouse, was up ahead. He heard music from beyond the barrier.

The skinny guitarist wore a denim jacket with jeans and dirty white tennis shoes. His brown hair hung long and lank, entirely covering his ears. The man's face was gaunt and unshaven, apparently not having encountered a razor in days.

Eric sat listening to the folk songs, most of which were unfamiliar to him. He recognised *Freight Train* and *Blowin' in the Wind,* and they sounded good. At the musician's feet lay a cap with a few copper coins. In the fifteen minutes he sat on the wall listening, Eric noted that the singer had made fourpence. Halfway through Woody Guthrie's *This Land Is Your Land*, the boy walked over and threw a sixpence into the cap. The busker smiled and nodded his thanks. A few more of those, and he would eat well today.

Finishing his song, the beatnik crouched and scooped up the coins. He turned to Eric on the wall. 'Could you take care of this for a minute, man?' he asked, handing Eric his guitar.

Eric watched the busker walk to a fish and chip kiosk. Resting the guitar on his lap, he quietly strummed a G chord. The strings were old and dull, but there was something about the battered instrument that made it feel alive, as if after their years together, the guitar had become endowed with the personality of its owner. A policeman ambled by with his hands behind his back.

'Chip?' The busker offered Eric the open bag as he sat alongside him, watching the policeman walk away into the distance.

'Thank you.'

'I see you're a player,' the beat said, smiling at the boy. 'Thanks for holding Louise; I coulda got busted. Lucky I can spot a pig from half a mile.'

'Louise?'

'That's her name,' replied the man. 'Only polite to know her name if ya gonna sleep with 'er ev'ry night.'

Eric smiled at the cobblestones, wondering if he should be annoyed at being conned into holding the guitar. 'What if he'd arrested *me?*'

'Aww, don't be mad,' soothed the beat. 'No way he woulda done that. Here, 'ave another chip.'

Eric relaxed. The man had a rough endearing charm about him, even if he smelled a bit.

'Are you a beatnik?' enquired Eric, immediately feeling silly for asking.

'I'm an art school dropout who travels around playin' his guitar. Yeah, I s'pose you could call me a beat,' replied the man. 'But you can call me Ricky.'

'Eric,' said the boy.

Ricky pointed to Louise. 'Go on then, play somethin'.'

It was early evening when Eric and his new acquaintance made their way up the grassy hill that overlooked St Ives. Ricky was the first real musician the boy had met. As they approached the wooded brow, the man nodded to a small encampment near the edge of the tree-line. Between the orange and blue tents, a trace of smoke rose vertically in the still, warm air.

'Looks like somethin's cookin',' observed the beat. 'Hope we're not too late for the feast.'

Ricky and Eric entered the camp.

'Everyone, meet my good friend Eric,' the busker said, resting his hand on the boy's shoulder. 'George, Andy, Rita and over there is Sandy.' He pointed to a flaxen-haired teenage girl removing clothing from the guy-ropes and folding the laundry into a rucksack.

'Draw up a log,' said Andy, smiling warmly at Eric and motioning to the sections of wood that surrounded the campfire.

'Make any bread today?' inquired George, the eldest of the group.

'A whole one-and-nine,' replied Ricky. 'Guess the holidaymakers at St Ives don't know great music when they hear it.'

'I liked it,' said Eric.

Rita looked over her shoulder, examining the boy. 'You've got good taste, then,' she said, turning her attention back to the campfire.

Eric gazed at the attractive longhaired girl crouching in front of him. Rita wore a long red T-shirt which served as a dress. He didn't know you could cook Cornish pasties in a frying pan.

The atmosphere in the camp was friendly, and Eric soon relaxed in the unconventional company. These people were different to any he had met before, except perhaps for Julia Ramsey. The eldest man, George, was dressed entirely in black and sported a grey-flecked goatee. With his long hair, sunglasses and black beret, George had the appearance of a jazzman. The others were all in their late teens or early twenties and clothed in the road-worn casual clothes favoured by the so-called *Beat Generation:* denims, cotton slacks and T-shirts.

'They're done,' announced Rita, placing the frying pan on the grass. 'There're six of us, so half a pasty each.'

'Oh, thank you, but not for me... Thanks though,' Eric said, over-politely.

'It's okay, man, share our food with us,' insisted Ricky. 'There's plenty to go round.'

Eric hesitated. 'Well, the thing is, thanks, but I don't eat meat.'

'No meat? It's okay to eat meat – it's natural. Look at the food chain, man. Big animals eat the smaller ones; it's nature's way. We're at the top of the chain, man.'

George, who had been sitting quietly, came to Eric's defence: 'Look at it this way, Rick. If there was a species above us on the ladder – more intelligent, more powerful – would it be okay for them to eat us?'

Eric filed George's argument away for future use.

When they had finished their meagre meal, Andy crawled into one of the tents and reappeared with a long hand-rolled cigarette. Tearing off the twisted paper tip, he lit-up and inhaled deeply. Eric watched as the cigarette passed around the campfire. It smelled different to the Park Drive he had smoked in Gunnersbury Park. The perfumed aroma hung in the still evening air.

From the encampment high on the grassy hill, Eric looked down at the miniature white houses and the tiny wooden boats bobbing gently in the harbour below. In the golden light of the midsummer evening, the tranquil Cornish fishing bay was the most beautiful place he had ever seen.

George had been observing the boy. 'Top of the world, man,' he said quietly. He addressed the group, 'Maybe it's time for another reading.'

'Oh, not again, George,' groaned Andy. 'We sat through the entire length of *Howl* last night. That'll keep us going for a few days.'

The older man smiled, clearly unoffended. Peering over his dark glasses, he raised his eyebrows at Ricky, 'A little music then, maestro?'

The busker picked up Louise, who had been resting against the log at his side. Ewan MacColl's *Dirty Old Town* was followed by *Where Have All The Flowers Gone?* the latter occasioning soft vocal accompaniment from the small bohemian gathering. As they sang, the first of the nighttime stars appeared in the evening sky.

'I could do with a little help here,' Ricky said, offering his plectrum to Eric. 'Been at it all day, and me fingers are screamin'!'

Finding Louise sitting on his lap, Eric's mind raced. He looked down at the battered guitar, picturing expectant eyes upon him.

In a broken arpeggio style, he played the introductory chords to *The House of the Rising Sun:* Am, C, D, F... *'There is a house in New Orleans...'* Ricky sang the first verse while Eric played. Then Andy took the second, *'My mother was a tailor...'* Sitting together and swaying gently, Rita and Sandy sang the third verse in unison, *'Now the only thing a gambler needs...'* The plaintive lament of George's blues harmonica drifted across the campfire. Bending tortuous single notes, the soloist conjured soulful emotions from the tiny instrument to which Alan Price's electronic organ could only aspire.

'I got one foot on the platform...' For a split second, Eric wondered who was singing, then realised it was him! *'The other foot on the train... I'm going back to New Orleans... To wear that ball and chain.'* From somewhere outside the camp, an expressive female voice intoned the reprise, *'There is a house in New Orleans...'* Their faces raised, everyone smiled as a beautiful raven-haired woman drifted into their midst, her long purple dress floating as she passed gracefully among them. When the song finished, the party burst into spontaneous applause. Seating herself beside him on the log, Rita slipped her arms around Eric and kissed him full on the lips.

'Watch out, she'll 'ave you in 'er tent in a minute!' laughed Ricky.

Rita stood in front of the boy with her arms akimbo and wiggled her hips.

Blissfully nonplussed, Eric just grinned.

The camp lapsed into quiet conversation. The dark-haired woman in the purple dress was seated next to George. She was closer to his age, and Eric guessed they were a couple. Ricky was laid out on the grass, snoring.

Eric stood up. 'I'd better get back. Thank you... It's been great.'

As everyone said their goodbyes, George rose and joined the boy. 'I'll walk with you a little ways,' he offered. 'Sun'll be down soon.'

'Your mouth organ sounded brilliant,' Eric said, as he and George walked down the hill. 'I played one once, and it sounded, I dunno... Nothing like that!'

'I'll let you into the secret,' replied the man. 'You were playing in the key of A, right?

'A Minor, yeah.'

'So I blew a harp in the key of D. That's how you get the blue notes.'

George explained the *cross-harp* method, saying something about sucking when you would usually be blowing.

'That's our cottage.'

'Okay,' replied George. 'Good luck with your folks,' he added wryly.

'Thanks, I'll need it! It was... I mean, I really enjoyed meeting you all.'

'You too, man. Try to hang out with people who bring out the best in you. And keep up that guitar playing; it'll make you lots of friends.' George waved and turned back up the hill.

Eric walked hesitantly towards the cottage. It was almost dark, and he would have some explaining to do.

Seated at the side of the boat, Eric trailed his hand in the water. Friday being their last full day at St Ives, Bill had suggested the family take a pleasure-boat trip around the bay. The motorboat sat low in the water, and the spray felt refreshing in the hot summer sun.

Halfway up the hillside, Eric could see the white cottage where they would soon spend their last night at St Ives. He knew that around the curve of the hill were the tents belonging to the beats. The atmosphere of the previous evening had been tinged with magic, and Eric had lain awake in his bed reliving every verse of *The House of the Rising Sun*. He would always remember the flirtatious beat girl's unexpected kiss and the feeling of her soft embrace. That night she took the place of Julia Ramsey in his secret imaginings.

'Penny for your thoughts,' said Mary.

'It's been a great holiday,' replied Eric.

Sweeping around in a wide arc, the captain steered the motorboat back towards the jetty. Taking a last look from their nautical vantage point, Bill, Mary and Eric surveyed the picturesque fishing village.

The boat approached its mooring, the engine chugging quietly, and Eric looked up at the quayside. Standing in a loosely huddled group were the six beatniks.

'Oh, look at that scruffy bunch!' exclaimed Mary.

'It takes all sorts to make a world,' sighed Bill.

Disembarking, they climbed the worn stone steps on the harbour wall. Eric dawdled behind his parents as they walked in the direction of the beats. When they drew close, Eric smiled at his new friends.

Preoccupied, the beatniks completely ignored the passing boy, talking amongst themselves and gazing out to sea.

Eric's heart sank. Pushing his hands in his pockets, he followed his parents to the promenade, staring dejectedly down at the cobblestones. Spinning on his heel, he looked back at the beats.

Eric's mood switched in an instant as the smiling group waved animatedly. Stepping forward, the man in black drew back his arm, and with the stance of a tenpin bowler, tossed a small glittering object to the boy. Catching it neatly, Eric unclasped his fingers and grinned, examining the silver harmonica in his hand.

7

Reg

Eric strolled down Leighton Road in the warm August sunshine, his mind hundreds of miles away on the hillside at St Ives. Hearing his name, he looked above the hedge to see Reg leaning out of an upstairs window.

'Hello Eric,' called the spikey-haired postman. 'Have you got a minute?'

It took well over a minute for Reg to get downstairs and open the front door.

With a cup and saucer balanced on his leg, Eric looked up at the framed photograph of the recently completed Post Office Tower. Reg had been prattling on about the Liverpool – Arsenal game he had watched on the BBC's new football programme, *Match of the Day*. The postman described each of the goals in detail and was now airing his views on the drop in gate receipts that might follow due to the TV coverage. Eric sipped his tea, wondering when Reg would get around to the real reason he had invited him into the house. Having heard enough football talk to last him the rest of the season, Eric slid in with a well-timed two-footed tackle,

'So Reg,' Eric said, eying the man's plastered leg. 'What happened?'

The invalid refocused. 'I've been in hospital again.'

I'd never have guessed, thought Eric.

'I was minding my own business, crossing the road,' explained Reg, 'and this car comes belting round the corner doing about four hundred miles an hour... And the next thing I know, I'm looking at the ceiling in Emergency Ward Ten.'

'In Hartlepool?'

'How did you know that?'

'The letter you sent me. The hospital's address was on it.'

'Ah.' The postman slid a knitting needle beneath his plaster cast, 'Would you like a biscuit?'

'No thanks. What's all this about Sid?' Eric asked, determined to stay on the subject. 'I'm guessing it was him you were writing about?'

'Yes.'

'So why should I stay away from Soho?'

Reg shifted in his chair. 'I did a lot of thinking in the hospital, and I decided to fill you in on a few things.'

Eric nodded.

'How about another cup of tea?' suggested the postman.

Eric sighed. 'Okay, I'll make it.' He was in no hurry to get home, and Reg obviously believed he had something important to say.

When the boy returned from the kitchen with the hot drinks, the postman was smoking another cigarette, his fourth. Eric sat in his armchair and waited. Finally, the man was ready to talk.

'Eric, when I invited you up to the office last year, it was about more than repayment for your dad fixing my bike.' The postman's eyes were now keen and alert. 'It was a test, Eric.'

'A *test?*'

'Yes. It's part of my job, part of Sid's job, too... to recruit people who can work the transmitter. It doesn't happen very often, only once in a blue moon. And it's extremely rare to come across someone with your talent.' Reg sat back, 'Unprecedented, actually.'

'*Talent?* All I did was speak into a microphone!'

Stubbing his cigarette and lighting another, Reg continued: 'The machine – the transmitter – was constructed during World War Two. *The Scientist* – that's what they called him – locked himself away in an outbuilding in the grounds of Bletchley Park. There were rumours that he had found a way to send subliminal radio messages. He worked on it for years. It was all very *hush-hush*, of course... And you should know that it still is. Anyway, to the amazement of the people involved in the project, the machine worked. But only one man had the ability to use it.' Reg raised an eyebrow, 'That man was me.'

'What does *subliminal* mean?'

'Um... getting something into somebody's mind without them knowing.'

Eric nodded, 'Okay, go on.'

'The clever-clogs bunch at Bletchley... they said I had *the Knack*. It turned out that a few people have it – this *Knack* – but only in small amounts. I have a little of it, and so does Sid. And so do you, Eric. You have it, and far more than the rest of us.' Reg drew a long breath, 'The fact of the matter is, Eric, you've got a bloody-great shed-load!'

Eric sipped his tea, finding it difficult to swallow.

'They developed the transmitter for propaganda purposes,' Reg explained. 'And to confuse the minds of the enemy. But it came too late. By the time they had it working properly, the war was over. Bletchley was being dismantled, so they hid the machine where they thought no one would find it: in plain sight. In an office in West Ealing.'

Reg sat back in his chair, allowing Eric to process the information.

'Why are you telling me all this? It's *top-secret*, isn't it?'

'Yes,' replied the postman. 'It's as top-secret as top-secret gets, and I could find myself in a lot of trouble for telling you about it – a lot! You see, Eric, I was doing my job. I'd suspected for years that you had the Knack. Sid guessed it the moment he met you. Don't ask me how; let's just say that it takes one to know one. So we went ahead and did the test. Having someone actually *use* the transmitter is the only way to be certain. But we didn't for one moment expect you to have so much of it. The meter was fluttering into the red!'

'Do they know about me in Hartlepool?'

Reg shook his head, 'No, not yet. I don't think so, anyway. We took a chance, Sid and me. If we find a new recruit, we're supposed to report it right away, but we made an exception with you. Your gift is so strong, Eric; they'd do whatever it took to have you work for them.'

'*Whatever it took*? Like what?'

'Like... I don't know, but they'd find a way.'

'But what if I said *no?*'

Reg looked gravely at the boy, 'They'd find a way.'

With Reg's change jangling in his pocket, Eric left Parker's bakery carrying a white cardboard box containing the four strawberry tarts that the postman had requested. Once after Saturday morning pictures, Paul had dropped a stink bomb on the crowded shop floor. Today, the memory of the schoolboy prank was blown away by the bombshell that Reg had just dropped. Eric picked anxiously at the thin red ribbon on the cake box.

Using the key that the postman had lent him, Eric re-entered the house in Leighton Road.

'Any questions?' Reg enquired past a mouthful of strawberry tart.

Eric thought for a moment. 'Who *are* these people in Hartlepool? Do they work for the government?'

'Sort of, yes. The office is run by MoD2, a breakaway group from the Ministry of Defence. Even the present government is unaware of the department's internal affairs, and over the years, it's become untouchable. In the event of all-out war or some kind of dire national emergency, there are channels in place waiting to be reopened.'

Eric looked over at the postman, 'You've got strawberry jelly on your nose. Are you going to tell them about me?'

Reg wiped his big nose with the back of his hand. 'Not if you don't want me to. There are things you should consider before committing to MoD2. We'll discuss that later... maybe in a year or two. In the meantime, if you feel the need to talk about it, talk to *me*, not to anyone else. Not to Sid, not to your friends, not even your parents. Okay?'

'Yeah, I understand.' Eric stared down at the swirly green-and-yellow carpet. 'Why did you send me that warning letter about Sid?'

Reg struggled to his feet, 'I'll make us another cuppa, then we can polish off those strawberry tarts.'

Eric nodded. He was becoming used to the pace at which things proceeded in the postman's house.

'There you go.' Reg banged his plaster-cast leg against Eric's chair.

Eric levelled the saucer, pouring the tea back into the cup. 'So why should I stay away from Soho?'

'Ah, back to where our conversation started.' Reg grunted, falling clumsily back into his armchair. 'Okay. Now don't get me wrong, Sid's a great bloke, one of the best. But he can be overenthusiastic about his business ideas. There are a couple of East End gangsters operating out of a snooker hall, and I've heard he owes them money.' Reg sighed, 'Believe me, Eric, that makes hanging out with Sid something to avoid.'

'Okay, but why did he want my help in the first place?'

'The Knack, Eric. Sid calls it *Grandmama's Gift*. You see, people with the Knack often share something else... I suppose you could call it *intuition*. That's what Sid wants from you. I'm certain he'd like to involve you in all his business plans, his decision-making.'

Eric nodded, 'Okay, that makes sense now. Though I haven't seen or heard from Sid for ages.'

'I'm not surprised,' said Reg. 'Neither has anyone else. Sid's gone.'

8

The Quartet and the Barbershop

Goldfinger was the blockbuster film of 1964. Like Beatlemania, the James Bond series hit a peak that year, firing expectations and bolstering Britain's growing sense of pride and optimism. While the Beatles' *A Hard Day's Night* established their endearingly irreverent persona, Goldfinger's gadgetry ushered-in an age of technology. Behind a veneer of playful facetiousness, the Bond series blew away the barriers. The future was fast: fast living, fast cars, and fast women.

James Bond and the Beatles personified the nation's post-war transformation, transcending generational boundaries and taking the world by storm. The two disparate forces spearheaded an army of emerging liberalist talent, bestowing the battle-worn Union Jack with an image of *cool*.

Tired of the grey austerity and stifling conformity of the previous decade, someone in a bed-sit in Camden reached for the knob and turned up the colour.

It was the beginning of *the Swinging Sixties*.

Eric examined the acoustic guitar on his lap. As his proficiency on the instrument increased, so did his awareness of the cheap guitar's limitations. Barre chords, where the forefinger is required to depress all six strings across the fretboard, had now become second nature. The problem with Eric's low-budget guitar was the wide gap between the strings and the neck: a lot of pressure was needed to hold down chords, and doing this for any length of time made his hand ache.

Figuring out the Kinks' hit *You Really Got Me* had been easy enough, but continually sliding the barre chords back and forth was a killer. Eric persevered. He heard something new and exciting in the song: a raw guitar-driven energy. It had to be mastered.

Flexing his grudging left hand, Eric's thoughts returned to his meeting with Reg. Could the transmitter in West Ealing really infiltrate people's minds? It seemed too fantastic to be true, yet his own short broadcast – *Bill Grimes can fix anything* – had apparently energised his dad's business. And then there was Butlin's. The stunning blonde had been the hot favourite to win the contest, but Susan, with her big blue eyes, had won the prize. Susan... It all seemed a long time ago. He had felt so much younger then.

'Your gift is so strong, Eric; they'd do whatever it took to have you work for them... They'd find a way'.

The postman's words echoed in the boy's head. Eric felt sure he could trust Reg not to tell the faceless men in Hartlepool about him, but what about Sid? *Sidney Mars DJ to the Stars*. Reg said the American had people after him: dangerous people. Perhaps Sid was the kind of person that Eric's mum would describe as *a loose cannon*.

*

'There you go, mate.' Ron Hillman pushed a sack of newspapers towards Eric with his foot. 'Now, do you think you know where you're going?'

'Yeah, I've got the route written down.'

'Good,' replied the ginger-haired goalkeeper. 'It'll get easier when you've done it a few times. By the end of the week, you'll be delivering newspapers with your eyes closed.'

Eric's eyes were almost closed when he left the newsagent shop on the South Ealing Road. He squinted up at St Mary's and saw the clock click to 7am. The air felt fresh. Mounting his bike, Eric set off towards Ealing Common in the blue morning light. An Express Dairy milk float whirred by, the glass bottles clinking musically as the electric vehicle bumped over a pothole, dislodging a carton of eggs.

Someone won't be going to work on an egg today, thought Eric.

Delivering his first newspaper, Eric glanced at the front page. Harold Wilson stared back at him. The pipe-puffing leader of the Labour Party had recently pocketed the keys to number ten. Behind the public smile, Harold worried that his five-seat majority would not be enough.

Eric slotted the Sun newspaper into the letterbox. 'One.' It was the first of a large bundle.

The paperboy was five minutes late for school that day. Bony-faced Mr Styles wriggled his Hitler moustache as Eric entered the classroom flushed and fatigued.

*

The three boys sat talking in the front room of the Ramsey house. Paul and Eric cradled their guitars while Tony sat on his heels, surrounded by cardboard boxes.

'Do you think you'll stick with the paper round?' Paul asked, tuning the high E string on his acoustic to his friend's guitar.

'Got to,' answered Eric. 'My guitar's rubbish. I've worked it out; if I keep delivering those papers, in forty-two and a half years, I'll be able to afford a Fender Stratocaster!'

'Nah, Fender's are out,' said Paul. 'Why do you want a Hank Marvin guitar? Get yourself a nice German one: a Gretsch or a Rickenbacker.'

'I still like Hank's sound best,' replied Eric. 'But right now, I'd settle for a nice acoustic like yours.'

Tony clicked his mother's seldom-used knitting needles, 'Let's do *Wipe Out.*'

'Again?' said Paul. 'We've already played it four times.'

Eric pulled a face, 'What about the neighbours?'

'Oh, sod the neighbours,' scoffed Tony. 'And Mum's at Uncle Jack's till late.'

For the fifth time that evening, they launched into the surf classic. Eric played the lead lines to Paul's rhythm while Tony bashed manically on the cardboard boxes with the knobbly ends of the knitting pins. *Wipe Out: Version Five* lasted nearly seven minutes, featuring a Chuck Berry style improvisation from Eric and an extended two-minute *box* solo. Tony punched holes in the Scalextric lid and demolished a carton of Daz, spraying light-blue washing powder into the air and across the front-room carpet. The instrumental ended with a spirited crescendo.

'That sounded great!' called a voice from the hall.

'Hello Mum, how's Uncle Jack?' inquired Paul.

'Fine,' Julia replied, walking up the stairs.

Paul laid his guitar down next to him on the sofa, 'Maybe we'd better call it a night. And *Z-Cars* is on soon.'

Tony launched into an impromptu version of the programme's theme tune, *da-da-ing* loudly and bashing his battered boxes.

Eric stood up, sliding his guitar into its cover. 'Okay, I'll take a leak before I hit the road.'

Reaching the upstairs landing, Eric glanced into Julia's bedroom. Laid out on the bedcover was a white tennis skirt. He had seen it once before, pushed down in her handbag. Eric stared at the short pleated skirt. Though Julia was slim and petite, it looked about two sizes too small.

'Eric!' Julia exclaimed, holding her palm to her chest and smiling. 'You frightened the life out of me!' Even as the words left her lips, Julia realised she had caught the boy ogling the skirt on her bed.

Eric knew it, too. 'I didn't know you played tennis,' he said, trying unsuccessfully to hide his embarrassment.

Julia's pale cheeks flushed. 'Oh. No... I was thinking of taking some lessons. I was at the Broadway this afternoon, and I saw the skirt in a sale.' Glancing back over her shoulder, Julia wondered if Eric had noticed her fine needlework.

Eric wondered why she was lying. 'My mum plays tennis; she could teach you.'

Julia smiled through the narrowing gap as she closed her bedroom door.

*

Ron *Marmalade* Hillman and his crew of young paperboys called it *the Knowledge:* the pragmatic familiarity that comes with delivering the same newspapers to the same houses and flats day after day. Eric imagined that as a postman, Reg would have known similar experiences: the door with no number on it, the hidden entrance down the side alley, the house with the screaming baby and the mad Springer Spaniel. But along with the Knowledge came complacency, the kind that snuggles up with you beneath the warm blankets and drops sleepy-dust onto your eyelids on chilly autumn mornings.

Eric entered the classroom with seconds to spare. Another minute and he would have set Bony Styles' toothbrush moustache twitching. Paul smiled at Eric from his desk by the window. Bony opened the register and selected a pen from the 1953 Coronation mug in front of him,

'Ainsworth.'

'Sir.'

'Beaching.'

'Sir.'

Paul slid a note to the adjoining desk,

Got any plans for Friday night?

'Coats.'

'Sir.'

Eric read the note. Looking sideways at his friend, he shook his head. Paul reached across and turned the paper over,

Want to see the Beatles? Mum's got 4 tickets.

'Fisher.'

'Sir.'

'Grimes... Grimes?'

*

Hearing the front door close behind her son, Mary turned to her husband, 'I'm still not happy about Eric going to a pop concert with that Ramsey woman.' Mary invariably prefixed Julia's name with *that*.

'Oh, he'll be all right.' Bill stared at the clock on the mantelpiece. 'He knows he can call us if he's in trouble.'

'It's just that *Julia Ramsey*... And how on earth can she afford to pay for four tickets?'

Bill shrugged, 'Maybe she came into some money.'

Julie Andrews watched from a Mary Poppins poster as Eric, Julia, and her two sons, approached the bus stop on Northfield Avenue.

'Supercalifragilisticexpialidocious,' intoned Tony.

'Very good,' Paul said flatly.

Boarding a 97 double-decker, they went upstairs where Julia sat next to Tony on his favourite seat at the front. Eric and Paul sat behind. With the early evening rush-hour having come and gone, they had the upper deck almost to themselves. Two men sat smoking near the back.

The conductor leaned on the seat-backs, peering down at the empty stop. He stamped on the floor, signalling to the driver below. As the bus pulled away, overhanging branches banged and scraped the metal roof.

It was almost dark when the bus reached Ealing Broadway. Turning left into Springbridge Road, the driver headed clockwise around Haven Green, approaching Ealing Broadway Station.

Paul pointed to his left as the bus passed Mount Park Road, 'Uncle Jack lives somewhere up there. That's right, isn't it, Mum?'

Julia rested an elbow on the seatback, 'Yes, at the top of the hill near the disused reservoir. Jack lives in one of Ealing's oldest houses. It's a lovely place, but it's seen better days.'

Tony stared ahead at the traffic queue below. 'Don't talk about it, Mum.'

Julia tapped her youngest boy with the back of her hand, 'Oh, stop it, Tony. There are no ghosts at Uncle Jack's.'

Ealing Broadway Station being a terminus, there was already a red Central Line train waiting at one of the platforms with its doors open. Julia selected a *No Smoking* carriage, and the four sat together on facing seats. The electric doors closed, and the train set off towards London. Tony made faces at his distorted reflection in the window.

'What time are they on?' Eric asked as the train left Holland Park.

Julia glanced at her watch. 'In about twenty minutes, I should think.'

'Twenty minutes! But –'

Julia smiled, 'Our tickets are for the second show. It starts at nine o'clock; we have plenty of time.'

Lulled by the monotonous *clickety-clack* and the featureless black tunnel, Eric drifted back to the outings with his mother. The tube took on a different atmosphere at night. The clamorous voices of the city seemed to call down into the tunnels, inviting the travellers up to the historic streets and hidden alleyways above.

'Oxford Circus; we have to change here,' Julia said, rousing Eric from his dream.

The group made their way through a labyrinth of passages, and Eric wondered how many thousands of glazed tiles lined the walls of the underground network. A rush of cool air hit them as they turned a corner towards the northbound Bakerloo Line platform.

On the last leg of the journey, there were no vacant seats on the train. Every compartment was filled to bursting with Beatles fans. Flattened against the sliding metal doors, Paul and Eric grinned at one another: the carriage was jam-packed with teenage girls.

The Gaumont State Cinema in Kilburn resembled the ground level of an Art Deco New York skyscraper. The audience from the first performance spilt out of the 1930s theatre as Julia and the three boys joined the queue for the second show. Reactions on the faces of the predominantly female fans varied from joy and excitement to stunned shellshock. Few appeared unmoved by the experience.

The line slowly advanced, and eventually, they reached the entrance.

'Oh, I love it!' Julia exclaimed, surveying the lavish foyer.

Joining the queue on one of the two staggered staircases, the three boys received a lecture from Julia outlining Art Deco's history, beginning with the influence of technology. By the time they reached the balcony, Julia had taken them through Cubism, Functionalism, Constructivism and Modernism, and had begun to expound upon the relevance of Futurism in the Deco movement.

'Argh, it smells of piss!' Tony exclaimed, as they entered the cavernous auditorium.

Checking the tickets, Julia led the boys down to their seats, three rows from the front of the large balcony. An air of anticipation filled the 4,000 seat cinema.

Paul turned to his right, grimacing at Eric, 'Errk, my chair's wet!'

'Here, sit on this.' Leaning past Tony, Julia handed Paul an open concert programme.

Paul slid the souvenir booklet under this bottom, 'Seems a shame to ruin it.'

'Well, it's better than having a wet bum,' replied his mother, privately musing that the female urine might endow the concert programme with an added degree of authenticity.

The house lights dimmed, signalling an outburst of screams, cheers and shouts from the expectant audience. Veteran compère Bob Bain strode onto the stage. His usual job of winding-up the crowd took on a different aspect at Beatles shows. Bob strived to appease the impatient fans, maintaining an air of anticipation, as the supporting groups and singers battled gamely to win over the partisan mob.

Opening act, the Rustiks were followed by Sounds Incorporated, then Michael Haslam, the Remo Four, and Tommy Quickly. All five were signed to Brian Epstein. By special invitation from the headliners, American singer Mary Wells also appeared on the bill. She was the first Motown star to perform in Britain.

'They're on next,' Paul said, gingerly peeling the pages of the sodden programme.

Eric noticed that the girl's legs next to him trembled uncontrollably as she twisted her handkerchief on her lap.

'And here they are, *the Beatles!*'

The auditorium erupted in a cacophony of high-pitched screams. The enormous sound was everywhere at once: behind, below and on either side, echoes raining down from above. Eric sat looking at a row of backs, feeling like a seven-year-old at a football derby. Then he was on his feet, clapping and cheering along with Paul, Tony and Julia.

Eric stared down at the four mop-topped figures and the noise and chaos seemed to fall away. In that timeless surreal moment, he stood alone on the balcony of an empty theatre: empty except for himself and the Beatles. It was really them.

Twist and Shout. John Lennon sang, adopting his tuning-fork stance. His voice was barely audible above the unabating din. The crowd had morphed into a two-thousand-headed creature, the life-force paying homage to the earthly gods to whom it owed its existence.

Money, another rasping Lennon vocal. Then two from Paul: *Can't Buy Me Love* and *Things We Said Today*.

Between the songs, John stomped around the stage, contorting his face and affecting jerky spasms. Immune to the tastelessness, the audience screamed and cheered. Perhaps it was Lennon's assertion that he could do no wrong. Yet.

'Their hair is getting really long,' Julia shouted, looking along the row of boys and running her fingers down her black hair.

Next, it was George's turn to sing: *I'm Happy Just To Dance With You*, another from the latest LP. John's *I Should Have Known Better* followed, and Eric recalled the girls from the film's railway carriage scene. The harmonies of *If I Fell* were lost beneath the incessant screams. Ringo sang *I Wanna Be Your Man* from behind his drums, then John retook the lead for *A Hard Day's Night*. The set concluded with Paul McCartney's full-blooded rendition of Little Richard's *Long Tall Sally*.

It was after eleven-thirty when the black taxicab pulled up outside Eric's house. Julia stepped out to let him past.

'Thank you so much,' grinned Eric. 'I'll never forget tonight.'

Julia hugged Eric warmly, 'Oh, you're ever so welcome.'

Everyone waved as the taxi pulled away. Fumbling in his pocket, Eric found his key. As he walked up the crazy-paving pathway, he saw a curtain twitch in his parents' bedroom window.

*

Mr Cheddar was close to losing it. Chalking an algebraic formula next to the triangle on the blackboard, the mild-mannered technical drawing teacher indulged himself with a gory fantasy. Standing on his desk, he hacked mercilessly with the heavy end of a wooden set-square as the worst offenders cowered beneath his sweeping blows. He knew who they were. That ginger-headed Hillman kid would be the first to feel his wrath, then the snotty gang of troublemakers that hung around him. *If I hear one more farty noise, one more mouse squeak,* he thought. *One more —*

'*Eeeek-eeeeek!*' squeaked a mouse at the back of the classroom.

'*Eeeeeeeeeeeeeeek!*' squealed another.

Soon the room was filled with mice, squeaks coming from every direction.

Cheddar spun around, and the shrill rodent chorus fell mute. The teacher's face glowed red, his frame visibly trembling. Absolute silence. The chalk dropped from his quivering fingers, clicking on the floor. His darting eyes fixed on a set-square.

Opening his desk drawer, Mr Cheddar snatched a bunch of keys and marched stiffly out of the classroom. The door closed behind him, and a key turned in the lock.

The silence was broken by whispers, then chatter. The school bell rang, signalling the lunchtime break. Paul left his desk and walked to the door,

'It's locked,' he confirmed, looking back at the class and rattling the handle.

Five minutes later, the door was still locked.

Eric looked up at the louvre windows. The asbestos used in constructing the new extension had rendered the classroom fire-resistant, but not escape-proof. Following Eric's gaze, Ron Hillman climbed onto a desk and removed one of the tilting glass panels. Pupils gathered around the ginger-haired boy. When the strips were removed, he clambered through the frame and jumped down to the grass below. Boys followed like paratroopers exiting a plane. Two minutes later, the technical drawing classroom was empty.

Word of the escape spread like wildfire, and the story soon found its way to the ears of the headmaster.

The following morning, the entire class lined-up outside Mr Hunt's study, going in two at a time to receive a single whack each from his infamous cane. Eric and Paul stood last in line, Paul having reasoned that after thirty-odd swishes, the headmaster's arm might be tired.

Two by two, boys emerged from the study, those in the dwindling queue examining their faces.

Swish-thwack... Swish-thwack.

The last two boys waited apprehensively.

'His arm doesn't sound very tired to me,' whispered Eric.

'Do you think he'd notice if we buggered off?' asked Paul.

'May I be excused for the rest of the morning please, I have to change my library book,' Eric joked in a Charlie Drake voice.

'Too late now,' said Paul. 'You'd better shove that library book down the back of your trousers.'

Gallows humour, thought Eric.

The study door opened, and two red-faced boys came out rubbing their bottoms.

Side by side, Eric and Paul bent forward over the headmaster's desk. The two friends stared straight ahead, neither wishing to show or to see the grimace of pain integral to the disciplinary action.

Swish-thwack. 'Oop!' ejaculated Paul, as the slender cane whipped harshly across his buttocks.

Swish-thwack. 'Ek!' exclaimed Eric, his squeal conflicting pain with ironic amusement as he recalled the classroom of squeaking mice.

The boys rose slowly from their prone position, then both felt a heavy hand on their back.

'Down,' growled the sadistic headmaster, 'I'm not finished with you yet.'

Paul yelped as the flexing bamboo rod smote viciously, striking the same strip of aching flesh made tender by the initial blow.

Eric heard himself scream as the headmaster's malicious second lash sent shockwaves through his body.

Both boys remained prostrate. Stunned by the severity of Hunt's final assault, they stared down with blurry vision as tears pooled before them on the desktop. Mr Hunt circled the desk like a matador approaching his kill. Grabbing handfuls of their hair, the headmaster bent forward, pulling up the boys' heads. Inches from their tear-stained faces, in a hoarse voice, he whispered, 'Get your hair cut!'

Four days later, Eric's bruised buttocks were still recovering. Using his dressing-gown cord as a guitar strap, he stood practising in the front room. Eric was making his first attempt at slide guitar when the front-room door opened.

Bill nodded at the radiogram, 'Turn that racket off for a minute.'

The Stones' *Little Red Rooster* sounded nothing like Eric's idea of a racket, but he lifted the stylus off the record, at the same time slipping his mother's lipstick cap from his finger and hiding it next to the turntable. He had seen the letter in his father's hand and wondered what kind of trouble he was in this time.

'Here,' said Bill. 'Read it for yourself.'

When he saw the signature, Eric's heart skipped a beat.

Dear Parents,

    The personal appearance of some of our pupils is in a state of decline. The girlish hairstyles favoured by today's pop singers have recently become prevalent in our classrooms.

    Please ensure that your son is sent to school with hair cut above the ears so that our standards and respected position in the community may remain undiminished.

            Yours Sincerely,

                E. R. Hunt

                Headmaster

'Oh, right.' Eric handed the letter back to his father.

'Yes, *oh right*, indeed,' replied Bill. 'I'll leave some money in the dish on the sideboard. You can sort yourself out in your own time, but don't be too long about it!'

In the following days, Eric and Paul walked the school corridors with their hair tucked inside their collars, dreading a confrontation with Mr Hunt. Some of the boys had nightmares about the intimidating headmaster, while others went straight to the barber. The hard-core music lovers, along with a few nonconformist rebels, determined to hold out until the bitter end, whenever that might be.

Julia Ramsey's reaction upon receiving the headmaster's letter was to tear it up and throw it in the bin. 'Oh, for heaven's sake, your hair is barely over your collars. Anyone would think you were walking around looking like cavemen!'

'But what can we do?' griped Paul. 'It's Hunt's school, and he makes the rules.'

'I don't know, Paul,' replied Julia. 'Let me think about it.'

On the other side of the block, tensions over *the great hair dispute* were mounting.

Bill looked at the sideboard, 'I see that money's still in the dish.'

'Yeah,' replied Eric. 'I thought I'd see how things go.'

'*See how thing go?* See how *which* things go?' Bill's temper was rising again.

'Well, you know... things at school. I'm thinking it's a storm in a teacup and that it might –'

'Oh, is *that* what you're thinking?' Eric's father was now visibly angry. 'Well let me tell you what *I'm* thinking. I'm thinking you're going to get a bloody haircut if I have to do it myself!'

For a long moment, the father and son stared at one another. Then Eric turned abruptly, walked quickly down the hallway and out through the front door. Bill stood fuming in the living room.

Eric walked the backstreets aimlessly, his duffel-coat buttoned against the cold December chill.

When he came home, Eric made straight for the front room. He stared at the armchair. His dressing-gown cord lay discarded on the seat. Eric looked around, suspicion growing in his mind. There was only one way to be sure. He approached the living room, where Mary and Bill were watching *Take Your Pick*. Bob Danvers-Walker announced Eric's entrance with a cheesy organ flourish.

'Um, has anyone seen my guitar?'

Mary looked at Bill. Bill looked at the TV. *Open the box*, shouted members of the studio audience. *Take the money*, called others.

'You'll get it back when you've had your hair cut,' answered Bill.

This was precisely the reply that Eric had expected to hear.

'*Oh dear, you've won tonight's booby prize,*' commiserated Michael Miles. '*It's a mousetrap.*'

Hair or guitar, take your pick, thought Eric.

Bill spent the following day laying linoleum tiles on a kitchen floor in Perivale. When he returned home in the early evening, he glanced at the sideboard. The money he had left there for Eric's haircut was gone.

Three days later, an article appeared on page four of the local paper under the title, *HAIR RAID SIREN*. The piece outlined a controversy concerning a letter sent to parents of boys attending a local grammar school. According to sources, several parents were *angered and insulted* by the headmaster's assertions that their sons were being sent to school with unacceptably long hair. A quote from one young mother read: *Their hair is barely over their collars. Anyone would think they were walking around looking like cavemen'.* Accompanying the article was a head-and-shoulders photograph of a smiling Paul Ramsey, proudly displaying his neatly combed Beatle haircut and holding up a framed picture of Sir Isaac Newton. Paul's quote proclaimed: *'I want to be like my heroes'.*

When he saw his friend's photograph in the newspaper, Eric smiled and vowed never to have his hair cut again.

9

The Queen of the Suburbs
1965

On the 30th of January 1965, a grey Saturday, Bill and Mary sat in front of the television watching a live broadcast of Sir Winston Churchill's state funeral.

'I don't envy those pallbearers having to carry that lead-lined coffin,' said Bill.

Eric had something else on his mind. Telephoning earlier, Paul had told his friend that the Ramsey's had some news, but insisted he give it to him in person.

All very mysterious, Eric thought, as he turned the corner into the next road. Perhaps the boys' mother had bought tickets for another concert. It would be great to see the Rolling Stones. Eric's curiosity was perked. Whatever the nature of this disclosure, it was clearly important to Paul.

Sitting in the Ramsey's front room, Eric looked expectantly at the two brothers, 'So come on then, don't keep me in suspenders.'

'Well,' said Paul, 'we're moving.'

Eric felt a chill as it dawned on him that he may shortly be losing contact with his two best friends. 'Oh... Right. How come you... Where are you moving to?'

'Only to Ealing Broadway,' replied Paul. 'You know that Mum's been visiting our Uncle Jack for a long time now...'

'Yeah?'

'He's dead,' interjected Tony.

'Oh, I'm sorry,' said Eric. Aware that this was the first time in his life he had been given news of this kind, he felt satisfied with his response.

'Ah, it's nothing to us really,' said Paul. 'I've run into him a few times, but Tony only met him once.'

'Uncle Jack left his house to Mum,' Tony said glumly.

'What, the big house round the back of Ealing Broadway? The *haunted* one?' There was a trace of excitement in Eric's voice.

'Swinging,' said Paul, smiling and giving a thumbs-up.

'Dodgy,' his brother replied, pointing his thumb towards the carpet. 'Hello, Eric.'

Eric thought Julia's fair complexion looked even paler than usual. Her delicate high cheekbones appeared more pronounced.

'I just turned that stupid television off,' Julia said, sitting next to her sons on the sofa. 'Winston Churchill. I hate funerals. People talk about closure, but I'd rather find that in my own way, not through the archaic ritual of a morbid, depressing ceremony. I like to remember people at their best, but funerals always become part of the memory. You try to shut them out, but they're always there in the shadows, tainting your recollections.' She sighed, 'Maybe it's just me. Anyway, I don't want a funeral. I want you all to remember me smiling.'

In the light of Julia's recent bereavement, this was a little awkward. Eric decided to risk broaching the subject. 'I'm sorry to hear about Uncle Jack.'

Julia closed her eyes, smiling sadly. 'Thank you, Eric. Jack wasn't terribly old, but it was his time to go. People die at different ages.'

'Mum was there!' blurted Tony, 'Uncle Jack had a dodgy ticker, and it stopped, and Mum saw it happen!'

Julia breathed in deeply, 'Yes, all right, Tony. But remember what I told you: that's not the sort of thing we want to go telling people about. It's a private family matter.' She turned to the boy sitting opposite, 'I don't mean you, Eric. You're part of our family as far as I'm concerned.'

'Thank you,' Eric said quietly.

Julia addressed her two boys, 'If either of you feel you need to talk about Uncle Jack, you can always talk to me.'

Paul nodded. 'When will we be moving to the new house?'

'Oh, it'll be a while yet,' replied his mother. 'There's the probate and all the other legalities to deal with first.'

Tony remained silent. He wondered if Uncle Jack's ghost had joined the others in the old house on Hanger Hill.

*

Fortified by as many as five layers of clothing, Eric braved the cold winter mornings, building his reputation as paperboy extraordinaire. 'Here's the *Incredible Bulk*,' joked Ron Hillman, when Eric lumbered into the newsagents looking like the Michelin Man. Throughout the winter, the dream that he would someday be the owner of a Fender Stratocaster ousted Eric from his warm bed and powered his peddles through the worst the Weather Wizard had to throw at him.

Eric's paper round kept him up-to-date with the news, albeit mostly via osmosis. By way of this subliminal process, on a chilly February morning, he learned Sir Stanley Matthews had played his last football match aged fifty years and five days. *'It wasn't until I switched to Craven 'A' that I understood what smooth smoking meant'*, said Sir Stanley.

Eric finished his round in record time, which turned out to be a stroke of good fortune (or not, depending on your viewpoint). Cycling home to change into his school uniform, he spied a pink-and-white Hillman Minx parked a short distance from his house. There were many Minx's with the same colour scheme, but none looked quite like *that*.

Eric pulled up next to the open car window, 'Hi Sid.'

'Eric, my boy, my heart's filled with joy,' rhymed Sid, all smiles, teeth and Americana.

The boy on the bicycle grimaced at the man's cheesy greeting.

'Park your bike over there and pull up a chair,' Sid said, patting the worn leather passenger seat.

When Eric slid in, two empty wine bottles chinked by his feet. The car reeked of alcohol.

'Well, how do you do? Now tell me what's new.'

Eric looked at Sid. The man had been drinking, and it was 8:15 in the morning. 'I just finished my paper round,' said Eric. I'm saving up for a new guitar, maybe an electric one.'

Sid smiled, 'The life and times of Eric Grimes.'

Eric nodded. 'How about you, Sid? The last time I spoke to Reg, he said you'd disappeared. Are you okay?'

'Mm, yeah, yeah,' the man answered uncertainly. 'Bin havin' a few financial issues, you might say. Had t' close the nightclub, just till I get things straightened out with a couple o' fellas.'

Eric shifted on his seat. The bottles by his feet clinked, making him jump.

Sid drummed distractedly on the steering wheel, 'I'm gonna be out o' town for a while, and I may not get a chance to... Anyways, could you get a message to Reg for me?'

'Of course,' replied Eric, relieved that Sid had not asked him to go to Soho or to undertake something life-threatening. 'What shall I say?'

'Just tell Reg... Just tell him... the Scientist is back.'

'That's it?'

'Yep. The Scientist is back. He'll understand.'

'Okay.'

'Okay!' Sid's smile returned, 'Now get on your way and have a cool day!'

Eric stepped out onto the pavement. Resting his forearm on the open door, he leaned into the car, 'It was great to see you, Sid. I'll give Reg your message. I hope everything works out with your nightclub and –' From the corner of his eye, Eric saw a man running fast up the pavement towards them, 'Sid, it's my dad! He found out about Soho. Quick, *get going!*'

Eric slammed the passenger door and stepped back.

Sid turned the key in the ignition: the car groaned but refused to start. He fiddled frantically with the choke. The battery sounded like it was about to die, the engine turning over with agonising sluggishness.

'Stop!' shouted Bill, now only thirty yards away and closing fast. 'You wait right there!'

With a characteristic fart, black smoke belched from the exhaust pipe, and the Minx sputtered into life. Eric saw Sid's toothy white grin, then he was gone.

'If I see you talking to my son again, it'll be the last thing you do!' Bill shouted, shaking his fist at the pink-and-white Hillman.

The following Sunday, Eric walked to Reg's house to deliver Sid's message. Passing the Forester, he heard a loud *slap* followed by peals of laughter from the public bar where a lively game of dominoes was taking place, West Indian style. Reaching the postman's house, the boy heard music on the other side of the hedge. Eric chuckled. Arms and legs flying, Reg cavorted around his front room to *It's Not Unusual*, the first hit record for Tom Jones.

Endeavouring to keep a straight face, Eric sipped his tea. 'I see your leg's better.'

'Good as new,' smiled the postman, returning from the kitchen with a plateful of digestives.

The Post Office Tower picture had been joined by a signed photo of Dusty Springfield: *To Reg, With Love, Dusty x*. The singer's panda eyes stared down at Eric from beneath her bleached-blonde bouffant.

'I know Mary quite well,' said Reg. 'Often bumped into her on my rounds.' Reg neglected to mention that he had not seen Mary for two years and had ordered the photo from her fan club.

Eric had heard Reg's Dusty stories before and quickly jumped in, 'I saw Sid last week.'

'Really?' Reg reached for his cigarette pack.

'Yeah. I was cycling home from my paper round, and there was Sid, parked down the road from my house.'

'Did you speak to him? Is he all right?'

'Yeah, but he'd been drinking. We had a quick chat, but he was in a hurry to get away. He kept looking in the mirror, like he was being followed or something.'

Reg nodded, 'Like I said, there're people after him.'

'Sid asked me to give you a message.'

'Oh?'

'He said, tell Reg, the Scientist is back.'

The postman slumped back in his chair, blowing a stream of smoke at the ceiling. 'Is he now? I really thought we'd seen the last of him.'

'Is this the scientist you told me about? The man who invented the machine at your office?'

'The transmitter. Yes, that's him.' Reg was drifting, lost in thought.

Eric sat quietly, staring down at the swirly green-and-yellow carpet. Dusty's *I Don't Know What To Do With Myself* played in his head. *Go away!* he told her, but the song had stuck. *At least it's not Rolf Harris*, Eric thought, then reprimanded himself for implanting the suggestion.

Reg emerged from his contemplation, 'Did Sid say anything else about the Scientist, Eric?'

'No, just that he's back.'

'Sid didn't mention Head Office or Hartlepool?'

'Head Office? No.'

'Then maybe they don't know,' Reg speculated.

'Is this scientist a bad man?' asked Eric.

'Bad? No, no, he's just a bit... Well, he's...' The postman stubbed his cigarette. 'I'm sorry, Eric, maybe I've already told you too much. From now on, the less you know, the better. And what you *do* know stays secret, okay? You understand?'

Eric nodded, 'Yeah, I know, top secret.'

'Exactly,' Reg said, winking and tapping the side of his nose.

*

At the beginning of March 1965, America stepped up its war effort in Vietnam. The US had been bombing the country for many years, and more ground troops were being added to combat the communist north.

Cosmonaut Alexey Leonov became the first man to walk in space. Four years earlier, the Russians had put the first man into orbit, and they were winning the space race. As Reg put it, *The Ruskies have done the double'.* If the first satellite, Sputnik, were to be included in his tally, Reg might have observed that the Russians had *done the triple*. On the same day Alexey made his spacewalk, the Stones were arrested for pissing on a petrol station wall. Or was it just hype?

Absorbing snippets of news during his paper round, Eric found himself discussing topical issues with Julia Ramsey. It could be argued that Eric's mother had been right. Whether or not Ms Ramsey was a positive influence is a matter for conjecture, but there was no doubt her views were in tune with the times.

In the mid-nineteenth century, Ealing Broadway Station provided a rail-link to London. The market garden gave way to urbanisation, and Ealing acquired the name *Queen of the Suburbs*.

The warm weather at the end of March continued into April. Eric sat astride his bicycle by Haven Green, studying the directions Paul had written down for him. At the bottom of the page, Paul had scribbled, *The bell is inside the letterbox.*

'Inside the letterbox?'

'Yep', replied Paul. 'You'll see'.

Eric slid the note into the back pocket of his jeans. Around him, Ealing Broadway buzzed with the bustle and colour that accompanies the first sunny spring Saturday. Travellers filed in and out of the busy station, and taxicabs queued in the rank. Opposite the Feathers, the air smelled of freshly baked bread. Opposite the bakery shop, the air smelled of beer. On the green, locals sat in groups on the grass, enjoying the midday sunshine. Eric frowned. His bicycle chain had deposited an oily black streak on his Levi's.

Riding away from the curb, Eric watched two girls in summer dresses cross Haven Green. A bus whooshed by within inches, sending him wobbling towards the pavement. Adding insult to embarrassment, a pair of passing nuns tutted loudly.

The boy passed the Wheatsheaf, then continued up the hill towards Ealing Cricket Club. He rode by some of Ealing's most expensive properties: Victorian houses built for well-to-do businessmen seeking a quiet haven away from the city. Sweat beading on his forehead, he conceded defeat, pushing his bike the rest of the way up the incline.

Over the high wooden fence to his right, Eric saw the brick tower that Paul had sketched next to his directions. Straight ahead, where the road bent sharply to the right, was Fox Wood. Behind the tree-line was the enormous disused reservoir. Alongside it to the right, Paul's drawing showed a public footpath.

Eric wheeled his bike along the tree-arched walkway. *This can't be right. You couldn't get a car down here, let alone a removal van.*

Fox Wood loomed thick and impenetrable, pressing the wire-mesh fencing on either side of the path. Pencil beams of yellow sunlight pierced the arboreal roof, starkly illuminating the leafy green tunnel. Curving gently to the left, the footpath became brighter, and the blue sky came into view. To Eric's right stood a high wall topped by metal spikes. At the centre was a green door, crowned by an R set in a filigree design.

Eric stared up at the intricate green metalwork. *R for Ramsey.* Leaning his bike against the wall, he stood before the wooden door. *'The bell is inside the letterbox'. Well, of course it is. Where else would you put a bell?*

Eric pushed the flap and felt around inside the mail compartment. *No spiders, please.* Pressing the button, he quickly removed his hand. A few seconds later, he heard Paul speaking from inside the letterbox.

'Who is it?' enquired the muffled voice.

'It's me,' Eric said to the boy in the box.

Eric heard a click, and the big green door swung a few inches inwards.

'Close the gate behind you,' Paul instructed through the intercom.

Eric found himself standing in a huge overgrown garden enclosed by a high brick wall. Beyond the boundary on every side, the ancient trees of Fox Wood stood tall and green against the brilliant blue sky. A straight gravel path some twenty-five yards long bisected the badly neglected front garden, leading to the broad stone steps of a large arched porch. Eric understood immediately why Tony had imagined the run-down residence to be inhabited by ghosts.

Leaving his bicycle next to the heavy wooden gate, Eric approached the towering old house. The tall three-story building was noticeably older than the Victorian homes he had passed on the hill. Its design and dilapidated appearance exhibited the gothic hallmarks of a classic haunted mansion. Eric stood on the pathway, looking up at the high wooden gable. The house seemed to lean towards him as if curious of the young stranger about to enter its rooms.

'What do you think?' Paul called from the doorway.

'It's fantastic!' replied Eric. His friend joined him on the gravel path.

'It could do with some decorating,' Paul said, pointing at the flaking bottle-green woodwork. 'It's better inside, but the floorboards creak, and most of the rooms could use a coat of paint.'

'I like it as it is.' Eric stared up at the imposing façade. Over the front porch, two large round leaded windows stood one above the other. 'It looks like a tall English version of the Addams Family house.'

'There aren't as many rooms as you might think,' Paul said, as they entered the hall. 'But most of them are really big.'

'Wow! I see what you mean,' exclaimed Eric. 'You could get a herd of elephants in this hallway!'

It was cooler inside the house, and there was a faint odour of mould and damp: a barely discernible musty smell peculiar to buildings of substantial age. Eric looked down at the black-and-white tiles that ran the hallway's length, disappearing around a corner to the right. Doors stood ajar on both sides of the wood-panelled entrance hall.

Paul pushed open the door on their left, 'This is the living room.'

'Bloody 'ell!' exclaimed Eric. 'This room's as big as our whole house!'

Opposite the door was an elaborate fireplace that looked as if it belonged in a stately home. A gold-framed mirror hung above the mantelpiece, upon which stood an eighteenth-century French clock. Two traditional sofas faced across a dark-wood coffee table in front of the gaping hearth. A deep-red patterned Indian carpet added to the cosy feel of the room. Eric assumed this to be the heart of the house and pictured himself sitting next to a roaring fire with Julia and the two boys, talking and laughing and putting the world to rights. He turned to the row of recessed windows,

'Green velvet curtains like the ones in Northfield. A green house with a green R over the green front gate. Green seems to be popular in the Ramsey family.'

'The R stands for Russell,' said Paul. 'Ramsey is Mum's married name.'

'Oh, of course.' Eric juggled his friend's lineage in his head.

Paul grinned, 'But the R stands for *Ramsey* now.'

The far end of the long living room had fitted bookshelves on all three walls. The library area boasted thousands of titles. Heavy dark-oak and mahogany furniture had been the deceased owner's preference and a gothic influence, including crystal chandeliers, was prevalent throughout the house. Eric studied a gold-framed photo of Uncle Jack, taken in the nineteen-twenties or thirties. Wearing a white V-necked jumper and holding a tennis racquet across his chest, the aristocratic young Jack posed haughtily next to a potted aspidistra. The handsome man's chiselled features bore the beginnings of an impish smile, his eyes appearing to twinkle through the sepia.

'Jack Russell!' laughed Eric.

'I wondered how long it would take you to get that,' smiled Paul. 'Mum reckons the name suited him.'

'Where are Tony and your mum?' asked Eric. 'Ten minutes' walk away on the top floor?'

'Gone shopping. Do you want a drink?'

'Scotch and soda, please.'

'We've got some squash.'

'That'll do.'

Leaving the living room, Paul pushed the door on the opposite side of the hall. 'The dining room,' he announced in a posh voice.

'It's like a bleedin' Cludo board, this place!' Eric joked, admiring the eight-place dining table.

Paul pointed to the door at the end of the hallway, 'Have a shufti in there. It's the biggest room in the house.'

Eric pushed open the door, 'Crikey, this must be the ballroom, then!' He looked around the huge room. Double French windows faced out onto a desperately neglected back garden.

'And the kitchen's along here.'

Passing the impressive curved stairway, Paul led his friend down the tiled corridor behind the dining room. 'The bog's up there by the back door and the kitchen's here on the left.'

A sprawling aspidistra was bursting out of its pot on a jardinière by the bottom of the stairs. *Same china pot as in Jack's tennis racquet photograph*, thought Eric.

Sipping his squash, Eric stood by the kitchen sink, looking out at the big back garden. 'It's not every house that comes with its own jungle.'

Paul chuckled, 'I saw a couple of giraffes out there earlier.'

'And it's got a swing.' The rusty red frame faced the double French windows.

'Stick it up your arse,' said a voice from beside the kitchen door.

Eric jumped.

'This is Keith,' said Paul. 'He's an African Grey parrot.'

'Can he fly?'

'Yeah, but he's old, and he mostly stays on his perch.'

'Couldn't he fly away?'

Paul shrugged, 'This is his home. Why would he? Mum says if an animal has to be kept in a cage, it's not a pet; it's a prisoner. Ready for the rest of the tour?'

'Lead on,' said Eric, rinsing his empty glass and placing it upside-down on the draining board. Keith leaned forward on his perch, his yellow eyes following the two boys out of the kitchen.

The stairway wound back on itself. The blood-red stair carpet continued along the wood-panelled first-floor corridor leading to one of the enormous round windows at the front of the house. Passing a bedroom on his right, Eric recognised Tony's Mickey Mouse alarm clock. The striking red carpet had also been fitted in Tony's room.

'I take back what I said about all the green,' said Eric. 'It's very *red* up here!'

'You noticed the carpet, then.'

'Yeah. I like it, though.' Eric looked around, tapping his lower lip with his forefinger and adopting the persona of a flamboyant interior designer. 'Yes, yes,' he said in a silly voice, 'the Miss Scarlet carpet certainly complements the baroque wall panelling. It brings to mind a certain Transylvanian count whose name escapes me.'

'I'm glad you like the red carpet,' smiled Paul. 'It runs all the way up the stairs, and it's in every room on this floor *and* the one above!'

'Every room! Uncle Jack must've been a nutter!'

'Let's just say he was a little... *eccentric*,' Paul said in his posh voice.

Sunlight streamed through the round leaded window casting two shadows along the corridor. The boys looked down at the overgrown front garden below.

'That was a pond,' said Paul, pointing at a round stone structure to the left of the central path. 'I think it had a fountain once. Over there, on the other side, is a fallen statue of a Greek goddess or something. She's laying beneath that ivy and stuff. And Uncle Jack's tennis court is under there somewhere.'

'It just gets better,' said Eric.

'Oh, there's more to come,' his friend replied, raising his eyebrows.

The second-floor layout looked identical to the first, except only three doors led off the corridor.

'That's another bathroom,' said Paul. 'And that's Mum's bedroom at the end on the left. Uncle Jack's is opposite.'

'Uncle Jack's?'

'Yeah, I know, it's a bit weird. Mum says she wants to keep Uncle Jack's room as he left it. She keeps his door locked.'

'I bet Tony loves that.'

'Tony never comes up here.'

'It sounds a bit... Jane Eyre.'

Paul nodded, 'Except there's nobody in there. I offered to clear-out Uncle Jack's room, but Mum wants it left as it is.'

The two boys stared at the locked door opposite Julia's room.

'Anyway...' Paul clasped his hands, smiling at Eric. 'I saved the best till last.'

Opening his mother's bedroom door, Paul beckoned to his friend. 'Follow me,' he said, entering Julia's room.

'Blimey! This must be the biggest bedroom in England!'

'Could be,' grinned Paul. 'It's directly above the dining room, and it's about the same size.'

Eric looked around at the carved wood wardrobes, chest of drawers and dressing table. 'The furniture looks like it was made to last a thousand years.' The centrepiece of the room, festooned with cream and gold netting, was the big four-poster bed.

'Fit for a queen,' said Paul.

Eric agreed. *The Queen of the Suburbs.*

Paul turned to the back of the long room, 'This way.'

Eric followed his friend up a white spiral staircase. Up and up it went, beyond the ceiling of Julia's bedroom, passing through a dusty attic housing trunks and suitcases and a battered old rocking horse. Daylight filtered down from above.

'The attic's huge,' said Paul.

Eric could smell the dust. The winding staircase passed through a second circular opening. Looking up, Eric saw his friend step away from the metal helix.

'Welcome to the observatory,' Paul said, smiling broadly.

The view from the small octagonal room took Eric's breath away. He steadied himself whilst his eyes adjusted to the sunlight. Holding the solid metal staircase, he looked up at the domed ceiling.

'Top of the world, man,' said Paul.

Eric flashed back to the hill above St Ives; George, the harmonica-playing beatnik, had used the exact same phrase. 'It definitely beats the view from the roof of the ABC.'

'It certainly does,' agreed Paul. 'The house is at the top of the highest hill for miles.'

'Yeah, I pushed my bike up most of it.'

Eric walked slowly around the windowed observatory. Looking down, he saw that the high wall was entirely surrounded by Fox Wood. To the east, a narrow tree-line separated the overgrown back garden from Hanger Hill Park. Far beyond in the distance, Eric could make out the distinctive Post Office Tower in central London.

'Have a look through the telescope,' Paul suggested, pointing to the bronze instrument perched on its tripod by the staircase.

Eric swivelled the telescope towards the south-west, 'I can't see my house, but the clock on St John's Church tower says a quarter-to-two.'

Beyond the front garden on the other side of the public footpath was the empty reservoir. Bushes had taken root at one end of the vast oval bowl, and Fox Wood encroached around the curved perimeter. The glazed brick surface shone pale orange in the afternoon sunlight.

'Mum says the reservoir was drained during the war to stop the German bomber crews using it as a landmark,' said Paul, adding a little historical context to his tour.

Far below, the green gate swung open. Julia and Tony entered the front garden, each pulling a two-wheeled shopping trolley. Sunlight glimmered on Julia's jet-black hair as the two figures made their way up the long gravel path before disappearing from view behind the large protruding gable. The two boys went downstairs.

Tony unpacked a big bag of vegetables, spreading swedes, onions, potatoes, carrots and turnips across the kitchen table.

Julia placed two brown Hovis loaves in the enamel bread bin. 'So what do you make of our new home, Eric?'

'Fantastic! It's really... big!' replied the boy, wishing he had come up with something more insightful.

'It needs a lot of work,' Julia said, glancing through the kitchen window. 'One of these days, I'll invest in a proper lawnmower.'

She never did.

Eric eyed the beetroot and cabbage that Tony had added to the rest. 'That's a lot of veggies.'

'Yes,' replied Julia. 'I'm trying not to buy too many processed foods. Companies try to outsell one another, and to make their products taste nicer, they pack them full of salt and sugar. If it carries on escalating, we'll end up with a nation of fat people.'

The group moved to the front room.

Just how I imagined it, thought Eric, looking around at Paul, Tony and Julia. Paul stood by the living-room fireplace with his elbow on the mantelpiece and a glass of squash in his hand. He turned to Eric on the sofa, 'Have you heard of the Who?'

'The what?'

'No, *the Who*, as in Doctor.' Paul looked at his mother, 'Okay to blast it?'

Julia smiled, 'Well, the nearest neighbours are over four-hundred yards away, Paul, so I don't suppose there'll be any complaints.'

Paul turned the volume knob on the radiogram fully clockwise and dropped *I Can't Explain* onto the turntable.

On his perch in the kitchen, Keith hopped from one foot to the other, bobbing his head: a good indication that the parrot was not too old to recognise the emergence of a new and exciting musical era.

10

The Picnic and the Poet

On the first weekend of May 1965, Julia, Paul, Tony and Eric picnicked in the back garden of the *Ealing House*, as it had come to be called. Paul had unearthed an old hand-mower and had cut down the long grass around the swing, creating an oasis in front of the jungle.

'Deference is on the way out,' Julia said, gesturing with a cheese-and-cucumber sandwich. 'People used to respect authority with a kind of blind acceptance, but now the younger generation is starting to question it.'

'Is that a good thing?' Eric asked, helping himself to a macaroon.

'Definitely,' replied Julia. 'The old class systems have been disintegrating for decades, and now ordinary people are standing up and voicing their opinions.'

The Byrds' jangly version of Dylan's *Mr Tambourine Man* floated through the open French windows.

'Like how, Mum?' asked Paul.

'Well, through music for a start. Bob Dylan is making waves with his protest songs, and the Beatles are breaking down barriers with their irreverent humour. You know, like John Lennon addressing the Prime Minister as *Harold*.'

'And thanking him for the purple hearts,' said Paul.

'And telling the toffs at the Royal Variety Show to rattle their jewellery,' added Eric.

'Exactly. And David Frost and co did quite a job with *That Was The Week That Was*. There's that *Private Eye* magazine, and Peter Cook with his *Establishment* club. Satire – ridicule – is a powerful tool, and they've all used it to great effect.'

Peter Cook and Dudley Moore's *Not Only... But Also* television show had given rise to a multitude of silly voices and wacky conversations up and down the nation.

'And it's easy to forget,' added Julia, 'we've only really had television for about twelve years. Before that, radio was heavily controlled by the establishment, and before that, all they had was the printing press. For those with an eye on revolution, the technology is now in place to get their message out to the world: TV, satellites, and God knows what else.'

I know what else, thought Eric. The feeling in his stomach was similar to when his dad drove the van fast over a humpback bridge. He felt an urge to break the promise he had undertaken with Reg.

The picnic over, Julia disappeared through the French windows into the huge back room: *the ballroom*, as Eric had christened it.

Tony piped up, 'Eric, we've got something to show you.'

'Ah yes, right this way,' Paul said, getting to his feet. 'Bring your machete.'

The three boys fought their way through the invading flora that had long ago seeded itself in the big back garden. Tony led the expedition, hacking from side to side with a sturdy branch.

'I gather gardening wasn't high on Uncle Jack's priorities,' said Eric. 'Some of these trees look like they've been here a hundred years.'

'They probably have.' Paul stepped over a half-buried ornamental column. 'Mind the nettles.'

'Over here!' Tony had forged ahead and was crouching beneath the trees, examining the base of the wall. 'Here it is,' he said, with the air of an explorer uncovering the tomb of a Pharaoh.

A few inches above ground level, a two-foot-high rectangle had been chiselled into the old brickwork. At its centre, in detailed relief, crouched a gryphon-like creature, poised and ready to strike. Beneath the carving, a gothic inscription read,

If the people don't get you, the animals will.

*

'Hello stranger,' Bill said, entering the front room.

'Oh, hello Dad.' Eric was surprised to see his father home on a weekday lunchtime. 'No work today?'

Bill smiled as he sat opposite his son. 'A rare afternoon off.'

Eric leaned his guitar against his chair.

'I'm not here to have a go at you about anything,' Bill said, reading Eric's expression. 'You're doing all right at school. Well, considering the grammar school's high standards. And your A's in art are excellent.'

But? thought Eric.

'But it seems like your mother and I hardly ever see you these days.'

'I know, Dad. I go to Paul's after school and we do our homework together. There's a lot of it.'

This was partly true. The boys did collaborate on their homework assignments.

'Yes, but you're over at that house every weekend. You only come home to sleep, then you're off again.'

'Paul and Tony are my friends, Dad. We do music and things together.' Aware of his mother's reservations about Julia Ramsey, Eric deliberately omitted her name. He also neglected to tell his father that he had, at Julia's suggestion, left some of his clothes in the spare bedroom at the Ealing House.

'All right,' sighed Bill. 'Just remember where you live. Your mother and I worry about you.'

When his father closed the front-room door, Eric grabbed his guitar and picked the intro to the Beatles' current number one, *Ticket to Ride*. Driving his dad's words from his mind, he then applied himself to the more challenging riff from the group's previous hit, *I Feel Fine*.

*

'*Poetry?*' Tony whined, screwing up his face. 'Can't we go to a football match or something? We never do anything *I* want to do. I *hate* this house, I *hate* my school, and I *hate* poetry.' Throwing his Batman comic to the floor, the eleven-year-old stormed out of the front room and stomped angrily down the hallway heading for the back garden.

'He'll go, Mum,' Paul said quietly.

Eric stared into the empty fireplace.

'No, Tony's right,' Julia said, rubbing her brow with her fingertips. 'I'll take him to a football match. I should be doing more *dad* things instead of pushing my own interests on all of you.'

Eric looked up, 'Paul and I could do that. We could take Tony to see Brentford play.'

'Definitely,' agreed Paul. 'When's the poetry recital, Mum?'

'The eleventh of June; next Friday.'

'Right. I'll stay here and look after Tony, and you and Eric can go to the poetry thing. I'm not that bothered about going, anyway.'

'Oh Paul, that's so nice, but –'

'Just go, Mum. I promise I won't let Tony burn the house down.' Paul stood up and directed a double thumbs-up towards his mother, 'Good, that's settled then. I'll go and check on him.'

Paul stepped through the open French windows into the back garden. From somewhere in the jungle came the dull knocking of a branch being hit repeatedly against a tree trunk.

Eric saw no advantage in concocting a cover story, and as it turned out, Bill and Mary were pleased at the prospect of their son attending a poetry reading. They were less enthusiastic about his request to stay the night at the Ealing House. Eventually though, permission was granted.

On the warm Friday evening, Eric set off for Ealing Broadway with a carrier bag dangling from his handlebar containing spare clothes and a toothbrush.

'I'm not going to worry about the boys,' Julia told Eric and herself as they entered Ealing Broadway Station.

'You've no need to,' Eric replied reassuringly. 'Paul knows you've put your trust in him, and he won't let you down.' This sounded very adult, Eric thought. The evening was off to a good start.

As Julia gazed out through the tube train window, Eric stole a glance at the delightful young woman by his side. Julia had allowed her straight black hair to grow long over her shoulders, accentuating her pale complexion and enhancing her femininity. Beneath her deep-purple blazer, she wore a knee-length flower-patterned dress. Her sandals revealed purple painted toenails that matched her fingers and the jacket. Eric thought she looked lovely.

The rail journey was relatively short. Changing trains at Notting Hill Gate, they rode the Circle Line for one stop, getting off at High Street Kensington.

Orange evening sunlight lit the high street, casting long shadows across Kensington Gardens and Hyde Park. Soon the Albert Memorial came into view. Surrounded by artists and artisans and sculpted depictions of Victoria's empire, golden Prince Albert watched from his high throne as curiously dressed young people filed into the building bearing his name.

As they approached the Royal Albert Hall, Julia took her teenage companion's arm. Eric was now taller than his friends' mother, and he fancifully imagined that the attendees would assume the attractive young woman to be his girlfriend.

Entering the foyer, Julia and Eric were greeted by four enchanting young women wearing long cotton dresses. Their faces were painted with colourful swirling designs.

'Have a lovely evening,' smiled one of the nymph's, handing both visitors a single yellow flower.

On the tickets was printed: Poets of the World ¦ Poets of Our Time. A multi-coloured hand-written poster read:
Welcome to the
INTERNATIONAL POETRY INCARNATION.

'The International Poetry Incarnation?' mused Eric. 'That's an unusual name.'

Julia smiled, 'We may be in for an unusual evening.'

They climbed the stairs to the balcony, each with a yellow flower in their hand.

'This place is fantastic.' Eric gazed around the cavernous nineteenth-century auditorium. 'It's got so much atmosphere. I love all the red and gold.'

'I thought you might like it,' Julia replied, looking down. The seats were filling around the podium in the centre. 'Paul told me that when you first came to the Ealing House, all you could talk about were the colours.'

'Well, it's very green and red.'

'It is that,' smiled Julia.

'I've always had a funny thing about colours,' confided Eric. 'When I was young, and sometimes even now, I see colours in my mind.'

'In what way?'

'It's hard to explain... The colours are not really there. I mean, they're not coming in through my eyes, but... Well, for instance, I always used to colour the days of the week. Monday: brown, Tuesday: green, Wednesday: dark-red, Thursday: grey, Friday: bright-red, Saturday: yellow and Sunday: blue. Actually, I still do it. I know it sounds a bit mad. I've never told anyone before.'

'It's not mad,' replied Julia. 'It's called *synaesthesia,* and I have it too.'

'Really?' Eric looked astonished.

'Yes. Like you, I recall the associations being more pronounced when I was young, but they're still there. My synaesthesia is more related to sounds. The sound of waves breaking on a beach is yellow, birdsong is usually blue... I've never met anyone else who has it. You're the first.'

Julia and Eric were now facing one another in their seats.

Eric continued, looking directly into Julia's green eyes. 'I get colours from guitar chords. E is black, G's red, C is yellow –'

'So you could play a rainbow.'

'I never thought of that!'

The house lights dimmed. A bald-headed man with a bushy black beard and thick-rimmed glasses seated himself near the edge of the centre circle and began chanting in a low voice and ringing finger-bells.

Leaning close to Eric, Julia whispered, 'I told you the evening might be unusual!'

Eric smiled. He was ready for whatever Prince Albert had in store for them. When one of the poets read a piece entitled *To Fuck Is To Love Again*, any lingering doubts about the evening's *unusualness* were extinguished.

'Don't tell your parents,' whispered Julia.

Eric returned her smile and shook his head.

While a few of the readings resonated at some level, most of the poems failed to hold Eric's attention, and he found himself looking at the audience. The flower-decked ground floor and its surrounding boxes were packed with the disciples of a new creed. It was less full high up where he and Julia were, and people sat where they liked.

The aroma of incense hung in the air, blending with a smell that Eric could not place. The strangest among the bizarre assembly had gathered around the central podium. One man blew bubbles from a long wooden pipe while a slender girl in a short white dress danced to imaginary music. Her arms entwined above her head, she weaved and swayed like a fairy ballerina. Encircling the arena were three tiers of private boxes, each an impressionist vignette of spectral silhouettes. Wine and food were shared by the merrymakers, and cigarettes glowed orange-red in the semidarkness.

Eric saw that Julia was also studying the unconventional audience. 'What do you think of the poetry?' he whispered.

'Mm, some of it's okay. To be honest, I'm more interested in the event.'

Eric waited. He had spent enough time with Julia over the years to know that an inexplicit statement of this kind would be followed by a considered analysis.

'Something's happening,' whispered Julia. 'You know all the things we've been talking about: Bob Dylan's lyrics, the satirists, the long hair, the music, the rebellious young people; John Lennon and everyone. Well, it's not just *us* that have been taking notice, Eric.

'The Albert Hall holds seven or eight thousand people, and look around... It's almost full. And that's for a poetry incarnation! Young people in America are protesting against the Vietnam War, and I bet if you asked this audience, they'd be against it, too.'

As if to affirm Julia's point, English poet Adrian Mitchell entered the arena and began reading *To Whom It May Concern*.

Most of the preceding poems had eluded Eric, but this time, he understood every word; the anti-war message was heartfelt and clear. He became aware of someone approaching along the empty aisle, and a man sat next to him,

'Hello Eric, how've you been?'

'George!'

The elder beat looked just as Eric had last seen him on the seafront at St Ives. Dressed in black from head to toe, the man wore the same flat beret along with his Trad-Jazz grey-flecked goatee. All that was missing were the dark glasses. Eric later spotted them poking out of the breast pocket on his jacket.

George embraced the boy over the seat arms, 'Small world, man.'

'It's great to see you, George,' Eric whispered excitedly. 'I've often thought about you and Ricky and the others. You're a long way from St Ives.'

'Oh, I get around,' smiled the older man. 'I heard through the grapevine that Ginsburg was reading here at the hall, so me and my lady made the trip.'

'Is she here?' asked Eric.

'Downstairs talking to Indira Gandhi; Nehru's kid. There're all sorts here tonight.'

'This is Julia,' Eric said, pushing back in his seat. 'George and I met at St Ives.'

'Hello.' Julia reached across to shake the beatnik's hand.

George took Julia's hand and kissed it, 'A pleasure to meet you, milady.' The beat turned to Eric, 'Hey, how about we get some Cokes? I'll buy if you fly.'

'Okay.' Eric took the ten-shilling note. 'I'll be right back.'

When Eric returned with the drinks, he saw that George had taken his seat next to Julia. To his surprise, Eric saw that she was smoking. When the teenager entered the aisle, George returned to his original seat. Julia stubbed the cigarette on the underside of her sandal.

'Hey, thanks, man.' George took two Cokes and handed one to Julia.

'Thank *you*,' Eric whispered, giving him the change.

George produced a quarter-bottle of Bells from his jacket pocket. 'Care for a little livener?'

'Thank you.' Julia held out her cola.

'Eric?'

'Thanks, George.'

In hushed voices, the three spoke of St Ives, the beats, the magical properties of ginseng, and discussed at length the significance of the poetry evening. George encouraged Eric to pursue his guitar playing and employed poetic lines to charm Julia. Eric noticed that she was giggling a lot.

Ten minutes later, following mutual assurances that they would all meet again, the elder beat said his goodbyes.

'He's a really nice man,' whispered Julia.

'Yeah, and his friends are great, too.'

'You never told me you had beatnik friends.'

'I only knew them for a little while; one evening, really. I played guitar at their camp, and one of the girls kissed me.'

Julia grinned, her green eyes flashing.

Outside the Royal Albert Hall, Julia took Eric's arm. As they made their way through the London night, Eric pictured himself on Dylan's *Freewheelin'* cover, cruising a city street with a lovely longhaired girl at his side. Julia leaned in to him, clinging. 'Do you feel okay?' asked Eric.

'Never better.' The woman looked up, smiling prettily.

'I didn't know you smoked.'

'Only on my birthday.'

'Oh, I didn't... Happy bir –'

Julia laughed, 'It's not really my birthday, silly.'

The Circle Line train was full, mostly with people from the Albert Hall. Eric held on to a silver pole while Julia held on to him. They were the first to step off at Notting Hill Gate.

'Quick!' urged Julia. 'That's our train over there!'

Running across the station, they reached the train as the doors were closing. When Julia stepped into the empty carriage, one of her sandals slipped off, balancing precariously on the edge of the platform. Eric grabbed it in the nick of time.

'My hero.' Julia smiled as they entered the aisle. The train pulled away with a jerk, sending Julia tumbling onto one of the double seats. Eric sat opposite and handed her the sandal.

'Thank you, Eric. I saw it teetering, about to fall under the train. You were so quick, but it was like it happened in slow-motion.'

Eric looked down at the sweet wrapper lodged between Julia's purple painted toes.

'Oh, I'm a mess.' Julia placed the sandal down and flattened her flowery dress. She drew a Kleenex from her pocket and spat into it, smiling apologetically.

Eric smiled, shaking his head.

Julia lifted her foot onto the seat, and her dress fell back. When she lowered her knee, Eric knew he should look away. The young woman threaded the Kleenex between each of her toes, and Eric's pulse raced. She was taking her time, apparently unaware that he was looking. Julia wetted the tissue again and glanced up. Eric waited for her reprimand, but it never came. Cleansing the last smudge, she slipped the sandal on and placed her foot back on the floor,

'That'll teach me to go running for a train in sandals.' Julia crumpled the dirty tissue and pushed it into her jacket pocket.

Julia insisted they take a taxi from Ealing Broadway. When they stepped out of the cab at the top of Hanger Hill, Eric noticed that she was swaying and attributed it to the generous measure of whisky that George had poured into her Coke. He watched Julia take out a half-smoked cigarette. They entered the dark walkway. Her cigarette smelled like the Albert Hall.

'Have you ever walked down here at night before?' asked Eric. A soft yellow glow lit his companion's face as she drew on the hand-rolled cigarette and inhaled.

'Never this late,' Julia replied hoarsely, holding the smoke in her lungs. She exhaled a long stream, 'It's a little spooky, isn't it.'

There were no lamps along the footpath, and above their heads, the tangled branches blocked the light from the moon and stars. Julia slipped her arm around Eric's waist. The deeper they ventured into the overarched tunnel, the darker it became. When the pathway began its curve to the left, the diminishing amber light behind them disappeared, shrouding the walkway in blackness.

'I can't see my hand in front of my face!' whispered Julia.

A black cat in a coal cellar at night.

Their arms around one another, they walked on slowly in silence. Eric's thoughts returned to the tube train. Deprived of visual stimulus, vivid mental images appeared in his mind.

'Okay?' whispered Julia.

'Fine,' replied Eric, in some remote way, only then making the connection between the woman at his side and the one in his vision, peeking up at him over the hem of her dress.

A patch of night sky became visible, and they knew they were nearing the house.

'We're home,' Julia said quietly.

'Yes,' replied Eric. 'Thank you for tonight; I'm so glad we went.'

Julia moved around, facing him in the darkness. 'Give me a hug before we go in.'

Eric's arms slipped around her, and Julia's around him. He felt the young woman's breath on his cheek. Though his eyes were wide open, they may as well have been closed. Images from the tube train flashed across his internal cinema screen, playing in the blackness in full-blown Technicolor.

Pulling back, Julia placed her palm on Eric's chest, 'Let's go in now.'

11

Help!

Tony joined his older brother in the kitchen. 'What's for breakfast?'

'Fuck off,' said Keith, sidling along his perch and eying the butter dish in Paul's hand.

'Fuck off yerself,' snorted Tony. He looked out at the back garden where his mother was pegging washing to a rotating dryer. 'Where's Eric?'

'Still in bed, I think,' replied Paul.

'No he's not,' Eric murmured drowsily.

'Ah, good morning, my young friend,' Paul intoned in his mock aristocratic voice.

'Where were you last night?' asked Eric. 'I thought you'd be up when we got home.'

'Tony had the heeby-jeebys again. I sat with him and dozed-off in his room.'

'You heard it!' Tony replied angrily. 'If you say you didn't, you're a liar.'

'This is an old house,' replied his brother. 'Old houses creak at night. The wood expands during the day, then contracts when the temperature drops.'

'It wasn't that,' Tony said sulkily. 'Anyway, you weren't supposed to leave me on my own, so shut up about it.'

Julia placed an empty polythene washing basket on the flagstone floor. 'Shut up about what?'

'Show us your knickers,' said Keith. The parrot balanced on one leg, stretching the other beneath his extended wing.

Eric stared blindly out of the window.

'So tell us about last night,' said Paul. 'Was it good?'

Julia drew out a chair and sat beside her son at the kitchen table. 'Well, it was...'

'*Unusual*,' Eric and Julia said together.

Paul listened with interest as his mother described the evening at the Royal Albert Hall, appraising the poetry and, more significantly, the audience.

'It was an eye-opener for everyone, I think,' said Julia. 'The event may have been the catalyst required to mobilise a new generation of artistic and politically motivated young people.'

'It's no use giving a catalyst,' Tony said, pouring out a mountain of Sugarpuffs. 'Cats can't read.'

Eric smiled at the younger boy's weak joke.

'You could see it in their faces,' enthused Julia. 'They were looking around thinking, *there are thousands of people here that are just like me.*'

'So you think it might be the start of something,' said Paul. 'Like the mods and rockers.'

Julia nodded, 'Yes, but far more important. The mods and rockers don't really stand for anything, but these people do. If their ideas catch on, they'll probably try to change the world.'

Eric went out to the passage and made the phone call he had been putting off since he woke up.

'No, Dad, it was only for one night. I'll be home before it gets dark, definitely.' Holding the phone away from his ear, Eric leaned against the bannister flicking the big aspidistra's drooping leaves, 'Okay, will do... Right... Okay, see you later, Dad. Yeah, bye.' He replaced the receiver and breathed a sigh of relief. Turning back to the kitchen, he overheard Julia questioning the two boys.

'Well, *someone* had been in my room last night, and if it wasn't either of you, it must have been Uncle Jack!'

Tony sniffed, 'That's not funny, Mum.'

Eric waited silently by the stairs. Julia sounded agitated.

'Look, I don't mind you being in my bedroom, but someone has been going through my clothes.'

'I didn't go *near* your room last night,' said Paul.

'Well, it wasn't me,' Tony said bruskly.

'All right, we'll drop it now. But if either of you ever want anything from my bedroom, you only have to ask.'

'I told you about this house before we moved here,' muttered Tony. He scraped his chair back noisily on the stone floor and made for the door.

'Fuck off,' said Keith.

'*You* fuck off, you stupid parrot.'

The boy hurriedly left the kitchen, bumping into Eric in the passageway.

'Tony!' his mother called after him.

Eric joined Paul and Julia at the kitchen table.

Paul shrugged, 'Maybe Tony's right. Maybe the house *is* haunted.'

'Oh, stop it, Paul,' Julia said quietly. 'I'd expect more sense from *you*. Have you had some breakfast, Eric? There's Marmite in the cupboard, or cereal.'

'Just toast'll be fine, thanks.' Eric rose from his chair and headed for the bread bin.

'I'm going to Ealing Broadway this afternoon,' said Julia. 'Do you three have any plans?'

Paul turned to his friend, 'I thought we might go and explore the reservoir?'

'Fine with me,' Eric said, sawing off a doorstep of brown bread.

Julia looked at Eric, then at Paul. 'It's no use me telling you not to go over there because you'll go anyway.' Staring down at the kitchen table, she turned the butter knife with her fingertips. 'But please do be careful. And keep your wits about you. That place has a reputation as a pervert's paradise.'

An hour or so later, Paul closed the garden gate behind him and turned right on the public footpath joining Tony and Eric. A short distance from the house, the path curved more sharply to the left, skirting the steep embankment that formed the reservoir's boundary. The tall trees of Fox Wood enclosed the walkway. High above, a streak of blue sky stretched between the spreading green canopies.

'There it is.' Paul pointed to a gap where the chain-link fencing had been bent to one side.

As any spirited boy will tell you, there is always a way in. Ealing Council had chosen the likeliest spot for its warning sign, which was ignored by all but the hopelessly timid.

Squeezing through the opening in the wire fence, the three boys made their way up the steep wooded incline, emerging at the grassy edge of the empty reservoir. From their vantage point at the northern end, they looked down into the vast oval bowl. The orange-beige surface reflected brightly in the afternoon sunshine.

'It looks like the Colosseum,' Eric said, imagining Roman chariots racing around the arena-like basin.

'Or a swimming pool for dinosaurs,' suggested Tony.

Entirely surrounded by Fox Wood, the disused reservoir had succumbed to invading flora, particularly at the opposite end near the road. Weeds and bushes had taken root in the cracked surface, dotting the immense crumbling shell with bristling protuberances of green and brown and flowerings of purple and yellow.

Eric stood close to the edge. The fired-brick wall below him dropped vertically for about eight feet before sloping away to the floor. 'How do we get down there?'

Paul had wandered around the grassy perimeter to their left. 'Over here!'

Eric and Tony watched Paul disappear down a square manhole next to the rim. By the time they reached the rusty hatchway, he had climbed down the short metal ladder and was standing inside a small cubicle that opened into the reservoir. Moments later, Eric and Tony found themselves in the low-ceilinged chamber surrounded by the rudest collection of writings and drawings that any of them would ever encounter.

'Your mum was right about the perverts,' said Eric.

'Bloody hell!' Paul exclaimed. 'Have you read this one?'

Eric turned to Tony, 'Come on, let's get down the side.' He was the first to venture out through the opening.

Assuming sitting positions, the three boys inched down the sloping wall. Reaching the floor, Eric brushed the backside of his favourite jeans and looked around the enormous bowl.

'Knackers!' Tony shouted at the top of his voice. He smiled as a faint echo bounced back.

Walking the reservoir's length with his friends, Eric recalled the previous evening at the Albert Hall. He pictured the freaky crowd around the poet's podium, and Julia's expression as she surveyed the *'new generation of artistic and politically motivated young people'*. He visualised the train carriage. Green eyes regarded him, probing his thoughts. He felt Julia's embrace in the dark walkway. It seemed to Eric that he was outside himself. Floating high above the reservoir in the dazzling sunshine, he looked down at three tiny figures in the vast empty basin. In that infinitely small twinkling of time, he felt five years older.

A rusty baked bean can rattled across in front of Eric as the three boys made their way back to the north end.

'On me 'ead, son,' Paul shouted, then quickly ducked when Tony took his instruction literally.

A distant *pop* echoed around the reservoir. Eric sank to his knees, clutching his thigh. Paul and Tony froze, staring uncertainly.

Paul raced across, squatting and placing a hand on his friend's shoulder.

'My leg,' winced Eric, tears clouding his eyes. 'I think somebody shot me.'

Two older boys appeared from the opening in the rim and skidded down to the reservoir floor. One of them was holding a rifle. Paul stepped back warily as the two figures trotted towards them.

'Are you all right, mate?' asked the teenager with the rifle. 'I didn't mean t' hit ya; I was aimin' at the floor between yer legs.'

Eric remained on the ground, still clasping his thigh. Moving his hands, he was relieved to see no blood seeping through his jeans.

'It's only an airgun, mate,' said the sniper. 'Bet it 'urts though, dunnit.'

Fighting back tears, Eric looked up at the skinny teenager. He knew the boy's face.

'Ent I seen you at the paper shop?' asked the lanky older lad.

Eric nodded.

'Look, I'm sorry, mate.' The teenager offered Eric the gun. ''Ere, d'ya wanna 'ave a go?'

Eric shook his head, '*No...* thanks. I think I'd better get home.'

'C'n I 'ave a go?' Tony asked in a low voice.

'Course ya can, mate.' The skinny lad handed Tony the air rifle. 'Mind where ya point it, i's loaded.'

Tony aimed at the rusty baked bean can, fired, and missed. 'Fanks, mate,' he said gruffly, handing back the gun.

There was a light knock on the bathroom door. 'Are you all right, Eric?' Julia called from the first-floor corridor. 'Paul told me what happened.'

Eric looked down at the pitted swelling on his thigh. 'Yeah, the hot bath has helped. Thanks... I'm okay.'

'Good, all right... Stay in there as long as you like.'

Half an hour later, having changed into fresh clothes, Eric walked into the living room.

'He's very clean, isn't he,' Paul said in a Liverpudlian accent.

Eric joined Tony on the sofa. Eamonn Andrews handed over to Ken Walton for the wrestling as Big Daddy crushed another opponent.

'And you win a Crackerjack pencil... up yer arse,' said Tony, whose humour was becoming increasingly rude.

Julia leant on the doorframe with her arms folded. 'Teatime in five minutes,' she announced to the boys.

'What are we having?' asked Paul.

'Pizza and salad.'

'Pizza? What's that?'

Julia smiled, 'You'll like it – I hope. It's basically Italian cheese on toast.'

Crossing the hall, Paul, Tony and Eric seated themselves at the highly polished eight-place dining table. It was the first time Eric had sat in the long room. *Nice*, he thought, looking around at the period furniture and Jane Austin décor. The rarely used dining room was in better condition than the rest of the house.

After she had brought in the pizzas, to the surprise and delight of the three boys, Julia produced a bottle of Mateus Rosé from the sideboard and poured them each a glass. The pizza was an instant hit, which pleased the chef. Having searched high and low for the simple ingredients, she had ended up at an Italian deli in Soho.

Paul sipped his wine, 'Ah, the soft strawberry flavours of this little Portuguese beauty sit delicately on my palate.'

Julia raised her eyebrows, then lowered them when she saw her son reading the bottle. 'Well, I'm glad you like strawberries because that's what's coming up for dessert.'

'How was the trip to Ealing Broadway?' enquired Paul.

Julia smiled, 'Oh, fine.' She hesitated. 'Well, a little strange, actually.'

'You ran into a family of goats in Woolworths?' speculated Tony.

This raised a collective smile: a better reaction than the boy had anticipated.

'No goats today,' said Julia. 'I was in Bentalls, by the perfumery counter, and a snooty-looking lady bought an expensive bottle of Chanel Number 5. Then she turned to her friend and said, 'Well, you know what they say, Celia, *When life gets tough, buy more stuff*.''

'Why is that strange?' asked Paul.

'Well, it seemed... *out of character*. Anyway, I'm not finished. Ten minutes later, in W. H. Smiths, a man was carrying a big pile of books to the till. He must have had seven or eight. He winked at his wife and said, '*When life gets tough, buy more stuff*'. That's such an odd coincidence, don't you think?'

Icy-cold fingers tickled Eric's back, and he shivered.

'All right, Eric?'

'Yeah, fine.' Eric reached for his glass.

Julia continued, 'You know, it made me think...'

Choosing his moment well, Paul reached for the rosé and topped-up their glasses.

'It all started about forty years ago,' began Julia. 'There was this Austrian man named Edward Bernays. He was a nephew of the famous psychoanalyst Sigmund Freud. Anyway, Bernays moved to America, and with the help of his uncle's psychological techniques, he turned the world of advertising upside-down. Basically, he used psychology to brainwash Americans into buying things they didn't need.'

At this point, Tony would typically have left the table or attempted to change the subject, but the wine was flowing.

'Of course, the American government loved it,' continued Julia. 'Bernays was oiling the wheels of capitalism and creating work and wealth for the nation.'

'Well, that sounds good,' said Paul.

'Yes, in one way. But Bernays' brainwashing sells empty dreams. Psychological advertising convinces people that possessions equal happiness. They don't, of course; at least, not in the long term. But people are sucked in, and that leads to greed, and in many cases, selfishness and corruption.'

Eric thought of the poems he had heard the previous evening.

'And that,' Julia said, folding her arms, 'is what the people at the Albert Hall last night are against.'

Paul glanced at the clock, 'Mum, can we have our strawberries in the other room? It starts in a minute.'

Light-headed and stuffed full of homemade pizza, the party moved back across the hallway to the living room.

Paul walked to the television and turned up the sound. The news report began with the Beatles themselves.

Congratulating the group on their MBE nominations, the interviewer asked Ringo how he felt about going to Buckingham Palace in a morning suit. The drummer admitted he didn't have one and asked if an evening suit would do. Learning it would not, Ringo said he would go in his pyjamas.

'Go there with yer willy out!' Tony called, drowning his strawberries in double cream.

Julia frowned, 'Tony! Stop being so rude all the time.'

Public reaction to the Beatles' nomination ran the gamut from pleased, to ambivalent, to downright disgusted:

A lady who looked like Dora Brian thought the Beatles were lifting the spirits of the country.

Conversely, one old soldier vowed to return his medal, saying the MBE was being given to people who didn't deserve it.

Carrying empty plates and dessert bowls, Eric and Julia made their way down the wood-panelled hallway. When they reached the stairs, they heard the tinkling of cutlery hitting the kitchen floor.

'Better get in there before he breaks something,' muttered Julia.

They hurried to the kitchen in time to see a thirty-year-old floral-patterned teacup fall from the edge of the sink and shatter on the flagstones below. Tilting his head, Keith eyed the outcome of his destructive deed. Eric felt a waft of air on his face as the parrot flew at him, bounced off the top of his head, then landed on the kitchen door.

'He likes you,' said Julia.

'Really?'

Julia nodded, 'Keith only does that to people he's comfortable with. It's probably because you're calm.'

Placing the dessert bowls by the sink, Eric glanced up warily at the parrot on the door. 'Let me do the washing-up.'

'I'll wash, and you dry,' suggested Julia.

'Nice to see you,' said Keith. 'Nice to see you... Nice to see you.'

'It's strange hearing Jack's voice,' said Julia. 'It would be one thing hearing it on a tape recording or something, but when it comes from right behind you like that...'

'Especially from on top of the door.' Eric took an Isle of Wight tea towel from the counter.

The opening chords to *Eight Days a Week* drifted through from the living room.

'I was thinking,' said Eric. 'That phrase you overheard twice in a row when you were out shopping, *When life gets tough –*'

'Oh, it was a coincidence, Eric. These sayings catch on, and before you know it, they're in the culture. I'm pretty sure I've heard it before.'

Eric was pretty sure that he had heard it, too.

*

Eric and Paul saw *Help!* at the beginning of August 1965, a few days after its general release. The Northfield Odeon was packed with fans, just as it had been for *A Hard Day's Night*.

Although only thirteen months separated the two films, there were changes in both the production and the cinema audience. The new film was in colour, and more males were in evidence this time. Help! also differed in its approach, the tongue-in-cheek realism of A Hard Day's Night giving way to a zany comedy romp. As always, the songs were great, though *Yesterday* came too late to be included. Paul McCartney's timeless ballad wound up on side two of the soundtrack album.

Eric eyed the two blondes sitting next to Paul. 'Give 'em your best chat-up line,' he whispered, nodding at the girls.

'I haven't *got* any chat-up lines,' replied Paul.

Eric thought for a moment. 'Ask them, *Which one's Ringo?*'

Paul smiled.

To Eric's surprise, Paul whispered to the girl beside him, 'Excuse me, um, which one's Ringo?'

'The one with the rings.'

The girl's crisp retort threw Paul. 'What're you doing Thursday?' he blurted, alerting everyone within twenty feet.

A fat man with a bowtie leaned forward, glaring, 'Shush!'

'I'll have to check my diary,' whispered the blonde.

As they followed the girls towards the exit, Paul grabbed Eric's arm. They moved to one side, letting a group of noisy teenagers pass.

Eric looked quizzically at his friend.

'I got a look at them when the lights came on.'

'Dodgy?'

Paul pulled a face.

Eric watched the two blonde heads disappear. 'Are you sure?'

Paul stepped into one of the empty rows, 'Definitely dodgy.'

'Okay... Back exit by the toilets,' said Eric.

*

Replacing the roof on the house was a job beyond even Bill's ever-widening scope. 'I'd rather leave it to the experts,' he said, studying the cracked tiles and crumbling chimney stack through a pair of binoculars. Expensive summer holidays being low on Mary's list of priorities, the family booked a week in a caravan at West Bay.

'I can see the sea,' trilled Mary.

Sonny and Cher's *I Got You Babe* played on the radio.

Bill peered through the windscreen at the tiny harbour town. 'There's not much of it, is there. We'll have to get out and see some of Dorset.'

In the days that followed, the green van took them east and west, accumulating more window stickers along the way. Wandering along the beach at Lime Regis, Mary spotted an ammonite embedded in a rock. 'It's as big as my hand!' Bill exclaimed as they stared at the four-hundred-million-year-old fossil.

The shell-shaped bay at Lulworth Cove possessed a beauty to rival that of St Ives. Over the hill was Durdle Door, its natural limestone arch framing a photo of Eric's parents that he would treasure in later years. All agreed that Dorset's Jurassic Coast had impressed far beyond expectations.

On the final evening at West Bay, Eric spent some time alone with his thoughts. He smiled to himself, strolling by the small harbour, pleased that the week with his parents had been a good one. As he approached the cliff path, a tune surfaced in his head; the melody had been there throughout the holiday. Eric wondered if his synaesthesia spurred his tendency to attach songs to places. Holidays were especially poignant in these associations. At Skegness, it had been *She Loves You*. When he thought of St Ives, *The House of the Rising Sun* invariably came to mind. Even before the present holiday had ended, Eric knew that the song he would forever associate with Dorset would be Donovan's *Universal Soldier*.

Eric sat on the grassy crown above West Bay's sandy-yellow cliffs. As the blood-red sun sank in the west, he watched three white seagulls hover on the thermals above the placid English Channel. Donovan was singing again. The anti-war message reminded him of the poets at the Albert Hall, the people there, and the unforgettable evening he had shared with Julia. Eric remembered her story at the dining table and the coincidence that had sent shivers down his spine. Julia told of the Austrian man who sold empty dreams. Eric thought of Reg and the mysterious office in West Ealing. Somehow, they were all connected.

'Boy, you may not know it yet, but you got Grandmama's Gift'.

Eric knew that he, too, was connected.

12

Autumn Leaves

Back in class for the start of the new school year, Eric pencilled a horizontal line below the centre of the paper. The lower section he painted a medium blue, and above it on the far right, a red semicircle depicted the setting sun. Merging bands of analogous colours rose above the sea, beginning with a pale-yellow and culminating in deep-purple at the top. Rinsing his paintbrush, Eric mixed a thick white and added waves, a few high stars, and three seagulls in the middle-left.

'Very good,' said Scarecrow. He peered over the boy's shoulder, 'I'd have positioned the sun closer to the middle. It's a natural focal point, and in that respect, it's too far to the right.'

'Yeah, but that's where it was,' explained Eric.

'Doesn't matter.' The art teacher pushed his hands in his pockets, 'It's called *artistic licence.*'

Eric would have instinctively balanced the picture, but the view from the clifftop was emblazoned in his mind, and he wanted his painting to recall the scene as he remembered it.

When Scarecrow moved along to the next easel, Donovan unfolded his arms, picked up his acoustic, and started back at the beginning of the song.

*

The first signs of autumn had appeared in Fox Wood, the treetops exhibiting traces of yellow, brown and ginger. Further evidencing the changing seasons, freshening easterly winds brought cooler weather into the south-east.

Equipped with torches, Paul and Eric climbed the white spiral staircase at the far end of Julia's bedroom. Passing through the portal in the ceiling, they clambered over the handrail into the dusty attic. The afternoon sky was overcast, and subdued light filtered down from the observatory.

'Be careful where you step,' warned Paul. 'Some of the boards are loose.'

Eric directed his torch to the opposite end of the loft. 'Blimey, it goes on for miles. Tony should get his Scalextric up here. If he cleared some of this junk, he could have the longest racetrack in the world.'

'Yeah, the problem would be getting *Tony* up here. He's been up to the observatory, but he closes his eyes when he goes past the attic.'

Rain pattered on the roof tiles.

Eric nudged the old rocking horse. Painted wooden eyes regarded him as the head rose and fell. He threw his beam along a row of dusty trunks and suitcases, 'Have you been through these?'

'Pretty much,' replied Paul. 'They're mostly full of junk and old clothes. There're some by the hatch I haven't looked in yet.'

Squeezing past a brass headboard, Paul negotiated an obstacle course of cardboard boxes, some woodworm-infested furniture, four press-framed tennis racquets, and a pair of table lamps. Peering at the tilted tasselled shades, Eric saw two ladies at Ascot. Paul knelt on the dirty boards and opened a trunk.

Several painted canvases had been stacked against the curved metal staircase. Eric immediately identified the paintings as Julia's. Her distinctive artwork utilised surrealist techniques to create wild fantasy landscapes where elven kings and fairy queens dwelt in leafy grottos, surrounded by goblins and pixies, nymphs and brownies. Behind these dreamlike fairy scenes stood grand mansions or castles in the clouds.

Working through the stack, Eric shone his beam on the penultimate canvas. Although bearing Julia's hallmark, the subject had been realised in a conventional style. A wrought-iron R occupied the foreground, and beyond it was the Ealing House.

The final picture had been painted in the same orthodox style as the last but conversely depicted the rear of the house. Pale-green curtains hung in the kitchen. To the right, a shadowy figure stood at the French windows peering out at the artist.

'I was looking for a match and I found one,' said a chirpy American voice. 'My arse and your face!'

Paul peered between the two tilted lampshades. Wearing round glasses and a Groucho Marx moustache, he tapped make-believe ash from a make-believe cigar.

*

Eric was spending most of his free time at the Ealing House, and he now purchased his records from W. H. Smiths in the Broadway. Today, however, he found himself heading for British Home Stores, the sacred shop in West Ealing where he had first heard the Beatles. Recalling his epiphany two-and-a-half years earlier, Eric pictured the spot where he had stood transfixed by their sound. He envisaged a brass plaque embedded by the sock counter, the etched date appearing in his mind. Just two-and-a-half years. It felt like so much longer.

Passing Woolworths, Eric looked across at the corner office above Burton's. He saw the silhouettes of the two dancing men as his mother wiped his face with her moist handkerchief. Recollections of shopping trips with his parents carried their own distinctive ambience: watercolour images accompanied by a deep-seated sense of security. Even as a teenager, Eric was prone to spells of nostalgia.

Standing in the record department in BHS, Eric flicked through the LP sleeves weighing his options. He intended to buy one single and had narrowed his choice to either *(I Can't Get No) Satisfaction* or Dylan's *Like a Rolling Stone*. He wanted both, but knew in his heart that Bob would win-out over the Stones. After much deliberation, Eric elected to blow some of his savings on Dylan's new LP, *Highway 61 Revisited*, which included *Like a Rolling Stone* in its track listing.

The attractive female shop assistant slid Bob into a bag. 'Anything else?'

'Yes, and *Satisfaction*, please,' Eric heard himself say.

'You should be so lucky!' quipped the pretty shop girl's co-worker.

When Eric turned away from the counter – his electric guitar fund now two pounds, six shillings and tuppence lighter – he felt a tap on his shoulder. 'Hello, Sid.'

''Ello love,' replied an overweight old lady with lilac hair. 'I'm sorry to trouble you, dear. You're Eric, aren't you?'

'Oh, sorry.' Eric felt himself go hot under the collar. 'I thought you were... someone else.'

'Yes, ducks. Oh dear.'

The fat lady cupped her hand under Eric's elbow and ushered him away from the aisle. 'I do the cleanin' at the office across the road,' she said, standing between two rails of woolly winter cardigans. 'I knew it was you as soon as I seen you. I've clocked you through the window once or twice. Sid talked about you quite a lot, you know. Not to me, you understand, to Reg. But you can't 'elp over'earing. I'm very sorry.'

'That's all right,' replied Eric. 'It's quite a small office.'

'Oh, that's not what I meant... I'm all of a fluster.' The fat lady paused. 'You 'aven't 'eard, 'ave you.'

'Heard what?'

'I'm ever so sorry, dearie. Sid passed away a few days ago.'

Bill and Mary were out doing some shopping of their own, and the house in West Ealing was quiet. On any normal day, Eric would have played his new records the moment he arrived home, but that Saturday afternoon, they remained in their paper bag on the radiogram. Eric stared at the yellow-jacketed pirate on the mantelpiece. *Sid, dead! He can't have been very old; no more than forty-three or forty-four,* Eric thought. *Perhaps he looked younger than he was.* Or maybe there was something sinister afoot. Sid owed people money, bad people; Reg had said as much. And there was the mysterious organisation in Hartlepool...

Eric pulled out the slip of paper that the lady with the lilac hair had given him. *Hanwell Cemetery, Wednesday, 11:30.* He decided to skip school that day. Eric recalled the last time he had seen Sid. They had sat together in the Hillman, parked just up the road from the house. Sid had been drinking, and he seemed paranoid, continually checking the rear-view mirror. Eric's stomach churned. *'If I see you talking to my son again, it'll be the last thing you do!'* his dad had shouted, shaking his fist after the spluttering Minx.

Eric heard the front door open.

Bill came in holding a small paper bag.

'Hello, Dad.'

Conceding to his long-held desire, Bill had begun his collection of model cars with the Corgi replica that would become the iconic classic of them all: the James Bond Aston Martin DB5. Excitedly removing the packaging, he held the car at eye level, studying it from every angle. Pressing one of the tiny metal tabs, he smiled as the dual machineguns clicked out from beneath the radiator grille. Next was the bullet-proof shield behind the rear window. Saving the best for last, Bill engaged the ejector seat, firing the tiny plastic passenger through the roof. Eric was pleased to see his dad so happy and, for a few moments, felt himself to be older than his father.

Having seen Goldfinger with his dad, Eric remembered the Bond car as silver but kept this observation to himself; Bill was clearly delighted with the gold-finished model. *Artistic licence*, Scarecrow might have said. Corgi struggled to meet demand for the gadget-laden replica.

The next day, the DB5 appeared on the living-room mantelpiece parked at a jaunty angle. In the following weeks, the car would face different directions, including backwards, presumably denoting a silent protest following Mary's frequent dusting.

Eric had mentioned nothing to his parents about Sid's passing, and on Wednesday morning, he left home at his usual time. Cycling a few blocks, he pulled up and exchanged his school tie for the black one he had borrowed from his father's wardrobe.

The autumn of 1965 was well underway. Shrivelled brown leaves crunched beneath Eric's shoes as he wheeled his bicycle past the empty tennis courts in Lammas Park. October had been unseasonably dry, but low clouds blotted the sky. Leaning his bike against a shelter, the boy sat on the bench seat and checked his watch. There were two-and-a-half hours to pass before the funeral.

Eric closed his eyes and watched disjointed flashbacks fill his inner-vision. The stranger with the brown fedora. The Beatles looking down from a balcony. The pile of jazz LPs in the office: Miles Davis. *'Put your left hand there and prepare to swear'.* Sid held up his hand. Then they were in the basement club in Soho. Brian Jones tuned his white teardrop guitar, and Cola bubbles burst in Eric's nostrils. Sid looked at him and smiled: that big, white-toothed grin. His bright eyes flashed as he handed the boy a gold-edged card, *Sidney Mars DJ to the Stars.* Then he began to chuckle. Louder; he could not stop. Rocking his chair, Sid threw back his head and laughed helplessly at the ceiling.

Eric woke with a start. He stared at his watch, *11:15!* His bike had been stolen while he slept. Then he saw it where he had left it at the side of the shelter. Eric rode at full speed towards Northfield Avenue. His deception had backfired, adding precious minutes to the journey.

Taking the backstreets, the cyclist sped into Hanwell, joining the Uxbridge Road. He turned left into the cemetery, whizzing past the tall iron gates.

'Hey! You can't ride that in here!' shouted the attendant.

'Sorry.' Eric dismounted. 'Sidney Mars, DJ to... Sidney Mars's funeral. Any idea where it might be, please?'

Without the man's directions, Eric may have spent ages wandering the twenty-three-acre cemetery and would probably have missed the funeral altogether. As it was, he arrived as the presiding clergyman was concluding his reading.

Leaning his bicycle against a yew tree, Eric approached the small gathering then stopped. Joining the mourners halfway through the ceremony seemed intrusive. If Sid was watching from *the great somewhere*, he would at least know that Eric had attended.

Surrounded by monoliths and memorials, the group stood around the open grave. Eric saw Reg and the lilac-haired lady. Standing beside them was the office receptionist. Behind one of the headstones, a man sat filling-in a crossword puzzle. Facing towards Eric stood a middle-aged man in a black coat. Flanking him were two burly men wearing suits and dark glasses. Their military stances reminded Eric of soldiers at ease.

As the clergyman stepped back, closing his bible, wind scattered the fallen leaves. A grey-haired tramp appeared from behind a Victorian memorial and approached the open grave. Reaching into his tattered jacket, the vagrant pulled out a quarter bottle of whisky and poured the contents over the coffin,

'Here, Sid,' the tramp said in a road-weary voice. 'Have the last drink on me.'

A well-dressed black musician stepped forward and brought his tenor saxophone to his lips. The man screwed his eyes tight shut. With the breath of an angel and the soul of the devil, he blew a slow, impassioned verse of *Autumn Leaves*. Finishing with a wild glissando flourish, the musician stepped back from the grave and lowered his instrument. The ceremony was over.

Eric noticed that the man in the black coat was staring at him. Feeling uncomfortable, he turned and walked back to his bike. When he looked again, the man was gone, along with his two minders.

'Hello Eric,' Reg said, joining him under the tree. 'I'm surprised to see you here.'

Eric wanted to say *I'm surprised you didn't tell me about it*, but instead asked the question that had been in his mind for days, 'What happened, Reg? What happened to Sid?'

Reg leaned back against the yew tree, staring into the middle distance. 'Well, Eric, over the last year or two, Sid had got into booze in a big way. One night he went on a bender. He fell asleep and never woke up.' Shrugging, Reg faced the boy. 'That's all there is to it.'

Eric thought the postman seemed to be looking through him. 'So you don't think there was anything funny going on? The gangsters he owed money to, or –'

'I don't think so, Eric. Not as far as I know, anyway. Sid just... had one drink too many.'

Eric sniffed and turned away. Looking across the cemetery, he saw only a misty grey blur. 'Shall we get going, then?'

Reg hesitated. 'It might be best if we don't leave together.'

'What do you mean? Why?'

'Because,' said Reg. 'Because... '

'Because of the men from Hartlepool,' said Eric.

'How did you know?'

'Because I'm clever,' Eric replied, remembering his father's phrase.

Reg smiled weakly. 'Well then,' he said, looking sharp-eyed at Eric, 'you'll know that the *clever* thing to do, is to leave separately.'

Eric nodded.

Early that evening, Eric joined Paul in his room to catch up on some homework. Explaining that he had been to a funeral, Eric skipped over the details, saying only that the deceased had been a distant relative. The lie jarred, but an explanation was required.

The homework assignments completed, they went downstairs. Julia was in the kitchen, leafing through a pile of newspapers and magazines that Paul had brought down from the attic.

'Harold Macmillan: *'You've never had it so good',*' read Julia, flattening the creases from a 1959 Daily Mirror. 'Actually, he said something like, *'Most of our people have never had it so good',* but that's not as catchy, is it.'

'You're such a cynic, Mum,' Paul said, using his favourite new word.

Eric pulled out a chair and sat opposite Julia. 'How about this one. *A Communist in Space*, the headline says. *Soviet Union wild with joy at first trip outside of this world.'*

Paul nodded, 'Yuri Gagarin, April 1961.'

'Let's see,' Julia leant across the table.

Eric swivelled the paper, holding up the front page.

Julia laughed, *'The Daily Worker.* Definitely one of Jack's.' She leaned closer, reading the small print, *'The only daily paper owned by its readers.* Now that's a *real* red-top newspaper!'

They heard Tony drumming along with the intro music from the new Gerry and Sylvia Anderson puppet series, *Thunderbirds*.

Julia walked to the kitchen door. She leant out into the passageway, 'Don't break the coffee table in there.'

'No milady,' came the reply from the living room.

'This one's been folded open.' Julia slid a magazine from the middle of the pile. 'Oh, April Ashley. Do you remember all the fuss they made about her?'

Eric shook his head.

'She was the first British transsexual.' Julia checked the cover, 'Yes, Vogue. These must be some of her original fashion shots, David Baily, probably. This was before it all came out in the press.'

Eric looked at the photo spread, 'All *what* came out?'

'About her operation. She started life as a man.'

'Yeek!' Paul exclaimed, cupping his tackle with both hands.

'She's pretty,' Eric observed, picking up on Julia's use of the female gender.

'Mum,' Tony shouted from the living room. 'Someone's buzzing.'

Julia stood up and left the kitchen.

'Yes, who is it?' she inquired, speaking into the small box next to the living room fireplace.

'Sorry to bother you, I'm from the West London Department of Education. Could I have a minute of your time?'

Julia paused. 'Yes, all right, wait there.'

Paul followed his mother down the front path. He stood beside her as she opened the gate.

Julia regarded the two grey-suited men through the partially open door. 'How can I help you?'

'We're on the lookout for a teenage lad,' said the man without the sunglasses. 'About the same age as that young chap next to you. He's not in any trouble, but the school is concerned about him.'

'What does he look like?'

'Quite slim, medium-brown hair –'

'Oh, we all have dark hair in this house,' said Julia. 'Sorry... I hope you find him.' She closed the gate.

'Mum,' Paul asked, as they walked back to the house, 'did you see someone in the bushes on the other side of the pathway?'

Julia shook her head, 'Kids, probably.'

'Why would anyone be looking for me?' Eric asked Julia across the kitchen table.

'Because you've been a naughty boy and bunked-off school?' suggested Paul.

'No chance,' said Julia. '*The West London Department of Education?* That sounds made-up, doesn't it? And they didn't even mention the boy's name.' She leaned back, gathering her long black hair. 'They might have been a couple of weirdos. That's the trouble with living in a tucked-away place; you have to be so careful. Anyway, they've gone now.'

The next morning at school, Eric approached Bony's desk with trepidation. 'I'm sorry about missing yesterday, sir. I had to go to a funeral. My –'

'All right,' interrupted the teacher. 'But if anything like this crops up again, Grimes, you must inform me in advance. Understood?'

'Yes, sir. Sorry, sir.' Eric filed *funerals* alongside *diarrhoea* in his list of *likely to get away with it* excuses.

*

Ron dropped a bundle of newspapers on the counter with a *thump*. 'Seven o'clock, mate.'

'I'll try to make it.' Eric stifled a sneeze and looked up at his ginger-haired classmate. 'I'm not sure if –'

'Ah, come on, it's my birthday. All my mates'll be there. We'll have a laugh. And don't bother getting me anything. *I'm* giving out the presents, and I've got a special one stashed away for you.'

Eric forced a smile, 'Okay, seven o'clock.'

When he set out from the newsagents, it had already been snowing for five or ten minutes. November had been cold, but bundled-up in his Michelin Man gear, Eric could cope with that. Precipitation was the paperboy's nemesis, and on that frosty Thursday morning, the sky was white.

Within fifteen minutes of his leaving the shop, a white blanket had covered Ealing, slowing progress and icing the roads. *Ticket to Ride* selected itself on Eric's internal jukebox. At one point, visibility was limited to twenty feet. *Crap*, thought Eric, *I'm going to be late for school – again.* And to worsen his mood, he had said *yes* to Ron Hillman.

Twenty minutes late but true to his word, Eric arrived at Ron's house in South Ealing. Stamping the snow from his shoes, he rang the bell. Footfalls thundered on the stairs.

'Hello Grimsey,' grinned Ron.

'Happy birthday,' said Eric, handing his host a white envelope.

'Thanks. We're upstairs.'

Crammed into Ron Hillman's tiny bedroom were two paperboys and the two older lads Eric had encountered at the reservoir.

The spotty one raised his glass, splashing Ron's bed. 'It's 'im!'

'Ullo mate, anybody shot ya lately?' snickered his skinny friend.

Eric managed a half-smile. *I'm missing Top of the Pops for this.* He looked around for a television.

'There you go, mate.' Ron handed Eric a glass of cider. 'Knock it back; you've got some catching up to do.'

Eric stood by the wardrobe and sipped the sweet drink.

'Goo-on,' goaded the skinny teenager. 'Don't piss abaat, do it in one!'

'Five, four...' began the skinny boy's friend.

The other lads joined in, 'Three, two...'

Eric downed the cider without stopping for air. There were a couple of cheers that sounded more like jeers. He belched loudly.

'Now that we're all here...' Ron topped-up everyone's glasses. 'Since it's my birthday, I've got everybody a present.'

Eric moved out of the way as Marmalade opened his wardrobe. The top shelf was packed with cigarettes, cigars, and numerous chocolate bars, lighters and trinkets. Ron slid out five magazines and tossed one to each of his guests.

'Oo-ay, wank mags!' exclaimed the skinny teenager.

The glossy magazines were followed by cigarettes. Eric received a box of Dunhill's to accompany the three-month-old copy of *Parade*.

'Okay, before we go out, we've got to finish off the cider,' said Ron. 'And there's two more quart bottles, so we better get cracking.'

Three minutes later, Ron's bedroom was choked with smoke.

The spotty teenager nudged his friend's arm, spilling more cider on the bed. 'Fuckin' 'ell! Look at the bazookas on this one!'

Eric had heard that a few nights earlier, someone had said *fuck* on television.

When the cider was gone, Ron filled the outstretched glasses with beer. 'Right. Everybody... down in one!'

Filing past a row of empty bottles and cans, the six boys left the room.

Eric gripped the handrail, wondering which of the two staircases he was walking down. 'Where are we going?'

'Bit o' *mischief*,' the skinny marksman called up from the hall.

'Shut it!' hissed Ron. 'Me mum'll hear.'

Eric wished he had heeded his intuitive warnings. He could have been at home or at the Ealing House instead of taking to the streets with a gang of idiots. But he had accepted Ron's stolen gifts and drunk his alcohol; he was along for the ride. And it really didn't help matters that for the first time in his life, Eric was drunk as a skunk.

*

Eric opened the front door. 'Tony!' he exclaimed, surprised to see his friend. 'Is everything okay?'

'Yeah, fine,' said the boy, automatically walking into the front room.

Eric seated himself in his usual chair. 'Isn't it your scouts night?'

'Yeah, Paul's there now. He still likes it, but I've 'ad enough.'

'Have you told Paul? He'll worry if –'

'I told him earlier,' Tony said, taking off his coat.

'So how come you –'

'Blokes wearing shorts, doin' knots and waggling their woggles. Bugger that.' Tony seated himself, facing Eric. 'Cubs was all right, but scouts is shit. I 'aven't told Mum.'

Eric was surprised that Paul still attended the meetings, but he had kept this to himself.

'Mum's out with one of her art school friends,' said Tony. 'So I thought I'd ride over to where we used to live.'

'Nice idea.' *Better than the empty Ealing House*. 'I'll ride back with you if you like. Have you got keys to get in?'

Tony nodded, giving Eric a thumbs up.

Most of the recent snow had melted. The twenty-minute ride to Ealing Broadway was cold that November evening, but the roads were dry and free of ice. A light fog hung in the moist air, and the cyclists' breath froze.

Having wheeled their bicycles to the top of Hanger Hill, Eric and Tony remounted and rode slowly along the dark walkway. Two pale-yellow beams pierced the murky gloom.

Tony unlocked the gate.

Some of the downstairs lights had been left on, and a faint hazy glow lit the garden. Eric looked up at the spooky silhouette. The house appeared taller in the dark. He appreciated Tony's reluctance towards returning home alone. 'Are you sure there's no one here?'

Tony shook his head, 'Mum was havin' kittens on the phone. She'll probably be out all night talkin' bollocks.'

'Right.'

Tony closed the front door behind them and began to unbutton his coat. 'What's that?' he hissed, standing stock-still.

'What's what?' asked Eric.

'Listen!'

Eric walked slowly along the hall. 'It's coming from upstairs,' he called back. 'It sounds like music. I'm not sure which –'

Tony was through the front door before Eric could finish his sentence.

Two minutes later, they sat together on a wet bench in Hanger Hill Park. The world felt eerily quiet in the foggy darkness.

'It was probably your mum,' said Eric. 'I expect she came home early.'

Tony sniffed. 'Playing music upstairs? Why? How? There's no record player upstairs.'

'Paul has a radio in his room.'

'Why would she be in there?' Tony shrugged, 'The radiogram's in the living room. She'd use that.'

'Perhaps Paul's home, then.'

'His bike wasn't where he leaves it. Stop tryin' to make excuses.'

An hour-and-a-half later, Eric convinced Tony to return home.

Paul and Julia were sitting in the living room, watching *The Avengers*.

'You're missing it,' said Paul. 'Emma Peel just –'

'Oh, thank heavens!' exclaimed Julia. 'Thank you for bringing him home, Eric. Where on earth have you been?'

'Sitting in the park next door,' replied Eric.

Tony still had his coat on. 'How long have you been home, Mum?'

'Not long, I came in just before Paul. I –'

'We heard ghosts,' Tony said, teetering between anger and tears.

139

'I think it was music,' said Eric. 'Coming from somewhere upstairs.'

'Oh, silly, that was me,' said Julia.

'But what... I mean, it can't have been *you*,' protested Tony. 'There's no record player upstairs.'

There was an uncomfortable silence.

Julia smiled consolingly, 'I was cleaning on the first floor. I had Paul's radio on for company. Oh, Tony, you are daft. There are no ghosts here or anywhere else.'

Eric was on the telephone for ages. After repeated offers of a lift home, he eventually persuaded his dad to let him stay the night at the Ealing House.

Eric went upstairs and joined Paul in his room.

'Eric the ghost hunter!' joked Paul. He flopped back onto his bed with his acoustic on his lap. 'Why did you bring your coat up?'

Eric raised his eyebrows. Reaching inside his duffle coat, he slid out the Parade magazine. 'I thought you might like to borrow this.'

Paul grinned, 'Are the pages stuck together?' He flicked through the girly mag. 'One's been torn out.'

Eric's mind raced: *It's probably on Marmalade's wall.* He had lied to Paul about Sid's funeral. 'Well, there was one pic that I sort of liked,' Eric admitted. He refrained from describing the pretty topless model with long black hair and a short tennis skirt. 'Where's your radio?'

'In the ballroom,' Paul said, studying the magazine. 'I left it down there yesterday.'

Eric changed the subject.

Tony had been coaxed into bed. Julia, Paul and Eric sat around the kitchen table, each with a mug of coffee.

'It was 'orrible,' Eric said, intentionally dropping the h. 'But it was Ron's birthday. I'd have felt rotten if I'd left.'

'*And*, you were sloshed,' added Paul.

Keith ruffled his feathers, wishing they would all go to bed.

'So, what happened when you went out?' asked Julia.

Eric frowned, 'We walked the backstreets in the snow. And it was bloody cold. South Ealing Station's phonebox got smashed up, and there's now a street sign above Ron's bed saying *Alacross Road.*'

'But the *good* thing is...' said Paul, 'Ron gave Eric a dirty magazine, and he just lent it to me.'

Julia giggled, 'I'll take a look later.'

Eric considered the contrasting attitudes of Paul's mother and his own parents. Granted, Julia was more than ten years younger, but the two relationships were entirely different.

'Why would anyone want to go around destroying things?' reflected Eric. 'It's just stupid.'

'Frustration?' suggested Paul. 'Maybe they're not good at anything, so they take it out on a phonebox.'

'Perhaps that's one of the reasons,' acknowledged Julia. 'There are probably lots of others. Even Edward Bernays's empty promises might have a part to play. As far as I can see, the only solution is an intellectual one: education. To understand the root causes of aggression, you have to understand nature. Darwin showed us that *survival of the fittest* is the way life evolves. And that – at its most basic level – means killing-off the weak before they can pass on their ill-suited genes.'

'We should get a bit fitter then,' Paul said, flexing an unimpressive bicep.

'Fittest as in *fit for purpose*,' clarified Julia. 'That doesn't necessarily mean physically fit. As humans, *our* best weapon is our big brain.'

'Which brings us back to education,' said Eric.

Julia nodded, 'Precisely, Eric. We have the technology to blow-up the world. If we're to survive as a species, we must learn to transcend the darker aspects of our hunter-gatherer instincts.'

'If I ever write a book,' mused Eric, 'maybe it'll be about that.'

'Do it,' urged Julia. 'Call it, *The Life and Times of Eric Grimes*.'

Eric thought of his recently departed friend. In a different context, Sid had suggested the same title.

*

Aware of his frequent absences and despite being invited to the Ealing House, Eric spent Christmas Day at home. Excavating a silver sixpence from his pudding, he promised himself he would be there every year.

There was no snow on the 25th, but coloured lights threw fuzzy reflections across the frosted window. A fairy passed down by Mary's grandmother topped the tree, and cards hung along a string above the fireplace. Between pinecones and baubles, the gold Aston Martin now faced permanently out to the room. It felt a lot like Christmas.

Early that morning, with excitement akin to his childhood, Eric unwrapped *Rubber Soul*. John Lennon's contributions stood out on the new Beatles album. Eric particularly liked *In My Life* and *Girl*. George's sitar on *Norwegian Wood* added an exotic texture; the introspective *Nowhere Man* reminded Eric of himself. Paul's *Michelle* added a touch of lightness to the contemplative, understated LP. The writers were leaving behind the boy-meets-girl love songs, incorporating narratives and social observation into their lyrics. On hearing *Rubber Soul* once through, Eric immediately rated it as the Beatles' best work to date. The second listening was like falling in love with the group all over again.

Crackers dispensed coloured paper crowns to be worn during and after dinner. The Queen's Christmas Message at 3pm was followed by the annual screening of Billy Smart's Circus. In the evening, Max Bygraves met the Black and White Minstrels. Bob Hope and Bing Crosby set out on *The Road to Bali*, and Ken Dodd (the self-proclaimed head of Knotty Ash TV), introduced the nation to the Diddy Men. When Bill and Mary went to bed at 10:30, Eric helped himself to another chunk of Christmas cake and settled down to watch Top of the Pops. From the Beatles and the Stones to the Seekers' *I'll Never Find Another You*, the late-night Christmas special reprised every number-one song from 1965.

Six days later, as the rest of Britain prepared to welcome 1966, Eric celebrated his fourteenth birthday.

13

Rapier 33
1966

When they were giving out noses, I thought they said roses, so I asked for a big red one.

The problem was not deafness, nor was Eric incapable. The problem, Bony surmised, was the boy's infuriating tendency to park his brain in an entirely different location to that of his physical body. 'What did I just say, Grimes?' barked the skeletal teacher.

'Peas banned in Bash Street,' Eric replied, not stopping to think.

'*Please hand in your math sheets,*' repeated Bony, as the class erupted into laughter.

Eric would forever associate his *faux pas* with the new school term at the beginning of 1966. He had been reliving the holiday period, and he did not need to be Sigmund Freud to identify the factors influencing his reply. He reasoned that the peas had popped up in relation to his Christmas dinner. *Bash Street* was the unfortunate part, Bony's resemblance to the Beano comic's teacher being evident to all.

*

Julia stepped onto the pavement regarding the white Mini Cooper. 'She's very pretty. I might name her *Jean*, after Jean Shrimpton.'

'How about Jack?' Paul said, eyeing the painted British flag on the roof.

Eric came cycling around the bend into Hillcrest Road. 'Wow! It looks like it drove straight out of Carnaby Street!' He pulled up next to the entrance to Hanger Hill Park. 'I love the Union Jack.'

'Hello, Eric.' Julia stared doubtfully at the flag on the little car's roof.

'What's wrong with a Union Jack?' queried Paul.

'Well, don't get me wrong, I love where we live, but I don't think much good comes out of nationalism. In fact –'

'Oh, leave it out, Mum!' interrupted Paul. 'You've just bought a new car, and you're going on about –'

Julia smiled, 'Yes, you're quite right, Paul. But the car's not brand new. Pattie suggested I buy one that was a year or two old; you get better value for money.' A vehicle approached and Julia turned, 'Ah, talk of the devil.'

Julia's blonde art school friend drew up in her purple Volkswagen Beetle. Grabbing a Halfords bag from the passenger seat, she joined the others on the pavement.

'Hi, Pats,' Julia grinned, hugging her friend. With an arm around the attractive woman's waist, she turned to face the two boys. 'This is my son, Paul, and this is our friend, Eric. Guys, meet Pattie.'

'Hello,' Eric and Paul said together.

Eric regarded the two young women. Their looks, height and slight stature were strikingly similar. Aside from their contrasting hair colours, Julia and Pattie looked like they had been created from the same mould. Realising he was staring, Eric commented on the resemblance, 'You look like sisters.'

'Yes,' Pattie acknowledged, in a tone that said, *We've heard that a hundred times.* 'At college, they called us *the Twins.* They got us mixed-up all the time, which is why I bleached my hair.'

'You can't tell,' Eric said, immediately wishing he hadn't.

Pattie smiled. She was every bit as pretty as Julia; prettier, if you like blondes. She reached inside the Halfords bag, 'Make yourself useful, guys.' Pattie handed Eric and Paul an L-plate each.

Tying one of the plates to the Mini's radiator grill, Eric smiled to himself. He much preferred the term *guys* to *boys.* Straightening up, Eric looked through the windscreen at the Twins. He thought the petite longhaired girls looked great in the Mini; a Zephyr or a Jag would have dwarfed them. In their case, he preferred the term *girls* to *women.*

Eric and Paul stood by the park gate while Pattie gave her friend a few instructions. When Julia twisted the ignition key, the radio blasted the Rolling Stones' *Nineteenth Nervous Breakdown.*

Pattie looked at the driver, 'I hope that isn't an omen.'

*

When he dialled the EAL phone number from the *Musical Instruments* column in Exchange & Mart, Eric struck lucky. Elers Road was a ten-minute walk from his house. He had never heard of a *Rapier 33*, but the man on the telephone told him the red guitar had three pickups and looked like a Fender Stratocaster. And it came with an amplifier. The asking price was twenty-two pounds. If the electric guitar met his requirements, Eric was prepared to smash his paper-round piggy bank to buy it.

The terraced house was larger than the one he had just left, and backed on to Lammas Park. Eric approached a black front door with stained-glass panels. He drew back the brass knocker and rapped twice, much harder than he had intended.

The small man that answered looked to be nineteen or twenty. Tousled brown hair covered his ears, loose straggly curls framing a Hobbit-like face.

'Hello, I'm Eric.'

'Phil,' said the Hobbit man, smiling as he shook Eric's hand. 'Do come in.'

Although he was perhaps six or seven years older, Phil stood at the same height as Eric. He also had been granted the use of his parents' front room. Phil's radiogram stood in the same alcove next to the fireplace. It felt like a home from home, only bigger and a bit posh. Eric's eyes landed on a pale-yellow Fender Telecaster that lay propped against the sofa.

'That's it,' Phil said, gesturing towards the expensive Fender guitar. 'Twenty-two quid, and it's yours.'

Eric's mouth fell open.

'Sorry,' said Phil. 'My dodgy sense of humour.'

'That's okay,' smiled Eric. 'I've never actually seen one before. Only on Top of the Pops.'

Phil reached behind the arm of the sofa. 'Take a seat.' He lifted out a green-tartan guitar bag, 'Have you had an electric before?'

'No, just an acoustic,' Eric replied, staring at the bright-red guitar.

'Well, you've got one now.' Phil handed the instrument to Eric, 'I'm only joking. Give it a play and see if you like it.'

Eric sat with an electric guitar on his lap for the first time in his life. Although it had some weight, the guitar felt svelte, almost like a toy. Leaning back, he pushed his forefinger into the small pocket on his Levi's and slid out his plectrum.

'That's what they're for, those little pockets,' said Phil. 'Plecy pockets.'

Eric strummed an E chord, then fingering a barre shape, he moved up the neck, hitting a G, an A, and then a B. He glanced up at Phil, 'It's dead easy to play!'

'It's a semipro guitar, but it's a good one,' said Phil. 'I've mucked about with the string heights, tweaked the neck, and adjusted the intonation. And it's got light-gauge strings on it, so it's easy on the fingers. Here, let's plug you in.'

Eric loved the red Rapier, and the small amplifier that came with it as part of Phil's twenty-two-pound package. He tried every control on the guitar, fascinated by the tonal variations.

'I've used the amp while playing with a drummer,' said Phil. 'There's no problem being heard. It's small, but it's bloody loud.'

Eric handed Phil four five-pound notes and two singles. 'Thank you,' he said. 'I'll look after it.'

Phil smiled widely, 'I believe you will. Come on,' he grinned, reaching for his yellow Telecaster. 'Let's have a play.'

Plugging into the amplifier's second input, Phil tuned his new guitar to his old one. When they kicked off the opening riff to *Day Tripper*, it dawned on Eric that he had turned to a new and exciting page.

Half-an-hour later, Phil borrowed his dad's car and drove Eric home. The Rapier sat in its waterproof bag on the back seat alongside the small *bloody loud* amplifier.

'Have you seen many groups?' asked Phil.

'I saw one at Butlin's once,' replied Eric. 'I sat right at the front. They were great.'

Phil smiled his broad Hobbit smile. 'I'm going to Twickenham on the 20th to see a fantastic group. You can come along if you like. I guarantee they'll be better than the one you saw at Butlin's.'

Eric wondered why he had not told Phil that he had seen the Beatles in concert. Something held him back: deference to the older man, combined with an overactive sense of humility. If he found this flash of self-awareness disturbing, Eric might have been comforted by the counsel of an ancient Chinese philosopher:

'He who speaks without modesty will find it difficult to make his words good'.

The old khaki backpack that Paul had discovered in the attic was a perfect size; Eric's amplifier slotted in snugly, with room for a folded towel to serve as cushioning. *Where there's a will, there's a way*, thought Eric, as on a grey Saturday in March, he set off for the Ealing House with the Rapier dangling in its bag from his handlebar. Hanger Hill seemed twice as steep that day.

'Oh, Eric, you are silly.' Julia sat down next to him by the fireplace. 'I could have driven over in the Mini and picked up your amplifier.'

'He's too polite to ask.' Paul reclined on the smaller sofa on the opposite side of the coffee table, strumming the red Rapier, unplugged.

Eric peered past Paul into the front garden. Tony was haring up and down the long gravel path on his bike. 'The rucksack worked really well.'

'Good. Keep it then,' said Julia.

'Oh, thank you very much!' Eric replied with a smile.

Straightening up, Julia watched Tony enter a sideways skid, sending a hail of gravel stones rebounding off the steps and rattling into the porch.

Paul looked over his shoulder, 'He's gonna come off that bike in a minute.'

The buzzer sounded next to the fireplace. Julia leaned over the arm of the sofa and pressed the button on the intercom, 'Hello?'

'Hi Jules, it's me,' Pattie said from outside the front gate.

'I'll buzz you in. Watch out for the manic kid on the bicycle.'

Fortunately for the visitor, Tony was at that point standing on his pedals, scrambling through the weeds and bushes where the tennis court used to be. As Pattie closed the green wooden gate behind her, Julia went out to the hallway to open the front door. Paul and Eric stood back from the windows, admiring the attractive blonde. Pattie looked striking, dressed in a shiny red PVC mac and black knee-high boots. She held a sky-blue carrier bag.

'Wow,' Paul said, as Pattie neared the porch steps, her long blonde hair blowing back in the breeze.

'Wow,' echoed Eric.

'Wow!' Pattie exclaimed, entering the wood-panelled hall. 'Quite a place you have here!'

The Twins came into the living room. Pattie had slipped off her mac, revealing a simple black sleeveless dress. The tailored cut hugged her slight figure.

'Well, look at you!' exclaimed Julia. 'You put me to shame.'

Eric thought Julia looked great in her tight-fitting Levi's and baggy pink T-shirt.

'Oh, thank you, *darling*,' Pattie replied in a Fenella Fielding voice. 'Hi, guys. Oh, perfect!' she exclaimed, admiring Eric's guitar.

Julia laughed, 'You said the right thing there, Pats.'

'Glad you like it,' beamed Eric.

'It's a fabulous house, Jules.' Pattie looked around the room. 'In the olden days, they used to piss in fireplaces like that.'

'Cuppa?' offered Julia.

'Lead the way,' Pattie said, following her friend out of the room.

'She looks gorgeous,' whispered Paul.

Eric nodded. 'Like she stepped out of a fashion mag.'

A few minutes later, *the Twins* returned with four mugs of coffee. With their backs to the window, Paul and Eric sat together on the small sofa. Pattie craned her neck, peering into the garden,

'He's gonna come off that bike in a minute.'

Paul nodded, 'That's what I said.'

'Been shopping?' Julia enquired, trying to sneak a peek into the paper carrier bag.

'Not today.' Pattie pulled out a copy of the Daily Express. 'Have you seen this?'

'Not that article, but I know about Twiggy,' replied Julia.

'*The Face of 1966*,' read Pattie. 'She's a smash. And she's even skinnier than you, Jules.'

'Huh! You can talk. When you turn sideways, you disappear!'

Eric and Paul sat sipping their coffees and enjoying the banter on the opposite sofa.

'Well, my point is,' continued Pattie, 'that skinny is *in*. You've seen Mary Quant's stuff, right?'

'Of course, I love her look.'

'Have you noticed how skinny her models are? They get skinnier in every new spread.'

'I wish you wouldn't keep using that word.'

'Okay, sorry. Anyway, it's 1966 and sk... *thin* is in.' Pattie reached into the carrier bag, this time bringing out an expensive Pentax camera. 'Fancy taking some pictures?'

Julia smiled. 'The penny just dropped.'

'Okay, before you say anything, I know some people in the modelling business. Well, I have a friend who knows someone from an agency who –'

'Oh Pattie, I think it's a great idea! You're beautiful. Why not have a go? *Of course* I'll take the pictures, it'll be fun! Oh, and skinny is in.'

'*Thin*,' Pattie reminded her.

Two minutes later, the coffee table was strewn with every cosmetic imaginable: lipsticks, eye shadows, blushers, Pan Stik, mascara, mirrors, brushes, the works. Eric thought Pattie already looked perfect, but he and Paul watched with interest as Julia applied subtle touches, the artist inside her knowing instinctively where accents and highlights would be at their most effective. Pattie's pretty blue eyes received the most attention, the mid-sixties vogue dictating Julia's application of thick black liner embellished by tiny upward flicks at the outer corners. Applying a light mascara, the artist took a pin and deftly separated the false lashes. The deep-purple eye shadow complimented Pattie's natural colour. The attractive young woman's high cheekbones were shadowed with a touch of blusher, bringing the delicate features to the fore. *White lipstick...* No, today, the lips had to be red to match the PVC mac that the prospective model had chosen to wear in the photographs. The hair was easy: no curls or primping required. Pattie's long blonde hair was ubiquitous, perhaps timeless; a quick brush and a puff of hairspray would suffice. Leaning back and assessing her work, Julia pronounced her friend fit for the photographer's lens.

Pattie studied her face in a compact mirror. 'Nice paint job, Jules.'

Warming to her assignment, Julia examined the Pentax. 'Do you have plenty of film?'

'Rolls and rolls. Ready to shoot?'

Selecting a well-thumbed copy of *The Communist Manifesto* from the library at the back of the living room, Pattie stood at an angle to the camera, reading studiously.

'Looking good,' Julia said, inclining the camera vertically. 'Paul, would you turn on the overhead light and put some music on, please.'

'Can we have the Beatles?' requested the model. 'According to Lennon, they're bigger than Jesus now, and I could do with a miracle or two.'

Julia took half-a-dozen shots of Pattie posing in front of the bookshelves. *Drive My Car* played on the radiogram. Eric noticed that the blonde adjusted her stance and facial expressions between camera clicks without any direction from Julia. He thought of the *Hard Day's Night* LP cover.

Pattie slipped on the pillar box red PVC mac. 'Eric, may we borrow your beautiful guitar, please?'

When the session moved into the hallway, Eric stood by the front door with the red Rapier at the ready. Julia crouched in front of him, photographing Pattie down the wide corridor. The model became more animated, opening the mac and standing with her arms akimbo.

'Fabulous,' said Julia. 'The black dress and boots look great with the red mac. And the black-and-white floor tiles are perfect.'

Pattie struck pose after pose with Eric's guitar, holding the instrument every-which-way. Her long blonde hair hung down over the red body as she brought the Rapier up next to her face for Julia's close-ups. Eric pictured the photograph hanging on his bedroom wall.

'Okay, a few by the stairs,' directed Julia. 'Maybe lose the coat and the guitar. Paul, could you fetch a table lamp, please.'

'Why don't you use the flash?' suggested Eric.

'Oh, the flash would kill it,' replied Julia. 'It's all about light and shade.'

'Paint the light,' Pattie said, standing next to the jardinière with the big aspidistra.

Eric considered the advice. Not only did his artwork improve tenfold from that day, so too did his guitar playing.

'One or two on the stairs,' said Julia, 'then we'll move up to the next floor.'

'Would one of you lovely guys grab my carrier bag from the living room, please,' called Pattie. 'Jules, do you have anything to drink?'

When they re-joined the photoshoot on the first floor, Eric carried his guitar in one hand and Pattie's blue bag in the other. Paul brought a bottle of rosé.

Julia observed the wine glasses in Paul's hand with mock curiosity, 'I wondered what that clinking sound was.'

Downstairs, *Like a Rolling Stone* played at full volume.

'My bedroom's on the top floor,' said Julia.

'Okay.' Pattie took the carrier bag from Eric, 'We'll be back in a few.'

Eric and Paul sat side-by-side on the second stair, each cupping a glass of rosé.

Eric leant close to his friend, 'I'd love one of those pictures of Pattie holding my guitar.'

'Ask her, then.'

Eric stared down at the red carpet.

'Okay, *I'll* ask her.'

'That would be brilliant, but not in front of me.'

'No problem,' replied Paul. 'I'll have a word on the quiet.'

Eric brushed his finger across the guitar strings and turned to Paul. 'You're a really great friend,' he said, with more sincerity than he had intended.

'I'd be a better friend,' whispered Paul, 'if I could get you a pic of her wearing a few less clothes!'

'Photo session part two,' Pattie announced from the top of the stairs.

Eric and Paul stood up. Pattie was wearing the same black knee-high boots, but the dress had been replaced by a frilly white blouse and a black miniskirt. The session resumed by the big round window at the end of the first-floor corridor.

Ten minutes later, Julia took a few final pictures of her friend sitting on the stairs next to the aspidistra, 'Give me your best sexy look.'

Pattie leaned back on her elbows, draping herself casually on the red-carpeted stairway.

Bending her knees, Julia angled the camera, 'Great, looking good... Bring your chin down a touch... Hold it... Yeah. Now move one foot up a step.'

Patty obliged.

'Okay, lean back and face towards Eric.' Julia snapped a series of shots.

Pattie gave Eric an exaggerated wink, and he realised he had been staring.

Keith flew out from the kitchen, gaining altitude as he passed over their heads. Turning impressively in the air, the grey parrot sped off down the hallway and disappeared into the living room.

Paul sniffed, then looked questioningly at Eric. He glanced through the kitchen doorway, 'The back garden's on fire!'

They raced to the door at the end of the passage. In the garden, Tony was frantically beating the huge raging bonfire with a blackened branch.

'Stand back!' shouted Julia. 'You're too close!'

Smoke billowed as leaping orange flames consumed the tinderbox of paper and wood that Tony had spent the best part of an hour collecting. The charred skeletons of four discarded dining chairs glowed and crackled amid the ferocious blaze. Flaring red sparks spat onto the surrounding brown grass.

Julia grabbed her son, pulling him away from the flames, 'For God's sake, why don't you *think*, Tony! We live in an out-of-the-way place. The fire brigade couldn't get anywhere *near* this house if that got out of control.'

'But it isn't,' protested Tony. 'It's away from everything.'

Julia gripped the boy's bony shoulder, 'Yes, but it's too *big!*'

'I'll get a bucket of water,' Paul said calmly.

'Hold this, Eric,' said Julia. Handing him the camera, she followed Paul into the house.

Eric turned to Pattie, 'Quick, stand in front of the fire.'

Pattie ran over to the scorched grass. Standing as close to the flames as she dared, the blonde slipped into model-mode, striking poses while Eric snapped away like David Baily.

'You look great!' Eric said, adjusting the focus. 'Do you mind if I take a few mo –'

'Just do it!' urged Pattie. 'Before my knickers catch fire!'

Despite the size and intensity of Tony's blazing inferno, the Ealing House sustained no damage. Four days later, a fire extinguisher appeared by the bannisters on each of the three floors.

*

The clocks were not due to go forward until the following weekend, and it had been dark for almost two hours. Phil made a right turn at Brentford Half Acre, driving towards Syon Park,

'So where have you stashed it?'

Eric gazed out of the passenger window at the shabby shopfronts. 'Stashed what?'

'The World Cup. Didn't you see the news? *Police are interested in interviewing a fair-haired teenage lad who was seen in the area, busking with a red Rapier.*'

'I avoid the telly on Sunday evenings. It's when my mum gets her hymn book out and sings along with Songs of Praise.'

'Are your family religious?' asked Phil.

'Not really. Mum just likes the songs.'

Fifteen minutes later, Phil parked his father's blue Morris Oxford in one of Twickenham's narrow backstreets near the Thames. 'It's not far,' he told Eric, locking the driver's door and lighting a cigarette.

Leaving the high street by the fish and chip shop, they entered a short road that led down to the embankment. The water appeared glassy black at nighttime.

'Is the group playing by the river?' asked Eric.

'In it,' Phil said, pointing across to Eel Pie Island.

A single light was visible through the trees and bushes on the opposite bank. To the left, a big wooden boathouse opened onto the river. Behind it stood shabby sheds and workshops. The light appeared to be coming from a larger building situated near the centre of the river island. A curved footbridge spanned the Thames, providing the only access, other than crossing by boat or swimming.

Phil nodded at a grey-haired old lady wearing a heavy black coat and a bobble hat, 'You pay the bridge toll, and I'll get us into the club.'

'How much?' Eric asked as they approached the *sentry box* shelter.

'Sixpence each.' Phil flicked his cigarette butt into the river. 'If you ask her, she'll tell you the money's for a new bridge, but I bet she blows it all on biscuits and bingo.'

The old lady smiled as Eric dropped a shilling into the satchel on her lap.

Phil turned to Eric as they walked over the footbridge, 'I bet the roadies dread coming here.'

'Roadies?'

'The blokes who set up the equipment. There's no way to get a van over, so they have to carry it or wheel it on a trolley. Bad news if the group has a piano or a big organ or something.'

'What's the group called?' Eric asked, feeling a little silly for not knowing.

'*John Major's Bluesmakers,*' replied Phil. 'A mate of mine told me about them. He says they've got an excellent guitarist.'

'Lead or rhythm?'

'Oh, lead, I'm sure. They're a blues group.'

Attaining the island, they followed a pathway lined with trees and bushes, passing a row of padlocked boatsheds. The light that Eric had seen from the riverbank was on a big white building, set high above the raised entrance.

As they entered the old hotel's ballroom, Eric examined the ink stamp on his hand. When he looked up, he was surprised to see that the dingy hall was crammed full of people. The island had appeared deserted, but here in the derelict central building, a motley crowd of west London's blues hipsters had gathered *en masse*. Plaster had fallen from the dirty whitewashed walls, exposing crumbling nineteenth-century brickwork. The large dark room smelled of damp and mould, an odour similar to that of the Ealing House, but much stronger. Following Phil towards a row of arches, Eric noticed a meandering line of black footprints had been stencilled across the high ceiling. Sawdust, probably from a local boatyard, had been scattered on the cement floor. Wilson Pickett's *Midnight Hour* played, though no one danced.

'Looks like we've missed the first group,' Phil said, looking at the half-empty stage at the back of the hall. 'The headliners usually play at the other end, next to where we came in.'

An original feature of the old ballroom, the small stage was recessed and characterised by a curved pelmet set above the elevated platform. Stage right was a large organ resembling a battered wardrobe tipped over on its side. On the opposite side of the drums were guitar and bass amplifiers.

'*Marshall*,' said Eric, reading the name on the guitar amp. 'I've never heard of those.'

'You should've,' replied Phil. 'They're a local company. Haven't you seen the shop in Hanwell?'

My Generation, a recent hit for the Who, played through the house speakers.

'There you go,' said Phil. 'That's probably a Marshall on this record. The Who use them; they're locals, too. What do you want to drink?'

Eric stood beneath one of the arches watching his new friend climb a wooden stairway. The raised bar stretched along the opposite side of the hall.

The music being played that night was mostly unfamiliar to Eric. Occasional hits by the Kinks, the Small Faces, and the Rolling Stones were sandwiched between obscure blues records, none of which he had heard before. A number of these had come and gone when Eric noticed Phil standing halfway up the wooden staircase animatedly beckoning him over.

'This is Judy,' Phil said, smiling at the brown-haired girl standing at his side. 'And this her sister...'

'Linda,' said Judy.

'Yes, of course. Ladies, this is my friend, Eric.' Phil handed him a Coke.

Judy smiled at Eric. 'Shouldn't you be getting ready to go on stage?' she said, flicking her hair from her face.

'Sorry mate,' said a longhaired man carrying drinks down the stairs.

Seeing a gap open up, Eric squeezed in against the wooden handrail.

'Don't move from that spot!' called Phil. 'We've got the best view in the place.'

'Hello,' Eric said to the fifteen-year-old girl standing next to him.

Linda smiled shyly. She wore a white T-shirt and jeans beneath her long black coat. Eric adjudged her to be prettier than her older sister, though Judy looked nice in her yellow dress. Phil was making a play for Judy, so Eric set about turning on the charm with her younger sibling,

'Have you been here before?' This was marginally better than, *do you come here often?*

Linda nodded.

'Which groups have you seen?' asked Eric.

Linda looked to one side and shrugged, 'Different ones.'

Two lines into his charm-offensive, Eric was beginning to struggle. 'Do you and your sister live in Twickenham?'

Linda nodded again.

A murmur spread through the crowd, followed by cheers and applause. As Eric looked up, he heard the *thunk* of an electric guitar being plugged in. *Saved*, he thought, zeroing in on the cherry sunburst Gibson Les Paul.

'Good evening, Twickenham!' said the man behind the organ that looked like a sideways wardrobe.

The drummer clicked his sticks five times, counting in the opening number, *All Your Love*. It was loud! The chugging blues song sounded fantastic. Eric fell instantly spellbound, his eyes glued to the guitarist. After a couple of verses, the beat switched to a shuffle, and the guitar player fired into a solo. Eric felt shivers run down his spine. The young guitarist played with his eyes screwed shut. His style was fluid, edged with aggression and crying with emotion, the Les Paul singing beneath his fingertips. Eric gripped the handrail, unable to believe what he was hearing.

'Brilliant, isn't he?' smiled the man standing next to him.

'Who is he?' asked Eric.

'You don't *know?* That's Eric Clapton.'

The set seemed to pass in a flash.

Surrounded by buzzing blues fans, Phil, Eric, and the two girls made their way back along the dark pathway towards the bridge. Eric noticed that Phil and Judy were holding hands. As they neared the riverbank, Judy whispered something to her partner. Phil nodded and smiled at Eric.

'Fantastic show, eh?' Phil said, guiding him to one side.

'Brilliant,' replied Eric. 'That guitarist was –'

'Yeah, I know,' said Phil. He lowered his voice, 'Listen, I need a little favour.'

Moments later, Phil and Judy pushed through the bushes, melting into the darkness.

Ten minutes? thought Eric. *I bet they'll be gone longer than that.*

Finding a spot near the footbridge, Eric and Linda sat on the damp grass looking across the black river at the lights of Twickenham. On the opposite bank, a pair of drunks stumbled out of the White Swan. Falling into a two-tone Ford Anglia, the driver revved the engine and sped up Water Lane with the car's lights off.

Eric turned to the girl, 'I play the guitar, and I like painting. I'm thinking about being a photographer when I leave school. What do you do with your time?'

Linda stared at the inky river. 'I come here with my sister. She likes the groups.'

Eric abandoned the topic of music. 'What about films? I've seen the last two James Bond flicks.'

Linda shrugged, 'I think I've got a cold coming.'

'Oh?'

'Last week I felt, you know, *yucky*, and it's been coming and going ever since. I had the flu last Christmas, oh God, it was horrible; Mum got the doctor in, and...'

Eric smiled to himself. If the girl preferred to have a conversation about colds, that was okay. It would pass the time until Phil returned from his island adventure. Up to this point, eliciting a response from Linda had been a struggle. Now she was talking incessantly. Perhaps in a moment, she would ask for his opinion on something or invite him to comment. Four minutes later, he was still waiting.

'...because there was this rash on the back of my legs and I thought it might be some sort of disease, you know, so Mum got her medical book out, and...'

Eric watched a few dark stragglers walk over the curved bridge. The old lady at the shore end had gone. Light from the closing pub reflected on the endlessly flowing river. Linda seemed incapable of inserting full stops between her sentences, allowing him no opportunity to join in. Eric resolved to break the girl's flow by utilising the brutal tactic of interruption. *Okay*, he thought, *now!*

'What time do you think –'

'...and my head felt all prickly, like little pins were sticking in it, and my *hair* hurt, and...'

No good. Eric tried again,

'It's getting late, maybe we should –'

'...so I said, what about *me*? I've had glandular fever since I was *eleven*, and I told her...'

One of the lads at Eric's school had dated a hypochondriac. The relationship ended with a sigh and a whimper when the girl claimed to be allergic to rubber. 'I saw a flying moose in Cornwall,' said Eric.

'...little red spots all over my back, and I had to use a pencil to...'

Eric looked at his watch, hoping against hope that his parents would be asleep when he arrived home. Had it been a Friday or a Saturday, he might have got away with coming in after eleven, but...

'...couldn't stop coughing, and Mum said, *'Bill Grimes can fix anything,'* and *I* said, 'Well, if...''

Eric stood up and ambled slowly along the riverbank.

'Where are you going?' asked Linda.

The deep dark river flowed on.

In 1967, the ex-hotel on Eel Pie Island was temporarily closed after being declared unsafe and unfit for public use. Rumour had it that a girl had been injured while flushing a toilet when the cistern fell on her. When he heard the story, Eric pictured Linda sitting on the toilet floor with crossed eyes, tongue hanging out, and chirping budgerigars flying circles around her head.

A week after it was stolen, a dog named Pickles found the World Cup hidden beneath a hedge in south London.

14

Granny Takes a Trip

'Life sentences for Brady and Hindley, then,' Julia said from behind the Guardian. 'Six months ago, they'd have both hung, I expect.'

Pattie slid out the grill pan and turned over the two slices of bread. 'No doubt there'll be a lynch-mob campaigning to bring back the death penalty.'

Julia folded the broadsheet and tossed it onto the kitchen table. 'Well, I thought the reform was long overdue. Rule number one in a civilised society: *you don't kill people*. And that has to begin at the highest level.'

'I think God put it at number six.'

'It depends on which book you read,' said Julia. 'Five, six, or seven, I think. Unless you want to kill someone who happens to have been born into a tribe that worships the wrong deity. Then it's okay. But I'd make it Rule One – for everyone. Seems like a good place to start.'

'The gospel, according to Julia Ramsey.' Pattie dropped the toast onto two plates.

'You know me,' replied Julia. 'Always looking for ways to change the world.'

'Our world is already changing, Jules. Haven't you heard? We're living in *swinging* London, now.'

'Yeah, Time magazine. I read the article.'

'That's right, and it's not a catchphrase planted there by the British Tourist Board. London's *the* happening city, Jules. It's alive in the West End right now, and I'm concerned you're missing out. It's about time you and I hit the Kings Road.'

The buzzer sounded in the living room.

Paul came running down the stairs, 'I'll get it.'

'You have the perfect little car,' continued Pattie. 'Now we need to get you some groovy threads to go with it.'

'Uh-huh. And what exactly did you have in mind?'

'Oh, come off it.' Pattie smiled wryly, 'You couldn't wait to try on my miniskirt after our photo session. I saw you admiring yourself in your bedroom mirror. And don't think I've forgotten that fancy-dress party at college –'

'Shush!' hissed Julia, grinning at her friend.

'Hello.' Eric stood in the kitchen doorway with his guitar bag at his side.

'I moved your amp into the ballroom,' Paul said from the passage.

When he entered the huge room next to the kitchen, Eric stopped in his tracks. At the far end in front of the fireplace was a gold-sparkle Premier drum kit. Near the double French windows, a Hofner Violin Bass leaned against a brown-and-tan amplifier.

'A Paul McCartney bass!' exclaimed Eric.

'Nope, it's a Paul Ramsey bass!' Paul said, grinning from ear to ear. 'Let's face it, you were always going to be the guitarist.'

'Right,' Eric said, taking it all in. 'And the drums belong to?'

'Tony, of course.' Paul closed the door. 'Mum thinks Tony needs something to get involved in. She asked if I had any ideas, so...'

'That's brilliant!' enthused Eric.

'None of the gear is new,' said Paul, 'but it's all in good condition. Our old house in West Ealing was finally sold – for nearly three-and-a-half thousand pounds! So Mum got her car, and Tony and I got this.'

'Three-and-a-half thousand! You could live forever on that.'

'That's what I said, but Mum says it's less than we think, and we have to make it last.'

'I see you've got yourself a Bird, then,' Eric said, checking out Paul's amplifier.

'Yeah, it's a *Bird Golden Eagle*. Twenty-five watts with a fifteen-inch speaker. And it's got reverb, so if we get a microphone, we can plug that in as well.'

Paul flipped the power switch and handed Eric the Hofner bass.

'Wow, it's really light. And the neck's small; nice and easy to play.'

Five minutes later, the guitarist and the bassist stood facing one another playing *The House of the Rising Sun:* Paul with his back to the French windows, and Eric next to a big old sofa that had seen better days. These would be their respective locations for years to come.

Eric looked around the ballroom as they jammed through the song. Judging by its appearance, this had been the least loved of all the rooms in the old house. It was by far the largest. The damp, musty odour was more pungent here. The faded cream wallpaper had begun to peel, and the expensive patterned carpet had worn thin, its once vibrant colours lost to the ravages of time. Heavy green velvet curtains, identical to those in the living room, framed the French windows. In the overgrown back garden, the red swing stood in the early-May sunshine. A cloud of tiny insects hovered in the hazy yellow light.

Eric had played *The House of the Rising Sun* many times, and the chord changes and 6/8 arpeggio style had become automatic. While he was aware of passing milestones in his learning – barre chords being an example – the significance of consigning a song to the subconscious area of his mind had passed him by. This intellectual ability allowed Eric to detach himself from his own playing to appraise Paul's aptitude for the bass.

Despite his intense concentration, Paul looked comfortable with the Hofner. The guitar's violin-shaped body suited the teenager's slim build, and his boyish good looks befitted the image of a pop musician. Sitting on a sofa arm, Eric tried a solo. Deprived of the reference of a rhythm guitar, Paul upheld the song's structure. Eric felt pleased for his friend. It sounded good.

'So where's our drummer?' asked Eric. 'Still in bed?'

'Out with friends,' replied Paul. 'But Tony has some practising to do before anyone calls him a drummer. He's well into it, though.'

'Oh, I don't doubt that.' Eric recalled the flailing knitting needles and spurting blue washing powder at the Ramsey's previous house.

The ballroom door opened and Pattie breezed in, saucy and sexy, the epitome of a London dollybird. Made-up like a cover girl, the slender young woman wore an orange minidress with her trademark black leather boots. Black hooped earrings dangled beneath her long blonde hair. Eric thought Pattie looked fabulous, as usual.

'Sounding fantastic, guys! Listen, I've managed to talk Julia into driving up to town. It'll be girlie clothes shopping... but we wondered if you'd care to join us?'

Eric wanted to keep playing, but before he had time to reply, Paul answered,

'Yeah, we'd love to!'

'We'd love to,' smiled Eric.

On an unseasonably warm May Saturday, the white Union Jack Mini headed for London's West End with Julia at the wheel. Though dressed in her accustomed jeans and T-shirt, she looked different today. From his seat behind her, Eric studied Julia in the rear-view mirror. Accentuated by thick black liner, her pretty green eyes were shot with a clarity and depth that Eric felt he was seeing for the first time. Julia caught his gaze. Averting his eyes, Eric looked down between the front seats. Pattie's short orange dress had ridden up. *'Wonderful Radio London,'* announced the station jingle, crossfading into the descending bass intro to Nancy Sinatra's *These Boots Are Made for Walking*. Somewhere in Eric's mind, another image attached itself to a song. Joining the library of associations he had accumulated over the years, this one featured Pattie's black knee-high boots tapping to the music. Eric became aware that Julia was now studying *his* eyes in the mirror.

'Red light ahead!' warned Pattie.

'Yes, I see it,' said Julia.

'Not the next right, but the one after.' Paul turned a page in the London A to Z. 'That puts us on Regent Street. Then take the third on the left.'

Fifteen minutes later, twelve of which had been spent searching for a parking meter, Julia, Pattie, Paul and Eric walked along a busy Regent Street in glorious spring sunshine. The London traffic was heavy that day; red double-decker buses and black taxis crawled along the grand street with its impressive listed buildings, hotels, and expensive stores. Pedestrians in summer clothes lined the bustling thoroughfare.

'Tony would love that place,' Paul said, looking at Hamley's window displays.

Julia smiled at the pavement. They had just passed one of the world's premier toy shops, and while the merchandise was of little interest to Paul, his comment regarding his younger brother had been entirely genuine. For Julia, this was a defining moment: the pivotal point at which Paul left boyhood behind, becoming a young adult.

Sliding her arm around his waist, Julia kissed her son on the cheek, then continued along Regent Street clinched in a snuggled embrace.

Pattie and Eric looked at one another, then the blonde shrugged and took Eric's arm. In her high-heeled boots, she stood marginally above him, but with the gorgeous young woman at his side, Eric felt ten feet tall.

Turning right into Foubert's Place, the foursome entered Soho on the west side. A minute later, they were in Carnaby Street.

'It's tiny!' exclaimed Paul. 'If you leaned out of an upstairs window, you could almost shake hands with a person across the road.'

'Well, it's very narrow and only three blocks long,' replied Pattie. 'But it would lose its charm if they paved it over. Let's start with TreCamp.'

'Is that supposed to be a bloke or a bird?' Paul queried as they approached John Stephen's boutique.

Julia studied the painted figure beside the door. 'It looks like an androgynous, er, Greek or Roman – or maybe Egyptian – um, naked *girl-man*.'

'All those years at art school, and that's the best you can do?' Pattie slipped past her friend, entering the shop.

Eric surveyed the constricted Soho backstreet. Many of the small shop fronts had been painted in vibrant hues: reds, blues and yellows, rendering the old masonry with a fairground-like appearance. The little street was dripping with contemporary atmosphere, yet stubbornly unwilling to relinquish its long and colourful history. High above, a strip of bright blue sky bisected the shady road.

'How many Union Jacks can you see?' Eric asked, as Julia followed Pattie into TreCamp.

'Four hundred and twelve, I make it.' Paul stepped back, allowing a longhaired man in a frilly shirt and striped trousers to pass. 'And that's not counting the ones hanging on washing lines over the street.'

'There aren't as many dollybirds as I'd expected,' said Eric. 'I was hoping – Oh, hang on... Blimey! Look at her!'

Inside TreCamp, the Kinks' *Dedicated Follower of Fashion* played from a record player on the counter.

'How about this?' Pattie suggested, unhooking a red minidress from one of the rails.

Julia held the dress under her chin. 'Too short.'

'It's no shorter than the one I'm wearing now,' Pattie pointed out. 'Besides, you've got the sexiest legs in London, Jules. You'd look fab in that.'

'I... No, I don't think so.'

When Paul and Eric entered the shop, Julia was on her way out.

'Let's try Lady Jane next,' said Pattie.

Three Carnaby Street boutiques later, the four shoppers headed back to the car.

'The styles are... oh, I don't know, just too *modish* for my taste,' said Julia. 'They're great and everything, but they're not me.'

'Well, you're not going home without a bag if *I* have anything to do with it,' Pattie replied. 'There's Biba, Barbara Hulanicki's shop in Kensington, but time marches on. Maybe we should go straight to the Kings Road. Do you want me to drive?'

'No, I'm fine,' replied Julia. 'I have to get used to driving in the city sooner or later.'

The long Kings Road offered a very different shopping experience to that of Carnaby Street. Chelsea's upmarket retail district resembled an alfresco fashion show, the sunshine drawing London's swingers out of their coffee bars and vegetarian restaurants, sending them marching up and down the concrete catwalk like peacocks on parade. Scooters and convertibles shared the road with Mini's and Bentley's and an assortment of classic cars. Everyone watched a red open-topped E-Type Jag cruise by with three dollies in miniskirts perched behind the driver. Next was a green 1904 Darracq that looked like it had driven off the Genevieve film set. Behind it was a pink Bubble Car.

Inside Mary Quant's Bazaar shop, Eric stood beside the door girl-watching while Paul helped Julia and Pattie with their selections. Manfred Mann's *Pretty Flamingo* played: the perfect song, Eric decided, as a redheaded dolly stopped to look at Bazaar's window display. *Cripes, it's full of holes!* Eric was not alone in admiring the girl's underwear through her white crocheted minidress.

'Where's your mum?' Eric asked, joining Paul and Pattie.

'In the changing room,' replied Paul.

'We persuaded her to try something on,' said Pattie. 'I told her that if she wasn't going to buy anything, she could at least say she'd worn a Mary Quant dress, if only for two minutes.'

Two teenage girls stood next to Eric, browsing Mary Quant's spring collection.

'It's bloody expensive in 'ere,' observed one of the girls.

'When life gets tough, buy more stuff,' replied the other.

A curtain swished back, and Julia emerged from one of the cubicles wearing a lime-green minidress with a broad orange band around the waist.

'Yes!' exclaimed Pattie. 'You look like a million bucks, baby!'

'God, Mum, you look really sexy!' blurted Paul.

'It does fit very well,' Julia admitted, studying her reflection in a full-length mirror. She ran her hands down her sides, 'And it's beautifully tailored. But I –'

'No *buts*,' interrupted Pattie. 'It's just a dress, Jules. You're not signing up to buy a racehorse.'

'Get it, Mum,' urged Paul. 'You look fantastic.'

A short time later, Julia left Bazaar with a bag.

'Okay, one more shop before we go,' said Pattie, her spirits having lifted following Julia's purchase. 'It's on the way home anyway. Down the road at World's End.'

Looking through the Mini's side window, Eric caught a glimpse of one of the Kings Road's cul-de-sac mews streets: small roads lined with rows of stables that had been converted into cottages. He envisaged it as somewhere Emma Peel might live. A horn blasted angrily as Julia pulled into the curb without indicating.

A van sped past. 'Bloody women drivers!'

'Granny Takes a Trip?' smiled Julia.

'Great name for a boutique,' said Eric.

'This one's a little different,' said Pattie. 'Come on, let's go in.'

Climbing the short flight of steps, Eric examined the mural that covered the front window to his right. Yellow and white rays emanated from the head of a Native American Indian, the artwork completely obscuring the shop's interior. Passing through a beaded-glass curtain, Eric found himself standing in a dimly lit purple room that smelled strongly of incense. Bob Dylan's *Highway 61 Revisited* played from somewhere in the shadows.

'This is very weird,' said Eric. He stopped, his eyes adjusting to the light.

Paul looked around, 'How can you tell what colour the clothes are?'

Eric shrugged, 'Who cares, the music's great! Where are the girls?'

'Around the corner, I think,' answered Paul.

Eric realised he had referred to Paul's mother as one of *the girls*, but his long-time friend took no notice. Wandering through to the back, Eric stood beside Julia, peering up at one of the black-ink prints that hung around the strange esoteric shop.

'Aubrey Beardsley,' said Julia. 'He was a Victorian artist. Died very young. These prints are from his erotic collection.'

Eric wondered what his mother would say if she could see him standing next to *that Ramsey woman* looking at a pornographic drawing of three bizarrely dressed beings flaunting huge erect penises.

'Where's Pattie?' asked Eric.

'She ran into someone she knows. A friend of the owners, I think.'

Eric looked around. Apart from Julia and Paul, the dark shop appeared to be empty. Except for Bob Dylan, who was now complaining about having contracted a nasty dose of VD.

'I love this place,' declared Julia. 'It's nothing like the other boutiques. The clothes are so exclusive and interesting. And colourful! I suppose *Granny Takes a Trip* must be an LSD reference.'

Eric had heard of the drug but knew little about it. Julia was right about the colour: many garments featured paisley or flowered patterns, others displaying abstract swirling shapes or experimental avant-garde designs, some kinky in the extreme. Julia identified William Morris's work among the prints. The quality of the merchandise was high, and so were the prices.

Leaving Julia rummaging through a pile of vintage clothing, Eric gravitated towards the back of the shop. Mixed with the incense was a distinctive smell that triggered memories of the hilltop at St Ives and the poetry night at the Royal Albert Hall. Peering through a half-open doorway, Eric caught sight of Pattie's long blonde hair. She was sitting on a man's lap in a small dark storage room. Eric watched as Pattie carefully placed the lit end of a cigarette between her lips. Twisting to face the man, she blew a stream of smoke into his mouth through the coiled cardboard filter. Inhaling deeply, the man slipped his hand under Pattie's short orange dress.

Eric turned away. It occurred to him that the *swinging* side of London was intrinsically linked with sex. He knew also, that the heavy fragrant smell was that of marijuana.

15

Bobby, Martin and Geoff

A long black drip had run down from the A in the CLAPTON IS GOD graffiti on the fence in Islington.

Next on the left, thought Eric, checking the directions Phil had written at their jam session. Twanging away on his Telecaster, Phil had shown Eric his take on the Rolling Stones' Indian-influenced single, *Paint It Black.* The song was in Eric's head as he turned off the north London high street into a residential avenue. It was typical of the Stones, Eric thought, to write a song about painting everything black, just as the swinging capital was exploding into colour.

The basement flat brought to mind Sid's Soho club. Eric checked his watch: 1:59; right on time. The air felt cool as he descended the concrete steps and rang the bell. He hoped Phil's friend would remember he was coming.

A figure appeared behind the opaque glass, and the door opened.

'Hello, I'm Eric.'

'Ah, welcome to sunny Islington,' said an arty-looking man with a full beard and bottle-lensed glasses. 'I'm Roger. Come on in.'

It was difficult to estimate Roger's age. Hidden behind the fuzzy facial hair and thick horn-rimmed spectacles, the man could have been anywhere between twenty-five and forty.

Roger led the way to a pleasantly decorated front room: white, to compensate for the lack of daylight. An eight-armed Hindu statuette sat on the hearth. 'How's my good friend Phillip?'

'Phil's fine. We had a jam on Thursday.'

'So nothing changes at Bag End,' observed Roger.

'Er, no,' Eric replied, not yet having read *The Lord of the Rings.*

'I'd suggest the middle of the sofa,' said the thin man. 'That's the listening seat. Not that any of the records are stereo. Coffee?'

'Thank you, yes, please. White with two sugars, please.'

Eric's over-politeness often surfaced when meeting older people.

Roger smiled, 'I'll leave you with BB while I put the kettle on.' Lifting the record player arm, he carefully cued-up track four, *Ten Long Years*.

Eric began to understand the music he had heard at Eel Pie Island. The record sounded old, as if it had been recorded a long time ago in a dusty barn somewhere in the southern USA. The singing was soulful, the guitar playing fluid and inspired.

Roger placed two white mugs on the coffee table and sat in the chair beside the sofa. 'What do you think?'

'Brilliant,' replied Eric. 'I've hardly heard any proper blues music before.'

'I'm not surprised. You'll be hard pushed to find it in the shops,' said Roger. 'This is B. B. King's first LP, *Singin' the Blues,* from 1956. Like most of my blues LPs, I had to order it on an import.'

Over the next hour-and-a-half, Roger introduced Eric to *the Three Kings:* B. B., Albert, and Freddy. Eric soaked up the music like a sponge, particularly warming to the guitar playing of Freddy King.

Roger looked through the basement window as his girlfriend descended the steps. 'Ah, Carol's home.'

Eric had never met anyone with Julia's views before, but Roger's partner came close.

'Crowds are gathering in the high street for that boxing match at the Arsenal ground,' Carol said, lighting a stick of incense.

'Henry Cooper and Cassius Clay,' replied Roger. 'It's one of the biggest fights ever staged in this country.'

Carol scoffed, 'Yes, well, I think it's bloody barbaric. How can they allow two people to bash the hell out of one another and call it a sport? What kind of message is that putting out? While they're at it, they should send in the gladiators and throw a few hungry lions out there. Are we still in the Dark Ages? They banned cockfighting and bear-baiting; it's about time boxing went the same way. What the hell's the matter with people?'

Eric found himself agreeing with Carol lest he be beaten-up himself. But he did think she had a point.

*

In mid-June 1966, Eric quit his paper round.

Paul had been learning the bass part from the Beatles' new single, *Paperback Writer*. He leaned his unplugged Hofner against the sofa. 'How come you packed your job in now? I'd have thought you'd put up with it till winter.'

'It's not so much the weather…' Eric gazed out at the front garden. 'I've wanted to leave since I went out with Ron and his mates. His gang are always hanging around the newsagents.'

'Good for you, then,' said Paul. 'But you won't be buying so many records.'

'I thought I'd have a break, then look for another job. Besides, money isn't everything.'

'Hang on to that thought, Eric.' Julia entered the room wearing her green-and-orange Mary Quant dress.

Paul looked up, 'You look nice, Mum. So you finally got it out of the wardrobe.'

Julia smiled, 'Yes. And thank you, Paul.'

The sound of pounding drums filtered through from the ballroom.

'Tony's out of bed,' observed Paul.

'Thank heavens for those bookshelves.' Julia sat opposite her son and opened a windowed white envelope. 'I'm sure he's getting louder.'

Eric joined Paul on the small sofa. He watched Julia's expression change as she read the letter.

Paul picked up his bass, 'Who's it from, Mum?'

'From the bank,' Julia replied flatly. 'They're asking me to apply for something called a *Barclaycard*. It says they're hoping to recruit a million cardholders in time for its launch at the end of the month.'

Eric sensed a speech.

'What's a –?'

'It's a credit card. They already have them in America. It means… Well, it means they've devised a new way to separate us from our money. It's *The Cantos* – Ezra Pound – immoral moneylending.'

'What do you mean, *immoral?*' Paul asked cautiously, aware that his mother might go off on one at any moment.

'Immoral, because they're preying on people's weaknesses: desires that the system they live with created in the first place. I told you about advertising; how they try to convince people that possessions will make them happy.'

'What have these *credit cards* got to do with –'

'Oh, think about it, Paul! The manufacturers have coerced the population into wanting more and more *stuff*... And now the banks are taking advantage of these brainwashed people by making it easy to buy, and charging exorbitant interest on the cards. Look, it's right here in their advertising: *Our aim is to make shopping easier.* And by using a piece of plastic, you don't have the psychological wrench of seeing your empty wallet afterwards. Can you see where this is leading? To over-consumption, pollution and debt. It's cunning capitalist coercion. I'd call that immoral, wouldn't you?'

'Yes, I suppose it's... Nifty alliteration, Mum, but –'

'They've created a monster, and it'll make debt-ridden monsters out of *us*.'

Resuming his bass practice, Paul ran through a tricky phrase from *Paperback Writer*. Eric sat next to him, stealing admiring glances across the coffee table at Julia, who was still studying the letter from the bank. It was the first time she had worn the Mary Quant minidress, and Eric hoped she would wear it more often.

''Ello, ya bunch-a gits,' said Tony.

Eric looked up, 'Your drumming sounded good.'

'Ta.' Tony turned to his mother, 'How're you, you silly moo? Aren't you a bit old to be dressed like that?'

Julia pouted, 'I'm only twenty-nine, Tony. That may sound old to you, but I'm hardly ready for a walking frame yet.'

Tony shrugged his bony shoulders. He turned to Eric and Paul, 'How 'bout a play, then?'

Eric stood up.

'I'll be there in a minute,' said Paul.

Inside the ballroom, Tony closed the door and parked his skinny frame against the wall. 'I've got something to tell you,' he said quietly to Eric. 'But you can't say anything, okay?'

Another secret, thought Eric. 'Yeah, okay.'

'It's this house,' began Tony. 'It's *weird*.'

'Mmm.'

'No, listen. A couple of weeks ago, I was ridin' along the walkway past the reservoir... an' I saw Yogi Bear in the bushes.'

'Is this a joke?'

'No. Yogi was on the other side of the wire fence, right opposite our front gate. I mean, I know it wasn't the *real* Yogi Bear, but it looked just like 'im. He ducked into the bushes when he saw me.'

Eric refrained from pointing out that there was no *real* Yogi Bear.

'And that's not the worst thing.' Tony appeared agitated. 'I saw a blonde woman in Mum's bedroom window.'

'It was probably Pattie.'

'No, I'd just come home from school, and there was nobody in. I waited by the gate till Mum came home. Pattie wasn't there.'

'Has Paul seen her, this blonde woman?'

'No, he said he hasn't.'

Eric looked doubtfully at Tony, 'Are you having me on?'

'I'm not joking, I swear.' Tony walked dejectedly towards his drum kit, 'I hate living here.'

*

Pattie's modelling career had recently taken an upward turn, owing primarily to a series of catalogue jobs. She had appeared in various fashion items, including a pink-and-white polka-dotted pac-a-mac and a sequined bikini. Though she posed no threat to Jean Shrimpton and Twiggy, Pattie's newly acquired status gained her admittance to the exclusive world of London's *in-crowd*. Eric recalled the scene he had witnessed in the back room at *Granny Takes a Trip*. Perhaps encounters such as this had hastened the ascension of the model's rising star.

It was via Pattie that Julia learned of the Vietnam War Protest that was to take place on the 3rd of July. That Sunday, Tony opted to spend the day newt hunting at the Grand Union Canal.

Exiting Leicester Square tube station, Pattie, Julia, Paul and Eric found London basking in bright summer sunshine. Among the tourists on Charing Cross Road were protesters heading for Trafalgar Square. Denim was the uniform of this longhaired people's army, and it was easy to identify its troops. Julia and Pattie also wore jeans that day, in preference to the fashionable miniskirts they had both adopted that summer.

At Trafalgar Square, the Ealing foursome was confronted by a sea of blue. They paused to take in the scene. The crowd was enormous.

'That's the National,' Julia said, pointing to the nineteenth-century art gallery. 'If we become separated, we'll meet by the steps.'

Beneath a clear blue sky, Admiral Nelson looked down on four thousand protesters 170 feet below.

'I wonder what he'd make of it all,' mused Paul. 'If this lot had their way, he'd be out of a job.'

Shading her eyes with her hand, Pattie peered up at the English naval hero, 'He's probably more bothered about the pigeon shit.'

Eric read the placards held aloft by the protesters. Most displayed anti-war slogans, while some denounced capitalist greed. It was the first time Eric had encountered the moralism *Make Love, Not War*.

On the far side of the square, a section of the crowd began to move. Seemingly without leadership, a column formed and headed west in the direction of Mayfair. The march had begun.

As if in a dream, Eric and his three companions began walking, now part of a great river carrying them on. By their own volition, they were absorbed into the collective, united by shared conviction. There would be no turning back.

Eric looked to his left. Julia, Paul and Pattie stared straight ahead, alone with their thoughts and resigned to their assimilation.

As they passed through the sunny London streets, Eric's attention turned to the people around him. Watching the news with his mother, he had once seen footage of the Aldermaston marches: the Campaign for Nuclear Disarmament, CND, *Ban the Bomb*. He remembered the beatniks at St Ives and the audience at the Albert Hall. They were the body politic here today; if not in person, then in a spirit carried in every one of the protesters' hearts. The marchers were different from the *Swinging London* crowd, the *Jet-setters* and the *Neo-mods*, all of whom revered fashion for fashion's sake. At the core of this movement were the poets and students, the young intellectuals, the soldiers of a new order. Eric recalled Julia's summary of the poetry incantation, *'They'll probably try to change the world'*.

'Hands off Vietnam...' came a chant from the front. A moment later, the mantra was around them, then behind, snaking down the column like a burning fuse. As they neared Grosvenor Square, the procession gathered momentum, moving faster down the Mayfair street. A crowd of bystanders stepped back as a group of protesters ran past, impatient to join the affray. *'Hands off Vietnam...'* Pattie took Eric's arm; she was chanting too. They strode past the bordering trees onto the crowded grass plaza. The Stars and Stripes hung flaccid above the American Embassy, the bastion of capitalism and war. *'Hands off Vietnam!'* Louder now, as four thousand impassioned voices spoke as one. A dark-blue line of brave policemen stood resolute in front of the building. The

crowd surged forward. Something was happening at the front. Shouting punctuated the chants. Somebody screamed. Chaos ensued as protesters began pushing, some advancing towards the embassy, others struggling to escape.

'Let's get out!' Pattie shouted, grasping Eric's hand.

Eric looked for Julia and Paul, but they were gone.

'Stay on your feet!' warned Pattie as the crowd closed in.

Eric felt a jarring pain as an elbow thumped his head. Stars swam before his eyes. He and Pattie pushed through the jostling bodies, forcing their way towards the side. Their hands clasped tightly, they reached the trees at the edge of the square. A blue police van drove slowly towards them; protesters hammered the sides with clenched fists. A man staggered, blood bubbling from his nostrils. On the road ahead, a police motorcycle lay on its side, petrol spewing from its ruptured tank. Someone threw a match, igniting the fuel in a blinding orange flash.

'Fucking idiot,' spat Pattie as they ran past the flaming bike.

'This way,' urged Eric, pulling Pattie from the path of a mounted policeman. The big horse's steel-shod hooves clopped noisily as they passed.

Quickly crossing the road, the pair ducked into the service entrance at the side of a Mayfair hotel. Protesters ran past the alley, their shouts and footfalls echoing off the high brickwork. Pinning Eric to the wall, Pattie kissed him with an intensity he had never known.

Julia spread a thin layer of Marmite across her toast. 'How's your head today, Eric?'

'Oh, a bit of a bump, nothing serious.'

'Hello,' Keith said from his perch by the door.

'Hello,' Paul said, entering the kitchen.

Julia pushed Monday's Guardian across the kitchen table, 'There were thirty-one arrests at yesterday's demo, Paul.'

'I'm not surprised. Going on that march wasn't one of your best ideas, Mum. Is Tony out of bed?'

'Up and out,' replied Julia. 'He started his new job today.'

Eric looked up, 'Tony has a job?'

'Yes, didn't he tell you? He applied for your old job at the newsagents and got it.'

'Really?' said Paul. 'He kept that very quiet.'

Eric gazed through the kitchen window. Tony's involvement with Ron Hillman and his unsavoury crew was something he would have discouraged. Tony probably knew that.

Having spent the morning jamming in the ballroom with Paul, Eric said his goodbyes. The 4th of July was his father's birthday, and Eric had promised his mother he would be home in time for lunch. As he approached the end of the front path, the green gate opened. Pattie came into the garden holding a large manila envelope,

'Eric! Are you leaving?'

'Yeah, it's my dad's birthday.'

'Oh, then I caught you just in time. These are a little *thank you* for taking the picture that started my modelling career.'

Sliding three 12"x8" colour photographs out of the envelope, Eric smiled at Pattie. The first picture showed the blonde posing in front of the blazing bonfire that Tony had set in the back garden.

'That's the photo they liked at the agency,' explained Pattie. 'They went bananas over that one. You must have an eye for it.'

'Beginners luck,' Eric said modestly. He slid the photograph aside to reveal the second picture. 'Oh, brilliant!'

'Paul told me you wanted a copy of that one,' said Pattie. She smiled at Eric's reaction to the tightly cropped shot of her holding his red guitar up next to her face.

'It's fantastic,' Eric enthused. 'I'll get it framed and put it on my wall at home.'

Pattie studied Eric's face as he stared at the last photograph. This was one of the shots that Julia had taken near the end of the photo session. The model reclined on the stairs dressed in a frilly white blouse and a black miniskirt. The picture appeared to Eric as if it belonged in the risqué Parade magazine he had lent to Paul.

'Do you like that one?' Pattie's question was almost a whisper.

Eric could find no words and just nodded.

Pattie kissed him on the cheek, then turned towards the house, 'See you soon, Eric,' she said with a smirk. Walking away, she looked back over her shoulder and winked.

*

Eric had found further use for the canvas backpack that Julia had given him to transport his *small but bloody loud* amplifier. Since the amp had taken up permanent residence in the ballroom, the rucksack was now available to carry the red Rapier. Zipped-up in its water-resistant cover with a drawstring tied tightly around the guitar's neck, the old backpack proved an ideal conveyance method, come rain or shine. The extra protection was timely, given the wet weather that hit Britain in the middle of July.

Phil opened his front door to find Eric dripping in the porch. 'You look like a drowned rat. Blimey, your hair's getting long!'

In Phil's front room, Eric unzipped his guitar bag and pulled out the Rapier. The damp tartan bag smelled of rubber.

'Did you get over to Islington?' asked Phil.

'Yeah, Roger sends his regards. He must have the biggest collection of blues records in London.'

'Told you he was your man.' Phil clicked on the electric fire, 'We'll soon have you dried off. Have you been watching the football?'

'I've seen some of the England games,' replied Eric. 'Alf Ramsey said we'd win the World Cup, but we're struggling.'

'Our home advantage should help,' said Phil. 'And we've got Bobby Charlton and World Cup Willie.'

'Don't ask me to play the song.'

'Aw, come on... It's Lonnie Donegan.'

'I'll do *My Old Man's a Dustman* if you like.'

Perhaps inspired by the weather, Phil and Eric played *Rain*, the B-side of the Beatles' number-one hit, *Paperback Writer*. Phil took John Lennon's lead vocal. Eric's alternating 3rd and 5th harmonies on the choruses sounded so good, the rendition lasted for nine minutes. Eric sat close to the hot glowing elements, and his jeans were beginning to steam.

'I like *Rain* better than the A-side,' said Phil.

Eric agreed. 'Those guitars... It's got a great sound and a kind of weird atmosphere to it. I hope they do more like it on the next LP.'

Phil nodded, 'I think it's instrumentally their best song so far. And backwards singing at the end. Fantastic!'

'Yeah. Could you sing it backwards next time?'

'No, but I'll do *My Old Man's a Dustman*.'

So they did – start to finish, jokes included.

'Great stuff!' laughed Phil. 'As you might have guessed by the racket I've been making, my parents are away. I splashed out on some new records. Do you fancy blasting a few?'

First on the radiogram turntable was Ike and Tina Turner's *River Deep, Mountain High*.

'Phil Spector's *Wall of Sound*,' said Phil. 'I hope the neighbours like it.'

DJ Phil spun another disc.

'I was never a fan of the Beach Boys,' said Eric, 'but this is brilliant.'

'It's their new single, *God Only Knows*,' said Phil.

'It's got a kind of faraway *floating* feeling to it,' Eric said, struggling to explain what he was hearing.

Phil nodded, '*Ethereal*, might be the word you're after. I think one of the secrets is the bass guitar. She pretty-much avoids playing root notes. That's one of the tricks.'

Eric filed away the information to tell Paul. 'Can we hear it again?'

Three play-throughs of *God Only Knows* later, Phil slipped a new LP from its paper sleeve, carefully hiding the cover.

One guitar lick into the first song, Eric smelled the joss sticks, sawdust and damp walls of the hotel on Eel Pie Island. 'Eric Clapton!'

Phil handed Eric the cover, 'That's him reading the Beano. John Mayall and the Bluesbreakers Featuring Eric Clapton.'

The two guitarists sat at opposite ends of the sofa, listening intently. The guitar playing on the record was a masterclass. Their eyes met. No words were necessary.

'I've got one more to play you,' said Phil, 'but it's a long one. Up for it?'

A respectful silence prevailed as they listened to all four sides of Bob Dylan's new double LP, *Blonde on Blonde*.

'I packed in my paper round at the wrong time,' Eric said when the listening session ended. '*River Deep* is terrific, and I'd love to have it in my collection. But everything else you played me...'

'Is *essential*,' Phil said, finishing Eric's sentence.

'Well, it's been fun as always,' sighed Eric, stretching his arms towards the ceiling. 'But I'd better get going.'

Phil grinned his wide hobbit grin. 'Do you realise, you cycled down the Northfield Avenue in the pouring rain with your guitar on your back, and we only played two songs? And one of them was *My Old Man's a Dustman!*'

'Actually, I cycled from Ealing Broadway,' said Eric.

'Ah, no wonder you were soaked when you got here. How come you had your guitar with you in Ealing Broadway? Busking in the rain?'

Eric smiled, 'No, I kind of live there half the time.'

'Oh, with relatives?'

'No, with friends.'

Phil raised his Frodo eyebrows, 'You're bit young to be flying the nest, aren't you? I'm in my twenties, and I'm still living with my parents.'

'Well, it just kind of... *happened*,' Eric replied, shrugging. 'I'm not there *all* the time.'

The rain had stopped. Eric cycled slowly through the amber-lit backstreets, deep in thought. He pulled his key from his damp duffle coat and opened the front door, 'Mum, Dad, I'm home.'

*

On Saturday the 30th of July 1966, the football World Cup Championship final took place at Wembley Stadium. The rain held off that day, and thirty-two million UK viewers tuned in to watch England play their old rivals, West Germany.

In the living room at the Ealing House, Eric helped Paul move the smaller sofa to the end of the coffee table, setting up an L-shaped seating arrangement in front of the television.

'I like it better,' said Paul. 'Everyone can see the telly now. Maybe we should leave it this way.'

'Oh, I'd rather we didn't, Paul,' replied his mother. 'I much prefer to have a conversation area in front of the fireplace than a TV hangout. We can always move the sofa if, like today, there's something special on the television.'

Colour TV would not be available in Britain until the following year. Viewers did have the option of watching the match on BBC2, the 625-line broadcast providing superior picture quality to that of BBC1 and ITV's 405-line transmissions. The fact that the game was shown live on all three channels was indicative of the importance attached to the occasion.

'Some countries will be seeing the game as it happens via satellite,' said Julia. 'They send the signal up into space, then bounce it back to locations around the world. The technology has been around for a few years, but today is the first time it's been used on this scale.'

'Science fiction,' said Paul.

Eric sat quietly next to the fireplace. In the preceding years, he had pushed the transmitter in West Ealing to the back of his mind, and conversations of this kind were an unwelcome reminder. He wondered where Reg would be watching the Cup Final.

Julia turned to Tony, who was sitting on the Indian carpet with his back against the small sofa. 'When is your friend due?'

Tony glanced up at the clock, 'About now, I should think.'

Before anyone had time to enquire about Tony's friend, the buzzer sounded next to the fireplace.

Tony jumped up, 'I'll answer it.' He pressed the button on the intercom, 'Hello?'

'It's me,' said a voice next to Eric's right ear.

Eric and Paul immediately identified the disembodied voice as belonging to Ron Hillman.

'Push on the gate,' Tony instructed into the microphone.

As Tony left the living room to open the front door, the green garden gate swung inwards and Ron came through, followed by two tall teenagers with Union Jack flags draped around their shoulders.

Paul groaned, 'Marmalade.'

'Do you know who they are?' Julia asked warily.

'The one with the ginger hair is from the newsagents,' replied Eric. 'He's in our class at school. The other two are the lads who shot me in the leg at the reservoir.'

'Oh God,' muttered Julia.

Presenter David Coleman straightened his notes and handed over to Ken Wolstenholme and Walley Barnes at Wembley Stadium.

The gate swung in the breeze as the three teenagers approached the house. The Union Jacks fluttered from the two older boys' shoulders.

'I'll close the garden door, Mum,' offered Paul. 'Eric and I can keep an eye on things here if you want to disappear.'

'Thank you, Paul,' replied Julia. 'I might just do that. I'll shut the gate.'

Tony entered the living room, followed by Ron Hillman, flanked by his two tall friends.

'Hello Missus Ramsey,' Ron said politely. 'Thanks for having us over.'

Julia forced a smile. 'Have a seat; the match is starting soon.'

Tony squeezed onto the big sofa with his three guests, leaving the smaller settee for Eric and Paul.

'I'll leave you boys to it,' said Julia. 'Enjoy the football.'

As she turned to leave the room, the teenager who had taken Eric's seat by the fireplace nodded towards Hillcrest Road, 'There's a white Mini parked up there with a Union Jack on the roof. Fuckin' great!'

'Ing-ga-land,' chanted his spotty friend, grasping the corners of his flag and hoisting it up behind his back.

The first lad turned to Eric, 'Don't worry mate, I left me air rifle at 'ome today.' Craning his neck, he watched Julia walking down the path. 'Is that ya sister?' he asked Tony.

'No, she's me mum.'

'Yer *mum?* She don't look old enough.' Turning to his mate, he whispered loudly, 'I wouldn't mind givin' 'er a good seein' to.'

Eric sensed Paul's hackles rising.

The match kicked off at 3pm. Twelve minutes later, a tirade of abuse issued from the big sofa in response to West Germany's opening goal. Shortly afterwards, Geoff Hurst's equaliser had the visitors on their feet. Frantically waving their flags, they chanted, *'Ing-ga-land, Ing-ga-land,'* at a volume sufficient to alert anyone within the vicinity of Fox Wood.

During the half-time break, Eric saw Julia walking up the front path with a bulging carrier bag.

The second half saw the score remain at 1–1 until Martin Peters put the hosts ahead. It appeared that England would win until Germany scored at the death, sending the contest into extra time.

Eleven minutes after the restart, Geoff Hurst's shot hit the crossbar and bounced down next to the West German goalkeeper.

'Goal!' bellowed the occupants of the big sofa.

After consulting his linesman, the referee allowed the goal to stand. The decision would be among the most controversial in the history of the game.

Near the end of the extra-time period, with England one goal ahead, Ron began to repeat, *'1918, 1945, 1966...'* His friends failed to grasp the significance of the dates but joined in anyway. Julia stood in the doorway with her arms folded. Some English fans ran prematurely onto the pitch. *'They think it's all over,'* said BBC commentator Kenneth Wolstenholme. At that moment, Geoff Hurst fired a speculative long-range shot which found its way into the goal. *'It is now!'* exclaimed Ken. England had beaten West Germany by four goals to two.

Engaged in a red, white and blue wrestling bout behind the sofa, Tony and his three guests missed seeing the Queen present England captain Bobby Moore with the World Cup trophy. The vast majority of the television audience did witness the presentation, and a few remembered to credit Pickles the dog for making it possible.

The three visitors left the Ealing House shortly after the match. Walking past the white Mini on Hillcrest Road, Ron and his two friends noticed that the Union Jack on the car's roof had been obliterated by a thick coat of lime-green paint.

16

Every Colour There Is

Saturday afternoon shoppers hurried by on the rain-drenched high street. Ealing Theatre once stood on the spot now occupied by W. H. Smiths in the Broadway. Charcoal-eyed music hall stars on that lime-lit stage sang a Hollies song in Eric's head as he and Paul sheltered beneath the overhang outside the stationers. *Bus Stop* played in Eric's mind for much of the day, but the two friends had no umbrella to share.

Eric and Paul studied the cover of the Beatles' new LP, *Revolver*.

'Black-and-white and grey... It matches the weather.'

'That's an Eric comment if I ever heard one,' observed Paul.

'Oh, great! *Eleanor Rigby*'s on it. A black, white and grey song!'

Paul slipped the LP back into its paper bag and tucked it awkwardly inside his coat. 'Come on, let's get home and give it a play.'

The rain was still bucketing when Paul and Eric reached the top of Hanger Hill.

'Pattie's here,' Paul said, seeing the purple VW parked behind Julia's Mini.

Eric glanced at the little white car. 'Did your mum ever tell you why she painted over the Union Jack?'

'World peace,' replied Paul.

'Oh, of course,' Eric said sarcastically. 'When the soldiers see that lime-green roof, they'll all chuck away their guns and go home. That'll show 'em.'

'Mum reckons if there were no countries, there'd be no *them* to fight against,' explained Paul. 'And there'd be one government to keep an eye on the planet's resources and share them out sensibly.'

'I can see the logic,' said Eric. 'Imagine if a Martian looked at the way we run our world. He'd think we were crackers.'

Paul looked sideways at his friend, 'Try telling that to Ron Hillman and his mates.'

Rain dripped from the overarching branches as the two teenagers neared the house. Unaware of their impending arrival, Julia locked her bedroom door from the inside. Pattie knelt on the red carpet at the foot of Julia's four-poster bed,

'Okay to use the top of this trunk?'

'Of course,' Julia replied, arranging the cosmetics on her dressing table into tidy groupings. 'Do you want this stool?'

'No ta, I'm fine.' Pattie pulled three papers from an orange Rizla pack. She nodded at the gold monogram on the front of the old trunk, 'What does J.S. stand for?'

'Julia Stewart.'

'Your maiden name? I never knew.'

'Long ago and worlds away,' Julia said wistfully.

Pattie moistened a third cigarette paper, sticking it perpendicular to the other two. 'You never told me much about your past.'

Julia twisted a lipstick barrel. 'We can't go back there,' she said shruggingly. 'I'd rather look ahead and make the best of today and tomorrow.'

'Mm, fair comment,' replied Pattie. 'Can you toss over that pack of Benson's, please?'

Pattie removed a cigarette, located the seam, and moistened it with her tongue. Tearing the wet strip down its length, she emptied the tobacco onto the papers, spreading it with her forefingers.

'You've done that before,' smiled Julia.

'Once or twice.' Pattie placed a sugar-lump-sized block of hashish on the lid of the trunk.

Downstairs in the living room, Paul lowered the stylus onto the lead-in edge of Revolver and joined Eric on the big sofa.

'One, two, three, four, one, two,' counted a goofy voice, accompanied by studio noises and somebody clearing their throat. Taxman kicked in, setting up the LP with a killer bass groove punctuated by alternating guitar chops on the two and four beats.

'They gave George the opening track!' Paul exclaimed, as the Beatles' lead guitarist complained about Harold Wilson's Super Tax. The lyrical content was a long way from She Loves You.

'Amazing solo,' observed Eric. 'George must've been practising.'

Track two: Paul McCartney poetically lamented the tale of a lonely spinster, backed only by a doubled string quartet.

'Black, white and grey,' said Paul.

His wet shoes and socks having been left in the hall, Eric walked barefoot to the edge of the Indian carpet and stared out at the rain. *Eleanor Rigby* featured no guitar pyrotechnics or driving rhythm section, but the song reached the heart of what he loved best: *picture music*. In their own way, Eric thought, the Beatles had at last caught up with Bob Dylan.

Rainwater gathered on the open bedroom window's inner sill, forming little pools that dripped onto the blood-red carpet.

Julia gazed out at the rain misted grey-greens of Fox Wood. 'Can you smell the trees?'

Pattie blew a stream of smoke through the high window. 'I love the rain. I'd like to run naked through the woods and come home covered in mud, with leaves and little twigs stuck all over my body.'

'I'll go with you,' Julia said, accepting the joint. 'We'll give the perv's at the reservoir something to get excited about.'

Pattie laughed, 'You always were the exhibitionist, Jules.'

'I can't think what you could possibly mean,' Julia said, feigning affront. 'Anyway, it was your idea to run naked through the woods.'

'Yes, but it was *your* idea to flash the flashers at the reservoir!'

Julia leaned out of the open window, 'I can hear music downstairs. Paul and Eric must be home.'

Pattie reached forward, plucking the joint from her friend's fingers, 'You're getting the reefer wet.'

'I'll get *you* wet!' Julia moved back, shaking her long black hair in Pattie's face.

'Ee-yew! Shaggy dog bitch!' Pattie exclaimed, wiping rainwater from her cheek.

Downstairs, the record-player arm returned to its post.

Paul slid the Revolver LP back into its paper inner sleeve. 'So what did you make of it on first listening?'

'Really... *interesting*,' replied Eric. 'I think it might be one of those you have to hear a few times, and they're often the best. I thought George's sitar song was a bit strange, but they saved the weirdest one till last.'

'*Tomorrow Never Knows,*' Paul said, reading the listing. 'It sounded to me like it was about drugs.'

The Twins came into the living room, and Julia leant over Paul's shoulder, studying the reverse side of the Revolver cover,

'Oh, *Eleanor Rigby* is on it. I love that song! It makes me think of a rainy scene in an old black-and-white film.' She glanced over at Eric, tacitly acknowledging their mutual perception.

*

Tony's golf ball banged against the pole, bounced two feet into the air, then dropped down into the cup. 'Down in three!' he exclaimed triumphantly.

'Jammy,' said Paul. 'If the ball hadn't hit that oversized broom handle, it would've rolled halfway to the reservoir.'

Eric totalled the scorecard with his nubby pencil. 'Thirty-seven. Your round, Tone.' He smiled at the gangly twelve-year-old. Eric tactfully neglected to mention that it was the first time Tony had bested both Paul and himself at pitch and putt.

Hanger Hill Park sloped down from the road, dipping at the centre, before rising up steeply on the far side of the nine-hole golf course. The park always looked to Eric like someone had taken a giant shovel and sliced out an immense clod of earth. Silhouetted against the setting sun, the Ealing House's observation turret was visible above the trees of Fox Wood.

The late-September evening was the last they would spend on the golf course that year. Watching the first of Paul's abysmal five putts on the ninth, Eric reflected upon the summer of 1966. The shopping trip to London's West End and Chelsea districts filled his mind with blue skies, colourful clothes, cars and people. Hair was getting longer while skirts became shorter. Carnaby Street was like a multi-coloured picture postcard, touched up by a freaky experimental artist's rainbow brush. The peace march had been anything but peaceful, but Julia had been right about the new generation: they were trying to change the world. Although rumours circulated that the Beatles would no longer tour, their music continued to break exciting new ground, influencing and inspiring artists of every ilk. And just down the road at Wembley, England had won the football World Cup. It had been quite a summer.

'You three took yer bloody time,' grumbled the attendant. He tossed his cigarette end on the ground and shuffled back to his hut. 'Me dinner'll be in the dog.'

Paul resisted a smart-arse reply. Following Tony's club-wrecking tantrum, they had not returned to Gunnersbury Park, and it would be a shame to run out of golf courses. Handing in their clubs and balls, they joined the path leading up to Hillcrest Road. Shadows reached out like long dark fingers. Hanger Hill Park was quiet.

Eric handed Tony the scorecard.

'Cheers, mate. There's three birds on the swings.'

Eric looked ahead to the playground, 'He's right, you know.'

'Don't fancy yours much,' quipped Tony. 'Mine's the blonde in the light-blue dress.'

The girl on the middle swing raised her fingers to her lips. Her wolf whistle carried an ego-boosting invitation, one requiring swift appraisal. Like an athlete to a starting pistol, Tony cut across the grass.

'Blimey, he's eager!' smiled Eric.

Paul looked doubtfully at the three fashionably dressed girls. 'They look a bit young to me.'

'Ah, come on,' coaxed Eric. 'Do it for Tony.'

In a clumsy attempt to appear casual, Tony was gripping the frame, hanging over the blonde. 'Do you live round here?' he asked, swaying above the girl on the swing.

'A few roads away,' the blonde answered evasively. 'How about you?'

Tony pointed to Fox Wood, 'Just over those trees. You could hit our house with a stone from here. Well, you'd have to throw it pretty hard, but –'

'Do you live in the reservoir?' asked the girl on the middle swing.

'No, our house is in the woods between here and the reservoir. There's a high wall, but I know a secret way in, and –'

'Hello,' said Eric.

Names were exchanged, followed by chatter and impromptu humour. Encouraged by his success with the latter, Tony embarked upon a long joke concerning an old tramp with *Shorty* tattooed on his penis. When the three girls started to whisper, Eric and Paul exchanged knowing glances.

'...and when she looked at his willy again, it said: *Shorty's Bar and Grill, near Plymouth, on the south coast of Devon.*'

The blonde stood up, leaving her swing jiggling on its chains. Seeing her approach Eric, Tony steadied the seat and sat next to her friend.

'Stella fancies your mate,' the blonde said candidly as she and Eric sat on the cladded roundabout.

'Stella... The girl in the middle? Who does she like, Paul or Tony?'

'Paul. She said he looks like a skinny Elvis.'

Eric could see the resemblance. 'With longer hair.'

The girl nodded, 'Stella's got a thing for blokes with black hair. Is Paul a gipsy?'

Eric shook his head, 'No. I don't think so, anyway. Does she want me to drop a hint?'

Before the blonde could reply, Stella stood up and approached Paul. Tony shifted across to the middle swing and began telling the third girl another joke, this one involving a man, a chicken, and a brothel.

The blonde looked over and giggled, 'Third choice. Sorry Celia.'

The light was fading fast. On the brow of the hill, a streetlamp flickered. Eric looked at the girl sitting on the roundabout beside him. She was closer to Tony's age, though her heavy makeup and stylish blue dress made her look older.

'Are you a music fan?' asked Eric.

The blonde nodded, 'I've loved the Beatles since they first came out when I was twelve.'

Eric suspected she had added a few years to her age; there was no way the girl was sixteen. 'Nice dress. A friend of mine has a similar one by Mary Quant, though it's a different colour.'

'Oh, thanks,' replied the girl. 'This is a Mary Quant. I get all my clothes from Carnaby Street.'

Two lies in two sentences, thought Eric. Mary Quant's shop was on the King's Road, and Pattie had admired the same light-blue dress in the window of Marks and Spencer's.

'Carnaby Street is very expensive,' continued the blonde. 'But you know what they say, *When life gets tough, buy more stuff.*'

The phrase sent a shiver down Eric's spine. He felt dizzy. He slid down the wooden panels, seating himself on the footplate that girdled the roundabout. The girl was speaking, but her words were lost to him. Unbidden recollections engulfed his mind; a locked door in his brain had burst open. He saw Reg, the office above Burton's, the faceless scientist, and the dark-suited men at Sid's funeral. Standing by the big grey transmitter, Reg shrugged, 'It works; I proved it to you.' Sid was laughing again.

Eric stared blindly at the dark rocking horse. Maybe his father's business would have succeeded without his broadcast? Would Susan have won the contest at Butlin's anyway? These things had happened years ago. He was younger then, susceptible to the influence of adults; gullible, even.

A distant whistle cut through the evening air. At the top of the hill, four figures stood by the gate in an amber light triangle.

Someone was pushing the roundabout. Disoriented, Eric stared at his shoes and saw they were planted firmly on the ground. A pair of black leather boots stood toe-to-toe with him on the dark tarmac. The giddiness subsided, and Eric looked up. The blonde smiled down, coaxing him through heavily made-up eyes. Rising to his feet, Eric felt the girl's hands on his shoulders. He slipped his arms around her. Though taken by surprise, the girl responded willingly, kissing him amorously in the dwindling twilight. She had no way of knowing that the boy in her arms was standing in a hotel alleyway near Grosvenor Square.

'Whoa, take it easy, tiger!' The girl giggled. She hugged Eric tightly as their lips met again.

Nuzzling her bleached blonde hair, Eric whispered, 'Pattie, don't tell Julia we –'

The girl pushed Eric away, 'Who the fuck is *Pattie?*'

*

On Saturday the 15th of October 1966, Julia passed her driving test. That evening she celebrated with a bottle of rosé. Paul drew the green velvet curtains in the living room, shutting out the foggy front garden. A fire burned cheerily, the smokeless coke kindled by wood that had survived Tony's bonfire. Large scented candles glowed at either end of the mantelpiece, and a third stood on a wrought-iron stand beside the radiogram. At the back of the spacious room, the library area was shrouded in shadow. Julia's preference for minimal lighting had been apparent in West Ealing, and here it was no different. The fire-lit room reminded Eric of a setting from a Dickens novel. Glancing at the flaming grate, he pictured Miss Havisham and moved his hot leg away.

Had Tony known about the open bottle of wine, he may have chosen to join the others, but he had shut himself in the ballroom for the evening. Tony had set up the Ramsey's old television on a tea chest in front of the sofa. He had made for himself a refuge: a place of his own, away from his opinionated mother, his interminably older brother, and the ghosts that walked the upstairs rooms and corridors. He liked the TV loud. The snare drum at the end of the ballroom rattled during resonant passages, but Tony never bothered to turn it off.

Paul and Eric sat at opposite ends of the big settee. The Ealing House residents had adopted a policy of leaving their shoes in the hallway, and bare feet had become the norm. The fire blazed warm on Eric's blue jeans. He looked over at the facing sofa. Julia was a vision in black, the firelight shimmering on her hair. She had applied a thick mascara which, combined with a deep-purple shadow, endowed her green eyes with stunning depth and sparkle. Julia's wardrobe had filled over the summer of 1966. To Eric's beguilement, her new clothes included fashionable miniskirts, one of which she was wearing that evening. Julia's toes scrunched the Indian carpet. The purple nails matched her fingers and her eye shadow, a practice that both she and Pattie employed. Purple was the *in* colour.

Barefooted, and each with a glass of rosé in their hand, the three took turns to choose favourite songs. *Visions of Johanna*, from Dylan's *Blonde on Blonde* LP, was Julia's next selection. They sat listening in the firelight.

'That's one of his best; picture songs, I mean,' Eric said, as the track faded. 'It's... I dunno... It takes you somewhere magical, but I've no idea how.'

Placing his empty wine glass on the coffee table, Paul walked to the radiogram and drew the LP delicately up the spindle.

Julia looked thoughtfully at Eric. 'I have a few ideas about Mister Dylan. Have you ever stared into the embers of a dying fire and seen faces or looked up at cumulus clouds that form animal shapes in the sky? Most people do it, though some are more adept than others. It's a facet of our survival instinct, Eric. Humans – and probably animals, too – seek *patterns*. When the brain identifies, say, *a face* in the red-hot coals, it hits a mental alert button and focuses on the illusion, filling in the detail.'

Eric wondered what all this had to do with Bob Dylan, but it didn't matter. Julia looked beautiful in the firelight, and he loved her insights.

'But why do we so often conjure faces and animals?' Julia asked. She sipped her rosé. 'Why not trees or teapots?'

Eric shook his head.

'You see, thousands of years ago in Africa, where the human race began, that face-shape in the jungle may have belonged to someone from an enemy tribe or to a tiger that was seeing you as his dinner. The people whose brains recognised those facial patterns in the bushes had more chance of surviving. And that meant they could pass on their pattern-seeking abilities to future generations. That's how *natural selection* works. You can see it in lots of human and animal traits if you understand the basic principle.'

Julia continued, 'So, back to the faces in the embers. That's what Bob Dylan does. He jumbles together evocative words and phrases, and your brain does the rest, seeking patterns, and making sense of the words in its own individual way. Dylan puts his lyrical chaos in a musical picture frame, making it easier for the listener to focus. Music has patterns too, though they're more rigid; mathematical, really.'

'I sometimes get mental pictures from other people's songs,' Eric said quietly. 'But they're usually not as strong.'

'That's because Dylan gets your brain working. By feeding your mind *chaotic* verse, he stimulates your imagination. Your mind tries to make sense of the words, and it throws up random pictures and unusual feelings.

'Of course, he's not the first; poets use obscure imagery all the time. In many cases, if you try to translate poetry into prose, you'll end up chasing your tail. Also, putting it to music helps. Music carries its own emotional cues. Think of Jerusalem: *Bring me my spear, o clouds unfold.* Mind you, I suspect Bill Blake had one foot firmly in the cosmos.' Julia shrugged, 'It's a speculative theory. I hope my analysis hasn't killed the magic for you.'

Eric shook his head. Most of Julia's explanation had made sense to him, but lost in visions of his own, he had struggled to maintain concentration.

The intercom sounded by the fireplace.

'That'll be Pattie. Could you buzz her in, please, Eric.' Julia stood up, 'By the way, Pattie's staying the night. You can still have the spare room as usual; we'll share my bed.'

Pattie leant against the doorframe. 'We really are the Twins tonight,' she said, unzipping her high leather boots. 'At least we didn't turn up at a *party* dressed like bookends.'

Pattie followed Julia into the living room dressed in a virtually identical black top and miniskirt.

'No problem, Pattie,' said Paul. 'We'll know who you are by your green toenails.'

The blonde handed Julia a folded newspaper.

'*It?*' queried Julia.

'I T: International Times,' explained Pattie. 'Hot off the press. This is the first edition of England's first underground paper. And they've put your face on the header.'

Julia laughed, 'Well, the hair's right, Pats, but I don't actually own a tiara.'

The Twins sat opposite Eric and Paul. Angling the paper towards the firelight, Julia assessed the new publication.

'I went to the launch party at the Roundhouse in Chalk Farm,' Pattie said excitedly. 'It was an all-nighter and... Oh, hang on, I left my bag in the hall.' A moment later, she returned with her blue carrier. 'Wine,' she said, producing two bottles of Mateus Rosé. 'And someone gave me this. I haven't heard it yet.'

Paul picked up the single, '*Gimmie Some Loving,* the Spencer Davies Group.'

'This is great,' Julia said, studying the International Times. 'There's information on art exhibitions, theatre shows, concert reviews, poetry, pop music and upcoming events. This newspaper is exactly what the underground movement needs if it's going to get organised.'

'I know,' said Pattie. 'Last night, everyone was saying the same thing. Here's the flyer from the party.'

Paul picked up the leaflet, '*Strip Trip, Happenings, Movies, Soft Machine, Pink Floyd, Steel Band.* And it says there's a *Sur Prize for the Shortest-Barest.*'

'Marianne Faithfull won that,' said Pattie. 'She was dressed as a naughty nun – showing a little more flesh than the nuns in *The Sound of Music!* It was a pretty mad night. The Roundhouse is great; it used to house a turntable for railway engines. There's old Victorian machinery and iron girders sticking up all over the place. Lots of people were in fancy dress. Paul McCartney turned up in an Arab costume. A conceptual artist named Yoko Ono got everyone to touch each other in the dark. That was nice; a bit of a *happening*, really. There was a great big pile of jelly, and a man on a motorbike was whizzing around with half-naked girls on the back.' Pattie giggled, 'Some of the girls had their tits out. The Pink Floyd were amazing. It was their first big concert, apparently. They had a freaky light show and ended-up blowing the fuses. The place went pitch-black, leaving two-and-a-half thousand people in the dark. Well, you can imagine...'

Eric grinned, 'It sounds brilliant!'

Paul and his mother were grinning, too.

Pattie tugged at Julia's hand, 'I need to borrow you for a minute.' Replenishing their glasses, the Twins disappeared into the hallway.

Paul arched an eyebrow, 'May as well open another bottle, then.'

'Have you seen my guitar?' asked Eric.

'Oh... Yeah, it's in my room. Sorry, I –'

'No problem,' smiled Eric. 'Pour us a couple of glasses, and I'll run up and get it.'

Eric reached the first floor, having seen no sign of Julia and Pattie. Passing Tony's open door, he noticed a red, white and black Brentford FC rosette attached to the bedside lamp. Beneath it was the twin-belled Mickey Mouse alarm clock that Tony had kept at his bedside since early childhood. Entering Paul's room, Eric saw his guitar leaning against the unmade bed. One of the wardrobe doors stood ajar. Inside was the Parade magazine he had lent to Paul almost a year before. Deciding to sneak a peek, Eric knelt on the red carpet and picked up the dirty mag. When it fell open at the place where he had torn out the page, Julia's double stared back at him. Eric swallowed heavily. How could he have been so careless! The sexy photo of the dark-haired glamour model had been one of a set; a dozen pictures of the same girl continued over four pages – and his tear was right in the middle of the spread. The next thing Eric saw left him puzzled and inexplicably uneasy. In some of the photographs, neat oval holes had been cut where the girl's face had been.

'Where's your guitar?' Paul asked, when Eric came into the living room.

Eric's mind raced. 'Oh, I thought it might be unsociable if I started playing.'

Twenty minutes later, Paul and Eric heard giggling in the hallway. Julia and Pattie appeared, each holding an empty wine glass.

'A refill if you please, bartender,' Pattie said, swaggering into the firelit room.

'It's *far* too bright in here,' Julia declared, closing the living-room door and shutting out the light from the hall. 'What's happened to the music?'

Pattie gesticulated with her empty glass; 'See Jules, we leave the party for a couple of minutes, and the whole evening falls apart!'

'Let's try this, then,' Paul said, picking up Pattie's promo copy of *Gimmie Some Loving*.

The pounding intro kicked in. 'Crank it up, Paul!' called Julia.

Paul stood by the radiogram, and Eric watched from the sofa as Julia and Pattie sashayed towards the curtained bay window. Wide grins lit the lads' faces as the Twins launched into an enthusiastic go-go dancing routine. The girls' black and blonde hair flew from side to side, their arms in the air and their hips bucking in time with the music. Kneeling on the small sofa, Eric gulped down half a glass of wine: the Twins were putting on a show, and it would be rude not to watch! He glanced at Paul; he too was staring at the jiggling women. In the orange firelight, the girls' frenzied dance evoked a pagan mood. The air felt hot and clammy. In their black clothes, they appeared to Eric as pretty young witches performing a pagan ritual deep in the forest. The house walls seemed to melt away, the dancers now in a clearing surrounded by the dark trees of Fox Wood.

The record ended, breaking the spell.

'Play it again, mister deejay!' Pattie called, catching her breath. 'Come on, Jules, don't wimp out on me now!'

'Another drink first,' smiled Julia.

When the loud music resumed, Pattie grabbed Paul's hand, pulling him to the shadowed library at the back of the room.

Julia sat down and replenished her glass.

'You're a great dancer,' Eric said, smiling across the coffee table. 'I mean, you both are.'

Julia leant forward, pointing over Eric's shoulder, 'You're up next.'

Eric noticed that the whites of her eyes were bloodshot. He twisted around. The shadowy prancing figures reminded him of the jazzmen in the office above Burton's. He pushed the memory from his mind. Paul was moving well, he thought; better than most of the stiff young men on *Ready, Steady, Go!* When Eric turned back, his gaze dropped. Julia studied his eyes, then brought her knees together and leaned forward,

'Come on,' she grinned, nodding towards the back of the room. 'Let's show them how it's done.'

*

Tragedy befell the Welsh mining town of Aberfan on the 21st of October, when a colliery slag heap collapsed, engulfing houses and a school. It was the only notable occasion of sadness in an otherwise bright and optimistic year for Britain. Even cold November weather could not dampen the nation's spirits, particularly those of the younger generation in England's capital. The Beach Boys' *Good Vibrations* sent sunshine into the playgrounds and parlours. A string of acclaimed British films included *The Knack, Alfie,* and *Morgan: A Suitable Case for Treatment. Georgy Girl* provided comedic glimpses of London's swinging summer.

Pattie's purple Volkswagen sped past an amber traffic light in Oxford Street.

'Do you think they'll let me in?' asked Eric.

'No problem,' replied Pattie. 'With your long hair, you'll be part of the crowd. And anyway, I know one of the organisers.'

Eric watched the Christmas lights pass overhead. 'Organisers? I thought we were going to a club?'

'We are, but tonight's the opening night. If it bombs, it'll be the *only* night.' The blonde shot the teenager a smile, 'I'm sure it'll be fun.'

Eric felt good in the purple paisley shirt that Pattie had given him. As usual, Pattie wore her trademark black leather boots. Her minidress was radiant, the bold, swirling patterns displaying a myriad of colours. A string of purple beads hung around her neck, the colour matched by her eye shadow and nails. Three gold bangles jingled on her wrist.

Every colour there is, thought Eric.

Pattie turned left into Tottenham Court Road. 'Keep your eyes peeled for the Gala Berkeley Cinema; it's up here somewhere.'

When they pulled into the curb, Eric glanced at his watch. It was twenty minutes before midnight.

Pattie turned off the engine. 'The club's right there,' she said, pointing to the basement entrance below the old cinema. 'We may as well leave our coats in the car.'

Kneeling on the driver's seat, Pattie reached over and grabbed her gold purse. Eric noticed that she was surveying the quiet London street. Stepping out of the car, he turned to the shutdown cinema.

'Over here.' Pattie took Eric's hand, leading him into the doorway of an office building. She looked up and down Tottenham Court Road. Apart from a few passing cars and a lone couple, the area was deserted. The blonde stood close to Eric placing her hand on his shoulder. 'I shouldn't be doing this,' she said quietly. 'I hope you can keep a secret?'

Eric nodded. *Secret number 152.*

'Are you sure? Julia would go mad if –'

'It's okay,' Eric assured her. 'Secrets are my speciality.'

Pattie looked hard at Eric, assessing him, as if gauging his moral character while questioning her own. Stepping back, she glanced one way, then the other. 'All right, follow me.'

Pattie slipped into the alleyway that ran alongside the office block. Eric's mind raced as he followed her into the dark passage. Up ahead, Pattie squeezed past some rubbish bins. Eric recalled her passionate kiss by the hotel near Grosvenor Square. The blonde stepped through a doorway in a wooden partition,

'Come on... *Quick*, before someone sees us!'

Eric's heartbeat increased. When he stepped through the opening, Pattie closed the door quietly behind them. It was pitch black. Blindly, Eric stretched out his hand, finding Pattie's warm shoulder. She was leaning forward, reaching down. He felt her weight on his palm. Her long hair brushed his arm. *She's lifting her dress!* Eric's chest pounded as Pattie leant back against the wall.

The blonde's lighter clicked, illuminating her pretty face. The twisted end of the reefer flamed, then the light was gone. Green and yellow motes swam in front of Eric's eyes. He saw the glowing red tip trail down to the young woman's side. Pattie turned her head and exhaled,

'Did you tell anyone?'

Eric regained his composure. 'What do you mean?'

'About Granny Takes a Trip. I know you saw me smoking in the back room. Does Paul know?'

'No, I kept it to myself.'

'Thank you,' said the soft feminine voice in the darkness.

Eric saw the joint glow brightly as Pattie took another drag.

'Have you smoked before?' she croaked, holding her breath.

'Only cigarettes.'

Pattie paused, blowing out the smoke. 'So now I'm asking myself. Do I offer you this joint or don't I?' She drew again on the reefer.

'I thought you were going to offer me something else,' Eric heard himself say.

His timing was off. Pattie's smoke-filled coughing fit lasted all of fifteen seconds.

'Oh Eric, I'm so sorry! I'm such a bloody idiot,' panted Pattie. '*Fuck!* I'm so *stupid* sometimes.'

Eric laughed nervously, 'No, *I'm* sorry. I can't believe I said that.'

Pattie finished the joint. When she dropped the singed cardboard filter to the ground, Eric reached for the wooden door.

'Wait.' Pattie pulled back his hand.

Wrapping her arms around him, Pattie hugged Eric in the pitch-dark alleyway. She kissed his cheek, 'I can't... You know why.' Her lips brushed his ear; she whispered, 'But I'd really like to!'

The lingering kiss that followed was very different from their first. After that night, Eric and Pattie's friendship would take on new depth and intimacy.

'Hello,' Keith said, cocking his head.

The parrot's staring yellow eyes were the first thing Eric saw when he woke on the sofa in the ballroom. 'Morning, Keith,' he replied drowsily, focusing on the bird on his chest. 'Did you get that mask from the Lone Ranger?'

Keith's pupils contracted and dilated. He had never heard of the fictional western hero and knew nothing of his silver bullets or his good friend Tonto. Spreading his wings, Keith flew to the end of the room, landing on Tony's drum kit. Leaving a green streak on the side of the small tom-tom, he dinged happily on the ride cymbal with his hooked black beak.

Ten minutes later, Eric joined Julia and Paul at the kitchen table.

'So tell us all about it,' Julia said, handing Eric a mug of coffee.

'I wish you'd both been there,' Pattie said, breezing in and placing Julia's spare keys on the table. The blonde was wearing the psychedelic dress from the previous night.

'You look like you've had about three hours sleep,' said Julia.

Pattie glanced at the kitchen clock. 'Three and a half,' she replied, selecting a mug from the draining board. 'Well,' Pattie announced, 'I'm pleased to report that the underground scene is alive and well and happening just up the road in our fair city. Next time, you simply *must* find a babysitter, Jules.'

Tony spun on his heel in the doorway. The ballroom door slammed shut.

'Oh, crap,' muttered Pattie. 'I've been up five minutes, and I've put my foot in it already.'

Julia shook her head, 'Don't worry about it, Pats.'

'It was a fantastic night,' Eric said, rekindling the mood. 'The Pink Floyd were really weird, but great. Some people were dancing, but most of them just sat around on the floor. And they showed films and had poetry, mad lighting, bubbles – all sorts of way-out stuff. They kept playing two songs by a group called the Jimi Hendrix Experience: *Hey Joe* and *Stone Free*. Their guitarist is brilliant. And there was another one: *I Feel Free* by the Cream. The club was called *UFO*... or *Night Tripper*, I'm not sure which.'

'They couldn't decide,' explained Pattie, 'so they put both names on the advertising. One of the organisers, *Hoppy,* is something to do with the International Times. The audience were all hippies.'

'Is that what *we* are then?' asked Paul. 'The Ealing hippies?'

Blowing her hot coffee, Pattie looked over at Julia, 'I'd say your mum's always been a hippie, Paul.'

Julia smiled, 'I've been called worse.'

For his fifteenth birthday on the 31st of December, Eric received his own set of keys to the Ealing House. 'These are from the three of us,' Julia said, hugging him warmly and kissing him on the cheek.

Pattie had received her set of newly cut keys as a Christmas present.

17

The Ealing Hippies

1967

The automobile industry's shift towards minimalism had rendered the 1962 Ford Zodiac passé. Reg didn't care. Impervious to the dictates of fashion, the postman admired the space-age fins and chromium trim that adorned the black-and-grey car.

King of the road, thought Reg. Scraping a whitewall tyre against the curb, he parked his new purchase outside his house.

1967 had begun well enough, but the temperature soon dropped, bringing freezing sleet and snow. For the time being, the Zodiac's folding roof remained tightly secured. It would be months before Reg would feel the highway wind in his hair.

Opening his front door, Reg looked down at the envelope on the mat. His past stared up at him. He had not encountered the Scientist's spidery handwriting in almost twenty years. *Shame I missed Igor,* the postman thought, picking up the hand-delivered letter.

Tossing the envelope onto the table, Reg turned on the television and went into the kitchen. A few minutes later, he returned with a cup of tea, lit a Senior Service, and sat staring at *The Magic Roundabout* with the sound down. *Bollocks,* he thought. Like Eric, though to far less effect, Reg had consigned the MoD2 affair to the back of his mind. Hartlepool had been quiet for over a year, but the postman's second job made the spectre of the new regime impossible to ignore. Reg worried about the changing nature of the transmissions. *When life gets tough, buy more stuff.* He had reluctantly broadcast the propagandist message himself. To his dismay, it had spread like wildfire.

Leaning forward in his armchair, Reg turned up the volume on the television. *(Boing!)* Zebedee told him to go to bed. The postman stared at the unopened envelope while a newsreader informed the nation that

British record-breaker Donald Campbell had died. *His boat, Bluebird, crashed at Coniston Water, cartwheeling across the lake at over three hundred miles per hour...*' Reg turned the television off and read the Scientist's letter.

With the undercover help of his assistant Igor, the Scientist had intercepted several communications: top-secret directives revealing the plans of MoD2. Reg now understood why the crossword-obsessed linguist had been sent down from Hartlepool. MoD2 intended to send messages around the world in a multitude of different languages, using satellite technology. The plan had been on the table for some time. And the technicians in Hartlepool were on the verge of a break-through.

*

Portobello Road was packed with shoppers braving the chilly January weather. The west London street market was invariably crowded on a Saturday afternoon.

Julia checked the label inside her son's new greatcoat. 'WRAC: the acronym stands for Women's Royal Army Corps.'

'Oh, terrific,' replied Paul. 'Eric nabs the last blue RAF coat, and I end up with a greeny-brown ladies one.'

'Well, at two-and-a-half quid, you can hardly complain,' said Pattie, her breath clouding in the cold air. 'Rip out the label; no one will know. And the big gold buttons are cool.'

Ruby Tuesday played from a transistor radio tied to a pole on a stall. Eric eyed the colourful glass bongs and Middle Eastern hookahs with curiosity. It was the first time he had seen drug paraphernalia on sale. Julia and Pattie bought long Indian dresses decorated with mirrored discs. From the same vendor, they purchased beads and bangles, also in the south Asian style. Three-buttoned *grandad* vests completed the boys' shopping.

'What time do you have to be home for Tony?' Pattie asked as they reached Bayswater Road.

'Oh, not until tonight,' answered Julia. 'I'm picking him up from South Ealing at nine.'

Pattie smiled, 'Okay, good. Anyone fancy a trip to the pictures? My treat.'

They made for the tiny sandwich bar by Notting Hill Gate station.

Julia sipped her espresso. 'Just out of interest, what are you taking us to see?'

'Blow-Up. It's on at the Gaumont, down the road.' Pattie glanced at her watch, 'It starts in half-an-hour.'

'What's it about?' Paul enquired past a mouthful of egg and cress sandwich.

'The protagonist is a fashion photographer loosely based on David Baily,' explained Pattie. 'It's set in contemporary London, though the director's Italian: Antonioni. It may be a little weird.'

'Sounds good,' said Julia, 'I like weird. You can tell us afterwards if it's realistic.'

'Yeah, I know it's my thing,' admitted Pattie. 'Why do you think I offered to pay?'

Julia raised her eyebrows, 'Cos you love us?'

'That too,' smiled the blonde.

'It's a great old cinema,' Julia said as they approached the Gaumont. 'There's a story about a cashier who was caught with her fingers in the till. She ran upstairs and threw herself off the balcony... and her ghost has haunted the place ever since.'

Paul looked at his mother, 'Good job Tony's not with us, then.'

'I wouldn't have told you if he was.'

When he saw the poster for Blow-Up, Eric's heart skipped a beat: the film carried an X certificate. Entering the foyer, Julia verbalised her observations on the late-nineteenth-century structural embellishments, inadvertently providing a useful distraction for Eric and Paul. The two fifteen-year-olds nodded their heads, staring up at the ornamented ceiling, while Pattie paid for the tickets. The smitten male cashier gazed into her alluring blue eyes, paying no attention to the two young architectural students behind her.

Perhaps to thwart their staff's suicidal impulses, the cinema's owners had kept the gallery closed since 1950. Taking her pick from the sea of vacant seats, Julia led the way to the centre of the stalls. Eric followed Pattie along the empty row.

The usual string of adverts preceded a newsreel, which included a report from California detailing a 30,000-strong assembly of American hippies. *The Gathering of the Tribes* or *Human Be-In* had taken place earlier that month in San Francisco's Golden Gate Park. On the stage was Allen Ginsburg, the bearded poet Eric and Julia had seen at the Royal

Albert Hall in 1965. Eric wondered if his beatnik friend George had flown to America for the occasion. Judging by the music contained in the report, at least one of the groups had been decidedly dodgy. But like the Poetry Incantation, the event had been less about the show and more about the gathering's significance.

'*I bring you greetings from the tribes of the north.*' proclaimed a longhaired travelling hippie. '*I spent some time in New York, and I spent some time in London. And I'm here to tell you, it's happening all over!*' The narrator added that the hippie explosion was also *happening* in Amsterdam, Paris, and West Berlin. Attired in white pyjamas, Ginsburg sat cross-legged on the stage, striking finger cymbals and chanting. Brightly dressed young people watched through an LSD-induced haze, clinging to a tenuous sanity while striving for a higher state of consciousness. Political and cultural change, ecological sustainability, but above all, *peace and love* were the aims of this massed community. The hippies were going to make a new and better world.

Ex-Harvard doctor of psychology Timothy Leary, with flowers in his hair, urged everyone to '*Turn on, tune in and drop out*'. Galvanised by the televised horrors of the Vietnam War, most of them already had.

The red curtains closed, reopened, and a British Board of Film Censors certificate flashed onto the screen. *This is to Certify that Blow-Up has been Passed for Exhibition when no child under 16 is present*. Gaining admission to an X rated film was regarded as a rite-of-passage among Eric and Paul's classmates. Tall tales had recently circulated describing ghastly violence and juicy erotica.

Blow-Up featured a live performance by the Yardbirds and included a scene at a party where everyone was smoking pot. Eric identified with the fashion photographer played by David Hemmings. Since Pattie's photoshoot at the Ealing House, Eric had daydreamed about following up on his success behind the camera. A parade of female models and a couple of sexy scenes rekindled his muse. Eric imagined himself a few years hence, opening the door of his Chelsea studio to a bevvy of beautiful girls.

Dropping Eric and Pattie at the top of Hanger Hill, Julia and Paul set off for South Ealing to pick up Tony. When Julia pulled away, one of the Mini's front wheels dropped into a deep pothole, shaking the car's occupants in their seats. The roads were also poor in other parts of the country. Seven days earlier, the Daily Mail had reported an estimated 4,000 holes in Blackburn, Lancashire.

*

'Scouts on a Saturday?' queried Eric.

'It's a fundraising concert,' explained Paul. 'I have to be at the hall by half-five to help get everything set up.'

'I hope you're not going out in your shorts in the middle of February,' said Julia. 'You'll freeze your woggle off.'

Eric noted that Julia's sarcasm regarding the Scouts had escalated in recent months. Tony just took the piss.

Julia glanced up at the clock on the living-room mantelpiece, 'It's gone four. If the garage doesn't call in the next hour, we'll be without a car for the rest of the weekend.'

'What did you do before you had a car?' asked Paul.

'Yes, but I told Tony I'd pick him up from Ron's at nine. I don't like the idea of him walking home that late.'

'I'll go and meet him if the car's not fixed,' offered Eric.

Julia smiled, 'Thank you, Eric.'

Indifferent towards pop music before her introduction to Bob Dylan, Julia's interest in the genre had grown over the last three years. By the beginning of 1967, it had become a formality for Paul to persuade his mother to dip into her savings in the interests of the Ealing House's record collection. Financed by her modelling work, Pattie also contributed music to the commune. Recent additions included debut LP's, *Fresh Cream* and *The Doors*. Paul and Eric had purchased *Strawberry Fields Forever/Penny Lane* earlier that afternoon.

'I think it's their best,' Eric told the scout on the opposite sofa. 'Do you think *Strawberry Fields* is a drug song or just a nostalgic yearning for childhood?'

Deciphering lyrics to identify drug references had become a popular pastime. According to those supposedly *in-the-know*, Dylan had been disseminating drug messages for years. Eric had assumed Donovan's *Mellow Yellow* to be one such song until Julia informed him that saffron was powder obtained from a crocus, used in the flavouring of bread. A police raid on Keith Richards' *Redlands* home had heightened the public's awareness of drug use in the pop world.

'I love the Beatles' new record,' Julia said, entering the living room with three mugs of coffee. 'I think both songs are great. If *Penny Lane* is a Lowry, then *Strawberry Fields* is Dali.'

'High praise indeed, Mother,' the scout said in an upper-class voice.

Eric was not familiar with either artist's work, but both songs painted dreamlike pictures in his mind.

An hour later, when Paul left for the scout hall, the garage had still not repaired the rattle that had dogged the Mini for three weeks. Having recently mastered the art, Eric made two more cups of instant coffee.

'Did you hear about the drug raid on Keith Richards' house?' asked Julia.

'Yeah, it looks like the police have got it in for the pop stars.'

Julia smirked, 'There's a rumour going around they found Marianne Faithful masturbating with a Mars Bar. Do you have any old clothes upstairs, Eric?'

The spare bedroom on the first floor had become known as *Eric's room*, though he never referred to it as his. He rifled through a dresser drawer and pulled out the pair of oil-stained jeans he had left there after fitting a chain guard to his bike. His old *I've Got a Tiger in My Tank* T-shirt was a tight fit, but he squeezed into it. He heard a thump on the ceiling; Julia's bedroom was directly above. Leaving his room, Eric glanced through the opposite doorway. His electric guitar was propped against Paul's bed. Next to the instrument was a book of Beatles songs with lyrics and chord charts.

Eric walked down the long corridor on the top floor. Entering the open door on the left, he went into Julia's bedroom. She was kneeling by the spiral staircase spreading newspaper on the carpet. The room smelled of marijuana.

Julia smiled, 'You look like you're about to burst out of those clothes.'

'I've already started.' Eric raised his arm, ripping his T-shirt another inch.

'Here's a tip,' Julia said, handing Eric a paintbrush. 'When you paint stairs, start at the top and work your way down.'

'I'll remember that.'

'Good.' Julia passed him a tin of gold paint. 'Don't drink it.'

'I'll remember that, too,' replied Eric.

Half-an-hour later, the white metal staircase was starting to turn gold.

'We could do with some music,' suggested Eric. 'Music while you work.'

'There's no radio up here,' said Julia. 'I'll sing to you if you like.'

Julia proceeded to *da-da-da* the theme from the BBC's *Music While You Work*. Eric joined in.

'I've never heard you sing before. You have a nice voice.'

Julia frowned, 'If you *like* the sound of wailing cats.'

The pair then embarked upon a cat's chorus, each vying to out-meow the other. The goofiness continued with several silly songs, including *Right Said Fred* by Bernard Cribbins and Peter Sellers and Sofia Loren's *Goodness Gracious Me*. Eric loved to hear Julia laugh. Time passed quickly. Soon, the painting was almost finished.

'How well did you know Uncle Jack?' Eric asked when the joking had petered out.

Julia hesitated. 'Oh, Jack. Well, I... Yes, I knew him well.'

'It's such a great house,' said Eric. 'And all those books in the living room. Jack must've been an interesting man.'

'He was,' Julia said quietly.

The mood had changed. Eric felt awkward. Julia had mentioned Jack before, albeit only in passing. Eric searched for something to say. 'When do you expect Paul to be home?'

'I don't know.'

Julia's reply was distant, distracted. There was a faraway look in her glassy green eyes.

Eric glanced at his watch. 'I'd better go and meet Tony.'

'Yes.'

Approaching the bedroom door, Eric turned back, 'I'm sorry if... Are you okay?'

Julia didn't reply.

There was a cold wind that February night. Walking briskly along the South Ealing Road, Eric turned up the collar on his RAF greatcoat. He had considered waiting for a 65 bus at Ealing Broadway Station, but walking helped him think. Julia had seemed happy – exceptionally so – but her high spirits had evaporated when he asked her about Jack. The suddenness and depth of her melancholy had been disconcerting, almost scary.

Eric lowered his head as a chilly gust shook the trees in St Mary's churchyard. Ron Hillman's house was off the main road, a few streets ahead on the right. It was almost nine o'clock. *Get your coat on, Tony,* Eric thought, cringing at the prospect of an invitation to socialise with Ron and his friends.

Eric's fears were allayed when he turned the corner, though he could hardly have predicted the circumstance. A blue-and-white Ford Anglia Panda Car was parked outside Ron's house. Behind it was a van. A couple of policemen were loading an assortment of warning lights, road signs, and street nameplates. Leaning back against a garden wall with his hands in his coat pockets, Tony watched the repossession from a distance.

Eric tapped the thirteen-year-old on the shoulder.

Tony turned his head slowly, 'Erich!' he slurred. 'Where'sh Mum?'

Before Eric could explain about the unrepaired Mini, Tony twisted and spewed a watery stream of projectile vomit across the front garden, drenching a hapless gnome who had chosen the wrong spot to go fishing that night.

Eric ushered his young friend towards the South Ealing Road, 'If you're going to be sick again, aim it away from me.' Supporting the inebriated boy like he was aiding a wounded soldier, Eric hailed a black cab. To his surprise, it stopped.

'I'll take you, mate,' said the driver, 'but if 'e pukes in the back, you clean it up. All right?'

The taxi had them home in double-quick time. Eric added the coins he had found in Tony's coat pocket to his own and paid the fare. A few minutes later, he inserted one of the shiny new keys that Julia had given him into the Ealing House's front door.

'They're upshtairs!' Tony exclaimed as Eric helped him down the hallway. 'I'm not goin' up there; you can't make me. Fuck that.'

Eric held Tony by his armpits, preventing him from sitting down in protest on the hall floor. 'Okay, okay.' He dragged the sozzled teenager into the ballroom.

Tony staggered to the old sofa and flopped.

'I'll get a blanket,' said Eric.

'Fanks,' replied the drunk. 'I'm a bit pished.'

No kidding, thought Eric. Draping his coat over the bannister rail, he breathed a sigh of relief. *Okay, now where's Julia?* Climbing the stairs, he heard music from above.

The muffled sound was coming from somewhere at the top of the house. He recognised the song: *Fever* by Peggy Lee. He looked up; there was no light on the landing. Instinctively sensing that something was amiss, he scaled the stairs slowly. *Fever* ended, then there was silence. The top floor was in darkness. Eric looked down the corridor towards the front of the house. Moonlight shining through the round leaded window cast an elongated crisscrossed shadow along the passageway. All three doors were closed. The distinctive aroma of marijuana hung heavily in the air.

Creeping down to the middle floor, Eric went into Tony's room, stripped two blankets off his bed, and grabbed a pillow. He took the Mickey Mouse clock from the nightstand.

Downstairs in the ballroom, Tony was already fast asleep. Eric draped the blankets over his leggy young friend and placed the alarm clock on the tea chest next to the television. With the gentleness of a doting parent, he slipped the pillow under the sleeping boy's head then turned out the light.

A short time later, Julia entered the living room wearing her red Japanese robe, 'Eric! I didn't expect you back so soon.'

'We flagged a taxi on the way home.'

'Oh, good. How much do I owe you?'

'Oh, don't worry,' said Eric. 'Tony and I went halves on the fare.'

*

'I knew Brian Jones for a while,' said Scarecrow.

At the next easel, Paul's ears pricked up.

'He had a flat in the house next to mine at World's End – the unfashionable end of Chelsea. Keith Richards lived with him, and so did Mick, on and off.'

'Really?' Eric said, washing out his paintbrush. 'Was he –'

'I was talking to Brian over the back-garden fence,' the art teacher continued, 'and I asked him how his window got smashed. He said they'd had a party and some of the guests left without using the door.'

Pushing his hands into his pockets, Scarecrow strode between the easels. 'I won't be long,' he called, without turning back. 'Be good boys while I'm away.'

Eric leaned sideways, examining his friend's painting, 'World War Two?'

'More topical,' replied Paul. 'It's RAF planes bombing the Torrey Canyon.'

On the 18th of March, the supertanker had run aground off the coast of Land's End, spilling 120,000 tons of crude oil into the sea.

'Did you see Top of the Pops last night?'

'Of course,' replied Paul. 'It's a travesty if you ask me.'

'What, Pete Murray's suit?'

'Well, first Engelbert Humperdink keeps the Beatles from number one with their best single ever, then Sandy Shaw does the same to Jimi Hendrix with bloody *Puppet on a String*.'

'*Purple Haze* didn't win the Eurovision Song Contest,' Eric pointed out. 'Pattie said Jimi set fire to his guitar and was taken to hospital with burns on his hands.'

'Yeah, she told me that, too,' replied Paul. 'Pattie gets all the inside news. Did she tell you about this all-night rave-up thing at Alexandra Palace next weekend?'

Scarecrow returned to the classroom and sat with his feet up on his desk. Opening a drawer, he pulled out a glossy DC comic book. '*Zap! Kapow! Wonder Woman! Why did you come to America?*' the art teacher read aloud. '*I was sent as a courier from Themyscira to bring a message of peace and love.*'

*

On the evening of Saturday the 29th of April 1967, Pattie arrived at the Ealing House with her mother in tow.

Julia was in the kitchen. 'You probably won't see much of Tony. He's made a little den for himself in the ballroom. That's the name we have for the big back room. Tony tends to hide away in there with the old television.'

'They're often reclusive at that age,' replied Angela, Pattie's fifty-something-year-old mother.

'Just help yourself to anything,' offered Julia. 'I hope you won't be too bored.'

The middle-aged lady eyed the pile of dishes in the sink. 'I'm sure I'll find something to do,' she said, with a Mona Lisa smile.

Julia turned to Pattie as they climbed the stairs, 'It's so nice of your mum to babysit.'

'I paid her electric bill last month. She owes me.'

Downstairs in the living room, Paul and Eric were blasting the Who's *Pictures of Lilly*.

'Do you think the boys know what this song's about?' giggled Julia.

'Oh, I'm sure they do,' replied Pattie.

When the record finished, Angela entered the living room, 'Hello.'

'Hello, I'm Paul.'

'Angela.' Pattie's mother shook the teenager's hand. 'You're Julia's son. The resemblance is striking.'

Paul smiled, 'Yeah. And this is my – *our* friend, Eric.'

'Pattie told me about you,' said Angela. 'You're the photographer.'

'I wish,' replied Eric. 'Maybe one day. The picture I took of Pattie was beginners luck.'

Angela's blue eyes wrinkled as she smiled, 'She told me you were a modest type.'

Sitting around the coffee table, Paul and Eric set about uncovering Pattie's past.

'Oh, Pattie has always been a lovely girl,' effused her mother. 'She never swore, never smoked, always dressed nicely...'

'Fuck!' Pattie muttered, kneeling naked on Julia's four-poster bed. 'I've dropped the hash on the floor.'

An hour-and-a-half later, Pattie's purple Volkswagen pulled up in a side street in north London.

Dusk was fast approaching when Julia, Pattie, Paul and Eric joined the colourful hippie procession on Alexandra Palace Way. A floating coral sky dominated the horizon, merging overhead into star-studded blue. Sprawling parkland fell away to their left as they made their way up the hill towards the grand Victorian building silhouetted against the sun. Incense perfumed the air, made particularly strong by a kaftan-attired man with burning joss sticks tucked into the band of his floppy yellow hat. Victorian and Edwardian jackets, dresses and gowns were prevalent among the crowd, many of whom accessorised with bells, beads and bangles. For the Ealing hippies, it was like coming home. The tiny mirrored discs on Julia's purple Indian dress reflected pink in the evening light. In her psychedelic minidress, Pattie personified Swinging London's fusion with the hippie movement. Eric had chosen the purple paisley shirt that Pattie had given him, and the short denim jacket he had received for Christmas. Paul had become increasingly attached to his WRAC greatcoat, which he wore open, over a red three-button vest. With so many clothing variations on display, an outsider might have mistakenly identified a number of different groups, but unifying the hippies, both female and male, was the now ubiquitous long hair. Most of those who did not subscribe to the colourful eclectic fashions would succumb as the year wore on: some due to their experience at *The 14 Hour Technicolor Dream*.

Julia saw the tickets in Pattie's hand, 'Where did you get them?'

'From Indica book shop in Charing Cross Road. It's on my list of places to take you, Jules. They publish the International Times from there. The guy that runs it is Barry Miles. If there's such a thing as a headquarters for the underground movement, it's probably Indica.'

'Paul McCartney helped put up the bookshelves,' said a man at the Alexandra Palace entrance.

'Welcome.' Suzy Creamcheese smiled, shaking Eric's hand.

'Thank you,' replied Eric. The attractive blonde's American accent fleetingly reminded him of Sid.

'The Queen and your Prime Minister were offered free admission,' Suzy said, turning to Julia. She feigned bewilderment, 'But they haven't shown up yet.'

A fairground helter-skelter stood near the centre of the long hall. Forty-foot high columns spread like tall metal flowers, supporting the vaulted churchlike ceiling: a testament to the Victorian age of industry and grandeur. At either end, a stage had been erected to accommodate the many musicians who had donated their services for the International Times benefit. To Eric and Paul's bemusement, both platforms were being used simultaneously, creating a discordant stereo cacophony in the middle of the hall. A lighting tower aimed spots at both stages, while UFO-style light shows projected liquid psychedelia on the walls and the dancers. Using bed sheets for screens, enterprising cinematographers showed low budget underground films, along with a diverse assortment of photographic slides. 10,000 people attended the hippie coming-out ball that night. *The 14 Hour Technicolor Dream* was the UFO club reimagined on a gigantic scale, drugs included.

'If we lose one another, we'll meet at the helter-skelter,' said Julia.

Pattie nodded, 'Okay, Mum.'

They followed Paul, who had been drawn to a strangely dressed troupe of performance artists called The Tribe of the Sacred Mushroom.

Pattie turned to Eric and Paul, 'By the look of the people here, there are some powerful drugs about. If anyone offers you anything, don't take it.'

Following *the Mushroom*, a group played on the low stage. A section of the audience sat on a flight of broad steps. Above them, scaffolding reached up to the high ceiling encasing huge organ pipes.

'They're repairing the organ,' explained a short man standing next to Eric. 'The group are good, aren't they. I think it's the Move.'

'The Pretty Things,' said his friend.

'You're both wrong; it's the Utterly Incredible Too Long Ago To Remember Sometimes Shouting At People,' said another.

'That's *two* groups,' said the first man.

To Eric, it sounded like five. The atonal stereo din at the centre of the hall was assaulting his senses, driving him to the point of delirium. He turned to Paul, 'Let's go all the way to the end.'

A gathering of poets readied themselves by a podium.

'We'll stay here for a while,' Julia said, slipping her arm around Pattie. 'Don't forget, the helter-skelter's our meeting place.'

Meandering through the milling crowd, Paul and Eric headed for the far side of the island-like stage, making their way past the group that was either the Move, the Pretty Things, or somebody else.

Framed by a mop of curly brown hair, a hobbit face appeared from the tunnelled door of a nearby igloo.

Eric halted Paul with a hand on his shoulder. 'Phil!'

'Eric, my good friend!' Phil grinned from ear to ear. 'I half expected to see you here.'

'This is Paul,' said Eric. 'Paul, meet my friend Phil. He's the guitarist I told you about. Phil sold me the Rapier.'

'Pleased to meet you, man.' Phil shook Paul's hand vigorously. 'Cool coat. Are you one of the Ealing Broadway people who stole Eric away from his parents at such a tender age?'

'I'm one of them,' smiled Paul. 'What's in the igloo?'

'A blonde chick rolling banana-skin joints,' answered Phil. 'They don't work.'

Eric studied Phil's darting eyes. Perhaps smoking banana skins didn't work, but something obviously had.

A plume of smoke emanated from the exit doorway at the top of the helter-skelter. Inside the cramped dome, Pattie passed Julia the reefer, 'Hurry, before someone comes up the stairs.'

Julia inhaled deeply. Part of the burning end fell away, glowing red on a dirty wooden step.

Beneath the high organ pipes, another fire hazard blazed as a heavily made-up Arthur Brown took to the stage with a flaming metal helmet strapped to his head.

Pattie's psychedelic minidress inched up as she sat on a mat at the top of the helter-skelter and pushed off. A longhaired man in a striped blazer gawped at the blonde as she rounded the bend at the bottom of the slide. He had been waiting expectantly for almost five minutes.

Arthur Brown's hit single *Fire* was still over a year away. His newly formed group rocked and wailed, led by a grinding Hammond organ, while the extrovert singer's head grew increasingly hot. Cavorting around the stage, the *God of Hellfire* gamely balanced his methanol-fuelled flaming crown, delivering a demonic performance that would be influential in the years to come.

'He's brilliant,' Paul shouted into Eric's ear.

Eric nodded. He turned to speak to Phil, who wasn't there.

'Maybe he went back to his igloo,' suggested Paul.

'No...' Eric pointed up at the organ pipes. 'There he is.'

Eric and Paul watched, along with hundreds of others, as Phil clambered up the scaffolding that surrounded the tall pipes. Higher and higher he went, climbing from one metal pole to the next with the agility of a chimpanzee. Two, then three young men joined him on the metal framework.

'He's bloody mad!' Paul shouted above the noise of the group. 'They all are.'

'He's mad *tonight*,' agreed Eric. 'Phil's on something.'

'What? Banana skins?'

Eric shook his head, 'More than that, I reckon. LSD, maybe.'

As more climbers clambered up to join the others, the framework began to shift. Tension grew among the crowd as the precarious metal structure swayed one way, then the other. Eric and Paul saw the expressions of the monkey-men change. Someone with a microphone politely requested that they come down immediately. In less than a minute, the scaffolding was clear, except for one man.

High above the audience, Phil stood stock-still, his arms wrapped tightly around a cross-section of the silver-grey poles. Behind him, the organ pipes lined the wall like giant tin whistles.

Eric stared up at his friend, willing him to take the first step. *Come on, Phil, you can do it. Just a bit at a time.*

'He's frozen,' said Paul.

'Someone needs to talk him down,' suggested a nearby girl.

Eric glanced back at Paul then pushed through the crowd. He picked his way up past the hippies on the steps. The band played on. Eric began to scale the scaffolding. Bereft of the army of climbers, the bolted metal structure felt sturdy enough.

Don't look down, Eric told himself, steadily working his way up towards his petrified friend. *Phil was okay until he looked down,* said a voice in Eric's head. *It's easy going up.*

The group below had finished their set, though music still played from the opposite end of the hall.

'Hello mate,' said Eric. Clinging to the metal tubing, he looked down at the hundreds of small upturned faces.

Julia stared wide-eyed at Paul. 'What in God's name is going on?' she asked, clutching her son's arm.

'He took LSD,' replied Paul.

'Who, Eric?'

'No – no, Eric's friend, Phil. The scaffolding was wobbling, and he froze. Eric climbed up there to talk him down.'

Minutes passed slowly. Julia, Pattie and Paul stood in a line with their arms around one another, staring silently up at the two small figures. Ignoring the drama unfolding above, unkempt longhaired roadies set-up drums and amplifiers.

'I feel like we should be praying,' said Pattie.

'Or sacrificing a goat?' Julia replied dryly. 'Sorry,' she said, smiling apologetically at her friend.

Pattie thought she saw tears in Julia's eyes.

'They're moving!' exclaimed a pink-haired hippie girl standing next to Paul.

Eric led the downward climb, continually looking up at Phil. 'Nearly there. If we fell now, we wouldn't have more than a few bruises.'

Spontaneous applause erupted as the two climbers dropped the last few feet. Amid back-pats and comments of '*Well done, man,*' and '*Welcome back to planet earth,*' they joined the others. Eric felt a sense of relief as Julia wrapped her arms around him, squeezing him tightly.

'You're a fucking hero!' Pattie whispered. Hugging Eric, she kissed him full on the lips.

The Ealing hippies sat on the floor near a corner of the great hall. Bubbling images from a light show spread across their faces. Since his rescue, Phil had been unusually quiet though he had thanked Eric and assured his new acquaintances of his stable mental state.

'Someone spiked my Coke,' Phil told Paul. 'That must have been it. I mean, I like a smoke, same as everybody, but I'm not a druggie.'

Eric sat between Julia and Pattie, trying not to feel too pleased with himself. The pink-haired hippie girl who had been standing by Paul drifted over and struck up a conversation with Julia. Before long, the two were chatting away like old friends. Paul and Phil were also deep in discussion.

Eric turned to Pattie, 'Fancy a walk?'

The blonde slid her arm around Eric as they strolled leisurely among the eccentrically dressed revellers. Eric reciprocated, gently squeezing Pattie and kissing the side of her head. He was about to apologise but changed his mind when he felt her arm tighten around him. Pattie was beautiful. She had kissed him and called him a hero. Eric had never felt so good.

'There's no one on the helter-skelter,' said Pattie.

With two coconut mats tucked under his arm, Eric followed the girl up the winding wooden stairway.

'Do you want to go first?' Eric asked when they reached the top.

'Hang on a minute.' Turning away, Pattie pulled up the front of her minidress.

Eric's eyes widened as the blonde slipped her hand down inside her shiny red panties. A moment later, she faced Eric, holding a joint and a book of matches,

'Saves carrying a bag around.' Pattie tore off a cardboard match and ignited it with one strike.

She had almost finished the reefer when they heard footfalls clonking up the wooden stairs. Pattie's lungs were filled with smoke. Hastily stubbing the joint on the wall, she pulled Eric to her and kissed him. From the corner of his eye, Eric saw two flower-bedecked girls pass by, then they were gone. Running her hands sensually over his back, Pattie blew a stream of smoke into Eric's mouth. Their lips touched lightly as Eric inhaled.

'Hold your breath,' whispered Pattie.

Procol Harum played on the main stage, while inside the dome at the top of the helter-skelter, Eric and Pattie slow-danced to *A Whiter*

Shade of Pale. Eric exhaled over Pattie's shoulder. Their dance lasted the entire length of the song.

'What's happening here?' Pattie asked, as she and Eric re-joined the others by a small stage.

'*Happening* is the operative word,' replied Julia. 'It's something by Yoko Ono, the conceptual artist you saw at the Roundhouse.'

Paul looked at the low white stepladder in the middle of the stage. 'She won't be able to paint the ceiling with that.'

'Maybe she'll paint an imaginary ceiling with an imaginary brush?' suggested Phil.

'In an imaginary colour,' added Eric. He was pleased to see his friend back to his usual self.

'Yeah!' laughed Phil. He looked surprised to see Eric holding Pattie's hand.

Nothing was left to the imagination in the performance piece that followed: *A Pretty Girl is Like a Manifesto.* The pretty girl in question walked onto the stage wearing a white dress and sat atop the short spotlit stepladder. Volunteers were then called upon to snip away her clothes piece by piece, using a pair of scissors with a tiny microphone attached.

Phil turned to Paul, 'I have to say, this is my favourite presentation so far.' He grinned as the last remnants of the dark-haired girl's dress fell away.

'Oh yeah!' Phil exclaimed as her severed bra dropped to the floor.

'Too tight,' whispered Pattie.

'Sorry.' Eric relaxed his grip on her hand.

'It's okay,' Pattie whispered, a mischievous smile turning the corners of her mouth. 'I hope I didn't spoil the moment for you.'

Eric smiled back and shook his head.

In a shadowed alcove at the side of the hall, John Lennon was also enjoying the moment.

The first rays of dawn shone through the high windows of Alexandra Palace as Pink Floyd commenced their opening song, *Astronomy Domine.* The audience rose as one to greet the new day. Dressed in satin shirts and flared trousers, the gods of the underground looked down from the elevated stage. As the long improvised piece approached its crescendo, sunlight struck the mirrored discs on Sid Barrett's Fender

Telecaster, sending radiant beams of light dancing wildly around the hall. This was the moment that everyone would remember ever after: the end of the beginning, the piper at the gates of dawn.

18

Flower Power

Rain spattered the big round window at the front of the house. Pattie called down the gloomy second-floor corridor, 'Jules?'

'In here,' came the reply from the bedroom on the far left.

Light from the crystal chandelier illuminated Julia's room on this dull May afternoon. An open copy of Aldous Huxley's *The Doors of Perception* lay face down on the fabric laden four-poster bed.

'Oh, I love it!' Pattie exclaimed, admiring the gold spiral staircase. 'Where did you get the marionettes from?'

'I found them in the attic.' Julia reached up from the stepladder, pressing another drawing pin into the ceiling. 'It's a treasure-trove up there. Could you pass me the old witch with the broomstick.'

Julia stood back by the bed and assessed her work. Five colourful wooden puppets hung at varying heights behind the gold staircase, with a further four suspended in front. She turned off the overhead light. 'Would you draw the curtains please, Pats.'

Kneeling behind the spiral staircase, Julia switched on the up-lights she had positioned earlier. The slowly revolving spotlit marionettes cast wavering shadows across the walls and ceiling.

'Yeah! They look great!' enthused Pattie.

Julia beamed, 'They do, don't they!'

'This should make them look even better.' The blonde produced two matchbox-sized packages from her bag. 'I paid a visit to Mister Nice.'

'Crikey, that should keep us going for a while!'

'Opportunity,' explained Pattie. 'It's Afghan Black. I thought I'd stock up while it was available. Here, one for you, one for me. Do you have any papers?'

Julia opened the monogrammed trunk at the end of her bed, dug around inside, and brought out a rusty Old Holborn tobacco tin. 'I found this in the attic, too.'

'Classic,' Pattie said, unwrapping one of the packages. 'Have a whiff; it smells like Afghanistan.'

Julia closed the bedroom door and turned the key. 'The boys won't be home from school for a few hours, but best to be on the safe side.'

Pattie stuck two Rizla's together. 'Better open the window, Jules. This stuff stinks.'

The Twins sat on the floor, reclining against the big four-poster bed. Raindrops dripped from the raised sash window.

'Wow,' Julia exclaimed, handing the reefer back to her friend. 'You weren't joking about this pot. It really creeps up on you.'

'Economical,' replied Pattie. 'One joint, and you're off with the fairies.'

'One hit, more like.'

'You know that girl at Ally Pally?' began Pattie.

'Oh, *that* girl,' Julia replied sarcastically.

'I mean the one on the white stepladder who had her clothes cut off.'

'Uh-huh?'

'Well,' Pattie said thoughtfully, 'I was wondering what it would be like. You know, being stripped naked by strangers in front of ten thousand people.'

'I'd love it.'

'I think I would, too.' Pattie burst-out laughing.

Julia looked at her friend, 'I've been meaning to ask you...'

'Yes?'

'Have you got a thing going on with Eric?'

'Well, if you must know Julia, he's asked me to marry him, and I've said *yes*. I mean, he's very nice looking, and after all, he's only twelve years younger than me.'

'Don't try to wriggle out of it,' persisted Julia. 'I saw you two holding hands. You've seemed very close lately.'

Pattie paused. 'Okay, yes, we have been close in the last few months. But no, we don't have a *thing* going on!'

*

'I can't say if joining the European Economic Community would be a good or a bad thing financially.' Julia folded the morning paper and placed it in front of her on the kitchen table. 'But I do see it as a step in the right direction – towards a unified world, I mean. They came up with the idea of a European union to discourage extreme nationalism from happening again on the continent. The EEC will help that peace process along. It's wonderful to see walls coming down, not going up.'

Pattie nodded. 'Mm, well, I admire your optimism, Jules. Maybe a common market would lead to a more peaceful world, little acorns and all that. But it's still a million miles from the revolution everyone's talking about. Are there any more Coco Pops?'

''Ello,' Tony grunted, entering the kitchen.

'Fuck off,' said Keith.

'*Aaaagh!*' growled Tony, raising his long arms and towering over the parrot like King Kong.

Keith leapt sideways from his perch, described a semicircle above the kitchen table, then disappeared through the doorway into the back corridor.

'Oh, do try to be kind, Tony,' sighed Julia. 'We're all struggling to get along in this life, and it's so much better if we make an effort to be nice to one another. And that includes Keith.'

'He told me to F off,' protested Tony, his recently broken voice reverting to its former high pitch. 'Why should I be nice to 'im?'

'He's only repeating what he's picked up from people,' Julia explained patiently. 'He doesn't know what he's saying.'

'Then he should keep his bloody beak shut!' Tony stormed out of the kitchen. 'Bollocks!' he shouted from halfway up the stairs.

Julia watched Keith fly back in and land on his perch. She knew that the parrot's intelligence extended well beyond instinct and mimicry.

'Coffee?' suggested Pattie.

'Please.' Julia held her head in her hands. 'I've tried to include Tony in our lives... I've tried talking to him so many times, Pats. But when logic fails, what's left?'

'I don't know, Jules. I'll have to think about that one.'

'Paul and Eric were so much *older* at his age.'

'Those two are mature beyond their years,' observed Pattie. 'Maybe it's not fair to make comparisons.'

'Morning.' Paul walked into the kitchen wearing the Groucho Marx mask he had brought down from the attic. 'Mum, I was thinking – ah. What's wrong?'

'Tony's what's wrong.'

'Right. Anything in particular?' Paul removed the mask.

'No, just the usual.' Julia took a breath and smiled at her eldest son, 'What were you going to say when you came in?'

'Oh, it'll keep for another time.'

'No, go on,' insisted Julia. 'You were about to suggest something. If it gets me out of the house, the answer's *yes*.'

'It's fine if the answer's *no*,' began Paul.

'My purse just screamed. Spit it out.'

'Okay. How would you feel about getting a stereo record player?'

Julia considered Paul's proposal for all of three seconds. 'Okay. Now?'

'When Eric gets here.'

'Great. I'll see if Tony wants to come. Where is he?'

By the time Julia had found Tony's scribbled note, he was halfway to South Ealing.

Eric turned to Paul in the back seat of the Mini, 'It starts at four.'

Pattie stubbed her cigarette and wound up the front window. 'What does?'

'*Where It's At;* the BBC Light Programme on the radio. Kenny Everett is previewing the Beatles' new LP.'

'Cool,' said Pattie. 'I read they banned one of the songs for having drug references.'

'I read that, too,' said Julia. 'The song's called *A Day in the Life.* There was a great public statement from the BBC: *We have decided that it appears to go just a little too far and could encourage a permissive attitude towards drug-taking*.'

Pattie smiled, '*Just a little too far.* Naughty Beatles.'

'Kenny won't be previewing *that* one, then,' Paul said, as the Mini neared Ealing Town Hall.

'It's a generous chunk of promotion from the BBC, in my opinion,' said Julia. 'The drug dealers will be pleased.'

A light rain began to fall. Julia switched on the wipers, sending smears across the windscreen. Eric noticed that *Casino Royale* was playing at the ABC. Though the James Bond film was a spoof featuring

Peter Sellers and Woody Allen, he felt sadness. Perhaps his dad would suggest they see the next Sean Connery release together.

Passing through the nowhere-land between the Broadway and West Ealing, Julia parked the Mini behind St John's Church. For a few seconds, Eric fantasised about making the short walk to his house and dropping in on his parents with his hippie friends. He was surprised by the preposterousness of the scenario.

Eric gazed out at the Uxbridge Road through Bensteds' shop front. Having listened to the Tremeloes' *Silence is Golden* seven times on seven different stereos, it was clear to him that there was really only one. With its separate amplifier/tuner, record deck, and large heavy-duty speakers, the Kenwood package delivered a huge warm sound with plenty of balls at the bass end. It was the highest-priced stereo system in the shop, but boy, did it sound great.

Leaving Paul to work on his mother, Eric wandered through to the record department at the back of the store. Bensteds' small record section was busy that Saturday afternoon. Soon Eric was standing in a listening booth, transported back to the top of the helter-skelter by his current favourite record, *A Whiter Shade of Pale*.

'They're playing our song,' Pattie said, joining Eric in the cramped enclosure.

'I'll always think of us when I hear this,' Eric told the girl as they slow-danced.

'Me too,' replied Pattie. 'Julia thinks we're having an affair.'

'And are you?' asked Bill.

'Dad!' Eric exclaimed, releasing the pretty blonde. 'No! Pattie's... Pattie, this is my dad.'

'Pleased to meet you.' Pattie smiled sweetly, extending her arm. 'Actually, Eric and I are just good friends.'

'Bill Grimes,' said Eric's father, a broad smile lighting his face.

Eric had never seen his dad melt before. 'What brings you to Bensteds?'

'Your mum wanted the *Sound of Music* LP.' Bill held up an orange-striped paper bag. 'I'd better get going; she's waiting in the car.'

'Okay, Dad.'

Pattie smiled, 'Nice to meet you, Mr Grimes. I promise I won't run off with your son.'

'Bill,' grinned Eric's father. 'Oops, sorry,' he said, bumping into a female shop assistant.

Eric and Pattie re-joined the others at the front of the store.

'Oh, hello,' said Paul. 'We just saw your dad.'

'Yeah, us too,' replied Eric. 'Did you decide on a stereo?'

'We're buying the Kenwood,' said Julia. 'But the floor model is the last one they have, and that's sold. The man's gone to check –'

'Right, madam,' said the grey-suited salesman. 'There's more stock due next week. We can deliver it to you on Thursday the first of June, at no extra charge.'

Julia paid for the purchase and began giving the salesman detailed directions to the Ealing House.

Eric whispered to Paul, 'Do you have any cash on you?'

'Ten or twelve bob. Why?'

Eric fumbled in his jacket pocket. 'They're delivering the stereo on the first of June. That's the day the new Beatles LP comes out. If –'

'I'll get it,' Pattie offered, producing a five-pound note. 'Excuse me,' she said, turning to the salesman. 'Would it be possible to have an LP delivered with the stereo?'

By mid afternoon, the sun had broken through. Julia joined the others in the living room, 'I've spoken to Mrs Hillman on the phone. Tony is out with Ron and some of their friends, but I've arranged to pick him up later.'

'Mum,' said Paul.

'Yes?'

'Thank you for treating us to the stereo.'

Julia sat beside her son on the big sofa. 'Oh, you're welcome, Paul,' she said, hugging him and kissing his cheek.

'Ahh,' murmured Pattie. 'Now you've made me go all squishy.'

Eric stood staring out of the bay windows. 'What's going on in the front garden? There are green shoots popping up all over the place.'

'I was wondering when one of you would notice,' Julia said excitedly. 'I found a big bag of seeds and scattered zillions out the front. I've no idea what they are.'

'It'll be a lovely surprise, then,' smiled Pattie.

Paul raised his eyebrows, 'I wondered what had happened to my Triffid seeds.'

'Jules?'

'Yes, Pats?'

'You know all that money you just blew on the new stereo?'

'Uh-huh?'

'How would you like to make it all back, plus a bit more on top?'

'Go on.'

'Well, I've been offered a job. Actually, *we've* been offered a job. It's a straightforward fashion shoot – probably housewifey cardigans and crap like that, but here's the thing: the client wants *sisters*.'

'The Twins.'

'Exactly. I told the agent about the blonde and black thing. He passed it on to the ad people, and they loved it. What do you think?'

'I'm three years older than you, Pats.'

'Well, you don't look it!' said Pattie. 'Anyway, it's not for trendy teen clothes. It's only a single day's work, and it's well paid. Think of it as a free stereo.'

'You'll have to give me some pointers.'

'Yay!' cheered Pattie, bobbing and clapping her hands. 'We'll have a blast! One little thing though: the photoshoot's scheduled for the first of June.'

'The day the new stereo's being delivered.'

'Yeah.'

'No problem,' interjected Paul. 'I happen to be off school that day.'

'*There's* a coincidence,' said Eric. 'So do I.'

The dreary grey clouds that blighted spring had finally given way to sunny blue skies. It looked and felt a lot like summer. Early on the first of the month, Eric arrived at the Ealing House. Pushing his bike through the green wooden gate, he stopped in his tracks and blinked. The front garden was a teeming mass of colour. Chrysanthemums, Campanulas, Carnations, Calla Lilies, Cockscombs and Cosmos' – to name only the C's – bloomed brightly amongst the clumps of long grass, bushes and nettle beds. Eric smiled as a small brown rabbit scampered across the path, then disappeared into the thick flora.

'Good morning!' Paul called from the porch. He spread his arms wide, lifting his face to the glorious blue sky, 'Welcome to Wonderland, my friend!'

Eric smiled, 'Then you must be Alice, I presume?'

'Yeah, I fell down a rabbit hole and ended up here.'

'I met the rabbit,' said Eric. 'Could you ask the Hatter to get the tea kettle on, please?'

'It'll cost you ten-and-six.'

'Oh, then I'll have coffee instead.'

'Coming right up!' Paul spun around and walked back into the cool, tiled hallway.

Propping his bicycle against the big arched porch, Eric went up to the middle floor and changed out of his school uniform. He returned barefooted, in jeans and a yellow T-shirt. A mug of coffee was waiting for him in the living room.

'Your mum's already gone, then?'

'Yeah, Pattie picked her up half-an-hour ago,' Paul told Eric from the opposite sofa. 'Um... Is she your girlfriend now?'

'Who?'

'Pattie,' Paul said, half-smiling and studying his friend's face. 'You were holding her hand at the Technicolor Dream, and recently you've seemed –'

'My *girlfriend*? I wish!' replied Eric. 'We're just good friends.'

'Oh, don't give me that old chestnut.'

Eric reached for his coffee. The *old chestnut* had sounded okay when Pattie had used it on his dad. 'All right, here's how I see it. I think Pattie was really chuffed when she got her first modelling job, and she thinks I helped. But anybody could have taken that photograph. And there was the riot at the anti-war protest. Remember when we got separated? That was pretty scary. Pattie and I seemed to share a bond after that day. Anyway, you know what she's like: friendly and a bit touchy-feely.'

'Not with me, she isn't,' smiled Paul. 'Well, not like she is with you.'

'Tell you what, if I get her in the back of her Volkswagen, you'll be the first to know,' grinned Eric. 'But let's face it, it ain't gonna happen.'

'We've got the house to ourselves today,' Paul said secretively. 'And I've hatched a little plan.'

As Eric followed his friend into the hallway, the buzzer sounded by the fireplace. Hurtling back into the living room, Paul was the first to reach the intercom. 'Hello?'

'Bensteds delivery for J Ramsey.'

'I'll buzz you in, push on the gate.'

Eric and Paul watched through the windows as the gate swung open and the man came through pushing a porter's trolley loaded with four boxes. On top of the packages was a flat orange-striped paper bag.

221

'I hope it's in stereo,' said Paul.

I hope it's not The Sound of Music, thought Eric.

Midway through the twelve days they had waited for the stereo to arrive, Paul and Eric had brought two wooden packing cases down from the attic. The boxes were then positioned against the walls on either side of the wide bay windows to serve as speaker stands. Extra-long speaker wire, purchased from City Radio in Ealing Broadway, had been run beneath the large Indian carpet. The previous evening, the radiogram had been demoted to the ballroom.

'On this one, he's talking about his friends helping him to get high,' Eric said, reading the lyrics on the red back-cover of *Sgt Pepper's Lonely Hearts Club Band*. 'I'm surprised the BBC didn't ban that one, too.'

Paul checked the speaker connections one last time, then switched the new stereo's selector knob to TUNER. 'Wow, the amplifier's got separate controls for bass and treble! Okay, here we go.'

Paul pressed the ON button, and Scott McKenzie's *San Francisco (Be Sure to Wear Flowers in Your Hair)* blasted from the two speakers, filling the big front room with melodic West Coast hippie pop. The audio quality was fabulous.

'It sounds fantastic!' shouted Paul. 'And the volume's only on four!'

Eric grinned widely. 'It's brilliant! Ready for Sergeant Pepper?'

'Nearly.'

Dragging the smaller of the two sofas to a central position facing the stereo speakers, Paul slipped the shiny black LP from its inner sleeve and carefully placed it on the record deck. Switching the selector to PHONO, he brushed the tip of his forefinger gently across the stylus. A low amplified scrape emanated from the angled speakers.

'Right.' Paul lumbered towards the living-room door as if his limbs were made of rubber, 'Walk this way.'

Eric offered the standard reply, 'If I could walk that way, I wouldn't need the talcum powder.'

Paul scaled the stairs two at a time. No words were exchanged as they walked along the red-carpeted second-floor passageway. Beneath a summery blue sky, the sunlit treetops of Fox Wood became visible through the big round window at the end of the corridor.

'Okay.' Paul turned to his right, facing Jack's bedroom door. 'How's your shoulder feeling?'

'My shoulder? Fine thanks. Why?'

'Cos we're going to bash Uncle Jack's door down.'

'We're *what?*'

'Only joking,' said Paul. Flashing Eric a quick grin, he turned to the opposite side of the corridor and walked into his mother's bedroom.

'This is no time to be bird watching from the observation room,' said Eric. 'The *new* Beatles LP is sitting on the *new* turntable of the *new* stereo downstairs.'

'Precisely,' Paul said, maintaining his air of secrecy. 'Have a seat at the dressing table.'

Eric looked at the gold spiral staircase at the far end of the room. He counted nine puppets suspended around it. Paul knelt on the floor, fumbling inside the trunk at the foot of Julia's four-poster bed.

'Got it!' Paul announced triumphantly. He held up an Old Holborn tobacco tin.

Though Eric had never seen the rusty tin, he guessed immediately what his friend had in his hand.

Paul opened the tin and showed Eric its contents. 'As you so rightly said, my friend, *Sergeant Pepper* is waiting downstairs. And if the Beatles were stoned when they made it, *we* should be stoned when we hear it!'

When Paul pulled a packet of ten Gold Leaf cigarettes from one pocket and a box of matches from the other, Eric surmised that his friend's plan had been some time in the making. Paul stuck three Rizla papers together, then removed the tobacco from one of the cigarettes. He might have guessed that Pattie had used the very same trunk top for the very same purpose.

Paul sniffed the large lump of Afghan Black. 'You heat a corner, then crumble it onto the tobacco.'

'Where did you learn that?' asked Eric.

'I saw it on the telly.'

'Where, on *How?*'

'Yeah, *'Okay kids, today I'm going to teach you how to roll a joint using three Rizla's, some tobacco, and a big smelly lump of hash'.'*

'HOW!' they said in unison, holding up their right palms.

'You forgot to mention the cardboard filter.'

'Oh, yeah. Here, you can do that bit.'

Both Eric and Paul suspected that the other knew more about smoking marijuana than they were letting on.

'Is that enough, do you think?' asked Paul.

'I dunno. You missed a bit at the end.'

Unaware that it already contained approximately twice the national average, Paul added more hashish to the joint. The rolling process was the trickiest part.

'It's a bit loose,' Paul observed, eyeing the sagging reefer.

'Twist the end and give it a shake,' suggested Eric.

Paul shook the joint. 'Oh, that's much better. How did you know to do that?'

'I saw it on the telly. Well, the twisted end. The shaking part was basic logic and a smidge of natural genius.'

'We'd better smoke it outside,' said Paul. 'The room already smells like a family of gorillas stayed the night.'

Burying the tobacco tin at the bottom of the trunk, Paul followed Eric out to the corridor and closed his mother's bedroom door.

'Do you ever go into Uncle Jack's room?' asked Eric.

Paul shook his head, 'Mum keeps the door locked.'

Eric chose not to pursue the subject, although he did think it a little mysterious. Julia's mourning period – if that was the reason for the locked door – seemed unusually long and quite out of character. Now that Pattie had become an integral member of the commune, another bedroom would be pragmatic. And perhaps redecorating the deceased man's room would help lay Tony's ghosts to rest.

The two teenage lads trotted down the stairs.

Sitting out the front on the top step, Paul offered Eric the marijuana cigarette. 'Spark her up, my friend.'

'Oh no, your honour,' insisted Eric. 'You rolled the hash; you strike the match.' He thought of Sid.

Paul lit the reefer, inhaled, then blew out the smoke. 'Your turn,' he said, handing it to Eric.

'You have to hold your breath,' Eric said, taking the joint. 'Like this.'

'How long for?'

Holding in the smoke, Eric shrugged. Tiny tendrils trickled from the corners of his mouth, then a long stream emanated towards the garden, dissipating in the still, warm air.

Paul tried again, this time holding the smoke in his lungs. 'Long enough?' he croaked.

Eric nodded. A goofy grin spread across his face.

Paul exhaled. 'I can't feel anything. I wonder if this stuff's any good.' Two lungfuls later, Paul changed his opinion on the potency of the marijuana. 'Cripes, I can feel it now!'

'Me too,' smiled Eric. 'Shall we save the second half for later?'

'Good idea,' said Paul. 'One more puff.'

The sun emerged from behind a gilt-edged cloud, revealing the colourful garden in all its splendour. Butterflies fluttered above the dazzling array of flowers. Somewhere in the greenwood, a songbird tunefully hailed the arrival of summer.

'The sun feels great,' said Eric.

'And the wild garden looks amazing,' added Paul.

'Yeah.'

'I feel euphorical rhetorical.'

'Is that like a persuasive happy euphonium?' asked Eric.

'Yeah, I bought one from a cycling rabbit.'

'Never trust a bunny on a bicycle.'

'There he is,' said Paul, pointing to the overgrown fallen statue of Aphrodite.

'I see him,' said Eric. 'I met him when I arrived.'

The small brown rabbit sat on its haunches, twitching its nose and studying the two teenagers, then hopped down from the broken statue and scurried into the undergrowth.

Wiggling his toes, Paul turned to his friend on the step beside him, 'Could it be *Pepper time?*'

'Nah, let's stay here and look at the garden for a few weeks.'

Paul leaned back on his elbows, an expression of serenity on his face. 'Sounds great to me.'

When they entered the wood-panelled hallway, the musty odour propelled Eric back to his first visit to the old house two years earlier. It felt like ten years, or was it yesterday? Time had always been a mystery to him.

Sitting on the sofa in front of the stereo speakers, Eric studied the *Sergeant Pepper* cover while Paul opened the row of windows. A fresh, delicate fragrance permeated the room.

'The people at Kew could learn a thing or two from that garden,' said Eric. 'Your mum had the right idea: chuck the seeds any-old-where and see what happens.'

Paul walked over to the record player, 'If you see one of my Triffids coming up the path, close the windows quick.'

Side by side on the sofa, Eric and Paul gazed out as the orchestra tuned up. Then the most famous group in the world launched into the title track, *Sgt Pepper's Lonely Hearts Club Band*. If the singer were to be believed, it was not the Beatles playing on the record that bore their name, but Sergeant Pepper's band.

The opening song segued into *A Little Help from My Friends*. 'Who's Billy Shears?' asked Paul.

The two friends agreed that this was undoubtedly Ringo's best vocal track. The album's first blockbuster, *Lucy in the Sky with Diamonds,* was up next. John Lennon sang this one. Underpinned by a haunting keyboard motif, the lyrics conjured colourful, surreal images of a weird and wonderful fairyland world. Eric loved it immediately. Half closing his eyes, he watched the sunlit flowers outside merge into a giant kaleidoscopic cluster. As the final chorus faded, the two teenagers turned to one another,

'Drugs.'

Neither had yet noticed that if the nouns in the title *Lucy in the Sky with Diamonds* were written as an acronym, they spelt LSD. Three Paul McCartney songs followed: *Getting Better, Fixing a Hole,* and *She's Leaving Home.* Backed by a lush string arrangement, the latter told of a runaway girl and her parents' distress upon discovering that their daughter had left home to meet a motorcar salesman. Side one concluded with *Being For the Benefit of Mr Kite,* an atmospheric trip to the circus, courtesy of ringmaster Lennon.

Paul raised his eyebrows enquiringly, 'Well, well, my friend, what do we have here?'

Eric shook his head. 'I don't know how the Beatles do it, but it's getting better every time.'

'I was going to suggest another smoke, but...'

'But we might go for a walk on the ceiling,' said Eric.

'Yeah. Let's put on side two.'

George's only song on the LP was another Indian-inspired offering. *Within You Without You* featured sitar, tamboura, swarmandal and a dilruba, augmented by a traditional western string section. No other Beatles were in evidence.

'What's he singing about?' asked Eric.

'It's a dream he had after getting hit over the head by a Bombay duck.'

'Ah, it all makes sense now.'

McCartney then sang a jolly vaudeville song about getting old, called *When I'm Sixty Four.* Paul's *Lovely Rita*, a song about a parking attendant, was followed by another of John's. *Good Morning Good Morning* was full of odd musical bars.

'Sounds like the Corn Flakes advert,' observed Eric.

The penultimate song on the album presaged the end of the show with a sped-up reprise of the opening track, *Sgt Pepper's Lonely Hearts Club Band*.

An acoustic guitar strummed the opening chords to *A Day in the Life*. 'This is the one they banned,' said Paul.

The lyrics might have been jumbled up and picked randomly out of a hat, but the effect was mesmerising.

Paul raised an eyebrow, 'So, he'd love to turn us on, would he? Not much doubt about the connotations there.'

'Then he went to the top of a bus, lit up, and started dreaming,' added Eric. 'Maybe we should have another smoke and try our hands at songwriting.'

'Great idea, but not right now.' Paul pointed through the window.

Wow, they're short, Eric thought, admiring Julia and Pattie's matching black miniskirts. The two women walked up the path in the sunshine. Both wore sunglasses. Pattie was holding a white paper bag that could only contain an LP. The heavily made-up Twins entered the living room and kicked off their shoes.

'You're home early,' said Paul. 'How did it go?'

'Great, I think,' beamed Julia. She turned to her friend.

'Bloody fantastic!' said Pattie. 'Your mum's a natural, Paul. We had the whole thing done and dusted in a couple of hours. The photographer was raving about your mum's legs.'

Eric was not surprised; the photographer obviously knew his trade. 'Where was the photo session?'

'Up the road in Acton,' replied Pattie. 'Not exactly Mayfair, but the studio was state-of-the-art.'

'I see the stereo's arrived,' observed Julia. 'Are you pleased with it?'

'It's stunningly amazingly fabuloso,' answered Paul. As the words left his mouth, he remembered he was stoned.

'That good!' grinned Julia. 'Ah! Look at the cover!' She held the Sergeant Pepper sleeve up in front of the open windows. 'It looks like it belongs out there among the flowers!'

'Eric did that with the last one,' said Paul. 'When I took Revolver out of the bag, he started comparing Eleanor Rigby to the weather.'

'Oh dear, it appears you're surrounded by artists, darling,' Julia said theatrically. 'Come on, Pats, let's go upstairs and get ourselves sorted out.'

Don't change your clothes, please, thought Eric.

'The photographer was playing this during the shoot,' Pattie said, holding up the LP bag. 'We stopped at Smiths on the way home and bought a copy. Don't play it till we come back downstairs.'

The Twins' laughing voices echoed down the hallway.

'Blimey, they're happy,' Eric said quietly.

'Just as well,' said Paul. 'I thought I'd blown it with *stunningly amazingly fabuloso.*'

'Oh, don't get paranoid,' replied Eric. 'You often say things like that.'

'Do I? Oh, okay, good.' Paul breathed an exaggerated sigh of relief. 'Any guesses?' he asked, eyeing the paper bag on the coffee table.

'My money's on Val Doonican.'

'I don't think you'll find *Paddy McGinty's Goat* on here,' Paul said, sliding out the record.

Eric and Paul sat outside on the porch steps while Jimi Hendrix waited on the coffee table. High above to their left, they heard the sound of a sash window being raised. Paul peered up and watched a cloud of smoke emerge from the second-floor bedroom. He beckoned to his friend. The two longhaired lads walked quickly past the open living-room windows and turned the corner. Nettles bordered the trodden pathway that ran between the side of the house and the high garden wall.

'What if they know?' Eric asked warily.

'They won't.' Paul reached into his pocket, 'They'll be stoned themselves by now, guaranteed. And I'll bet you anything Mum'll crack open a bottle of wine. If they notice us acting funny, they'll put it down to the booze.'

Having finished the heavily loaded reefer, Eric and Paul returned to the living room. Taking an end each, they moved the small sofa back to its usual place by the coffee table. 'The pot's creeping up again,' Eric whispered.

Pattie came in first with four clinking glasses, followed by Julia, holding a bottle of rosé. Paul gave Eric a look that said, *I told you so.* Eric noted that the Twins had not changed their clothes.

Julia sat facing the window and began opening the wine. 'So what's the new Beatles LP like?' she asked Eric.

Eric thought for a moment. 'It's incredibly visual: like a scrapbook of sketches from everyday life, given a twist, and put to music. I think you'll really like it.'

'That's a lovely description, Eric.' Julia poured out four full glasses of the sweet pink wine, 'I'm sure I shall.'

'Here's to Julia's modelling career and to Sergeant Pepper,' Pattie said, raising her glass.

'My modelling *day,* you mean,' replied Julia. Smiling, she consented, 'Oh, okay then.'

A spontaneous cheer was followed by brief silence as all four drank to Julia and the eponymous moustachioed sergeant.

'Right,' said Pattie. 'Before we listen to the Beatles, how about a bit of Jimi?'

'Loud as you like!' Julia called, springing to her feet and draining the wine from her glass. Paul cued up the first track on *Are You Experienced.* Julia quickly poured herself another. Paul edged up the volume.

Feedback howled through the big speakers. Pattie and Julia ran to the open area in front of the door. Draping themselves across one another, they affected a camp melodramatic modelling pose. Paul crouched in front of the two women taking pictures with an imaginary camera. Eric wished he had a real one. The song kicked in, Jimi leading the band with a grinding mid-tempo guitar riff: tortured yet dulcet and charged with a demonic sexuality. Interpreting the music with their bodies, Julia and Pattie twisted and writhed, their hips jerking and swaying, their arms entwining like courting cobras above their heads. *Foxy Lady!*

Paul danced with them. Rooted in his seat, Eric could only sit and watch.

As the song neared its conclusion, Julia sashayed towards the sofa where Eric was sitting. She stepped up onto the coffee table, her green eyes flashing as she registered Eric's glance. Julia danced above him on the table, weaving her raised arms hypnotically and gyrating her hips. Though he was aware that the others were watching, Eric had to look up. He had glimpsed Julia's panties many times, but never had he been so obviously invited to look at them. Laughing, Julia skipped down to the floor.

'Oh, now you're just showing off!' grinned Pattie. 'Just because the photographer said you had nice legs.'

Julia placed her hand on her hip, feigning offence. 'Showing off? Do I detect a teensy-weensy touch of jealousy from the little blonde bombshell?'

Pattie struck a haughty pose. 'Me? Jealous of your legs? Hardly, darling,' she jibed. 'Anyway, mine are every bit as good, if not better.'

Betty Grable would be jealous of these,' Julia said, hiking up her already short skirt.

Eric stared at his friend's mother, stoned and utterly convinced that Julia was lifting her skirt for him.

The boys settled the lovely legs contest by declaring an amicable draw.

The high spirits gradually died down. Following Pepper's second play-through, Pattie and Eric sat together on the small sofa opposite Paul and his tipsy mother. The Kinks' *Waterloo Sunset* played quietly in the background.

Pattie picked up her wineglass from the coffee table, 'You have your foot in the door now, Jules. If you're offered more modelling work, will you take it?'

'That's a big *if.*'

'Nonsense,' said Pattie. 'You were fabulous in front of the camera today, and they have your photo on file now. So *if* one day the phone rings, will you say yes?'

Julia gazed out at the flower-filled garden. 'I felt ten years younger today, Pats. Time marches on, and it's unlikely an opportunity like that would ever come my way again. So yes, being honest, *if* I were offered more modelling work, I'd probably take it.'

'Well, that's fantastic,' said Pattie. 'You're a long way from middle-age, Jules, let alone the other.'

'Oh, I know that,' replied Julia. 'But I think it's always wise to look ahead.'

Pattie shrugged, 'All we have is today, Jules. Why worry about tomorrow?'

'I take your point, Pats, but if we don't make some provision for the future... Ultimately, the world will become like a big Easter Island with warring tribes fighting over arable land. And eventually, like the people on the island, we'll all die out.'

'Do we care?'

'Apparently not.'

'No, really, I'm just asking the question. Does it *matter* if the human race survives?'

Julia thought for a moment. 'I think you've got me there, Pats. Well,' she concluded, 'it's probably best if we *pretend* it matters.'

'And on what do you base that assumption?' asked Paul.

Pattie laughed, 'You sound like your mother.'

Julia held her hands up, 'Guilty! Anyone for coffee?'

Pattie shook her head, 'Jules, only *you* could turn a conversation about modelling into a debate about saving humanity.'

'Don't take any notice, Mum,' said Paul. 'You can save the planet *and* look gorgeous at the same time.'

Julia smiled, 'Thank you, Paul. What do you say we postpone the coffee and open another bottle?'

Five minutes later, Julia and Paul followed Pattie and Eric out into the sunny front garden. Birds sang in the surrounding trees.

'It's beautiful, isn't it,' Paul said, sitting on the warm porch step and looking at the multi-coloured garden.

'Glorious,' agreed his mother. She joined him on the step. 'I'm sure Jack would be pleased to see his lovely flowers in bloom.'

Paul shaded his eyes, watching Pattie and Eric amble slowly along the central path. 'Mum, do you think those two are –'

'No,' said Julia. 'I think they like each other, that's all.'

Paul nodded and sipped his rosé.

'So what do you think of it, Paul?' inquired his mother.

'The wine?'

'No, the marijuana.'

19

The Summer of Love

Swivelling agitatedly on his garden seat, Paul McCartney admitted to having taken LSD, then told the ITN news reporter that he didn't think his fans would be inclined to take drugs because he had.

'Well, Paul,' Julia said to the television, 'you've just made arguably the greatest, most *creative* pop album ever, and everyone believes that you were on drugs when you did it. I have to say that with Sergeant Pepper, you and your mates have unleashed the most persuasive advertisement for recreational drugs the world will ever know.'

'The references are quite subtle,' said Paul.

Julia shrugged, 'Subliminal advertising is the most insidious kind. I wouldn't be surprised if, in the long term, the Beatles' association with drugs turns out to be a bigger part of their legacy than their music.'

'You smoke pot.'

'Yes,' said Julia. 'And between the Beatles and me, we're responsible for you trying it, too. I have to live with that, and in a general way, so do they.'

Eric sat quietly next to Paul. He thought Julia's criticism of the Beatles a little harsh, but her phrase, *subliminal advertising is the most insidious kind*, carried deeper connotations for him. Suppressing the thought, he pushed MoD2 back into a dark recess of his mind.

Ron Hillman was the only pupil to leave Paul and Eric's school at the earliest opportunity. Commencing an apprenticeship with his uncle's building firm, the former paperboy traded in his satchel for a brickie's hod and set off to cement his future.

The summer break stretched before Eric like an endless golden road. Paul made plans for riverside walks and trips to the seaside. Even Tony, who had been troubled following the move to the Ealing House, showed glimpses of his former self.

Tony tapped the drum break from *Wipe Out* on the edge of the kitchen table. 'Fancy a jam when Eric gets here?'

'Definitely,' replied Paul. 'We're overdue a good thrash.'

'No prob. Drop yer trousers, and I'll get me sticks.'

Eric's lead guitar playing had taken a giant leap forward in recent months. Having mastered the intro lick to Johnny Kidd and the Pirates' *Shakin' All Over*, he realised that by playing the same notes in a random order, he could improvise solos *ad infinitum*. Moving the pattern up or down the neck enabled him to solo in any key. Eric had discovered *boxes:* imaginary shapes on the instrument's fretboard comprising related notes in major and minor scales. This led to a search for more boxes, three or four of which he committed to memory. *Bends, hammer-on's* and *pull-off's* augmented his playing. He found finger vibrato challenging at first, but his technique was improving with every practice session. Eric listened carefully to Eric Clapton's playing on John Mayall's *Beano* album and Cream's *Fresh Cream*. He also learned parts from Jimi Hendrix's *Are You Experienced* LP, though the American guitarist's distinctive touch was difficult, if not impossible, to emulate. And Jimi seemed to play outside the boxes.

'Nice crash pad you've built for yourself,' Eric said, inspecting Tony's collection of miscellanea by the ballroom sofa. 'I see Mickey's still here.'

'Mick gets me up for my paper round,' Tony replied from behind his drum kit. 'Some mornings I want to kick his fuckin' 'ead in, but he keeps me in the job.'

Tuning his bass, Paul eyed the old-fashioned twin-belled alarm clock. 'Doesn't the ticking drive you nuts?'

'I've had it since I can remember,' replied Tony. 'I can't sleep without it now. I'd be lost without me clockwork mouse.'

'That's it!' exclaimed Eric.

'That's what?'

'The name of our group – Clockwork Mouse.'

All three agreed that the rendition of *Wipe Out* that followed was the best ever. Apparently, having a name made you play better.

That Sunday evening, Julia and the personnel of Clockwork Mouse gathered in the living room for the first live global television link-up. Conceived by the BBC, the transmission would enable viewers worldwide to watch the same live television programme simultaneously.

Made possible by satellite technology, Our World's objective was to feature contributions from every corner of the globe. It would be a celebration of international unity. Protesting against western involvement in the Arab-Israeli Six-Day War, the Soviet Union elected to pull out.

'It's such a shame about Russia,' said Julia. 'Bringing everyone together like this was such a lovely idea.'

'I didn't want to see a bunch of smelly Cossacks doing their stupid dancing anyway,' said Tony.

'It's not just about the entertainment,' Julia explained patiently. 'It brings to mind something Thomas Paine wrote: *My country is the world, and my religion is to do good*. If we all saw the world as one country –'

Tony scoffed, 'Oh, give over, Mum. We're only watching this to see the bloody Beatles.'

'Well, I'm glad we're all watching it together,' Julia said, snuggling up to her youngest son. 'I'm looking forward to seeing *the bloody Beatles*, too.'

On the other side of Ealing, Reg was snuggling up with a cup of tea and a cigarette. The postman winced as Cliff Michelmore explained about the satellite link-up that would make the worldwide broadcast possible.

Paul yawned. They had sat through a tedious two-and-a-half hours of babies being born, steel manufacturing, fishing, swimming, show jumping, canoeing, scuba diving and opera. The Beatles finally appeared on the monochrome television clothed in Pepperesque hippy garb and surrounded by friends and flowers. A pack of Embassy cigarettes stood prominently on the mixing console at Abbey Road. Producer George Martin directed the small orchestra to take their places in the studio. 'The Beatles get on best with classical musicians,' said BBC reporter Steve Race.

Paul folded his arms, 'Not by the look of the people sitting around them, they don't.'

Eagle-eyed viewers may have spotted pop luminaries Mick Jagger, Keith Richards, Marianne Faithfull, Eric Clapton and Keith Moon, sitting on the floor among the cross-legged observers. All looked resplendent, dressed in their flamboyant hippie regalia.

'Even the Stones have turned on to flower power,' observed Eric. 'I wonder what their next LP will sound like.'

'Echoey, I expect,' Julia said dryly. 'There's no wallpaper or soft furnishings in jail cells.'

The message that the Beatles sent worldwide to four hundred million viewers was *All You Need is Love.*

Reg had tired of the television programme hours before the *Fabs* came on. 'That's disgusting,' he muttered, watching old Flo down a pint of milk stout at a corner table in the Forester. Laughter erupted from the public bar, followed by the sound of slapping dominoes. The postman meandered unsteadily towards the door. The numbing effects of six pints and four shorts had failed to erase the Scientist's letter from his mind. *Bloody satellites*, he thought. *They should shoot 'em all down.*

*

'Who Breaks a Butterfly On a Wheel?' Julia read from the first of July edition of the Times. 'The editor has come out on the side of Mick and Keith. I have to say, sentencing Keith Richards to a year in prison was quite over the top.'

'It just serves to widen the gap between the establishment and us,' said Pattie. 'Bring on the revolution.'

Keith flew down to the kitchen table and began nibbling the remains of Julia's toast.

'The BBC are beginning their colour transmissions today,' said Julia. 'Wimbledon's to be the first. I suppose Paul will be asking me to buy a colour television next.'

Pattie picked up a crust that Keith had flung onto the floor, 'They say that money can't buy happiness, but a colour telly would be nice.'

'Oh, I'm not concerned about Paul in that way. He understands that you can't buy happiness over a shop counter.'

'Unless it comes in a box marked *colour telly.*'

'We all enjoy the new stereo,' replied Julia. 'The problems arise when people lose perspective and start buying any old thing just to cheer themselves up for five minutes. It's an easy trap to fall into, and the availability of credit opens the door.'

'I wonder if you're underestimating Joe Public,' said Pattie. 'Do you think people are that gullible?'

'Actually, yes.'

'Really? Everybody *knows* that advertisers are there to persuade –'

'Yes,' said Julia. 'But we've become desensitised to it. To deflect their brainwashing, we have to *think!* And too many people can't be bothered. Maybe that's changing with the arrival of the counter-culture.'

'*I've* been thinking,' Paul said, entering the kitchen. 'How would you feel about us getting a colour television?'

Julia looked up at her son, 'We'll wait till the prices come down.'

*

In the early hours of Sunday the 16th of July 1967, Paul lay awake in his darkened room listening to *The Perfumed Garden* on pirate station, Radio London. The air was warm and still on that clear summer night. Paul gazed through the open window at the twinkling stars above Fox Wood.

In this edition of his radio show, John Peel's sounds from the underground would include Freddie King's *Driving Sideways*, the Doors' *Crystal Ship*, the Beatles' *Lucy in the Sky with Diamonds* and Roger McGough's poem *The Day Before Yesterday*. Between his selections, disc-jockey-to-the-hippies Peel announced that a *happening* was to take place in Hyde Park later that day. He claimed ignorance as to the nature of the event but urged his audience to attend. The DJ said listeners to his Perfumed Garden show would be identifiable by the light emanating from their foreheads.

The following morning, the occupants of the Ealing House gathered in the living room. Eric looked out at the sunny flower-filled garden while Pink Floyd's *See Emily Play* played quietly on the radio.

Tony had accepted his mother's invitation. 'Oh, good,' Julia said nonchalantly, while inwardly falling through the floor. 'Hyde Park's lovely, especially in the summertime.'

'I'll drive,' offered Pattie. 'My Beetle's roomier than your Mini. A bit, anyway.'

A short time later, the two young women and the *three* lads left the house.

The two smallest of the four passengers, Tony and Julia, got in the back of Pattie's VW.

Paul turned to Eric, 'I'll let you sit next to your girlfriend,' he whispered, squeezing in next to his mother.

Eric smiled. His friend's suggestion added a fanciful touch of validity to his daydreams. And if Paul believed there to be some truth in his witticism, that was perfectly fine.

July 1967 had been particularly hot, and that sunny Sunday was no exception. The lads wore T-shirts and jeans, though Paul and Eric's long hair identified them as followers of the hippie path. Tony was getting there, his dark-brown ruff now partially hiding his ears.

A string of top-thirty hits elevated the Ealing crowd's spirits as they drove through Acton, Shepherds Bush and Notting Hill. Permanently tuned to Radio London, the purple Volkswagen's radio blasted current chart-busters including, the Monkees' *Alternate Title*, the Hollies' *Carrie-Anne*, Dave Davies' *Death of a Clown*, Nancy Sinatra's James Bond theme song *You Only Live Twice*, and Cream's psychedelic blues single *Strange Brew*. Pedestrians on the Bayswater Road were treated to a full-throated sing-along to the Turtles' *She'd Rather Be with Me*. Predictably, the Beatles currently occupied the number-one spot with their hippie anthem *All You Need is Love*. Parking on the north side near Lancaster Gate station, they entered Hyde Park by the Serpentine's end.

Groups of extravagantly dressed hippies headed towards the main gathering at Speakers' Corner. Their homemade placards disclosed the nature of the event: the Ealing crowd had arrived at a rally organised by the underground to promote pot's legalisation.

Julia pointed in the direction of Kensington Gardens, 'Let's take a detour first.'

Following the sunlit path on the west side of the Long Water, they came upon the bronze statue of Peter Pan. Covertly commissioned by author J. M. Barrie and recessed in a bushy clearing, the figure marked the spot where young Peter would begin his adventures.

Pattie delved into her tapestry shoulder bag and pulled out her camera. Eric's eyes lit up when he saw the Pentax.

Pattie removed the lens cap. 'Right, let's have you three guys around the statue. This'll be the first official shot of Clockwork Mouse.'

'Great idea!' Julia combed Tony's hair with her fingers.

Pattie's first two photographs would show the group cracking up in response to Tony's joke involving Peter Pan, Tinkerbell, and a bottle of dog shit. The third shot met with the photographer's approval. With a parting glance at the fairytale statue, the party continued through Hyde Park towards Speakers' Corner.

Five-thousand people attended the *Legalise Pot Rally*, the majority of them high on the illegal drug. Despite a high-visibility police presence, demonstrators smoked defiantly in front of the uniformed officers, who showed no interest in enforcing the disputed law.

'We should be wearing hats,' Julia said as they approached the large hippie gathering. 'We'll all end up with sunstroke in this heat.'

Pattie pointed to a giant leafy oak tree, 'How about over there? We could sit in the shade and watch from a distance.'

'I'm glad you said that,' Julia confided. 'I'd prefer to give Tony the impression we're here as spectators. I wouldn't have invited him if we'd known what the event was about.'

Pattie nodded, 'Five minutes people watching, then we'll head for the lake.'

Bearded Allen Ginsburg appeared on a stepladder surrounded by placard-carrying demonstrators. *Love Love Love,* read one sign. *Flower Power Now*, said another. *Legalise Pot, Pass Joy*.

A *Free Hoppy* banner referred to the jailing of affable counterculture organiser John Hopkins for possession of a tiny amount of marijuana. Sentencing Hopkins to nine months in Wormwood Scrubs, the judge described the political activist as *a pest to society*. Their infuriation compounded by Jagger and Richards' arrests, the audience at Hoppy's UFO club spontaneously marched to Fleet Street to protest over The News of the World's involvement in the scandal. Confronted by a longhaired legion armed with bongos and flutes, the police were totally unprepared.

'There's not much to see except a big crowd of people,' said Julia. She sat beneath the green outstretched branches of the oak tree. 'Let's rest here for a few minutes, then go and have something to eat.'

Accompanying himself on a portable harmonium, Ginsburg stood on his stepladder singing and chanting. Waving his finger in the air, he dedicated his next poetic offering to the god Shiva, god of meditation, aestheticism, birth, death, change, creation, destruction... and ganja.

'Is that two blokes *kissing*?' exclaimed Tony.

'Parliament has just changed the laws on homosexuality,' said Julia. 'You can't blame them for celebrating.'

'Being a homo should be illegal,' argued Tony.

'That's like making it a crime to be over six feet tall,' replied his mother.

'Hey baby,' said an American hippie in a short red military jacket. Grinning lopsidedly, he seated himself on the grass next to Pattie. 'Ya look like ya could use a smoke.'

'Oh, no thanks,' Pattie replied, eyeing the joint in the man's hand.

'Suit yourself,' shrugged the longhaired American. He took a deep drag and wobbled. 'I wus at Monterey last month. Two hun'red thousan' people... Jimi Hen'rix, Janis Joplin, the Who... Man, that Ravi *Shanker*. Somethin' else, man.' The stoned American leaned-in close to Pattie. 'You look like Michelle Phillips from the Mamas an' the Papas. Man, that chick –'

'Hello,' said a girl in a blue Indian dress. Smiling sweetly at Pattie, she handed the blonde a business card and walked on.

'Release,' read Pattie. *I could do with your help right now.*

'Git-outta-jail-free card,' explained the American. 'Caroline Coon. Keep it with ya in case y'ever git busted. Far out, man.'

Julia stood up, brushing her dress. 'We should be going.'

'Oh, okay.' Pattie glanced back, 'Nice talking to you.'

'Peace,' said the man, flashing the two-fingered sign.

'Ommm,' said Allen Ginsburg

Painted pedalos and wooden rowing boats shared the sparkling Serpentine with swans, mallards and white-capped coots.

Eric and Julia sat together on the concrete bank, dangling their feet in the lake. 'The water feels lovely,' the teenager said, tossing his bread crust to a nearby swan.

'You've got knobbly knees,' teased Julia, looking down at Eric's rolled-up jeans.

'You haven't.'

'Okay, you haven't either then. Penny for your thoughts?'

'My mum brought me here once,' Eric said, enjoying the memory. 'It was sunny, like today. We had cheese and tomato sandwiches made with white bread.'

'This was her world then.' Julia circled her feet in the rejuvenating water. 'It belongs to you now.'

'To us,' replied Eric.

Julia's green eyes flashed, her fringe wavering in the breeze. 'Yes, to us,' she murmured. 'To us!' she called, twisting and raising her cup.

'To us!' replied Paul, smiling and spilling his Pepsi.

Beside him on the grass, Tony and Pattie lay nose to nose, locked in an arm-wrestling bout.

'*Gyyyerk!*' Pattie rolled onto her back as Tony forced her forearm to the ground.

'She let you win,' said Paul.

'Not a chance,' said Tony. 'Did you hear the one about *Little Billy*?'

'No, but I think we're about to.'

'Little Billy looks into his parents' bedroom. His dad's sitting on the edge of the bed putting a rubber Johnny on his willy. Billy's dad sees his son at the door and quickly leans forward. *Why are you leaning forward, Dad?*' asks Little Billy. *'I thought I saw a rat on the floor,'* says his dad. And Billy says, *'Oh really? Were you gonna fuck it?'*'

Pattie made light of Tony's dirty joke: 'That was a trifle *blue*, young man,' she said in a posh accent. 'I'll have you know I'm a fucking lady!'

Everyone laughed.

'I'd fuck you in a second,' quipped Tony.

This was awkward.

Pattie preempted Julia with her reply, 'I'll take that as a compliment, Tony, but I've had nicer ones.'

The difficult moment passed.

Julia walked ahead, flanked by her two sons.

Eric and Pattie followed the three Ramsey's along the path by the lake. 'Well done,' Eric said quietly.

'I didn't think,' replied Pattie. 'It just came out.'

Julia took her sons' arms.

'Camera,' Eric said, reaching into Pattie's bag.

*

'Tournament?' enquired Eric.

'Yes,' replied his mother, taking her tennis racquet from the arm of the sofa. 'A semifinal against one of the top seeds. I'll have to be at my best. Oh, that friend of yours, Phil, called yesterday. His number's on the pad by the phone.'

'Thanks, Mum.' Eric followed her into the hall.

Mary shouldered her kitbag, 'Bye, see you later.'

Eric sat on the stool next to the telephone table. 'Bye Mum, good luck.' He glanced up at her white tennis outfit and flashed back to his childhood, remembering the tennis matches he had watched from the sidelines with his father.

As usual, Phil was in good spirits. 'Right now would be a good time,' said the voice on the phone. 'We'd have the place to ourselves for a few hours.'

'That's fine with me,' replied Eric. 'But my electric guitar's in Ealing Broadway.'

'No problem,' answered Phil. 'Except you've spoiled my surprise.'

'How do you mean?'

'I've just bought a Gibson SG, so you can play my Telecaster if you like.'

'I'll be there in ten minutes,' said Eric. 'Make that five!'

Eric cycled through the backstreets enjoying the hot July sun on his face. He thought of strawberries and cream. When he arrived at Phil's house, the happy hobbit-man was waiting in the doorway, his curly brown hair cascading onto his shoulders.

Having introduced Eric to his brand new cherry-red Gibson, Phil led the way upstairs. Opening his bedroom window, he sat on the edge of his bed, placing his Sergeant Pepper album flat on his lap. 'Eric, thanks again for helping me down from that scaffolding.' Phil opened the drawer in his bedside cabinet, 'You saved my life, man.'

'I wouldn't go that far,' smiled Eric. He looked out of the open rear window into Lammas Park. Freed temporarily by the summer holidays, boys played football, watched by girls in white socks. 'Anyway, you would have done the same for me.'

'I'd like to think so, man,' replied Phil. He opened an Indian trinket box and began arranging its contents on the colourful LP cover.

Eric noted that Phil had called him *man* in his last two sentences.

Phil pulled three cigarette papers from an orange pack. 'Your girlfriend's beautiful. Long blonde hair, blue eyes, the face of an angel. She must've been made in hippie heaven. Is the little black-haired babe her sister?'

'No, but they were known as *the Twins* at art college.'

Phil looked up, 'If you feel inclined to arrange a double-date, I'll be sure to cancel any previous engagements.'

'I'll keep that in mind,' replied Eric. He decided he had enjoyed Phil's mistaken assumption for long enough. 'The problem is, Pattie's not my girlfriend.'

'Oh... Damn. Just good friends?'

'Yep.'

'Well, you have great taste in companions, man.'

Joining Eric by the open sash window, Phil lit the joint.

Ten minutes later, in the front room, Eric fiddled with the tone controls on the muscular sounding Gibson SG.

'Have you seen this?' Phil passed Eric a recent copy of the Times. 'My mate Harry told me about this advert.'

The full-page advertisement featured a box bearing the line: *The law against marijuana is immoral in principle and unworkable in practice.* All four Beatles had signed the petition, along with their manager Brian Epstein. Fifty-three prominent others included, David Bailey, Francis Crick, David Dimbleby, David Hockney, Graham Greene and George Melly. Several doctors were among the signatories, as well as renegade MP Tom Driberg.

'Paul McCartney paid for the advert,' explained Phil. 'Pot'll be made legal soon. By the way, did you like the joint?'

'Brilliant,' grinned Eric. 'I don't remember coming downstairs.'

'Let me know if you want any,' said Phil. 'My friend deals a bit. Only to mates – nothing bigtime – but I can get it for you.'

'Thanks,' said Eric. 'I may take you up on that one day.'

'Anytime,' said Phil. 'Here's a little lump to be going on with.'

Eric studied the brown ball of hashish on his palm. 'Oh, that's really nice of you, Phil, but –'

'No buts,' replied the hippie hobbit. 'It's a little *thank you* for getting me off that scaffolding. Besides, we gotta spread the love, man.'

*

Aside from a brief spell of unsettled weather in the middle of the month, the long hot summer of 1967 continued throughout August. Temperatures approached eighty degrees Fahrenheit during the final week.

Eric cycled past Haven Green on his way to the Ealing House. The Flowerpot Men's infuriatingly catchy hippy hit *Let's Go to San Francisco* resisted his attempts to eject it from his head. The summer had been a good one for girl-watching, and some of Ealing's prettiest were in evidence that Saturday lunchtime. A longhaired young man with an acoustic guitar sang for a group of them on the green. Even Bob

Dylan's *Love Minus Zero/No Limit* failed to budge the Flowerpot Men from Eric's internal record player.

At the top of Hanger Hill, Eric stopped as Julia's white Mini pulled up alongside him. She opened the driver's door, scraping the pavement with the lower edge.

'Can I take your bag, madam?' asked Eric.

'Thank you, young man.' Julia passed him the large carrier.

Eric watched her slide out of the car. In her orange minidress, he thought Julia eclipsed every one of the girls on the green. He hooked her bag onto his handlebar.

'How did it go last night?' Eric asked as they walked through the leafy shaded tunnel.

'It went well, I think,' answered Julia. 'It was strange at first, doing the modelling session without Pattie. But I soon got used to it, and the photographer seemed pleased. We finished the shoot with another session this morning.'

'Yeah, I thought you looked heavily made-up,' said Eric. 'What were you modelling?'

'Tights, mostly,' replied Julia. 'Which is ironic as I never wear them.'

'You don't need them,' Eric said, glancing down at Julia's legs.

'Why, thank you. Compliments are always welcome. Actually, the photographer said the same thing.'

Eric decided that fashion photography was, without a doubt, the best job in the world.

Julia opened the green wooden gate.

Pushing his bicycle into the garden, Eric was once again struck by the multicoloured mass of flowers. 'I bet John Peel would appreciate *this* perfumed garden.' He wondered if one day, someone would invent a way to transmit smells through the radio.

Julia squinted up at her bedroom window, 'Oh, Pattie's here. I wasn't expecting her till later.'

Leaving their shoes in the hallway, they went into the living room. Eric placed the carrier bag on the carpet.

'I'll go up and find Pattie,' said Julia.

'Okay. Could you tell Paul and Tony I'm here if you see them.'

'Will do.' Julia left the room.

Eric looked out at the sunlit flowers, remembering that he and Paul sat on the porch steps sharing their first joint. The low throb of a bass guitar rumbled from behind the bookshelves.

'Hello squire,' Eric said, entering the ballroom and closing the door behind him.

'Welcome, my friend,' Paul replied in his mock-aristocratic voice. 'I forgot, you now have a key to this crumbling abode. Is this the first time you've had occasion to use it?'

'I met your mum on the way in,' said Eric.

'Ah, my mother, the famous fashion model.'

'That's the one.' Eric slipped his finger into the plectrum pocket on his Levi's. He held up the foil-wrapped ball, 'I come bearing spliffs.'

'Yeah!' Paul exclaimed, improvising a swift crescendo on his bass.

'The thing is, you're gonna have to go up and pinch some Rizla's and a cigarette from your mum's room.'

'You're looking at the craftiest cat burglar in London,' said Paul. 'I've burgled cats from the rich and famous.'

As Paul and Eric left the ballroom, Julia was coming down the stairs.

'Hello Mum, how was the photo session?' asked Paul.

'Very good,' smiled Julia. 'And there'll be a cheque in the post on Monday which may go some way towards that colour television.'

The front door swung open and Pattie walked into the hall wearing a bright-green minidress. 'Oh, a welcoming committee! You shouldn't have.' She bent down, unzipping her boots.

'That's strange,' said Julia. 'I thought you were upstairs.'

'Mm, I don't think so,' Pattie replied, looking down at herself.

'Perhaps it was Tony you saw?' suggested Eric.

Paul shook his head, 'Tony went out ages ago.'

Julia shrugged, 'I was probably hallucinating.' She smiled, 'It's a beautiful day. Shall we go out somewhere nice?'

An hour later, Julia, Pattie, Paul and Eric found themselves in the gardens of Chiswick House. A tall white obelisk stood in a circular clearing near the gate on Burlington Lane. This corner of the sixty-five-acre estate was deserted, save for a scurry of grey squirrels and a pair of warring crows. Sunlight dappled the pathway as they passed along an avenue of beech trees, heading towards another of the park's neoclassical features.

Eric saw Julia look about her, then nod to Pattie. The two women veered off the path, making for a bushy thicket near the high perimeter wall.

Maybe this is our lucky day, mused Eric, in a hopelessly optimistic rush of wishful thinking.

Paul looked at his friend, 'Are we supposed to follow?'

The answer came when Pattie half-turned, motioning for them to hurry.

Pushing through the foliage, Eric looked down into a little green bowl. Silver-birch trees and buddleia bushes surrounded the small grassy hollow. At a hidden spot like this in any other public grounds, there would typically be empty beer cans and discarded food wrappers; this estate was pristine. Julia sat on one side of the dell while Pattie perched on the opposite bank holding a book of matches and a joint.

Eric knew where Pattie concealed her stash and wished he had arrived a few seconds sooner.

'Come and sit down,' urged Julia. 'And everyone keep your eyes peeled. They haven't legalised it yet.'

Pattie lit the reefer.

Julia turned to Eric, 'Paul and I have smoked together a few times. I expect he's told you that already.'

Eric shook his head.

'Okay, I'll tell you what I told Paul. I thought long and hard about this marijuana business. You're old enough now to make your own decisions; many people your age are already working for a living. And you'll do what you want to, whether we talk about it or not. So rather than keep up a silly pretence, I think it's best if we're open with one another. Oh, but for God's sake, stay off the hard stuff. There's a big difference. Tell me you know that.'

'Yeah, I know that,' Eric said, accepting the joint from Pattie.

'Okay, good. That's it, speech over.'

'People!' hissed Pattie.

Four pairs of eyes watched through the bushes as a young woman with a pushchair passed on the pathway.

For the very first time, all four Ealing hippies shared a joint.

Paul turned to Eric as they followed the Twins towards the hothouses, 'Good old Mum. She always manages to turn a party into a drama.'

'Yeah, but she's still very cool,' replied Eric.

'True,' agreed Paul. 'If she wasn't my mother, I'd marry her.'

Exquisitely manicured flowerbeds blazed with colour in front of the glass-panelled eighteenth-century Orangery. Inside the long white building, potted palms and shrubs stood on a Romanesque mosaic floor.

Eric looked around thoughtfully, 'I feel like I know this place.' He stared up at the powder-blue sky through the iron-framed glass roof.

'Maybe you were here in a past life,' suggested Paul.

Eric snapped his fingers, 'The Beatles! This is where they did the promo films for *Paperback Writer* and *Rain*. Look at the statues.'

Outside in the sunshine, they walked among the flowers enjoying the quirky Palladian gardens and the hot summer day.

'I've got one more joint,' whispered Pattie. 'Shall we find a quiet spot before we visit the house and the lake?'

Locating Pattie's *quiet spot* proved easier said than done. The four hippies eventually returned to the secluded dell. This time Eric made sure to be present when Pattie retrieved the reefer.

Adjusting her dress, the blonde turned around and handed Julia the joint and a warm book of matches. 'By the way, what made you think I was at the house?'

'I thought I saw you in my bedroom,' Julia mumbled past the joint in her mouth. Striking a cardboard match, she lit the reefer.

Paul glanced at his mother, 'You must've seen one of Tony's ghosts, Mum.'

'It was probably clouds reflecting on the windowpane,' Julia replied, passing the joint to Eric. 'The mind plays tricks like that sometimes.'

Eric handed Pattie the reefer and exhaled a stream of smoke. 'Well, if that's what it was, Tony saw the same blonde clouds. Mind you, in his next breath, he told me he'd seen Yogi Bear looking at him from the bushes by the walkway.'

'Yogi Bear?' grinned Paul. 'That's the best yet! Was he serious?'

'Crap!' said Eric. 'That was supposed to be a secret.'

'Then let's keep it that way,' Julia said, looking at Paul. 'Tony's been coming out of his funny-phase. The last thing we want is to send him back into his shell.'

Pattie turned to Eric, 'Don't worry about Tony's secret. Marijuana loosens tongues. I'm the worst one for putting my foot in it.'

'We all do it,' said Julia. 'Alcohol is my downfall. One drink too many, and I lose my inhibitions *and* my common sense.'

Eric smiled. He could think of a few alcohol-fueled occasions when Julia's behaviour had been surprisingly extroverted. Since the day Tony had accompanied them to Hyde Park, Julia's drinking had lessened.

Leaving the concealed hollow, the Ealing foursome made for Chiswick House. They took a shortcut through the trees. Julia and Paul walked on ahead, deep in conversation, Julia's vibrant orange dress presenting a strong focal point among the soft greens and browns. Eric saw Paul put his arm around his mother's waist and resisted an urge to do the same to Pattie. A moment later, he felt her hand slide across his back. Wrapping his arm around the pretty blonde, he squeezed her gently, holding her to him as they walked.

'We're you surprised?' asked Pattie. 'I mean about sharing a joint with Julia.'

Eric considered his reply. 'I felt like I *should* have been surprised, but somehow, it seemed, well, normal.'

'The pot thing was a dilemma for Julia,' confided Pattie. 'Though she's since told me that getting stoned with Paul has made them close.'

'It's the love drug,' said Eric. 'Pot makes you loving.'

'And sexy,' added Pattie. 'Talking of which, I wonder how Julia got on at her photoshoot.'

'She said it went well.'

'Oh, I've no doubt it did,' replied Pattie. 'But I'd like to have been a fly on the wall.'

'What do you mean?'

Pattie giggled. 'He's a fabulous photographer, but he's a dirty bugger. I bet he loved seeing Julia in those stockings.'

'Mm,' mumbled Eric. Julia had told him that she had been hired to model tights. Stockings were far more risqué. Having committed one *faux pas* already that afternoon, he let the discrepancy pass.

Julia and Paul were waiting when they reached the edge of the wood. The open grass beyond was bisected by a long river-like lake that ran beneath a white stone bridge. A waterfall cascaded in an Italian-style grotto. On the other side of the lake was Chiswick House. Surrounded by classical white statues, the Roman-inspired villa stood proudly in the orange sunlight, a testament to the eighteenth-century eccentricity and vanity prevalent in the European nobility of that time.

'This is a great place to get high,' Paul whispered to Eric as they approached the bridge. 'I wonder if the bloke who dreamed all this up was smoking Mary Jane.'

'He missed out if he wasn't,' said Eric. 'Still, it's nice of him to leave it for us to enjoy.'

A large terrapin swam beneath the white bridge. Pattie cuddled up to Eric as they leaned on the parapet. They gazed out at the sparkling lake stretching away before them.

'They're calling this *the Summer of Love*,' Pattie said softly. 'I like that name, don't you?'

On the grassy bank to their left, the Small Faces' *Itchycoo Park* played on a radio while its owner fed ducks with a bun.

20

The Red Swing

On the night of the Chiswick outing, Eric slept at the Ealing House. A fractured dream in which Julia was surrounded by attractively dressed fashion models left him determined to pursue a photography career.

Eric's head felt fuzzy. As he made his way down the stairs, the sitar introduction to Traffic's *Hole in My Shoe* drifted up from the hallway.

'Hello,' said Keith. Gripping his perch with one foot, the grey parrot stretched a feathery white leg and extended his wing.

Eric smiled at his four friends, 'I see I'm the last one up again.' He drew out a chair at the kitchen table.

'I hear I missed a good day out yesterday.'

Eric hesitated. Coming from Tony, the comment resonated like a psalm at a sabbat. 'Yeah, Chiswick House is a mad place,' replied Eric. 'The Beatles did some filming there.'

A little girl in the living room said something about a giant albatross.

Julia smiled, 'We'll revisit Chiswick, Tony, and you must come with us next time.'

Tony nodded, 'I'll treat you to a round of lollies if yer lucky.'

Pattie smiled at the younger boy, 'Spend some money and make the day sunny.'

'That's what they say,' responded Paul.

Eric wondered if he had woken up in a parallel universe.

That Sunday, temperatures rose into the low eighties. When Tony announced that he would take a bath, Eric and Paul headed for the spare bedroom and locked the door. Directly above them on the top floor, a similar key turned in Julia's lock.

'I've got two rolled,' Eric said, reaching under his pillow. 'Did you put the Rizla's back in your mum's trunk?'

'Yeah, a few minutes ago,' replied Paul.

Eric glanced up at the creaking ceiling. 'Just in time.'

Paul shrugged, 'Now that the pot business is out in the open, it doesn't really matter.'

'True.' Eric raised the window and thick paint flakes dropped onto the sill.

A minute later, the window above slid open. Eric looked up and waved to Pattie.

Paul managed to suppress a giggling fit until he made it downstairs to the ballroom. He fell onto the sofa and erupted in fits of laughter.

'What's so funny?' grinned Eric.

Paul shook his head, 'I've completely forgotten. He wiped his eyes with his wrist. 'Shall we plug in and have a play?'

Halfway through the first song, entitled *Quiet Jam in E*, Eric sat on a sofa arm and gazed out through the French windows. The overgrown back garden looked fantastic in the sunlight. In Eric's elevated mental state, it appeared particularly fantastic. A golden haze tinted the hot air, haloing the foliage and softening the edges like a marginally unfocused camera. The rusty red swing brought to mind the painting he had seen in the attic.

Eric looked across at his friend. Sitting on his amp with his back to the garden, Paul stared at the threadbare carpet, lost in a world of improvised music and grimy woollen fibres.

Ten minutes later, the ballroom door opened, and Tony walked in. 'Jam time!' announced the young drummer. Water dripped from his hair, forming dark patches on his Superman T-shirt. As he turned to shut the door, Keith flew into the ballroom. The parrot circled, then landed halfway up the green velvet curtains. Climbing steadily, the old grey bird grabbed the pelmet with his hooked beak and hauled himself onto the highest perch in the room.

'Let's start with a slow blues,' suggested Eric.

'Okay, *Red House*,' said Paul.

Eric stared blankly at his guitar neck. 'I can't remember the intro.'

'You knew it last week.'

'I'll just count it in,' Tony said from behind his kit.

Paul took the vocal on the Jimi Hendrix blues song, singing gamely into the cheap ribbon mic he had bought from the electrical shop in Ealing Broadway. The guitar solo began quietly. Looking up from the Rapier's rosewood fretboard, Eric saw Julia and Pattie in the garden unfolding a pair of loungers. When Julia bent forward in her yellow sundress, Eric's solo faltered briefly, then kicked into overdrive. Turning the volume knob to ten, the guitarist ventured into previously unchartered melodic territory, the trajectory of which he would never travel again. He felt the band lift behind him, each musician inspiring the others in a surging spiral of sound. His solo teetering between the sublime and the ridiculous, Eric watched his fingers fly across the fretboard, as in a bizarre reversal, the guitar appeared to be playing *him*.

When the song ended, Pattie and Julia stood in the long grass, smiling and clapping. For a few magical minutes, the band had attained musical nirvana. It was a plateau to which the three musicians would aspire, now that they knew it was there.

Teatime could not come quickly enough for Paul. He and Eric had sneaked off mid-afternoon and smoked the second joint, and at five o'clock, the bassist was beset by a severe attack of the munchies.

Paul returned to the living room with a second plateful of strawberry-jam sandwiches. The news was starting on BBC1, and a Beatle-related story dominated the headlines.

Travelling to Wales for a weekend of Transcendental Meditation, the four Beatles had settled in at a rented boarding school in Bangor, expecting to be joined by their manager Brian Epstein. Surrounded by flowers, they sat with the Maharishi Mahesh Yogi and talked about the meaning of life. Paul McCartney answered the phone the next morning to be told that Brian had died the previous night from a suspected drug overdose.

'People who take drugs are idiots,' said Tony.

No one disagreed.

*

Reg drummed his fingers on the Zodiac's big red steering wheel. Sitting alongside Hanwell Cemetery with the top down, he glanced at his watch. Today, punctuality was important. Reg peered past a Tate and Lyle sugar lorry at the roadworks ahead. The workman swivelled his lollypop sign from STOP to GO. *At long bloody last!*

It was cool inside the Catholic church. Reg grimaced. Whenever he entered an old church, he imagined he could smell dead people. The tall man walked up the central aisle between the rows of vacant pews, his eyes scanning the high stone nave. Aside from a lady polishing the altar's brass candlesticks, the building was empty. Reg entered the confession box and pulled the door closed. 'Forgive me, Father, for I have sinned.'

'That's okay,' replied a voice from the other side of the partition. 'Tell me all the best bits, then drop a fiver in the plate on your way out.'

'Hello Igor,' said the postman.

'Walls have ears,' said the Scientist's assistant. 'I'll make this quick. There've been some developments.'

'Good ones, I hope,' replied Reg.

'Not good at all.'

'How did I know you were going to say that.'

'Okay, Reg, listen up,' said the man in the adjoining cubical. 'The technicians at Hartlepool have constructed a machine capable of establishing a satellite link-up.'

'I gathered that from the Scientist's letter. Are you telling me they've built another transmitter?'

'No, not a transmitter,' said Igor. 'The consensus is that it can't be done.'

'What then?' sniffed Reg.

'They plan to send their messages from the old transmitter in West Ealing, then bounce the signal up into space using the new machinery in Hartlepool.'

'And how will they do that?' asked the postman.

'Buggered if I know, you'd have to ask the Scientist. Anyway, here's where *you* come in...'

Reg groaned quietly.

'A technician is working on the transmitter at the Ealing office right now.'

'Yeah, I've seen him,' said Reg. 'He's installing a new component of some kind.'

'Yes,' replied Igor. 'That's why the Scientist arranged this meeting. He wants you to nobble it.'

'*Nobble it?*' exclaimed Reg. 'How am I supposed to disable it without them knowing?'

'The Scientist obtained photographs of the blueprints,' explained Igor. 'He's written instructions for you. Follow the directions carefully, and they'll never know it's been tampered with.'

'Sounds like a job for James Bond,' muttered Reg.

'He's busy. Right, I'll walk out of here now, and I'll leave the Scientist's instructions under the seat. Okay?'

'Okay,' Reg muttered irritably.

*

Scarecrow had always been the black sheep in the staffroom. Through the years, the art teacher's hair had remained an anarchistic inch or two longer than that of his colleagues. His corduroy jacket and frayed cuffs hinted at a streak of rebelliousness lurking just below the surface.

Eric sat on Scarecrow's desk next to the teacher's feet.

'Well, Eric, you're a *senior* now, one of the *big boys*.' The teacher leaned his chair back, his fingers clasped behind his head. 'You know they'll never give you a prefect badge with your hair that long.'

'I don't want to be anyone's boss,' replied Eric. 'As long as I'm my own, that'll do me.'

'Good for you,' said Scarecrow. 'Now, you've got an O Level coming up, and I'm expecting you to pass with flying colours. So don't flake out on me, okay?'

'I won't. I've got to pass the art exam; it's the only subject I'm any good at.'

'You'll sail through if you apply yourself.' The teacher looked up, 'Stay clear of hard drugs, Eric. I'm telling you that as a friend.'

'You're the second person to say that,' said Eric. 'Have I got *junkie* written across my forehead?'

'No, but you're a natural artist, and you're a musician, right?'

'Point taken,' said Eric. 'I won't screw up.'

'Good. Have you decided what you want to do when you leave school?'

'I like the idea of being a photographer.'

'Great! Have you got a camera?'

'No.'

The teacher bounced a chalk nub off Eric's stomach, 'Then get one, you bloody idiot!'

*

The hot summer of 1967 came to an end in September with the arrival of grey clouds and showers. Determined to restore her family to its former closeness, Julia proposed an outing to London's Tate Gallery. She was delighted when Tony agreed to go.

'I know art's not really your thing, but it's somewhere to make for in this rotten weather.' Julia sounded almost apologetic.

Tony shrugged, 'I don' mind, Mum. I like goin' to London. Even if it's to see art with a capital F.'

Julia laughed, 'Maybe you'll be pleasantly surprised. And the four of us going out together will be like old times. Remember the Beatles concert?'

'I remember the pissy seats.' Tony smiled at the memory of his older brother's wet bottom.

Paul thought a visit to an art gallery was hardly comparable to a Beatles concert, but he grasped his mother's meaning. 'I've still got the wrinkly booklet.'

Pattie was absent that day. *'I'm hosting a Tupperware party',* she told Julia with a wink. The blonde was probably hobnobbing with one of her high-flying acquaintances.

Eric spent the morning helping his father install an immersion heater. When he met the Ramsey's at Ealing Broadway Station, the rain had receded to a light drizzle.

Eric gazed out of the misted window of the District Line train as they approached Hammersmith. 'This reminds me of when the four of us went to the Beatles concert.'

Julia smiled.

Paul felt a cold sensation on his bottom.

Changing trains at Victoria, they journeyed south to Pimlico.

'It's named after Sir Henry Tate,' Julia said as they approached the broad steps of the classically inspired building.

Less than three weeks earlier, Reg had sat in traffic behind one of Sir Henry's sugar lorrys.

'The gallery's home to paintings by some of Britain's best artists,' said Julia. 'I hope you'll all see at least one or two that you like.'

Tony groaned inwardly. Art was his mother's long-held passion and field of expertise. He braced himself for a tedious afternoon of boring lectures.

The collection of J. M. W. Turner canvases drew Eric's attention. 'He got there long before the impressionists.'

'That's true,' agreed Julia. 'And his interpretation of light was quite revolutionary.'

'Looks like someone's been sick on that one,' said Tony.

Paul smiled, appreciating both points of view.

'Oh!' Eric exclaimed, when they entered the next room. 'I saw a print of this at the art shop in the Broadway. But the real thing is so much bigger, and –'

'*The Lady of Shalott*,' said Julia. 'John William Waterhouse. He was associated with the Pre-Raphaelites. Do you like it?'

Eric nodded.

'Me too,' said Paul.

'It's not too bad,' admitted Tony.

A smile lit Julia's face. 'I guessed if any of the paintings were to make a favourable impression, it might be this one.'

Eric sat on a viewing bench, his eyes fixed on the painting of the red-haired young woman, beautiful yet forlorn. In a flowing white dress trimmed with gold, she sat upright in a small boat, looking towards the river ahead. She clasped a slender chain. What fate awaited when she released her grip?

Julia sat beside Eric. 'Her name is Elaine of Astolat. According to Arthurian legend, she was cursed by her love for Sir Lancelot and destined to see the world only in the reflection of a mirror. Temptation overcame her, and she dared to look directly at the handsome knight, activating the curse. In Victorian art, candles often represent life. Two of the three candles on the boat have already blown out...'

The world around him faded as Eric stared at the painting. Julia's soft voice soothed him like a lullaby. She told of the tapestry into which the young woman weaved the story of her life, and of the sad song she sang as she drifted towards Camelot at the ending of the day.

Julia looked around the big room, 'We've lost Tony and Paul.'

In an adjoining hallway, the two brothers stood in front of a busily composed painting. Tiny fairy-like people bustled about their business amongst long grass and flowers in a disturbingly sinister micro-world.

The instant he saw the picture, Eric thought of the canvases in the Ealing House's attic. Although Julia's work had its own distinctive style, there was little doubt that she had been inspired by this painting.

'*The Fairy Feller's Master-Stroke*,' said Julia. 'It's by Richard Dadd. He went mad and killed his father. They put him in a mental asylum. He was one of Broadmoor's first patents, and they never let him out.'

'I'm not surprised,' said Paul. 'You'd *have* to be nuts to paint something like that.'

'I like it,' said Tony. 'It's the best thing I've seen since we got 'ere.'

Before leaving the Tate, the Ealing crowd stopped at the gallery's gift shop. Eric selected a postcard depicting *The Lady of Shalott*.

'It's awfully costly,' said a large woman, admiring a print of Constable's *Flatford Mill*.

'Spend some money and make the day sunny,' her fat husband replied with a fat smile.

'That's what they say.' The woman slid the print from the rack.

'That sounds like something Viv Nicholson might have said,' whispered Julia.

Paul thought for a moment. 'Oh yeah, the lady who won umpteen-thousand pounds on the football pools.'

Julia nodded, 'She told the press she would *'Spend, spend, spend'*. Then she became alienated from her friends and ended-up broke and on the verge of going barmy.'

Eric repeated the fat man's words in his mind: *'Spend some money and make the day sunny'*. Pattie had used the same phrase a few weeks earlier. Why would she say that? It sounded so corny, like something Sid might have come out with. *He probably did.*

That night, Eric dreamed he saw Julia drifting past him in a small black boat. Strangely dressed fairy-people danced and sang on the bank. Unmoving, Julia stared straight ahead into the distance. The boat passed a weeping willow and disappeared around a bend in the river.

*

As part of his precise commando-like planning, Reg had chosen a night on which the new moon was in its darkest phase. Short of blasting it with a shotgun, there was nothing he could do about the streetlamp.

'I'm too bloody old for this lark,' the postman muttered, scrambling over the wooden door. He lowered himself into the tiny backyard behind Burton's. *And all because the lady loves Milk Tray.*

Clambering onto the brick annexe's roof, Reg crouched beneath the upstairs rear window and scanned the lamp-lit sidestreet. He slid a screwdriver from his back pocket. That evening, Reg had been the last to leave the office, and he had switched off the alarm on his way out. He was about to find out if anyone had been there and turned it back on. Holding his breath, he jammed the screwdriver between the window and the outer frame. Four seconds later, Reg was standing in the upstairs back room, looking at the enormous metal-cased transmitter.

So far, so good. The postman pulled a torch out of his jacket and re-read the Scientist's instructions for the twenty-fifth time. He eyed the suitcase-sized box that the MoD2 technician had attached to the transmitter.

'Right,' muttered Reg. Pulling on a pair of rubber gloves, he picked up the screwdriver. 'Time to get nobbling.'

*

'It's starting, Mum,' Tony called from the living room.

'I'm here.' Julia placed a sewing needle and a reel of beige cotton on the coffee table. She sat between Eric and her youngest son.

'I can't believe Paul's missin' the first episode for the bloody Boy Scouts,' said Tony.

I can't believe Paul is still going to the bloody Boy Scouts, thought Eric.

Finding himself in the village with the title Number Six, Patrick McGoohan protested that he was not a number but a free man.

'This is going to be another of those programmes like The Fugitive,' Julia surmised, half-an-hour into The Prisoner. 'You keep expecting it to end, but it never does. It's good, though. Very *swinging, groovy, hip, far out* and all that. And a touch surreal.'

Tony sighed, 'It's not as good as The Man from U.N.C.L.E.'

'I still like The Avengers,' Eric said, joining the telly debate.

Tony wrinkled his nose, 'Even that's gone weird.'

'That's what I like about it.'

Tony prodded his mother in the ribs, 'When are we getting a colour telly, Mum? Ron's mum got one on the HP and it looks brilliant.'

'I've already told your brother,' replied Julia. 'We'll wait until the prices drop.'

When the programme ended, Tony went upstairs to bed, leaving Julia and Eric alone in the living room. Julia picked up Eric's empty backpack and placed it on her lap.

'Where shall we put Sergeant Pepper?' she asked, holding the cotton bass-drum patch against the canvas bag. 'Should it go next to the CND emblem or on the opposite side?'

'On the same side, I think,' said Eric.

'Yes, that's what I thought.'

Eric watched Julia moisten the cotton and thread it deftly through the eye of the needle. *Only a short time ago, she would have had a glass of wine on the table.* 'I notice Tony's sleeping upstairs.'

'Yes,' smiled Julia. She pushed the needle through the canvas. 'There's been no talk of ghosts and ghoulies for ages. It's taken a while, but Tony's getting used to living in a big old house.'

'And he came with us to the art gallery.'

'Yes, and he almost enjoyed it!'

Eric remembered the fat man in the Tate Gallery's gift shop. The phrase he had used, *Spend some money and make the day sunny*, had lodged in his head. 'I was wondering... I know the hippies are against capitalism, but I don't really know how it works.'

'What makes you ask that?' smiled Julia.

'Something someone said.'

'Okay. To understand hippie politics, you have to know how the world operates.'

Eric nodded.

'There are basically two ways of running things: capitalism and socialism. In a capitalist system, everything is owned by individuals. With socialism, the state owns the country's industry. The state is *us*, the people.'

'That's it?'

'That's it. But the pros and cons are what everyone argues about. You've heard people talk about left and right-wing politics?'

'Yeah?'

'Okay, that's basically an equality scale. At the left end, all the people would be equal; on the right, there'd be class systems – divisions between the rich and the poor.'

'So which side are you on?' asked Eric.

'I'd like to see a more even balance between the two extremes. We have that to some extent in Britain, but we could do better. And heaven help us if a right-wing loony comes into power and starts privatising everything. I do worry that the utopian hippie ideals could initiate a backlash.

'Capitalism looks great at a quick glance,' explained Julia. 'And it does provide incentives, which we need to stay motivated. But money is power in many people's eyes, and it becomes like an addiction: they want more of it. Businesses compete with one another. Capitalists will tell you that this keeps prices down and quality up. But it becomes a rat race, which leads to exploitation of workers, a widening gap between the rich and the poor, and advertising that uses psychological techniques to convince people that buying will make them happy.'

'So people are sucked in by all the advertising and get into debt,' said Eric.

'Yes, but it's not really debt that the hippies are worried about,' explained Julia. 'Obviously, debt *is* a problem, and ironically, one that could backfire on the capitalists: they need people to keep spending to keep the system going. But the *big* worry is the pollution from the factories that churn out all this stuff. We're screwing up the planet.'

Eric nodded, 'And that's what the hippies are trying to say?'

'Yes. It's the same thing that Jesus was saying two thousand years ago, but without the mumbo-jumbo. He was the original communist.' Julia looked up from her sewing, 'But we may be fighting a losing battle. Nobody needs thirty pairs of shoes, but we're using up the planet's resources and poisoning the atmosphere so they can have them. People are generally disinterested in thinking about these things, which leaves them vulnerable to enticement. The capitalist machine is powerful and very persuasive.'

'It certainly is.' *More powerful and persuasive than you know*, thought Eric.

*

At 6:58am on Saturday the 30th of September, Eric was woken by his clock-radio. *'Now, with the clock ticking slowly up to seven a.m., it's going to be time to welcome Radio One's first daily show on 247 metres medium wave... Stand by for switching... Five, four, three, Radio Two, Radio One, GO!'*

Six weeks earlier, the *Marine Broadcasting Offences Act* had passed, outlawing the pirate stations. To curtail the inevitable public outcry, the BBC had set about a radical overhaul of its radio programming. At the vanguard of this rethink would be the new pop-orientated station, Radio One. Pirate radio DJ's joined the ranks of Britain's maternal socialist establishment. The BBC had loosened its moral guidelines, and John Peel was welcomed at Broadcasting House.

Eric lay in his warm bed, lulled by the knowledge that today was a Saturday, and he could remain in his cosy dream world for as long as he wished.

'*And good morning, everyone,*' chirped Tony Blackburn. '*Welcome to the exciting new sound of Radio One.*' A thunderclap split the airwaves, '*If this one doesn't wake you up, nothing will.*' The Move's *Flowers in the Rain* was the first song to be played on the new radio station; an appropriate choice given the summer's flower-power motif and the rainy September that followed. Next on the turntable was *Massachusetts* by the Bee Gees. '*Come on, up you get out of bed... twist the old kneecaps round a bit – bedroom twisting time,*' said Blackburn, introducing the Tremeloes' *Even the Bad Times are Good.*

Getting out of bed was the furthest thing from Eric's mind. In the coming winter months, waking to the unbearably cheerful voice of Tony Blackburn would frequently be edged with foreboding. Central heating was yet to be installed in the Grimes' house.

*

The autumn of 1967 was productive for Clockwork Mouse. When Ron Hillman left the newsagents, Tony began to see less of the South Ealing boys, spending more time at home. Though he continued to work his paper round, Tony's associations with his dubious friends were mostly limited to Brentford FC home matches and the occasional alcohol-fuelled night in Ron's bedroom. Incorporating a frenetic Keith Moon influence into his drumming, young Tony had recently become the most enthusiastic of the three musical mice.

Paul stood by his amplifier, cradling his bass. 'Does it change keys at the end?' he asked, scratching his head.

'Yeah. The Eifel Tower/Taj Mahal bit modulates to A and stays there for the rest of the song,' explained Eric.

'Oh, I was expecting it to go back to E.'

'I wish it did,' replied Eric. 'It's too bloody high to sing in A.'

Tony prodded his nostril with a drumstick. 'Roger Daltrey manages okay.'

'Yeah, well, I'm not him. Can we do something different to finish the song?'

'No problem,' the drummer replied. 'When it gets to the high bit at the end, stop singing, and I'll smash-up me kit.'

That Sunday evening, Pattie joined Julia and the three lads for a trip to the Northfield Odeon.

Pattie hung back with Eric as they entered the cinema, 'I know you've got school tomorrow, but come back to the house after the film. I've got some lovely grass.'

Fifteen minutes into *To Sir with Love*, Paul whispered to Eric, 'They're worse than the Bash Street Kids.'

'Judy Geeson's a bit gorgeous, though. Better looking than Toots.'

'I like the title song.'

'Me too,' agreed Eric. 'I think it's Lulu's best by a mile.'

When they arrived back at the house, Tony let loose some choicely worded comments regarding the cold November weather and the hour he was required to begin his paper round, then made a beeline for his bed. Eric sympathised. If his photography career took off, early morning sessions would be off the agenda. With Christmas and his sixteenth birthday on the horizon, Eric had already dropped a hint, truthfully telling his parents that his art teacher had suggested he get a camera ASAP.

Pattie patted her bag, 'Time for a smoky treat?'

Julia turned on the television. 'Let's wait a few minutes, Pats. I'd feel more comfortable if we give Tony time to get tucked up in bed.'

'It does not mean that the pound here in Britain, in your pocket or purse or in your bank, has been devalued,' said Prime Minister Harold Wilson.

Standing in front of the TV, Julia rested her hands on her hips and sighed. 'Tell you what, let's go up to my room and smoke that joint.' She turned the television off. 'Everyone be quiet on the stairs.'

Eric and Paul followed the two women up the winding stairway. Julia wore orange and Pattie lime-green, but their bright minidresses appeared colourless in the dark. Four pairs of bare feet stepped silently. At the end of the second-floor corridor, moonlight beamed through the big round window.

Opening her bedroom door, Julia turned on the light. 'We'll soon have it warmed-up. I've put an electric fire at each end of the room.'

'Oh, that's nice, Mum.' Paul closed the door behind him. 'I'll know where to come next time an icicle drops from my bedroom ceiling.'

Ducking beneath the suspended marionettes, Julia crouched behind the gold spiral staircase and switched on the up-lights. 'Turn off the chandelier, would you please, Paul.'

Yellow and red spotlights illuminated the slowly twirling puppets, throwing shifting shadows across the walls and ceiling.

'Yeah, brilliant!' exclaimed Eric. He stood by a glowing electric fire with his back to the window. 'It looks like a fairy grotto.'

Sitting on the trunk at the foot of Julia's four-poster bed, Pattie was busily rolling a reefer.

Paul admired Pattie's masterpiece in the low red and yellow light, 'Blimey, that's a monster!'

'It's my five-skin special.' Pattie tied a knot in the marijuana bag. 'It was the core presentation for my Girl Guide's badge in *Jointery*.'

'Shall we smoke it in the observation room?' suggested Julia. 'It's a lovely clear night, and we can look out at the stars.'

Lucy in the Sky with Diamonds played in Eric's head as he gazed down at the black reservoir and the still trees of Fox Wood. Lucy's diamond stars sparkled in the early-winter sky. On the opposite side of the high octagonal turret, Pattie peered towards London through the mounted brass telescope.

'Here,' Paul croaked, handing his mother the long joint.

Pattie swivelled the spyglass to the centre of the city. 'There must be a million-zillion lights out there.'

'At least,' replied Julia. 'A million-zillion and six last time I counted.'

They're both well on their way, thought Eric. He smiled at Julia as she handed him the reefer. She looked delectable in her short orange dress.

'I'll roll another,' Pattie said as they descended the spiral staircase.

'Um, *phwey*... not for me, thanks,' replied Paul. 'I'm already climbing Mount Everest with a tadpole.'

'No more for me, either,' said Eric. 'I've got a darts match with Sherpa Tenzing in five minutes.'

Julia contributed to the nonsense, 'That's why you ended up with the tadpole, Paul.'

The atmosphere in Julia's dimly lit bedroom was tinged with magic.

Eric sat cross-legged by the window. He looked at Paul stretched out on the carpet next to him, then up at the two pretty young women lounging on the four-poster bed. Everyone had a contented smile. Eric realised that he did, too.

'Did we all enjoy the film?' asked Julia.

'Mm, smashin'.'

'Super-duper.'

'I liked it, too,' said Eric. 'Though the best part of the evening for me was when Pattie whispered, *'Come back to the house after the film, I've got a lovely arse'.*'

'Some lovely *grass!*' Pattie's well-aimed pillow sailed across Julia's bed, slamming into Eric's face.

Everyone laughed.

'Oh, I'm sure Eric doesn't need reminding of his girlfriend's delightful bottom,' said Paul.

'Well, that's it then,' said Julia. 'It's finally out in the open.'

Paul looked up, 'Pattie's bottom?'

'You should be so lucky!' Pattie hurled a pillow at Paul.

Scrambling to his feet, Paul grabbed the pillow and stalked theatrically towards the fabric-draped bed.

'Okay, okay!' Pattie held her palms out to her would-be attacker. 'Jules... Help! A scary man is coming at me brandishing a fully loaded pillow!'

Julia reached behind her and snatched another pillow. 'I've got you covered, Pats,' she said, kneeling next to her friend on the large double bed. 'But watch out for his friend; I think he has designs on your bottom.'

'My bottom?' Pattie turned to face Julia and raised her eyebrows, 'Oh, really? Do you think so?' She smiled, fluttering her lashes.

Paul raised his pillow and brought it down squarely on Pattie's head. The blonde dived towards the headboard, narrowly avoiding Paul's follow-up blow. Julia countered with a full-blooded swipe across the back of her son's head, sending him sprawling face-first across the mattress. Julia's bed turned into a battleground as Eric joined the fray. Grabbing a pillow, he whacked Julia, then Pattie from behind, as the Twins assailed Paul with a frenzied attack. The pillow fight intensified, arms swinging, all four rolling and tumbling on the rumpled bedcover. Catching her son off guard, Julia scored a direct hit, forcefully wrapping her pillow around his face. Paul fell flat on his back, his head bouncing off the mattress perilously close to the headboard. Julia leapt astride her son, flailing mercilessly. When Eric twisted to look at his friend, Pattie pushed him backwards, and he found himself lying next to Paul with a manic blonde on his stomach. Eric looked up between the blows. Black and blonde hair flew above him as the relentless buffeting continued.

'Swap!' called Julia, and after a brief flurry, Eric found himself lying beneath his best friend's mother. They bounced as Julia straddled him, raining blows down on his smiling face. The lacy canopy shook and rocked above them.

'Wait, wait!' called Paul, holding his hands up in submission.

Their pillows raised high above their heads, Julia and Pattie sat astride the two teenagers, pinning them to the mattress.

'What?' said Pattie, bouncing playfully on Paul's stomach.

Paul gasped as she knocked the air out of his lungs. 'I just wanted to say... *Uh, uh, uh*... I just wanted to say...'

'*What?* Come on, out with it!' demanded Pattie, her pillow poised and ready to pummel.

Paul took a breath, 'I just wanted to say... that I love you all.'

'*Ahhh,*' purred Pattie, tossing her pillow over her shoulder.

The group cuddle that followed was an experience Eric would cherish. The outpouring of mutual affection felt like a consummation of their already close bond. For Eric, the physical sensation of the Twins laying huddled on top of him was nothing short of girly heaven. Everyone hugged warmly. The amorous kiss between Pattie and Julia was the cherry on the cake.

Pattie swung her legs over the side of the bed. Flattening her tousled hair with her hands, she turned back to Julia, 'Right. I think it's time for that second joi –'

Everyone followed Julia's gaze. The bedroom door had been closed before the pillow fight, and now it stood half-open. Eric's eyes landed on the ripped Rizla pack and the knotted bag of marijuana on the lid of the trunk.

Julia went to the doorway and peered down the moonlit corridor. No one was there.

*

Paul, Tony and Eric were at school when the delivery man arrived with the colour television. An hour later, a contractor came to install the roof aerial that Julia had ordered.

'It's a good job you told us about needing tall ladders,' said the workman. 'It was a bit of a bugger getting them down that long public walkway. How come they built the house so far from the road?'

'There *were* no roads when this house was built,' replied Julia. 'Just dirt tracks.' *The more hints you drop, the less your tip is going to be.*

The man nodded, 'Anyway, I guarantee you'll get great reception up here on this hill.'

Julia switched between the three channels. The workman was right. The picture on the colour television screen was excellent. And there would be no more fiddling around with the frustrating set-top aerials she had used for the last nine years.

When the man had gone, Julia stood in front of the big sofa assessing her expensive purchase. The television suited the room. In its polished mahogany encasement, it looked more like a piece of antique furniture than a television set. Dragging the small sofa around to face the fireplace, she set up an L-shaped seating area, ideally suited to viewing the new TV in the corner. *So much for my conversation area.*

'It'll never be the same, Julia', she heard Jack say.

Julia shrugged, confident that her sons would like the new furniture arrangement. She smiled to herself. Her surprise was complete.

'Oh, it's stunning, Mum!' Paul exclaimed, dropping his school bag next to the stereo.

'Fantastic!' agreed Eric.

'Good,' smiled Julia. 'I hope it'll cheer Tony up.'

Don't go down that road, thought Eric. 'I'm going up to get changed.'

'Me too,' said Paul. 'Then we can settle down and watch the new *colour* telly! Brilliant, Mum.'

When Paul and Eric re-joined Julia in the living room, Tony was still not home.

Julia glanced up at the clock, 'It'll be dark soon. Did Tony say anything to either of you about going out?'

Paul shook his head, 'Not to me. He's been flashing his savings around. Maybe he's gone on a spending spree.'

'I hope he hasn't bought a colour TV,' said Eric.

'Not unless he's backed a winner at a hundred to one,' replied Paul.

The lead story on the evening news featured a report on the first human heart transplant.

'Shame it came too late for Uncle Jack,' said Paul. 'If I remember rightly, you knew he had a weak heart, didn't you, Mum?'

'No, of course not,' Julia shot back. 'You can't predict these things, Paul. Nobody can.'

Paul started to say something, then changed his mind.

Twenty minutes later, a bicycle headlamp appeared in the darkness at the front gate.

'Tony's home,' said Julia. 'Thank heavens for that.'

The front door closed quietly.

'Helloo,' intoned Julia.

'I'm going upstairs,' Tony called back from the hall.

Julia rose quickly and hurried to the living-room doorway, 'Tony, wait! There's something –'

Tony stood at the foot of the stairs facing his mother. Beneath a short green Harrington jacket, he wore a yellow-and-white striped Ben Sherman shirt. Red braces were clipped to his jeans, and his shoes had been replaced by a pair of Doctor Martens boots. Julia stared at her son's head. It was completely bald.

*

Eric's occasional work with his father paid far better than his old job at the newsagents. Bill's reputation as a reliable all-round handyman had spread over the years. Eric found himself employed in work ranging from plumbing, which he hated, to carpentry, which he quite liked. Painting and decorating was his speciality, and he had recently helped his dad finish a big refurbishment job in Wembley.

On the second Saturday in December, armed with a crisp ten-pound note, Eric walked through a snow-covered Walpole Park. Their watery world now a sheet of thick ice, the ducks huddled on the two narrow islands in the long pond. Pulling his woolly hat down over his ears and turning up his greatcoat collar, Eric looked up at the featureless white sky. There was more snow on the way.

Ealing Broadway had that Christmassy feeling. Shoppers lined the streets, and Bentalls' window displays glittered with traditional reds, greens and golds. The snow completed the seasonal picture, the old church at the Broadway centre looking especially pretty with its white-capped roof and tall fairy-lit tree. Carols played from a nativity box near the main road.

W. H. Smiths was crowded that Saturday afternoon, the basement record department particularly so. Eric made straight for the C's and picked out Cream's *Disraeli Gears*. Moving along to the H's, he found Jimi Hendrix's *Axis: Bold as Love*. The Rolling Stones' *Their Satanic Majesties Request* had been released the previous day, but something told him to wait for the reviews. The two psychedelic LP covers gave Eric plenty to look at while he stood in the queue. As it turned out, the music contained on both records would provide a great deal for him to listen to over the coming years. He need not have worried about the money he was spending; Jimi's *Little Wing* alone was priceless.

'And one of those, please,' Eric said, pointing up to the row of *Magical Mystery Tour* EPs displayed along a shelf behind the counter.

The new double EP included the Beatles' recently released single *Hello, Goodbye/I Am the Walrus*. Being an avid reader of Britain's weekly music press, Eric had not bought the single, even though he rated it as one of their best. He wondered if the Beatles' Christmas marketing strategy would have been different had their manager still been around. *Spend some money and make the day sunny*, he thought, then swiftly banished the phrase from his mind.

Eric walked quickly to the Ealing House. While he had been inside the shop, the snow had begun to fall again. And by the look of the sky, there was more to follow.

By the time Eric arrived at the front porch, the air was filled with large white flakes. His knocking having elicited no response, Eric used his key.

The fire in the living room had burned low, and an open bottle of wine stood next to an empty glass on the coffee table. A half-smoked joint lay in the ashtray. Leaving his new records by the stereo, Eric hung his coat on the rack and walked down the hall. 'Hello?' He noticed a faint hollow echo. The old house always seemed bigger when there was nobody home.

Eric entered the ballroom, half-expecting to see Paul sitting on his amp with his bass on his lap. The instruments lay where they had left them after the previous night's session. Hearing faint metallic creaking, Eric crossed the room. He peered through the French windows into the steadily falling snow,

'Wha...' The involuntary exclamation died on his tongue.

Julia faced the house, swaying on the red swing. Her frozen white fingers gripped the chains. Eric stood open-mouthed, clinging to the handle on the glass-panelled door. He rubbed a pane with his hand. Snow settled in Julia's hair and on her skimpy yellow sundress.

Eric saw a surreal winter scene inside a swirling snow globe. He pushed down on the handle, and the lock sprang open. Julia looked up, staring wide-eyed. Startled by her expression, Eric watched as she kicked forward. Julia was wearing no shoes. Her summer dress rode up as she swung higher; she leaned back, her long hair hanging. When Julia's legs parted, Eric stared spellbound. In different circumstances, he would have been excited; even now, he could not look away.

Julia's bare feet brushed the frigid grass, and the swing came to a stop. Rising from the seat, she walked slowly towards the house, a trail of footprints following behind her in the snow. Eric pushed the brass handle; he felt a rush of cold air,

'Julia?'

Trancelike, she approached the open door. The saturated yellow dress clung limply to her skin, snowflakes melting in her tousled black hair. Her green eyes stared, unseeing. She drifted into the ballroom.

Never wake a sleepwalker.

Following her up to the second floor, Eric watched Julia walk down the red-carpeted corridor and enter her bedroom. The door closed behind her.

A little while later, Paul arrived home, and he and Eric listened to the new records together. Unsure of himself, Eric said nothing to Paul about his mother. When Julia entered the living room dressed in jeans and a floppy pink jumper, it was as if nothing out of the ordinary had happened.

*

Paying Phil a visit, Eric made an arrangement with his guitarist friend. Although Paul and Eric had only been smoking for six months, the prospect of Christmas without any pot was unthinkable. They should have known – and probably did – that Pattie would restock the Old Holborn tin for the holiday.

Remaining faithful to his pledge, Eric spent Christmas Day with his parents.

On Boxing Day, he cycled to the Ealing House with his new Pentax camera in his backpack. Although a step down from Pattie's top-of-the-range model, the camera came equipped with extra lenses and a case. The art teacher's suggestion had done the trick, and Eric looked forward to honing his photography skills.

That afternoon, Tony joined the others to watch the television premiere of the Beatles' *Magical Mystery Tour*. Shown in black-and-white, the Fab Four's Christmas offering undoubtedly lost some of its lustre, though even a full-colour screening could not have saved it in Tony's eyes. Before disappearing into the ballroom ten minutes from the end, he dismissed the Beatles' avant-garde film as *a load of bollocks*. When Eric heard *Hello, Goodbye*, he was reminded of Paul and his younger brother's polar-opposite perspectives.

Tony was not present on Eric's sixteenth birthday, preferring to see in the New Year with his friends from South Ealing. That afternoon, Julia and Pattie had prepared a fire in the living room.

Following a late candlelit dinner, Julia, Pattie, Paul, and Eric sat around the kitchen table, sharing the evening's first joint. The Ealing hippies had all dressed-up that night: Eric in his purple paisley shirt and Paul, looking particularly flamboyant, in a shocking-pink three-button vest with a string of Indian beads. The Twins looked fabulous. Pattie wore her psychedelic minidress – which she knew was Eric's favourite because he had told her. Julia had chosen a silver sequined top with a pleated black miniskirt. Both women were heavily made-up with dark eyes and jangly accessories. All four were barefooted, as usual.

'We have a double celebration tonight,' Julia announced, raising her wineglass. 'The coming of a new year, and more importantly, Eric's sixteenth birthday!'

Keith bobbed his head. 'Show us your knickers.'

'Oh, do be quiet, Jack,' Julia said, shooting the parrot a sideways glance. 'Here's to Eric!'

Pattie and Paul raised their glasses, 'To Eric!'

'Thank you,' grinned Eric, 'I love you all.'

As the words left his mouth, Eric regretted saying them. Everyone recalled Paul's sentimental line from the pillow fight, but the half-open bedroom door had cast a shadow over the night.

Paul came to Eric's rescue with a swift reply, 'We love you too, man!'

'Yeah!' Pattie and Julia exclaimed in unison.

Paul raised his glass a second time, 'And here's to the two beautiful girls!'

'Drink up, everyone,' said Julia. 'It'll soon be time to say goodbye to 1967.' She leaned back on her chair, 'And it's been quite a year! What does everyone remember about it?'

'A blur of swirling colour,' said Paul. 'And that's about all.'

'The flowers in the front garden,' said Eric. 'And Sergeant Pepper.'

'Dangling our feet in the Serpentine.' Julia smiled at Eric.

'Chiswick House,' said Pattie. 'The terrapin under the bridge.'

'The boy slipping a flower into the soldier's rifle by the Pentagon,' said Eric.

'The decriminalisation of homosexuality,' said Julia. 'At long last.'

'The first black headmaster.'

'Good one, Paul,' smiled Julia. 'Legalising abortion.'

'The helter-skelter at Ally Pally – *A Whiter Shade of Pale*.' Pattie winked at Eric.

Julia raised her eyebrows, 'Hmm, did we miss something there?'

'Yes,' replied Pattie. 'Next subject. Colour telly.'

'The Beatles' Apple boutique.'

'The white bicycles of Amsterdam,' said Julia. 'Provo's free pedals for the people.'

'What was that all about?' asked Paul.

'The White Bicycle Plan. Provo believes that freeing ourselves of possessions will eliminate greed, so they left hundreds of bikes around the city for anyone to use.'

'Cool. The Naked Ape – Desmond Morris.'

'The Festival of the Flower Children.'

'Harold Wilson suing the Move.'

'The Electric Garden, Middle Earth.'

'Radio One.'

The list went on, finally ending with contributions from Eric and Julia:

'The Summer of Love,' said Eric.

'Our *love-in* on my bed,' smiled Julia. 'I love you all.'

The party moved into the living room, the four hippies spending the final hour of 1967 smoking pot and drinking wine. Away from the hot fire, the dark library area became the dancing spot that night. Four shadowy figures shook, shimmied, jiggled and jerked to the Doors' *Love Me Two Times*.

Julia toppled backwards into her son's arms, spilling her wine.

'All right, Mum?' Paul shouted above the music.

Julia regained her balance, 'Just as well I've switched to *white* wine,' she said, prodding the squelchy wet carpet with her toe.

Pattie slipped out of go-go mode and tapped her wrist with her finger. Eric flopped over the back of the big sofa and peered closely at the French clock on the mantelpiece. Turning to his friends, he raised one finger to signal a minute, then sped over to the stereo.

The BBC announcer commenced his countdown to 1968. Eric rejoined the others at the end of the room, taking Pattie's outstretched hand.

'Five, four,' they all counted together, 'three, two, one, *happy new year!*'

The group cuddle was this time performed standing. They separated into pairs. Eric watched Julia kiss her son on the lips, hugging him in the darkness.

Pattie slipped her arms around Eric, 'We really must see about our marriage this year.' Her kiss was long and tender, more like that of a lover than a friend.

'Switch!' called Julia, recalling another moment from the pillow fight.

Startled by the sudden exchange, Eric felt a surge of excitement as Julia fell into his arms. Although small and slender like her friend, her body felt entirely different. Eric's heartbeat quickened as he kissed Julia passionately, holding her close as he did in his dreams. All too quickly, it was over.

'Happy new year, my friend,' Paul said, offering Eric his hand.

Eric hugged Paul and kissed him on the cheek. 'I'll always be your friend.'

'Come what may?'

'Come what may,' replied Eric.

'I might hold you to that one day.'

'New year joint,' Pattie announced, heading for the kitchen.

'New year black coffee,' said Paul, following her into the hall.

When Eric turned to join them, Julia grabbed his wrist and led him back into the shadows. *Nights in White Satin* played on the radio.

'We haven't had our birthday dance,' Julia said softly.

Guiding Eric to the darkest corner, Julia draped her arms around him. She had assumed a gentle femininity: more like Pattie, yet entirely Julia. Their slow dance, tentative at first, seemed to gain intensity as they found their rhythm, their bodies locking together as one. Julia drew her head back, her green eyes flashing in the firelight, 'We haven't had our birthday kiss.'

Their lips met, and Eric felt Julia's embrace tighten. She held him close as they kissed. Eric felt her pressing and pressed back. Julia's soft, moist tongue brushed sensually across his lips.

'Do you want your coffee black or white, Mum?' Paul enquired from the doorway.

21

Rainbow
1968

At odds with the hippies' peace and love philosophy, in the coming year, the world's superpowers would find themselves locked in a struggle for global dominance. Following the Prague Spring, Russian tanks rolled into Czechoslovakia, while in Vietnam, America stepped-up its crusade against communist expansionism.

The violence and political unrest provided a focal point for a young generation already questioning the values and ethics of a system to which it had been subjugated by birth. Distrusting the establishment and detesting its reliance upon consumerism, its prejudices, corruption, and corporate greed, militant student-led demonstrations were organised across America and in European capitals, including London, Paris, Amsterdam, Rome and West Berlin. In hippie circles, 1968 would be remembered as *the Year of the Barricades*.

'Western Australia.' Paul rattled three dice along the kitchen table.

'Me *again*?' complained Pattie. 'I've never even *played* Risk before. You could have let me warn the poor Aborigines.'

'There's no room for sentiment when you're out to rule the world,' replied Paul.

'What will you do with the world if you get it?' Eric fanned three cards, eyeing them Maverick-style.

Paul narrowed his eyes. 'I still have *you* to deal with before I decide upon the future of the planet. Have you got a set?'

Eric threw his cards face-up on the table, 'Nah, two cannons an' an 'orse.'

'Fuck off,' said Keith.

Tony clomped into the kitchen, 'Afternoon, 'ippies.'

Paul stared at his brother's shiny black eye, 'Blimey, what happened to you?'

'We 'ad a bit of bovver last night,' Tony replied, scraping a clod of mud from his Doctor Martens boot. 'You shoulda seen the uver bloke. I 'ope 'e likes 'ospital food.'

'And you're proud of that, are you?' Julia entered the kitchen with a glass of white wine.

Tony shrugged, ''E was askin' for bovver an' 'e got it.'

'That's all right then,' Julia said sarcastically. 'Oh, and by the way, I've been up to the first floor, and I see you can't be *bovvered* to clean your bath.'

'*You* don't have to use it.'

'No, but Paul does. Besides, it looks horrible.'

Paul looked up at his mother, 'I've given up. I've been using yours.'

'And another thing.' Julia's temper was rising. 'There are muddy boot-prints all over the living-room carpet and...'

Pattie tugged discretely on Eric's sleeve. Slipping past Keith, they retreated to the ballroom and closed the door. They heard raised voices on the other side of the wall.

Slumping back on the couch, Eric stared out at the swing. 'Do you know anything about sleepwalking?'

'A little,' answered Pattie. 'My aunty Vi used to raid the kitchen at three in the morning. She'd make a bowl of cornflakes, scoff jam sandwiches, and polish-off the fairy cakes, and she never remembered a thing about it. My uncle ended up tying her to the bed because of it. That was his excuse, anyway.'

'Julia's drinking again,' said Eric. 'More than ever.'

'Yes,' sighed Pattie. She looked directly at Eric, 'You know why, of course?'

'Tony.'

Pattie nodded. 'Why did you ask me about sleepwalking?'

Eric was still staring into the gloomy garden. He needed to talk to someone and had decided to confide in Pattie. 'One afternoon before Christmas, I let myself into the house. Remember that Saturday when it snowed a lot?'

'Oh... Yes?'

'I thought there was nobody home.' Eric gestured towards the back garden, 'Then I looked out there and saw Julia on the swing.'

Pattie raised her eyebrows, 'In the snow?'

'Yeah, with no coat, just a sundress.'

'Oh... right, I see.' Pattie looked hesitant, 'Go on.'

'I opened one of the doors, and Julia walked past me like I wasn't there. When she came down later from her bedroom, I don't think she remembered any of it.'

Pattie paused. 'Have you told anyone?'

Eric shook his head, 'Only you. It seemed... weird. Well, it *was* weird!'

'And this was after Tony saw our love-in on Julia's bed?'

'Yeah.' *And your pot on the trunk*, thought Eric.

Pattie gazed out at the swing. 'It was a heavy time for Julia. When Tony shaved his head, she really hit the bottle. Maybe she freaked out. Or maybe, as you said, she was sleepwalking?'

'She *looked* like she was sleepwalking.' Something in the back of Eric's mind suggested there was more to it. 'The brain's a funny thing. I've had a couple of strange things happen. Not like that, but similar.'

Pattie half-smiled, 'Eric, you're the sanest person I know.'

'Sometimes I wonder. The first time was after they moved into this house. I was –'

Pattie raised her hand, 'Wait. Is there a key in your bedroom door?'

'Yeah, why?'

The young woman stood up, 'Let's go upstairs.'

Following her to the ballroom door, Eric admired the little blonde's pert bottom through her Indian skirt.

'To smoke a joint,' Pattie said over her shoulder.

Eric wondered if women had invisible wing mirrors.

The pair sneaked quietly up the stairs. The argument in the kitchen had cooled, Julia's shouting having given way to an earnest lecture.

At least Tony's still in there, thought Eric.

Perched on the handrail, Keith watched Pattie and Eric disappear down the first-floor corridor.

Eric sat on the edge of his bed in the guest room. When Pattie stood facing the locked door, he knew what to expect. The long skirt made her retrieval of the joint less sexy than usual, but it was sufficient to quicken his pulse.

'Okay.' Pattie sat on the bed next to Eric and lit the reefer. 'Carry on where you left off; something strange happened to you after they moved here.'

Eric resumed his story: 'We were walking across the reservoir –
Paul, Tony and me. You know, exploring. It was summertime, and it
was scorching. The heat was reflecting up off the glazed bricks; maybe
that was it. Anyway, I felt like I was *floating*. I was high up in the air
looking down, and I could see the empty reservoir below, and Paul and
Tony were little dots.'

Pattie blew out a stream of pot smoke. 'Could you see yourself?'

'Maybe, I'm not sure. I can now, but that may be my mind playing
tricks.'

Pattie passed Eric the joint. 'Go on.'

'It only lasted a few seconds, maybe less. But it seemed very real.
And when I found myself back on the ground, I felt *older*, like I'd been
drifting around up there for years. How's that for weird?'

'And this is pre drugs?'

'Oh yeah, ages before.' Eric took another puff, inhaled deeply, and
handed the joint back to Pattie.

'Maybe you were astral travelling? Lobsang Rampa, *The Third Eye*
and all that. You've heard about people dying for a few minutes on the
operating table, then telling the doctors that they'd watched it from the
ceiling?'

'Yeah, I read about that in a Readers Digest.'

'Must be true then,' said Pattie. 'Was your other freak-out the same?'

'No, completely different. This pot's pokey.'

'Yeah. Carry on. What happened the other time?'

'Okay. That was at the park next door... With Paul and Tony again.
We'd just played a round of golf, and the attendant was pissed off cos
it was late and he wanted to go home.'

'Shame.'

'Yeah. So, there were these three girls on the swings, teenagers. I
ended up talking to the blonde. She had a dress like Julia's – the Mary
Quant one.'

'Lime-green-and-orange.'

'Blue, but it was similar. There you go.' Eric gave Pattie the joint.
'So we were sitting on the roundabout in the dark, and the girl said
something...'

'Yeah?'

Eric paused. 'Well, it's too complicated to explain, but she said
something that dragged up some stuff from my past... and I lost it.'

'You mean you lost your temper? That doesn't sound like –'

'No, no, I just went a bit nuts. My head started spinning, and I didn't know who this girl was. I'm not sure I knew who *I* was!'

'What happened?' Pattie asked, taking another hit.

'I started kissing her.'

'Now it's getting good. Was she okay about it?'

'Oh yeah. I... got carried away, but it was fine until...'

'Until?'

'Until I called her Pattie.'

Pattie's wide-eyed smile was one of surprise and amusement.

Eric nodded, 'I thought she was you.'

'If it was anyone but you, I'd say they were making this up.'

'It's true,' said Eric.

The bass from Love Affair's *Everlasting Love* rumbled up through the floorboards causing the sash window to vibrate against its frame.

'Sounds like the bust-up's over,' said Pattie.

When Pattie and Eric walked into the living room, Julia was by the windows with a large glass of wine, swaying to *Judy in Disguise*.

'Status Quo next,' DJ Paul shouted, waving his *Pictures of Matchstick Men* single at Eric.

Tony had left the house.

*

Drizzly snow fell in London near the end of February.

'Wonderful Radio One,' chimed the jingle.

Fire Brigade, the Move's song about a female pyromaniac, came on Phil's car radio. The hobbit man bobbed in his seat, his unruly mop of corkscrew hair bouncing on either side of his central parting. He turned left by the Lido cinema, heading west on the Uxbridge Road.

'The pirate stations wouldn't have made us sit through *What a Wonderful World* and *Delilah* before they played something decent,' said Phil.

'True,' replied Eric. *Even short-term nostalgia can be rosy.*

'Harry's a great bloke,' said Phil. 'He only deals to close friends: strictly small-time. I told him about you, and he knows you're coming.'

'That's good, thanks.' Eric felt nervous at the prospect of making his first drug purchase. They passed Woolworths, and he looked up to his left through the frozen rain. A light was on in the office above Burton's. Eric flashed back, seeing the monkey-like silhouettes of Reg and Sid dancing in the window. He recalled the shock-stricken faces of the Beatles after hearing of the death of their manager. Eric felt a wave of sadness pass over him. It was hard to believe he would never see Sid again.

Passing Hanwell Cemetery, Phil turned right. This was the route Eric had taken to the sports ground as a boy. The next instant, he was sitting in orange sunshine, watching his mother fly across the court in her white tennis outfit.

'Harry's place is down here by the viaduct,' the driver said, turning left into York Avenue.

Phil parked the car and turned off the wipers. Sleet spattered the windscreen. An elderly couple shuffled past under a black umbrella. Eric watched the man open the front gate of their Edwardian terraced house. *I wonder if you know that you live a few doors from a drug dealer?* The air felt cold as Eric stepped out onto the slushy wet pavement. Harry stood in the doorway.

Psychedelic posters lined the landing of the upstairs flat, lending some colour to the dreary décor. Eric identified a familiar damp smell that he had come to associate with hippie living. In the smoky room at the front of the house, the odour was masked by incense. There was no furniture. Beanbags and Indian cushions lay scattered by the walls and yellowed net curtains hung in the street-facing windows.

Phil and Eric settled on cushions facing the fireplace, where a skinny girl with long brown hair sat in a lotus position inside a pyramid. Christmas lights had been wrapped around the wooden frame, which Eric noted was held together with Sellotape and string. With her eyes closed and her hands resting on her lap, the girl remained inside her pyramid for the entirety of Phil and Eric's visit.

'Crystal's an amazing chick,' Harry said, stuffing a mixture of tobacco and hashish into a large embossed chillum. 'A couple of nights ago, she dreamed a new colour. She spent the next day with a box of water paints, trying to mix it. We're off to India in a couple of months; might run into the Beatles if they're still there. Ganja by the Ganges, man.'

Eric watched Harry wrap a tobacco-stained handkerchief around the tapered end of the conical clay pipe. The longhaired man reminded him of Phil's blues aficionado friend in Islington, though Harry's beard was less full.

'Gis a light, man,' Harry said to Phil, nodding towards the matchbox on the carpet. Cupping his hands around the pipe, Harry drew deeply between his thumbs. The mixture hissed and crackled, glowing orange-red.

Accepting the chillum, Phil did the same, then handed the pipe on to Eric. Eric drew two lungfuls of fresh air. Adjusting his hands, he soon got the hang of smoking Asian style. A short time later, he sat contemplating the life-enhancing potential of pyramid power.

'Your dope'll be here any minute,' Harry said, knocking out the ash and reloading the chillum.

Half-an-hour later, Eric and Phil were still listening to Pink Floyd's *The Piper at the Gates of Dawn*, while Harry told them everything he knew about Indian mystics, levitation, and the influence of the Freemasons on the British government. He also said that in the event of Crystal emerging from her pyramid, she would be willing to read their tarot cards and crack their necks. Eric hoped she would be meditating for some time.

Five minutes into the Velvet Underground's first album and fifteen minutes into Harry's tales of the Illuminati, the doorbell rang. The drug dealer went downstairs, leaving the two friends with the pyramid girl.

'Have you arranged that double date yet?' asked Phil.

Eric shook his head, 'Don't get your hopes up. Those two are... complicated. Well, Julia is, anyway.'

Harry came back into the room, followed by a surly unshaven man with a carrier bag and an *I'm Backing Britain* badge. Huddling in the corner by the door, the two dealers completed their transaction, then the man left.

Harry placed a set of scales on the carpet and dropped a weight into one of the pans. He reached into the carrier bag and produced a block of hashish the size of a house brick.

Blimey Phil, Harry must have a lot of close friends, thought Eric.

*

'What do you think of *Lady Madonna*?' Paul asked, as the two sixteen-year-old hippies approached Ealing Broadway Station.

'I like it, as always,' said Eric. 'But compared to what the Beatles have been putting out in the last year or two, it's a bit... *ordinary*.'

Paul nodded, 'Not much in the way of psychedelic mind-pictures.'

'Exactly.' Eric looked across the road towards Haven Green, 'Cor, look at her with the green polka dots. It's only the end of March, and the girls are looking good already.'

'Paul smiled, 'Nice dress.'

'I kind of like what's in it.' Eric walked backwards into the station with his hands in the pockets of his blue crushed-velvet jacket.

Changing at Notting Hill Gate, Paul and Eric boarded a southbound Circle Line train to High Street Kensington. London was buzzing that Saturday afternoon, and there was standing-room-only in the stuffy smoking carriage.

Paul leant close to his friend, 'Don't look now, but I think you've pulled. That redhead in the Afghan coat has been eying you up since we got on the train.'

Eric looked over his shoulder. A pretty hippie girl turned away.

'I told you not to look!'

'Wow!' exclaimed Eric. 'Long red hair like Jane Asher. You don't think it *is* Jane Asher, do you?'

'Probably not,' replied Paul. 'Her friend looks like Cathy McGowan, but I don't think it's her either.'

The busker in the station's arcade made Eric think of Ricky. He recalled playing *The House of the Rising Sun* by the campfire on the hill. The holiday at St Ives seemed like a dream from a hundred years ago.

Leaving the station, Eric and Paul turned right on Kensington High Street. The sunshine had brought out the shoppers, and the London thoroughfare was crowded. Cars, buses and taxis lined the busy road.

'According to Pattie, it's a block or so down on the right,' said Eric. 'Though she was totally out of it when she gave me the directions. We may have to ask a policeman.'

'It would be easier to ask a hippie,' Paul said as they walked past Derry & Toms. 'There are plenty about.'

'Here it is.' Eric pointed up at the red lettering above the entrance, 'Kensington Market.'

Opening its doors in late 1967, the indoor market catered to a select clientele. The three floors were full of hippie-orientated merchandise. Segregated stalls lined the long narrow corridors, where customers squeezed past one another in a tightly packed insular world. The large premises had become a meeting place as well as a market.

Bob Dylan's *Blonde on Blonde* LP played from somewhere at the back as Eric and Paul entered the building. The music and the market seemed made for each other. Merging with the aroma of incense, the sights, sounds, and smells cajoled the senses, inviting the visitor to venture deeper into the fairyland world of Kensington's hippie Aladdin's Cave.

'Fancy having your palm read?' Eric asked, glancing down at a hand-painted folding sign.

Paul shook his head, 'I saw into the future last summer when we sat on the porch steps looking at the flowers. Madame Gypsyknickers might tell me something different.'

Eric smiled, 'It was good then, your glimpse into the crystal ball?'

'Brilliant,' replied Paul. 'You and Pattie had fifteen kids and were living in a treehouse in Chiswick.'

'Must've been a pretty big treehouse.'

'Had to be, to have room for the albino rabbit sanctuary,' Paul said, brushing past a stuffed gorilla with sunglasses. They turned into another narrow aisle. 'How about one of those Zulu military jackets?'

'I'm going off army stuff,' said Eric. 'I don't want to be a soldier.'

'You've been hanging around with my mum for too long.'

'Well, of all the things you could choose to do with your life... Would *you* want to go out and kill people?'

'God no,' replied Paul. 'If they bring back conscription, I'll hide in a treehouse in Chiswick.'

'I've got a treehouse in Mayfair you could rent,' said a female voice.

Paul stood face-to-face with the Cathy McGowan girl from the train. He kept his cool, 'Your treehouse sounds very up-market.'

'It's up a tree, actually,' replied the Cathy McGowan lookalike.

The pretty Jane Asher redhead eyed the CND badge on Eric's jacket. 'We were at the anti-war demo in Berkley Square last week. There were two hundred people arrested, but we hid behind a bush.' She turned to her friend, 'Scary, wasn't it, Cathy.'

Cathy!? Eric didn't tell her that the protest had taken place in *Grosvenor* Square. Besides, it was all he could do to contain himself after hearing the other girl's name. *The weekend starts here!* 'Are you shopping or browsing?'

'Oh, shopping,' replied the redhead. She smiled sweetly, 'Actually, we could do with a male perspective. All the clothes here are so groovy, it's hard to know what to choose.'

Eric could not believe his luck. As far as he was concerned, the lovely twenty-something girl could say *groovy* all day long. Perhaps she had been a dollybird in a previous incarnation. 'Well, I have done some fashion photography,' said Eric. 'Does that qualify me to help you with your shopping?'

'Definitely,' smiled the redhead.

Fashion photography? She'll think I'm an idiot. Gazing into the pretty young woman's grey-blue eyes, Eric hoped the dream he was having would last a while longer. He looked around for Paul. Further along the aisle, his friend was skimming through a rail of fancily embroidered blouses. Cathy (not Cathy McGowan) stood attentively at his side.

An hour-and-a-half flew by as Eric, Paul, and the two hippie girls explored the sprawling bohemian market. All kinds of outrageous clothing, costume jewellery, posters, cosmetics, exotic perfumes, drug paraphernalia, records, boots, books, ornaments, and hippie-related miscellanea were on offer. The stalls were painted in bright colours, as was the tiny psychedelic café, where the four stopped for coffee. Paul and Eric exchanged glances when the redhead slipped in one of her passé expletives. *Groovy, fab, gear* and *swinging* randomly punctuated her sentences. Bewitched by her stunning looks, Eric found the girl's outdated expressions endearingly quaint.

A labyrinth of confined winding passageways twisted throughout the large, low-ceilinged basement. The market's mysterious underworld was muddled with nooks and crannies, small side rooms, and dimly lit enclosures, where weirdly dressed hippie traders plied their wares. It felt a universe apart from the London streets above. There were fewer people down here, visitors perhaps wary of the claustrophobic tunnels and dark recesses. Exploring the maze of pipelined corridors, the two couples soon became separated.

Eric smiled when he heard Jimi Hendrix's *Little Wing* playing from somewhere below. He peered through a low arched doorway. A single red bulb lit a descending flight of steps leading to a subterranean room. Rails of exotically fashioned dresses stood in purple fluorescent light. As Eric and his companion entered, a young woman looked up from a wooden counter. With her twisted white hairband and gold-trimmed medieval dress, the slender merchant girl reminded Eric of *The Lady of Shalott.*

Tall pampas plumes softened the room, the feathery white fronds arching overhead beneath a low dark-blue ceiling. While the redhead inspected a rail of Arthurian dresses, Eric looked around at the framed fairy pictures. Scantily clothed winged nymphs and nymphets flew among leafy forests and danced upon green velvet riverbanks.

Rising from her seat, the willowy woman drifted gracefully across the floor, her long white dress flowing behind. She indicated to the curtained cubicle next to the steps. 'Try on anything you like,' she said in a refined whispery voice. 'I'll be back in five.'

'Do you like this?' The redhead unhooked a white chiffon dress and held it up for Eric's appraisal.

'I love it,' said Eric. 'It's like a fairy dress. It floats in the air.'

The girl ran her hand down the flimsy white fabric, assessing the delicate garment's design. 'Shall I try it on?'

Leaning against the counter, Eric focused on the unusually large gap between the changing-room curtain and the floor. He drew a breath as the girl's Afghan coat sagged to the floor in the corner. The small room was suffused with feminine sexuality, and Eric wondered if the curtain had been intentionally cut short. The facilities in Kensington Market were very different from those of Marks and Spenser. The redhead's blue Indian blouse landed on top of the Afghan. Stepping out of her shoes, she pushed them to one side with the edge of her bare foot. Eric stared beneath the high curtain. The girl's knees bent as she lowered her jeans. He had never witnessed a real striptease, but this came very close. A white bra dangled below the curtain. This was unexpected and surely unnecessary, but it added extra spice to the spectacle.

The curtain drew back. A vision in white, the lovely girl stood with her head bent forward. Her fiery hair hung down as she reached back over her shoulders,

'Eric, could you help me with this top button, please?'

Eric's jaw dropped. The layered chiffon dress slanted up from above the knee. It looked like a fairytale negligée.

'Eric?' the girl glanced up at him as she struggled with the button.

Eric stepped towards the cubicle.

The assistant wafted back into the room.

'It's okay, I've got it,' said the redhead. 'What do you think?'

'You look fantastic,' gushed Eric, looking through the revealing fairy dress rather than at it.

The two young women travelled with Paul and Eric as far as Notting Hill Gate. Before they went their separate ways, the redhead produced a biro from her coat,

'Here,' she said, handing Eric the pen.

Eric wrote his parents' phone number on the girl's hand and smiled as she wrote on his.

The redhead passed her friend the biro, 'There you go, Katy.'

Katy? It was not so much the name change as the Cathy McGowan girl's expression that rang alarm bells in Eric's mind. The instant the redhead addressed her as Katy, Cathy had shot her a look that said, clearly and unmistakably, *You've blown it!*

The lads boarded a red Central Line train bound for Ealing Broadway.

'How come you didn't give Cathy your phone number?' asked Eric.

'*Katy*, you mean? She's not really my type,' said Paul.

Eric shook his head, 'Blimey, beggars can't be choosers. She was really nice looking. Opportunities like that don't come along every day.'

Paul shrugged, 'I dunno... I didn't feel good about her. There was something funny about the pair of them.'

Eric gazed at a Harrods bag held by a man on the opposite seat. He checked the back of his hand. The redhead had written *Rainbow* above her phone number. She was gorgeous, but something was telling him that Paul was right. Eric searched his memory. He could not remember telling the girl his name, yet when she called to him from the cubical, she had addressed him as *Eric*. And there was the question he had been asking himself all along: why would a pair of pretty young women in their twenties come on so strongly to a couple of sixteen-year-olds? Eric remembered his dad's maxim: *If something seems too good to be true, it probably is.*

Opening the front door of the Ealing House, Paul glanced at his watch, 'Right, gotta rush, I'm already late. I'll be back in a couple of hours.'

Eric followed his friend down the hallway, 'No problem, I know the scouts would collapse without you.'

'I'm the only one who knows how to set-up the PA,' Paul called, climbing the stairs two at a time. 'And charity bingo is big business these days!'

Eric entered the kitchen.

'Hello,' said Keith.

'Hello,' replied Eric. 'Where is everyone?'

The tatty grey parrot cocked his head, regarding Eric with his yellow eyes.

Eric walked back down the hallway, took off his shoes, then went into the living room. At the centre of the coffee table, an empty wine bottle stood on a folded copy of the International Times. *There's no need for Paul to see that.* Eric hid the bottle behind the end of the sofa.

'See you in a few hours,' Paul called from the hall. 'I'll be home in time for Morecambe and Wise.'

'I'll tell them not to start without you.'

When the front door closed, Eric felt suddenly alone. He had never encountered the same sense of solitude at home, but the vastness and tangible history of the empty Ealing House brought on the feeling every time. Standing in the wide bay window, Eric watched Paul wheel his bicycle out through the front gate. Remembering the empty wine bottle, he wondered if he should check the swing. Eric shrugged; Julia's sleepwalking had been a one-time occurrence. Dismissing the thought, he walked back and sat on the big sofa. He recalled painting the spiral staircase in Julia's bedroom. When he had asked her about Uncle Jack... Perhaps he should check the swing after all.

'Oh, hello Eric!' Julia drifted into the living room.

'Uh!' Eric flopped back on the sofa with a shocked smile. 'Cripes, I thought everyone had gone out.' He twisted around, 'You frightened the life out of me!' *She's wearing her black miniskirt.*

Julia made her way unsteadily into the L-shaped seating area with a glass of white wine in one hand and an unlit joint in the other. 'Tony's out for the evening.' She stood in front of the small sofa facing the fire and carefully placed her wineglass on the coffee table. When she sat down, Eric was treated to an eye-catching glimpse of her white panties. Julia crossed her legs.

Wow, first a see-through dress at Ken Market, and now the shortest skirt in Julia's wardrobe, thought Eric. *It's a good day!*

Julia held up the joint. 'If you look behind the far end of that sofa, you'll see a lighter and an ashtray. You may also find a bottle of white wine.'

Eric slid along towards the fireplace, *Yes, I know. There's also an empty bottle that I hid there earlier.*

Julia lit the joint and inhaled. 'How was your outing?' she croaked, holding the smoke in her lungs.

'Good,' replied Eric. 'Kensington Market's well worth a visit. There are three big floors packed full of great hippie stuff. Clothes, mostly.'

'So the underground has caved in and joined the capitalist ranks.' Julia handed Eric the joint, 'Would you like a glass of wine?'

'Oh, no, this'll do me, thanks,' Eric said, raising the reefer. 'As for the market, you can call it capitalism, but people have to make a living.'

Julia smiled, 'Yes, of course, you're right; I'm being cynical. But I'm sure it won't be long before the big corporations latch on to hippie merchandising. The music industry has already started.'

Switching on the lamp on the end table, Julia stood up and walked to the windows. As she drew the long green velvet curtains, her black pleated miniskirt wavered attractively. Eric brought the joint to his lips and took a deep drag. He was already feeling stoned.

Julia turned off the overhead light, then returned to the low-lit seating area. She flashed a curious smile, 'So who's Rainbow?'

'Ah, you read my hand.' Eric passed Julia the joint.

'Come on, don't be coy.' Julia sipped her wine. 'Did you and Paul chat up a couple of hippie girls?'

'No,' said Eric. 'As a matter of fact, they chatted *us* up.'

Julia giggled, 'Were they pretty?'

'*Very*, actually.' Eric's mannerisms were becoming increasingly extroverted as the effects of the marijuana intensified. 'Rainbow tried on a fairy dress.'

Julia uncrossed her legs, and Eric's gaze dropped. His involuntary voyeurism had lasted only a split second, but Julia was looking directly at him.

She's pretty tipsy this evening, thought Eric. He felt a tinge of guilt. Julia's drinking had been a cause for concern, and alcohol tended to put her in a sexy mood bringing her tarty alter-ego to the fore. He was finding it difficult not to look down.

'The tin is by the end of the sofa,' Julia said, reaching across the coffee table and picking up the International Times. 'Why don't you roll us another joint while I finish reading this article.' She leaned back and opened the underground newspaper, holding it up in front of her. This afforded Eric a perfect opportunity to admire Julia's lovely legs without being seen. He knew she was doing it intentionally.

Eric heated the block. The sweet dark aroma piqued his nostrils. From the corner of his eye, Eric saw Julia's leg begin to sway. He felt his heartbeat quicken as the swinging motion increased. It was the kind of unconscious action that people did on trains or in waiting rooms, like clicking a biro or twisting their hair. The effect was mesmerising. Julia's leg swung wider, the hem of her short pleated skirt rising and falling. Eric stared as her slender legs parted, revealing the taboo flesh of her inner thighs. Stoned and aroused, he looked up Julia's miniskirt, studying the feminine contours of her white cotton panties. She had teased him in the past, but never like this, never so obviously.

'Have you finished that joint yet?' Julia asked, crossing her legs. She tossed the International Times to one side.

Eric knew he had been caught.

22

The Chalk Man

Eric stood in his parents' kitchen, studying a box of Shreddies. He recalled Sugar Puffs bouncing across the kitchen floor at the Ealing House as Tony rummaged inside the cereal packet, searching for the bicarbonate-of-soda powered deep-sea diver.

Bill leant against the doorframe, 'Your girlfriend called.'

'My girlfriend?' Pattie came to mind as Eric shook an avalanche of Shreddies into his cereal bowl, watching closely for the Napoleonic infantryman depicted on the box.

'What kind of a name is *Rainbow?*'

'It's just a nickname, Dad. Her real name's Moonbeam.'

Bill smiled, 'She sounded very well-spoken on the phone. If she's half as nice as that Pattie I saw you with in Bensteds, you should invite her for Sunday dinner.'

Eric indented the gold milk-bottle top with his thumb, 'It's early days. I only met her once.'

'Her number's on the pad by the phone,' said Bill. 'I told her you'd ring her back.'

'Okay, thanks Dad.'

Bill turned back to the living room, 'By the way, I've already had the soldier out of the Shreddies.'

Dismounting by Hangar Hill Park, Eric looked at the rainbow that had appeared over Wembley. April had been showery and this was the third rainbow he had seen in as many weeks. *Maybe it's a sign,* he thought, pushing his bicycle up the steepest section of the hill. For the ninety-second time, Eric cast his mind back to Kensington Market, picturing the redheaded girl in the revealing fairy dress. He approached the entrance to the public footpath, *Maybe I will ring her.*

'Hello Eric,' called a familiar voice.

'Reg!' Leaning his bicycle against some wet bushes, Eric walked over to the black-and-grey Ford Zodiac.

The postman smiled through the open window, 'Climb aboard.'

'Nice car,' Eric said, admiring the plush red interior. He slid in next to the driver and closed the door. 'It looks like a spaceship.'

'Drives more like a boat,' replied Reg. 'Not that I've ever flown a spaceship. How're you doing? It's been ages. You look all grown up.'

'I'm fine,' smiled Eric. He thought the postman looked older, too. 'How about you?'

'Fine, fine.' Reg gazed through the windscreen at the looming grey clouds. 'It's going to rain again.'

'Yeah.'

'I've got a fiver on West Brom to win the FA Cup this year. That Jeff Astle's no George Best, but he's a hell-of-a player. Do you think they'll do it?'

'I haven't been following the football,' replied Eric. He waited. The moment he heard the postman's voice, Eric had felt a sinking feeling in his stomach. The location of the parked car was more than coincidental.

'Old Charlie Biggins reckons Everton will pull it off, but I saw them on Match of the Day, and I still fancy the Albion.' Reg paused. 'You can almost see Wembley Stadium from here.'

Eric determined to speed things along. 'What's happened, Reg?'

'What do you mean?'

'Something's going on, isn't it?'

Reg nodded, 'Yes.'

Eric waited.

'I need to...' Reg faltered. 'If you're free sometime soon, could we arrange a day to meet up?'

'What's this about?' Eric asked bluntly.

Reg ran a long forefinger over the knobbly grip on the red steering wheel, 'It's about... everything we've talked about. The transmissions. You've probably heard some of the recent ones; *Spend some money and make the day sunny.*'

'Yeah, I've heard that,' Eric said quietly. 'I guessed it was one of theirs.'

'It was,' said Reg. 'It is.' He looked at the gathering clouds. 'I'll explain everything when I see you. How about next weekend? Are you free Sunday?'

The postman was trying to appear casual, but Eric detected a sense of urgency. 'I have dinner with my mum and dad on Sundays. It'll be finished by half-one, but –'

'That's fine. I'll be waiting at the end of your road. Is two o'clock all right?'

Eric nodded, 'Two o'clock next Sunday.' He heard the reluctance in his voice. The postman must have heard it too. In truth, Eric had wanted him to hear it.

'Great,' said Reg. He tapped the steering wheel with his palms. 'That's great.'

Pulling his bicycle away from the wet bush, Eric wiped the rainwater from the saddle. He cycled slowly down the public footpath. Why had Reg been so enigmatic? A part of Eric wished he had not agreed to meet him, but he had never forgotten the postman's warning about the people in Hartlepool: *Your gift is so strong, Eric, they'd do whatever it took to have you work for them ... they'd find a way*. Eric had always believed that Reg had his best interests at heart. The postman was his friend, his ally.

Eric took a seat at the kitchen table.

'The fourth Ealing hippie joins us,' announced Paul. 'Welcome, my friend. May your hair flow long, and your beard grow soft and curly.'

'Don't hold your breath,' said Pattie. 'He's only just started shaving.'

'Last Wednesday,' said Eric. It had actually been three months ago.

Simon and Garfunkel's *Mrs Robinson* came on the radio. Eric looked over at Julia, who was reading that day's edition of the Guardian. He was glad to see her sober.

'More flak for Enoch Powell following his *Rivers of Blood* speech,' said Julia. 'I'm sure he's right about immigration changing the character of the country, but our horizons will broaden, and that can only be good.'

'I won't be complaining if they open more Indian restaurants,' said Pattie. 'Yum!'

Julia lowered her newspaper. 'Pattie thought I was being overoptimistic about the Common Market, but I believe it's a step in the right direction,' she said to no one in particular. 'If the union leads to borders softening in Europe, that will show the way forward for the rest of the world. I think a United States of Europe would be a good start.'

'I understand where you're coming from,' said Pattie. 'But how can that happen when some European countries are richer than others?'

'Good point,' replied Julia. 'It'll be difficult at first. Integration is a slow and arduous process. But as long as people appreciate the long-term interests, it'll settle down after a while. You don't get friction between the states in North America. A united world is more likely to be a fair and peaceful one. I don't see any other way.'

'Any other way to do what?' asked Pattie.

'To preserve humanity.'

Yep, Julia's definitely back to her old self today, thought Eric.

*

The following Saturday evening, Eric made his way to Hampstead. Exiting the Northern Line station, he checked his A to Z. The teenager turned right into Heath Street in the early evening sunshine, *This is a bit posh. I bet it costs a few bob to live here.* He recalled his telephone conversation with Rainbow. The pretty redhead had sounded particularly pleased to hear from him. Despite his uneasy feelings after their first meeting, Eric looked forward to seeing her again. *Norwegian Wood* played in his head and he pictured himself crawling off to sleep in her bath. It would probably be an old Victorian tub with little cast-iron feet.

Replenished with the arrival of springtime, the verdant trees of Hampstead Heath crowned the hill above the red-tiled rooftops. Hazy yellow sunlight lit the leafy canopies. Eric slowed his pace, gazing up at the softly illuminated woodland. This was his first real date and the attractive young woman was at least five years his senior. Steadying his nerves, he thought of Pattie and Julia. They were in their late twenties and he always felt comfortable in their company.

Eric stopped outside the small, well-appointed house. *Just do it,* he told himself, focusing on the black front door. He rang the doorbell. *Shit, I should have brought her something!* Leaning over the rail into the next garden, Eric plucked a daffodil. The front door opened. Rainbow was as pretty as he remembered.

Eric looked out into the back garden. Long shadows stretched across a recently mown lawn. The last rays of evening beamed directly onto the dining table, reflecting off the silver cutlery, and Otis Redding's

Dock of the Bay played quietly. Against the opposite wall was a gold-and-white traditional-style sofa. If things went well, maybe he and Rainbow would end the evening cuddled up there. The song on the radio faded. *Otis was a great singer, but his whistling was a bit dodgy.*

Rainbow glided into the room wearing a long green Indian dress with a matching headband. The colour suited her, accentuating the scintillating tones of her long red hair. She smiled, 'Sit down and make yourself at home.'

'Thanks.' Eric seated himself on the sofa. 'It's a nice house. Do you live here alone?'

'I share it with Cathy,' replied Rainbow. She placed a vase with the single daffodil at the centre of the small table. 'There, it looks fab.'

Eric wondered who owned the impressive brown leather cowboy boots he had seen through the front-room doorway. They were far too big to fit either of the women. Perhaps the boots belonged to Cathy's boyfriend. Perhaps Eric's Beatle boots would stand beside them one day soon.

Rainbow turned around and smiled. 'Cathy's out,' said the pretty redhead.

'Out with her boyfriend?'

'Oh, Cathy doesn't have a boyfriend,' replied Rainbow. 'She was disappointed that your friend Paul didn't give her his number. He's quite dishy – like a skinny young Elvis.'

'It's been said before,' said Eric. 'Shame he can't sing like him.'

'That would be groovy for your group.'

'How did you know I was in a band?'

'Oh, you just look like you should be,' replied Rainbow.

Half smiling, Eric looked out of the window. He had only been in the girl's company a few minutes, and already he felt a sense of unease. *So if Cathy doesn't have a boyfriend, who do those fancy boots belong to?*

'Dinner will be a few minutes.' Rainbow smiled and disappeared into the kitchen.

'Can I help?' enquired Eric.

'You can light the candle on the dining table,' called the redhead.

Dinner went smoothly enough. Eric had remembered to tell her he was vegetarian. The girl had told him that she was veggie, too. Eric had never heard of *ratatouille*, but the French vegetable stew tasted good. As the evening progressed, conversation flowed more easily, and Eric found himself warming to the attractive hippie girl. She told him about her job as a solicitor's receptionist, and he told her of his ambitions in photography. When Eric mentioned Pattie, Rainbow wanted to know about her modelling career and how they had met. Then she asked about Julia, expressing an interest in her politics.

Rainbow took a pack of Dunhill's from her handbag. 'I tried to buy some marijuana for tonight,' the girl said apologetically. 'I was hoping we could get high together, but my drug pusher was on holiday.'

Eric reached into his jacket pocket, 'That's okay, mine wasn't.'

'Oh... Groovy,' said Rainbow. She stared at the two joints in Eric's hand.

'Here.' Eric handed the girl one of the reefers. 'Dinner was lovely. I'm glad to contribute something to the evening. It's pretty good stuff; we may not need the second joint.'

'Oh, far out.' Staring at the marijuana cigarette, Rainbow rolled it between her fingers.

The sun had dipped below the horizon, leaving dwindling traces of red and yellow in the night sky. Eric stood up and drew the curtains. 'We don't want the neighbours watching us pass the joint across the table.' He pushed the candle towards the girl.

Rainbow lit the reefer.

Eric smiled, 'You'll have to inhale deeper than that. It's good pot, but not *that* good.'

Rainbow inhaled. A short time later, she and Eric were grinning like Cheshire cats. *I Can't Let Maggie Go* came on the radio.

Eric stood up. Bowing like Sir Walter Raleigh, he offered his hand. 'Would you care to dance?'

'I'd love to,' the girl replied, taking Eric's hand and sauntering to the centre of the candlelit room. 'Who sings this?' she asked as they slow-danced.

'Honeybus,' answered Eric. 'Does having our first dance to this make it our song?' *Bloody hell, that was smooth,* he thought, though he realised he had got the idea from Pattie.

'I was wondering,' said Rainbow, 'Is Julia a communist?'

Eric's delusion of being London's answer to Don Juan was instantly shattered. 'Um, no, Julia just wants a shift to the left.' Eric felt pleased with his response. He had managed a coherent reply.

'Is that what you want, too?' asked the redhead.

'Er, I wouldn't want the world to go too far the other way.' Eric hoped the girl's next question wouldn't send him out of his depth.

'I'd love to meet your Ealing friends,' said Rainbow. 'They sound fascinating.'

'Yeah.' The girl's fishing seemed overly inquisitive. And even Julia refrained from political discussion when she was dancing.

'Is Pattie a communist?'

'No. Pattie's just... Pattie.'

Mr Tambourine Man put an end to the slow dancing. Sitting on the sofa next to Rainbow, Eric searched for a topic that would steer the conversation away from his friends.

'The words to this don't make sense,' Rainbow said, picking up on the Dylan song. 'Trees aren't haunted or frightened.'

'*I* know what he means.' Eric surprised himself with his abruptness. *Julia would, too,* he thought. *And so would all the others at the Ealing House, even Tony. No Rainbow, I don't think you'd fit in there; not at all.*

'Oh, of course, I get it,' reneged the redhead.

Eric sensed an atmosphere. Beside him on the sofa, Rainbow was staring. It was as if she was looking into his mind, reading his thoughts. Women could do that. Perhaps it was one of those evolutionary self-preservation things that Julia had talked about.

'I'll be back in a moment.' Rainbow touched Eric's arm. 'I have a surprise for you.'

The girl's mood had shifted again. Her grey-blue eyes regarded Eric as she rose from the sofa. The door clicked closed behind her.

Eric went to the dining table where his jacket was hanging on the back of a chair. Taking the second joint from the table, he dropped it into the inside pocket. *Change of plan,* he told himself. *I'll smoke it when I get home.* He heard Rainbow speaking in the hallway. Hastening to the closed door, he drew close, eavesdropping.

'*Ten minutes, yes.*'

Eric heard the receiver go down.

Ten minutes? What did that mean? Had she called for a taxi to whisk him away? Eric's instincts told him to leave, but he sat on the sofa and waited.

Julie Driscoll's *This Wheel's on Fire* segued into the Lemon Pipers' *Green Tambourine.* The door opened, and Rainbow floated to the centre of the candlelit room. All thoughts of leaving vanished from Eric's mind as the girl danced in front of him wearing the white translucent fairy dress.

'It was so pretty, I went back to Kensington Market and bought it,' explained the lovely redhead. 'You do like it, don't you?' she whispered, gyrating like a bellydancer.

This is it! thought Eric. He wished he had summoned the nerve to purchase condoms from the chemist shop on the Northfield Avenue, but she was probably on the pill; most young women were nowadays.

Taking small stuttering steps, Rainbow danced towards the sofa. Eric slipped his arms around her as she straddled him. Running her fingers through his long hair, the girl guided his face to hers. The ensuing kiss was soft at first, then suddenly passionate. As if in a dream, Eric found himself lying flat on his back. He looked up at Rainbow. The semi-naked girl was on top of him, her long red hair falling across his face. Eric felt her flesh through the open back of the fairy dress. She kissed him harder, her tongue darting into his mouth. Rainbow reached between their bodies and unbuttoned his jeans. Eric's breath quickened.

'Oh!' Cathy exclaimed loudly, staring wide-eyed at the couple on the sofa.

Rainbow sprang to her feet, 'Cathy! I didn't expect you home so soon!'

Eric laid back and closed his eyes. *Yeah, Cathy, I'd say that was dead-on ten minutes.*

*

At two o'clock the following day, Eric left his house and walked up the road to meet Reg. A light drizzle deposited tiny droplets in his hair, the rainwater beading on his blue RAF coat. The previous evening's dinner date with Rainbow had been a distraction, but the day of the meeting had rolled around. It was with a mixture of trepidation and curiosity that Eric approached the Zodiac. The passenger door swung open, and he climbed in.

'You've got mint sauce on your lip,' grinned Reg.

Eric wiped his mouth. 'Why is it I have an urge to be back at home watching the telly?'

'What, *Wagon Train*, *The Golden Shot* and *Captain Scarlet?*' replied Reg. 'You're not missing much on a Sunday afternoon. I'll have you back in time for *The Saint.*'

Eric picked a dark-green speck of mint from his knuckles. He ducked as Reg drove past his house. 'Where are we going?'

'Stoke Poges. It's a village in Buckinghamshire,' said the postman.

Eric remembered Paul spending a weekend there with the scouts. 'Are we going camping?'

'No,' replied Reg. 'We're going to meet the Scientist.'

Reg turned left onto the Northfield Avenue, heading south towards Brentford. He glanced at Eric. The longhaired teenager was fiddling with a button on his greatcoat, apparently deep in thought.

'It was sad about Jim Clark,' said Reg. 'He was one of our best racing drivers ever.'

'Mm,' mumbled Eric.

'Did you hear about that American bloke who bought London Bridge? He thought he was getting *Tower* Bridge.'

'Yeah, I heard that.'

One more try, thought Reg. 'I see they finally nabbed the Kray Twins. I reckon they'll bang Reggie and Ronnie up for life.'

The Zodiac was on the A4 speeding towards Slough when Eric broke his silence, 'Why didn't you tell me we were meeting the Scientist?'

'I was afraid you wouldn't come,' Reg answered truthfully.

Eric nodded.

'Is there anything you want to know?' asked the driver.

'Yeah. What's this meeting about, and what's it got to do with me?'

'The Scientist asked to meet you.'

'Why?'

'It's best if I let him explain,' said Reg. 'But don't worry, he's not going to attach electrodes to your head and plug you in.'

'That's comforting.'

'I've known him for many years, and he's a good man,' continued Reg. 'I told you I worked with the Scientist at Bletchley during the war. He tried the transmitter with several people before he settled on me. Till Sid came along, I was the only one to have any success with it. Apparently, I had *the knack*.'

Grandmama's gift, thought Eric. He flashed back to Sid's basement club.

'After the war, when they moved the transmitter to West Ealing, me and Sid went with it,' explained Reg. 'You have to understand Eric; things were different then. They were rebuilding the country, and it was the start of a new era. Labour got voted in, and the new Prime Minister, Clement Atlee, had plans to make things fairer for everyone. He brought in a bit of socialism to narrow the gap between the rich and the poor. The National Health was the big one. Do you understand how the political systems work?'

'Julia explained it to me,' said Eric.

'Who's Julia?'

'Oh, a friend. Go on.'

'Well, we all had reservations about the transmitter, especially me and Sid. But we decided that if the right people were in charge, it could be used for the common good.'

Eric nodded, 'But now the *wrong* people are in charge?'

'Now a load of *nutters* are in charge,' replied Reg. 'And that's the problem.'

Eric watched the countryside go by. He asked the question that had been nagging at him, 'Reg, are you a communist?'

The postman shook his head, 'Oh no, I'm somewhere in the middle.'

'So's Julia.'

'I like the sound of this Julia,' said Reg.

'She's lovely,' replied Eric

Leaving the A roads behind, Reg steered the Ford Zodiac through winding country lanes. Thick forest lined the byways on either side, the trees broken occasionally by fields and isolated middle-class dwellings. Summer was late in arriving and a featureless grey sky imbued the Buckinghamshire countryside with an air of stillness and quiet.

Reg pulled up in front of a farm gate. A forest bordered the long muddy driveway beyond.

'This is it,' said the postman. 'Do us a favour and –'

Eric got out of the car. Opening the wide gate, he stood aside as Reg drove through. *Cheer up, mate*, Eric told himself. He had been short with the postman, saying little during the forty-minute journey. Closing the gate, Eric reminded himself that Reg was doing what he believed to be best for... For what? For him? For the Scientist? For the country, the world?

Reg manoeuvred the Zodiac up the muddy, rutted driveway.

'Sorry,' said Eric. 'I've wondered if something like this might happen one day. And now that it has, I feel...'

'Worried?'

'Yeah.'

Reg turned to Eric with a wry smile, 'Maybe I'm the one who should be apologising. When your dad fixed my bike all those years ago, I wanted to return the favour. I guessed that you had *the knack,* and Sid agreed. But neither of us expected you to have so much of it.'

'Which is why the Scientist wants to meet me.'

'Yes.'

'Well, it worked,' sighed Eric. 'Bill Grimes can fix anything.'

'That's what they say,' Reg replied flatly. He parked the car on the gravelled forecourt.

The impressive country residence looked to Eric like a giant doll's house.

Reg rang the doorbell. 'We may have to wait a while. Igor's in Hartlepool, and the Scientist is a bit on the slow side.'

'Who's Igor?' Eric pictured a hunchbacked dwarf from Transylvania.

'He's the Scientist's assistant. You'll meet him one day, I expect.'

I'm not sure I want to, thought Eric. Stepping back, he looked up at the two-story nineteenth-century building. Like the Ealing House, it was flanked by thick woodland, but unlike the Ealing House, it was in good repair.

The maroon front door swung inwards then juddered as it struck the Scientist's foot. Eric saw half a head of wild white hair, a wrinkled hand gripping a walking stick, and a blue carpet slipper.

'Mm,' grunted the old man, shuffling backwards and opening the door.

Eric wondered if all old scientists resembled Albert Einstein. This one wore a dark-blue dressing gown over yellow pyjamas and looked like he had fallen through a hedge backwards.

'Ah! You brought the boy!' the Scientist exclaimed, raising his stick and regarding Eric through round gold-rimmed spectacles. 'How long have you been in the RAF, lad?'

'I was nearly in the Women's Royal Army Corps,' replied Eric. 'This was the last RAF coat on the rail.'

The Scientist gazed skyward, a whimsical smile lighting his wrinkled face, 'Ah, those wonderful WRAC girls.'

'Yes, well could we continue this conversation over a cup of tea?' requested Reg.

'Yes, yes, come in.' The Scientist stepped aside. *'Igor!'*

'He's in Hartlepool,' said Reg. 'I'll make the tea.'

Copious bookshelves lined every wall of the Scientist's front-room study. From his comfortable armchair by the fire, Eric looked around the room; *The library at the Ealing House is big, but this one must have copies of half the books ever written. Saves on wallpaper, I suppose.*

'Are you a reader, Eric?' the Scientist asked from his armchair by the fireplace.

'I'm halfway through *The Lord of the Rings* at the moment,' replied Eric. 'I like anything that gets my imagination going.'

The Scientist smiled, 'Of course you do. Do you like music?'

'Very much.'

The Scientist nodded, 'I expect music conjures mental pictures for you.'

Eric stiffened. 'How did you know that? Usually, when I try to tell people about it, they –'

'Do you have out of body experiences?' asked the Scientist. 'Some call the phenomenon *Astral Projection*, though I find the term fanciful.'

Tiny prickles ran up Eric's neck; his cranium felt suddenly cold. 'Yes, I... Once, well, maybe a couple of times, I –'

'It's nothing to worry about,' the Scientist said reassuringly. 'The human brain is the most complex thing we know of. In a year or two, it'll be sending men to the moon.'

'But how did you know?' repeated Eric. 'I mean about my out of body experiences and the music pictures?'

The Scientist clasped his fingers. 'Reg tells me you have *the knack – the gift* – or whatever you choose to call it. Your experiences, your vivid imagination... they're part of the package. Your neural pathways are... We're all wired differently, Eric, and you happen to have been born with a rather fascinating set of circuitry. Perception is everything. You're very fortunate. Enjoy it.'

Reg entered the study with three cups of tea on a silver tray. 'Have you got any biscuits?'

'Eric, firstly, I would like to thank you for coming here today,' began the Scientist.

'That's okay,' Eric said, accepting a cup of tea from Reg. Eric's mood had changed. The Scientist's assurances had lifted a weight from his shoulders. He would never comprehend the workings of his sub-conscious mind, but at least someone understood. He was not alone in having these strange experiences, and according to the learned man, his neural wiring was okay – if a little unusual.

'I asked Reg to bring you here today,' admitted the Scientist. 'The reason, not to put too fine a point on it, is that we're trying to save the world.'

'Oh,' said Eric.

'I'm afraid the scenario is a little complicated,' said the old man. 'It has to do with many things: politics, ecology, and people's attitudes being at the forefront. We couldn't possibly expect you to understand it all at your tender age. I can only ask you to believe that our intentions are entirely honourable.'

Eric sipped his tea. 'You mean that MoD2 are using the transmitter you built to promote their right-wing ideology by turning people into mindless consumers with an upgraded version of the brainwashing techniques pioneered by Edward Bernays. And you're worried that this will turn everyone into greedy, selfish, miserable sods who don't give a monkey's about the future of the planet... Which is looking a bit dodgy.'

The scientist stared over his spectacles at Eric. 'Yes, that's exactly what I mean. Would you like a biscuit?'

'No thanks,' said Eric. 'And there's more, isn't there. You want *me* to send messages to counteract the ones that the people in Hartlepool have already broadcast.'

'Eventually, yes,' said the Scientist. 'But not today. First, we need to test the new transmitter. Will you do it?'

The new transmitter. Eric considered the Scientist's request. 'What do you want me to say?'

A patchwork of open fields stretched away from the back of the house. On a distant hill, the chalk outline of a male figure had been etched. A huge erect penis stood upright in front of the chalk man's chest.

'It's a fertility symbol,' the Scientist explained, joining Eric and Reg at the laboratory's rear window. 'Some of these Celtic hill carvings date back to around 500BC. Their gods were giants, and the depictions reflect that. The locals call him Big Ted.'

'They called me Big Reg at school,' said the postman. 'But I never got my picture on a hillside.'

'Yes, well, I've no doubt your legend lives on,' said the Scientist.

'What's that?' Eric asked, looking at a bazooka-like tube on one of the benches.

'Ah, it's a high-powered listening device,' replied the Scientist. 'This is the Mk1 prototype. The one Igor is using in Hartlepool is half the size. Open the window, and I'll give you a demonstration.'

The scientist grunted, hoisting the cylindrical instrument onto his shoulder. Squinting through the eyepiece, he levelled the listening device at a solitary sheep and pressed a green button on the side. The sheep remained silent. The Scientist aimed up at a nearby elm tree. The resident blackbird had nothing to say either.

'Oh, sod it.' The old man lowered the heavy instrument, resting it on the frame of the open window. 'It does work, but you'll have to take my word for it.'

'His cock's nearly as big as yours, Charlie!' a female voice said through the loudspeaker in the Mk1 prototype.

On a footpath below the chalk figure, a young couple strolled arm-in-arm.

'Where's the new transmitter?' asked Reg.

The Scientist pointed to a grey metal box on one of the benches, 'That's it.'

'That's it?' exclaimed Reg. 'The original machine takes up a whole bloody wall!'

'Electronic technology has come a long way in the last twenty years.' The Scientist shrugged, 'The first transmitter was a Heath Robinson job, cobbled together from whatever components were available at the time. I couldn't replicate it without those parts, even if I wanted to.'

'Will it work?' asked Reg.

'That's what we're going to find out,' replied the Scientist. 'Eric, would you take a seat in front of the new machine.'

Eric admired the Shure SM57 microphone on the benchtop. 'I'd like one of these.'

'When I flick the switch, read what's on that piece of paper,' said the Scientist. 'Just a minute, I forgot to plug it in.'

Eric looked down at the scrap of paper on the bench in front of him. The Scientist's spidery scrawl read: *Money can't buy you happiness; family and friends are best.*

Ahh, nice, thought Eric.

On the drive home, Eric discovered the SM57 microphone in one of his coat pockets.

23

Happiness Stan

Paul laid back on his sun lounger, 'Oh, deep joy.' He adjusted the angle to near-horizontal. 'The sun has got his hat on and he's decided to grinny-grinny down, all sintyladen and sunny beamleys to the world.'

'Much thinkly on that,' Eric replied, toppling his own lounger as he passed Paul the joint. 'Watch out for burny-burny of the skinly-most.'

Stanley Unwin's gobbledygook narrative on the Small Faces' *Ogdens' Nut Gone Flake* album had sent Paul and Eric off on a nonsensical tangent. The infectious gibberish had injected a shot of *quirk* into Tony's increasingly bawdy humour.

Paul screwed up his face, 'Burny-burny of the throatly-bold.' He reached into the long grass and pushed the singed cardboard end into the soil with his forefinger.

'Sorry about that.'

'That's okay,' wheezed Paul. 'It's my fault for instigating *The Night of the Long Roach*.'

'In the middle of the afternoon,' said Eric.

'*Afternoon* doesn't have the same ring to it.'

'True.'

Happy Days Toy Town played through the open French windows. Eric and Paul clapped twice, leant back on their loungers, and did the twist. They had been in and out of the back garden all day. Eric glanced at the red swing. Recalling Julia's painting, he turned his attention to the French windows and glimpsed a middle-aged man staring back at him through one of the small panes.

'A rather splendid bit of gear, this,' Paul said in his posh voice. 'What does it say on the packet?'

'Lebanese Gold: use sparingly and prepare to be silly,' replied Eric. 'I got it from Harry. I'm sorry to say that he's slipped a few rungs down the ladder of life.'

'Harry? In what way?'

'In every way. He used to have a nice upstairs flat in Hanwell. It was damp, but okay. And he had a groovy girlfriend who was into pyramid power.'

'Yeah, I remember you saying.'

'Now he's living in a crappy squat in Acton. His girlfriend's gone, and the place is a dump. The electricity goes on and off, and the living room is papered floor to ceiling with porno pictures.'

'What's the story?' asked Paul. 'Hard drugs?'

Eric nodded, 'Yeah, I think so. More than pot, anyway. Phil reckons Harry's heavily into speed. He looks like shit, and he can't stop talking. When I was there buying this Lebanese, he shoved a medicine bottle under my nose. I thought my chest was going to explode! Apparently, it was amyl nitrite.'

'You didn't like it, then?'

'It was bloody horrible,' said Eric. 'It felt... like it was *bad* for you, like paint stripper or something. They need to legalise pot to separate it from the nasty stuff. That's the problem. You go there to buy a nice bag of Mary Jane, and the dealer tries to sell you something nasty to go with it. It's easy to see how people get into trouble with drugs.'

'Mum says they'll legalise pot soon.'

'I think they'll have to,' replied Eric. 'People try marijuana and come to the conclusion that the government's wrong to make it illegal. That closes the door on their respect for authority and opens the door to the dodgy stuff: heroin, speed, and all the other crap. Harry's in a right mess. His brain's pinging about like a pinball.'

'All flart, fattang, and see you in Bedlam,' Paul said, reverting back to Stanley Unwin.

'Exactly,' said Eric. 'You go trundling along, happy as can be, then all of a sudden, wheels don't roll.'

Eric's eyes darted towards the house as Julia stepped out of the ballroom wearing a black bikini. The slender woman had the figure of a girl half her age. Julia's striking green eyes regarded Eric from beneath her black fringe, her long hair shining in the sunlight.

Paul sat up, 'Here, Mum, have your lounger back. I was keeping it warm for you.'

'No, stay put.' Julia held up a pair of cut-off Levi's. 'I came out to show you these.'

'They'll look great on you,' said Paul.

'No, they're yours,' replied Julia. 'I cut up those old jeans you'd thrown out. I thought they'd be good for the summer.'

'Shorts? Oh, no... Thanks, Mum, but I can't wear shorts.'

'Why not?' asked Julia. 'You don't have to wear them when you go out, but for times like this in the gar –'

'No, Mum, I'm not wearing them.'

Eric looked over at his friend. It was unlike Paul to be so abrupt.

'All right then,' Julia said quietly. 'Paul, I'm sorry I used to tease you about your Boy Scout shorts. I didn't give you a complex, did I?'

'I don't wear scout shorts anymore.'

'No, but –'

'Mum, I just... Can we drop it?' Paul's cheeks had coloured. Something had struck a wrong chord.

Walking past Eric, Julia sat on the swing. 'I've been watching a report on Robert Kennedy's assassination. It's what, only two months since Martin Luther King Junior was shot dead in Memphis.'

This is going to be an anti-gun speech, thought Eric.

'The Right to Bear Arms; why the hell do they keep *that* in their constitution?' began Julia. 'They should make it: *We all agree* not *to bear arms.* Do you know how many people died in America last year because of '

''Ello 'ippies! Sitting comfy on our bum-bums, are we?' Tony strolled into the back garden from the nettle-lined path by the side of the house. 'Is band practice still on?'

Eric thought Tony looked lankier than ever. Soon he would tower over all of them.

Paul rose from his lounger and walked over to the swing. 'I'm sorry about the shorts, Mum. What I said came out wrong.'

Julia stood up and hugged her son. 'Oh, it really doesn't matter, Paul. It took me all of thirty seconds to make them.'

Eric looked at Julia in her black bikini and wished it was him she was hugging.

Inside the ballroom, Eric unfastened his rucksack and brought out the microphone the Scientist had given him. 'Here, give this a try.'

'Where did you get it?' Paul asked, admiring the professional mic.

Eric was unprepared for the question. 'It was a present from my uncle. Well, he's not my *real* uncle...'

'Like our Uncle Jack,' suggested Paul.

'Yeah, one of those.' Eric hated lying, especially to his best friend. Maybe the next time he saw the Scientist, he would call him Uncle. Or maybe not.

The fourteen-year-old skinhead flailed manically behind his drums. His heavy boot slamming down on the bass drum pedal produced a chandelier-rattling thump.

'I was thinking we could try some new songs,' Paul shouted above the din.

Tony executed a procession of paradiddles, a couple of flams on the snare, caught his crash cymbal, then stopped playing. 'Let's do *Fire*. That's a fuckin' great one.'

Eric and Paul recalled *The 14 Hour Technicolor Dream*. Arthur Brown's performance had been unforgettable, even if he had fried his brain in the process. More than a year later, *Fire* was climbing the charts.

'It's all organ, really,' said Eric.

'Yeah, but don't let that stop you,' said Paul. 'What about *Jumpin' Jack Flash*?'

'Definitely,' came the reply from his bandmates.

'I like Donovan's new song, *Hurdy Gurdy Man*,' said Eric. 'We could hold back the verses, then crank up the volume for the choruses.'

'*MacArthur Park* is nice and weird,' said Paul. 'It might be hard to pull off, but –'

'Oh yeah, then we'll play *Congratulations* for an encore!' Tony shook his head. 'Let's do *Born to Be Wild* instead.'

'I thought you'd want to do that one, so I already worked it out.' Eric turned to Paul, 'It's in E. E for easy.'

'Let's do it in F for fuckin' loud,' quipped Tony.

On the other side of the adjoining wall, Keith bobbed from side to side, banging his beak on his perch.

*

The sunny spell was over almost before it had begun. Halfway through June, the unsettled weather returned, diminishing the attendance at St Mary's Church fete and scuppering Paul's plan to stage a Clockwork Mouse concert amid the flowers in the front garden.

Another school year was drawing to a close, and Eric again had the option to join the great British workforce. Art college was the obvious move, but Bill and Mary had their hearts set on A-Levels. It was this that occupied Eric's thoughts as he climbed the stepladder. He opened a tin of white emulsion and began stirring.

I should have done more with the camera. Eric looked down through the bedroom window of the semidetached Greenford house. A bicycle was sticking up from the shallow Brent River. *That old bike would make a nice black-and-white picture. I could call it River Bike. No, that's crap. Maybe —*

'Stirring a hole in the bottom of the tin?' Bill enquired from the doorway.

'Oh, hello Dad. Are you finished downstairs?'

'For the time being,' replied his father. 'I thought I'd come up and give you a hand in here.'

'Do you want the stepladder?'

'No, I'll roller the walls. You're better at cutting-in than me.'

'Does that mean I'll be getting a rise?'

'You'll have the shop steward on me next,' Bill said, pouring white emulsion into a metal paint tray.

'I will if you keep stealing the radio.'

'I'll go down and get it,' said Bill. Replacing the lid on the Dulux tin, he stood up and left the room. 'Anyway, it's *my* bloody radio!' he joked from halfway down the stairs.

Eric smiled. His dad rarely swore at home, especially when his wife was within earshot.

Tom Jones' *Delilah* played on the paint-spattered radio. Eric stood on the stepladder, cutting-in white emulsion against the Magnolia ceiling. He thought the colours should have been the other way round, but as his dad said, the customer was always right.

'Do you think the Common Market is a good idea?'

Bill filled the white V he had rolled on the back wall. 'Since when did you become interested in politics?'

'Since they put another five bob on the price of LPs.'

Bill smiled. 'Yes, I'm in favour of Europe. Harold Wilson came round to thinking it's a good idea, so that'll do me.'

'Do you vote Labour?' asked Eric.

Bill nodded. 'I've always voted on the left. Your Mum's been a true-blue Conservative all her life, but we agree to differ on that.'

'Are you bothered that even though Labour is in power, Mum's lot seem to be getting the upper hand?' asked Eric.

'Oh, we lefties said our piece after the war,' replied Bill. 'We got the NHS and a few other bits and pieces.'

'And you're satisfied with that?'

'Well, you don't want to rock the boat. Everyone's entitled to their opinion.'

Eric wondered if the old left's passive resignation was one reason his generation seemed so angry at their parents. While he was aware that Britain had its share of *Ron Hillman's*, the hippie doctrine made so much sense, soon everyone would see the light. The future was bright. Psychedelic bright.

Propping himself against the front gate while Bill locked the house, Eric looked at the green A35 van. The holiday stickers were still there. *Susan leaned out of her pink dodgem car, her blue eyes targeting him as Del Shannon's Runaway blasted through the loudspeaker.*

'Penny for your thoughts,' said Bill.

Julia had said that by the Serpentine. 'I was back in Skegness,' replied Eric.

'With that blonde girl, I suppose?'

'No, the dark-haired one, Susan.' *Blue eyes win the prize.*

Bill handed Eric a five-pound note. 'You've earned it.'

'Thanks, Dad. Can you drop me in West Ealing, please? Somewhere near British Home Stores.'

Eric emerged from BHS, having exchanged the big blue fiver for three pound notes, a few coins and Dylan's *John Wesley Harding* LP. The shops would be closing soon, and the high street was beginning to empty as people made their way home for tea. Eric glanced up at the office above Burton's,

Reg.

The postman stood at the window, waving his long arms. When the teenager waved back, Reg pointed a spindly finger towards the door at the side of the building. Eric hesitated, his raised hand suspended in the air. For three seconds, he toyed with the idea of misinterpreting the postman's gesture.

Ushering Eric inside, Reg closed the glossy red door. 'How've you been?'

'Fine, you?' Eric's shoes tapped the wooden stairs as he walked up to the first-floor office with Bob Dylan under his arm.

'There's no one else here,' Reg said, following Eric up the stairway. 'That's pretty rare these days. They've beefed-up the security in the last few years.'

Eric looked around the office. The last time he had stood there had been in 1963. He visualised his eleven-year-old palm on a stack of jazz LPs as he raised his right hand and swore to Sid, *'I ain't gonna tell nobody 'bout the shit I seen in this here office'.* Eric had kept the promise for five years, though there were times when he had been tempted to confide in Paul, and more especially, Julia.

Reg lit a Senior Service and rested his arm on the watercooler. 'Hasn't changed much, has it.'

Eric shook his head, 'No, but it's smaller than I remembered.'

'*You* were smaller,' observed Reg. 'And younger. The five years between eleven and sixteen are like the twenty between thirty and fifty. Time flies as you get older.'

Eric looked at Sid's old desk by the window.

'It's mine now,' said Reg. 'Here, have a seat. Not by the window, there's no point in advertising that you're here.'

Here it comes, thought Eric. Pulling out a chair, he looked over his shoulder. On the other side of the dividing wall was the troublesome transmitter. Eric felt no desire to open the door and take a look.

'I had a visit from Igor,' began Reg. He seated himself near Eric. 'The Scientist was pleased with the test on the new transmitter. He's expecting the first results to start filtering back anytime now.'

No football, thought Eric. *At least we got straight to the point.* 'I liked the message the Scientist wrote: *Money can't buy you happiness, family and friends are best.*'

Reg nodded, 'It's not as catchy as some of my past masterpieces, but the sentiment is good.'

'Gibbons don't do algebra?'

The postman smiled, 'That was one of Sid's.' Flicking his cigarette ash on the floor, Reg turned to face Eric. 'If the new transmitter works, we'll do one more broadcast to counter the messages that MoD2 has been sending out. The Scientist is working on the wording right now. All you have to do is drive to Buckinghamshire with me and read it into the microphone.'

Eric sighed, 'So I'm to be Lord Haw-Haw.'

'Just the opposite,' Reg explained patiently. 'MoD2 are the ones broadcasting the propaganda. All you'll be doing is counteracting what they've already put out.'

Eric stared at the column of ash on the floor. 'Yeah, I know; sorry.'

'It's okay,' smiled Reg. 'I understand your reluctance, and so does the Scientist. Believe me, if it weren't for your super-powerful *knack*, we would never have got you involved. But with your help, we can override anything that MoD2 broadcast. They don't have anyone to rival your *knack*, Eric.'

'So you said. Why did the Scientist have to build a new machine?' Eric gestured towards the back of the office, 'Couldn't we use the one behind that wall?'

'The broadcasts sent from here are being monitored,' explained Reg. 'We could try to jam their system, but that would mean breaking-in to the headquarters in Hartlepool. It's much easier – and safer – if we send our messages from the Scientist's laboratory.'

Eric looked at the empty desk by the window. 'I miss Sid.'

The postman nodded.

*

'Hello Mum.' Paul kicked-off his shoes and dropped his school bag next to the living-room doorway.

'Oh, hello Paul, Eric.' Julia smiled over her shoulder at the two teenagers. She placed her book down next to her on the sofa.

Eric stuffed his school tie into his blazer pocket. 'What are you reading?'

'*Silent Spring*, Rachel Carson,' replied Julia. 'It's about agricultural pesticides and the effect they're having on our environment.'

'Sounds cheerful,' said Paul. 'Are we all going to die from Weetabix poisoning?'

'Not directly,' answered Julia. 'But the chemicals we're pumping into our atmosphere and the nitrogen and phosphorus being carried into our oceans pose a serious threat to future generations.'

'People should have fewer kids,' suggested Eric. 'Then we wouldn't need to produce so much food to feed everyone.'

'I couldn't agree more,' said Julia. 'And the stupid Pope has just decided that birth control is upsetting God. If you ask me, he's an irresponsible bloody idiot.'

Paul nodded, 'I'm going upstairs to get changed.'

'Me too,' said Eric.

'Pattie wants to take us to the pictures tonight,' Julia called as they left the room.

Avoiding the numerous potholes in the car park behind Northfield Odeon, Julia parked the Mini in a space facing the railway. Pattie unbuttoned her jeans. Eric watched over Julia's shoulder as the blonde slipped her hand inside her panties and slid out a reefer.

Handing Julia the joint, Pattie refastened her Levi's. 'I have it on good authority that a pre-cinema smoke is essential for this film.'

Fifteen minutes into *2001: A Space Odyssey*, everyone agreed.

Thirty-three years hence, Arthur C. Clarke's conception of a manned voyage to Jupiter would prove premature. Still, a waltzing space station and evolution-altering monoliths made for thought-provoking entertainment. Near the end, the Ealing Hippies watched through a stoned haze as astronaut David Bowman was catapulted into a psychedelic vortex and reborn as a Star Baby.

Paul scrunched his empty Butterkist bag and dropped it into a bin by the side exit. 'That was a trippy ending.'

'You nearly missed it, dashing off to the foyer like that,' said Julia.

Pattie flicked back her long blonde hair, 'When the munchies hit, you just gotta split.'

Not one of Sid's. Eric pushed down on the metal bar, opening the exit door at the side of the cinema. He and his three friends passed out into the night. 'I'm not sure I understood it all,' admitted Eric.

'I'm not sure we were supposed to,' said Julia. 'We're all made of stardust, so perhaps it was about the eternal cycle.'

'Mind the potholes,' warned Paul.

An underground train rattled past, light from the carriages spilling through the chain-link fence, throwing shifting shadows across the fractured tarmac. The white Mini in the far corner was the only vehicle in the parking area.

'Oi, 'ippies!' called a male voice from behind.

Eric glanced back. Three skinheads were following them across the empty car park. They appeared to be at least two years older than him, and they were certainly much bigger.

'Keep walking.' Julia quickened her pace. 'And don't look back.' She pulled her car keys from her pocket.

Eric heard heavy footsteps approaching fast. He thought he should be scared but felt only numb. Then the three skinheads were among them. One of the ruffians barged hard against Eric's shoulder, sending him staggering to his right. Another snatched the car keys from Julia's hand and tossed them to his friend.

'We was finkin' you two birds might like to 'ave a drink wiv us,' said the skinhead with the keys. Swaggering over to the Mini, he turned and leant against the door. 'I don't mind drivin'.' He held up the keys, jangling them tauntingly.

'No thank you,' replied Julia. 'May I have my keys, please?'

'May I have my keys, please,' the skinhead mimicked in a falsetto voice. 'Oo ju fink you are, the fuckin' Queen?'

The four hippies stood in a row facing the skinheads.

'Oo you screwin'?' said the smallest of the three short-haired thugs. Clenching his fists, he stepped forward, glaring menacingly at Paul.

This is it, thought Eric. *If he hits Paul, the girls will wade in. It'll all go off and we'll lose.*

The smaller skinhead pushed Paul's shoulder, 'I said, oo you fuckin' screwin'?'

Paul said nothing.

There was a rustling from the bushes. 'Can I help you, gentlemen?'

The three skinheads spun around as one. Everyone watched as a tall figure emerged from the shadows. Walking around the Mini, the man confronted the skinhead who had threatened Paul.

He looks like Jim Morrison, thought Eric.

The aggressor backed away, re-joining his mates by the car.

The tall stranger held his open hand towards the biggest skinhead. 'Keys.'

The two stared at one another, assessing the opposition like pack animals contesting leadership rights on the plains of Africa. Fight or flee. With a flick of his hand, the big skinhead tossed the keys forcefully towards the man's chest. His reflexes sharp, the stranger snatched the keys from the air, nullifying the thug's last-ditch challenge.

'Thank you,' sighed Julia, looking up into the tall man's face.

Eric glanced back towards the cinema. The three skinheads sloped away across the dark tarmac.

A chorus of *thank you's* followed. Paul stepped forward and shook the man's hand. Dressed in jeans and an embroidered waistcoat, their rescuer appeared to be in his late twenties. He stood tall in Cuban-heeled cowboy boots. Loose curly brown hair covered his ears.

It is Jim Morrison, Eric thought, still slightly stoned.

'I'm Stan.' The handsome man smiled, handing Julia the keys.

Julia introduced everyone. 'Can we give you a lift? It's the least we can do.'

Pattie squeezed into the back of the Mini, draping herself across Eric and Paul. Julia steered the little car onto the Northfield Avenue.

'What do these skinheads get out of it?' mused Eric. 'I don't see the point.'

Stan half-turned, his knees brushing the glove compartment. 'Aggression releases dopamine in the brain, Eric. They get a buzz from it.'

'Violence can become an addiction,' added Julia. 'Like psychoactive drugs or sex, it can get you high.'

Stan grinned at the driver, 'Those last two are much better options.'

'Without a doubt,' agreed Julia.

Eric felt a pang of jealousy.

'Shall I drop you at home, Eric?' Julia asked as they approached Kingsdown Church.

'No, it's okay, thanks.' Eric searched for a reason to justify his going back to the Ealing House. He shifted. Having Pattie sprawled across him should have been a pleasure, but he felt uncomfortable.

'And another thing regarding the skinheads,' said Stan. 'It seems like everything has an opposite. Black/white, matter/antimatter... I suppose when us hippies came along with our peace and love philosophy, it was inevitable that an opposing movement would arise advocating violence and hate.'

'Newton's third law,' observed Paul.

'That's right,' said Stan. 'It seems to be true of people as well as physics.'

'Sorry.' Pattie shifted awkwardly. 'Is my hip poking your –'

'It's okay,' Eric grunted, pushing back on the seat. 'I wasn't planning on having kids.'

'Your *opposites* theory is an interesting idea,' Julia said, turning right onto the Uxbridge Road. 'Sometimes, even love can turn to hate.'

'I saw that happen in Paris last month,' said Stan. 'Do you know, a *million people* marched through the streets of the French capital. It was amazing, like an anti-capitalist festival, with people singing and protesting in a beautiful, peaceful way. Gandhi would have approved. But there was violence, too. I saw one kid get beaten-up by the French fuzz. Up until that point, everyone seemed so happy. That's all I want, you know? Just to see people happy.'

By the time they reached Haven Green, Eric's right leg was tingling and he had lost all feeling in his foot.

'I'll drop you here if that's okay,' said Julia. 'The station's across the road.'

'Perfect,' smiled Stan. 'Thanks a lot for the lift.'

'Oh, you're ever so welcome,' Julia said, pulling up the handbrake. 'You were our knight in shining armour tonight.' Leaning over, she kissed Stan on the cheek.

'Be happy,' called the smiling hippie. Stan waved back as he crossed the road.

Paul watched the tall man walk across Haven Green. 'Pleased to meet you, Happiness Stan.'

24

A Saucerful of Secrets

Pattie entered the living room wearing a powder-blue minidress she had borrowed from Julia's wardrobe. 'Will this do? I was looking for that green-and-orange Mary Quant number, but it wasn't there. This one matches my eye shadow, so I won't need to redo my makeup.'

Eric smiled up from the sofa, 'Perfect.' He wound-on the new roll of film. 'You look fab, as always.'

'Flattery will get you everywhere,' the model replied with a wink.

A gently swaying cluster of tall red hollyhocks peeped over the windowsill. Eric looked out at the colourful array of mixed flowers, 'It's a lovely day for a change. Shall we start in the front garden?'

The beginning of July 1968 had seen heavy rainfall with flooding in the south-west of England. However, the wet weather improved temporarily, coinciding with the school holidays and providing clear skies for Eric's photoshoot with his friend. Mindful of the recent rain, Pattie had selected her black knee-high boots. She probably would have worn them anyway.

The flower-filled front garden appeared glorious in the summer sunshine: a chocolate-box painting made real.

'That's great; you look gorgeous.' Eric focused the Pentax, clicking the shutter twice. 'Bring your left shoulder towards me... Yeah, hold it there... Beautiful.'

'You've certainly got the patter,' laughed Pattie.

Eric snapped, capturing the delightful blonde's natural smile. 'And I've got the loveliest model in London.'

'Oh, fuck off, you smarmy git!' Pattie grinned, twirling a giant Michaelmas daisy against her cheek.

This was Eric's best shot so far, the close-up of Pattie's face and the wildflower perfectly in focus against a blurred backdrop of deep-green and a cumulus-strewn blue sky.

As he and Pattie left the garden, the Kinks' latest single, *Days*, played in Eric's head, overwhelming him with a wave of anticipated nostalgia. Storing impressions and atmospheres for future recall felt more important than the pictures.

Closing the green wooden gate behind them, they turned right on the arboreal-arched walkway. Dust motes danced in shards of sunlight that cast laser-like beams on the puddled path. Pattie took Eric's hand as they followed the curve to their left, skirting the slope that led up to the reservoir. The warm summer air, the smell of the woodland, the camera in his hand, and lovely Pattie at his side, Eric committed the scenario to memory, reliving it in his imagining as an old man. And the Kinks' song played on. These were the special days.

Through the trees to their right came the crack of a golf ball being struck. Here at the back of the reservoir, the walkway ran straight, the high branches interlocking overhead like the nave of a great woodland cathedral.

'This is the stretch I had in mind.' Eric pointed down the footpath, 'If you go up there a few yards then walk back towards me...'

'Got it,' replied Pattie. 'By the way,' she whispered, more for effect than for secrecy, 'I have a joint tucked away if you fancy one.'

Eric smiled: partly at the promise of the reefer, but mainly at the thought of its hiding place. 'Okay,' Eric called. 'Just stroll towards me.' Turning the camera, Eric snapped a series of portrait shots. He held his breath as he zoomed in for a close-up of the model's boots.

'Joint time,' announced Pattie. 'I spotted a gap in the chain-link fence back there.'

'I know it,' replied Eric. 'But the reservoir may not be the best place to go. It has a reputation for –'

'Oh, don't worry about it.' Pattie spun around, walking back up the pathway. 'Julia warned me, but in my experience, perv's tend to keep their distance. Besides, I'm curious to take a look.'

The slender blonde slipped through the bent-back opening in the wire.

'Wait for me!' Eric called as Pattie picked her way up the muddy slope. Eric cursed as his T-shirt snagged on the mangled fencing.

Pattie stood on the crest of the rise with her hands on her hips. She looked out at the empty reservoir, 'There's a great view from up here!'

There's a great view from down here, thought Eric. He joined Pattie on the grassy rim. 'Blimey, look at those black clouds! And they're heading this way.'

'It's much bigger than I thought.' Pattie looked down into the vast empty bowl. 'It's like a bathtub for a giant Greek god. I can imagine Zeus laying back in a sea of bubbles playing with his rubber duck.'

'Is *that* what you call it?'

Pattie eyed the darkening sky. 'Those rainclouds are moving in fast. The light's gone weird; sort of pinky-yellow.'

Eric adjusted his camera, 'A couple of quick shots.'

Pattie slipped into model mode, striking poses by the bushes. Eric stood with his back to the empty reservoir, snapping speedily.

'Look behind you!' called Pattie.

Eric turned. A curtain of rain was moving towards them across the reservoir. Eric took a photograph of the strange phenomenon, then spun to his right, pointing his lens at a thicket.

'Eric, over here!' Pattie disappeared down the manhole in the concrete lip.

Eric was halfway down the short metal ladder when the rain reached them. Feeling the cold shower hit him from above, he dropped to the floor of the small brick cubicle. Torrential rain streamed loudly on either side, spattering the concrete below the ladder and dripping heavily off the rungs. Eric looked towards the portal that faced out to the reservoir. A wall of rain obscured the basin beyond. It was like standing behind a waterfall.

Pattie stared intently at the graffiti-covered bricks. 'Julia was right about this being a pervert's paradise; there's pornography here to cater to every taste. It's, um, very *extreme,* isn't it.'

'Yeah.' Eric puzzled over a detailed depiction of a pretty doe-eyed schoolgirl with an enormous penis. He recalled Paul's fascination with the lewd inscriptions and drawings. Pattie seemed equally captivated. 'How about that joint?'

'Definitely.' The blonde brushed against Eric as she turned to face him in the confined brick chamber.

Only inches separated them. The sweet exotic smell of the model's patchouli oil mingled with a musty, damp odour. Eric looked down as Pattie raised the hem of her short blue dress. He watched in the eerie pink light as the model slid her hand down inside her white panties and produced a book of matches.

Pattie passed Eric the warm cardboard folder, 'Hold these.'

The pretty young woman glanced up at him, and Eric's heartbeat quickened. This time, there was no pretence of modesty. Pattie's black boots parted, scuffing the concrete floor. She leaned back against the graffiti-covered wall and raised the front of her dress. Hooking the elastic waistband with her thumb, the blonde stretched her panties forward and delicately retrieved the joint.

Eric jumped as the elastic snapped back. His hands trembling, he struck a match and lit the reefer in Pattie's mouth.

The joint passed back and forth. There was only the sound of the rain. Minutes ticked by before either one spoke.

'Why did you take a photo of the bushes?' asked Pattie.

Eric returned from his dream, 'I thought I saw someone.'

'In the bushes?'

'Yeah.'

'A man?'

Eric took another drag and passed the joint back to Pattie. 'I think so,' he croaked.

Pattie nodded, 'I expect he was looking up my dress.' She scoffed, 'I hope he enjoyed his wank.'

Eric exhaled towards the rain and stifled a laugh. He decided not to tell Pattie that when he collected the photos, he was expecting to see a picture of Yogi Bear.

When Pattie entered the kitchen wearing her friend's sky-blue dress, Julia looked up from her seat at the table. 'It suits you!'

'Thanks,' replied the blonde. 'Actually, I think it looks much better on m – Oh... hello!'

'Hi Pattie,' said Happiness Stan.

Julia rested her elbows on the table, cupping her coffee mug. 'I popped into Fine Fare earlier, and we saw one another across the baked bean display.'

'How romantic.' Pattie pulled away as Keith helped himself to a beakful of her hair.

'How're you doing, Eric?' asked Stan. The fringed sleeve of his cowboy jacket brushed the tabletop as Stan reached forward to shake the teenager's hand.

'Good to see you,' said Eric. Remembering his father's instruction, he gripped Stan's hand firmly.

Pattie turned to Eric, 'I'll go upstairs and grab some gear if you make the coffee.'

'No need, I've got it covered.' Eric sat at the table and opened his camera case.

'Two sugars?' Standing behind Stan's chair, Pattie reached under her dress and pulled out the book of matches to light the gas.

'How was your photoshoot?' enquired Julia. 'Did Pattie do her thing for you?'

'Oh, she certainly did,' Eric replied, flattening the cigarette papers on the kitchen table.

Julia raised an eyebrow, and Eric made a mental note not to try to slip veiled jokes past her.

'Eric thought he saw someone perving from the bushes at the reservoir,' said Pattie. 'He took a photograph.'

'You went in *there*?' Julia smirked, 'Well, it'll be interesting to see the picture. It's a shame we can't see it now.'

Stan leaned back, 'One day, everyone will have computers in their homes, and we'll be able to plug our cameras in and see the photos instantly.'

'I've seen computers on *Tomorrow's World*,' said Pattie. 'They're huge. You'd need a spare room, and they'd cost a fortune.'

Julia shook her head. 'Religion is on the way out, and *commodities* are the opium of the people now. They'll make computers affordable enough for us all to have one.'

Pattie lifted the whistling kettle from the stove. 'What's religion got to do with computers?'

'Nothing, I just dropped it in to facilitate the paraphrase.'

'You *what?*'

'Karl Marx,' said Stan.

Bighead, thought Eric.

'It'll be amazing,' continued Stan. 'Owning a computer will be like having a library the size of the Albert Hall on your desk. And you'll be able to get any television programme, any film, or any music you want at the press of a button.'

'I dunno...' Eric paused, crumbling a lump of Pakistani Black between his thumb and forefinger. 'I got to hear about blues music through a friend, who put me onto a friend of his. I travelled halfway across London to hear it, and when I finally tracked it down, it was like discovering the source of the Nile.'

Julia regarded the teenager, a smile curling the corners of her mouth. 'Oh, you're so right, Eric! Technology promises us the world, but we lose something precious along the way.'

'Eric's instant-cake theory,' Pattie said, sitting at the kitchen table with two mugs of coffee.

Now I'm *the big head*, Eric thought, wiping hashish residue from his thumb and inserting a scrolled cardboard roach into the reefer. He detested his feeling of smugness but still enjoyed the moment.

'That's a great point, Eric,' said Stan. 'But there's no stopping progress. The capitalist system will see to that.'

'Which is what the hippie movement is all about,' said Julia. 'Yes, progress is inevitable, but we have to handle it properly. The emphasis needs to shift from coercive consumerism to things that really matter, like relationships, community, self-expression and creativity.'

'Which means throwing a spanner into the capitalist machine,' Eric said, lighting the joint.

Julia nodded. 'The capitalist brainwashing has to be stemmed. If we carry on pillaging the planet like we are now, we'll have blackened the sky and used everything up in a hundred years. You have to ask, is it possible to keep capitalism and save the world? I don't think so.'

Eric passed Pattie the reefer, 'But how can we change it?'

'Well, there's no point in storming Buckingham Palace,' said Julia. 'We have to go about it another way – by changing people's heads.'

'That's why I joined the Young Communist League,' said Stan. 'Some people call it *The Trend*. I saw Pete Townshend at one of the meetings.'

Oh really? thought Eric. *Don't tell me: you taught him to play the banjo and started the mod movement from a basement in Battersea.*

'That's interesting,' said Julia. 'Jack, who used to live in this house, was a Marxist. I learned a lot about politics from him.'

'Are you a communist?' asked Stan.

That question again!

'Not really,' replied Julia. 'A socialist, yes. At least, I'd like to see Britain hold on to the socialist institutions it already has. Financial incentives are all well and good, but I firmly believe that capitalism needs to be moderated. Some form of wealth cap, maybe.'

'Amen to that,' Stan said, accepting the joint from Pattie.

'We're being poisoned by industry,' Julia continued, now in full flight. 'We simply can't keep manufacturing disposable stuff. The system must change if we're to save the planet, and the sooner people realise that, the better.'

Eric and Pattie reached the first-floor corridor. Rainwater streaked the round window at the front of the house.

'What was the prod in my ribs all about?'

'Isn't it obvious?' replied Pattie. 'I thought we should leave Julia and Stan alone to get to know each other.'

'Oh... Yeah.' Eric opened the door to the spare bedroom.

Pattie followed him in and closed the door behind them. 'I thought we could have a cosy chat and another joint.'

'I'm pretty zapped as it is.' Eric sat on the side of the single bed. 'And I left my camera case on the kitchen table.'

'No problem, it's my turn,' Pattie said, lifting her blue minidress.

'You've got *another* one under there?' exclaimed Eric. 'I would have seen... I mean –'

'It was round the back. I moved it to the front so I wouldn't sit on it. I'm giving away all my secrets now.'

'I'm good at keeping secrets.' Eric watched as the blonde stood in front of him with her hand inside her panties. He knew she was teasing.

'Well, don't expect a fanny-flash every time,' said Pattie. 'What I did at the reservoir was a spur of the moment thing. Being in that dark place with all those filthy-dirty things on the wall... It just happened.'

'I loved it,' grinned Eric.

'Yeah, well... So did I.' Pattie burst out laughing.

'I haven't stopped thinking about it.'

'Mm... well, maybe it'll take your mind off Julia for a while.' The model placed the joint between her lips and struck a cardboard match.

'What do you mean?' asked Eric.

Pattie blew a stream of smoke, 'You really like her, don't you.'

'It's just that bloke,' Eric said, avoiding Pattie's question. 'There's something *wrong* about him. I'd hate to see Julia get hurt.'

'Wrong? In what way?' Pattie sat beside Eric on the edge of the bed.

'Oh, I dunno, little things.'

'Like what?' pressed the blonde. She handed Eric the joint.

'Like when those skinheads followed us into the car park. Why was Stan in the bushes? He had to have been hiding there. And it must've been three or four minutes before he...'

'Came to our rescue?'

'Yeah.'

'Could it be that you're a teeny-weeny bit jealous?' suggested Pattie. 'Stan seems like a lovely guy to me.'

'*Jealous?*'

Pattie gave Eric a knowing look. 'I've seen the way you look at Julia. She's sexy, isn't she.' Pattie giggled, 'If I were to have a girly affair, I'd want it to be with her.'

'Are you saying that –'

'Oh no,' Pattie chuckled. 'Julia's as straight as they come. I remember back at art school, she had all the guys after her. She loved the attention, and she'd tease the shit out of them. I knew Julia had a partner and a little boy at home, but no one else did. She was secretive about her private life. I didn't even know she was married.'

'She never talks about her past,' said Eric. 'Both her parents are dead, right?'

'Yeah. Julia lost her parents when she was fourteen. Apparently, they were travellers, adventurous types. They went sailing off the coast of Madagascar and disappeared. Murdered by pirates, or so the story goes. A girl at college knew Julia from school, and she was the one who told me. Some of it's probably bullshit – the part about the pirates, anyway.'

'Julia was orphaned at fourteen? I had no idea.'

'That's when she came to live here.'

'Julia lived here at the Ealing House?'

'Only for a few years, I think. When her parents died, Jack took Julia in. Jack was her mum's brother. Didn't you know?'

Eric shook his head. 'I don't think Paul and Tony know either.'

'Oh,' sighed Pattie. 'I've really opened my big mouth this time, haven't I. Julia never spoke to me about it, so I never brought it up. But I didn't realise... *Shit!*'

'It's okay,' said Eric. 'It seems strange that Julia never told anyone that Uncle Jack was her *real* uncle, but for whatever reason, she's kept it a secret. No one will ever hear about it from me.'

Pattie nodded thoughtfully. 'It's good that we had this conversation. I could easily have let something slip in front of Paul and Tony.'

'We'll put that one to bed, then.'

Pattie smiled, 'Yeah. Have you had any more astral projections?'

Eric watched Pattie's toes gripping the blood-red carpet. 'No, nothing for ages.' He wanted to tell her about his talk with the Scientist.

Pattie bent forward, stubbing the joint in the ashtray on the floor. 'I was remembering your story about kissing that girl in the park... and thinking it was me.'

'I shouldn't have told you.'

'Oh, no... Actually, I was flattered.' Pattie raised an eyebrow and leaned back on her elbows. 'I thought *Julia* was your fantasy girl.'

'She is. I mean *you* – I mean... I'm digging myself into a hole.' Eric caught himself looking at Pattie's legs. When she leant back, her dress had ridden up, and her panties were showing.

Pattie giggled, 'I'm sure all the boys fantasise about sexy Julia. And sexy Julia loves to tease.'

Eric nodded, 'I know.'

'She's got you wrapped around her little finger, hasn't she?' Pattie said playfully. 'One flash of her white knickers, and you're hooked. Have you noticed she always wears virginal white knickers?'

'Yeah.'

'Like these.'

Eric looked.

Sitting upright, Pattie clasped her fingers behind Eric's neck. As she laid back, pulling him down with her, Eric moved onto the bed. They embraced, and he felt her arms tighten around him.

Eric met Pattie's soft, moist lips. Their kiss was long and sensual. Pattie was beautiful.

'You're a naughty boy,' purred the lovely blonde.

'I was just looking for a joint.'

'Maybe you should look a bit harder,' Pattie whispered, raising her hips and pressing. She smiled wickedly, 'Shall I keep Julia's little dress on?'

*

Cream's *Wheels of Fire* was the summer album of 1968 for Eric and Paul. The double LP featured a studio and a live disc, neither of which were consistently brilliant, though track one on each of the records was outstanding: *White Room* and *Crossroads*. Tony loved Ginger Baker's fifteen-minute drum solo on *Toad*.

Tony was refused admission to the X-rated Hammer Horror film *The Devil Rides Out*, despite showing his mother's driving licence at the ticket booth. He did accompany Paul and Eric to see the Beatles' *Yellow*

Submarine, which he subsequently described as *a pile of shit*. Eric and Paul dismissed the film as *one for the kids*.

On Wednesday lunchtimes, the record department at Bensteds was quiet. Reg stood in listening-booth number two, watching a bob-haired secretary peruse the LP bins.

Dusty Springfield's *Where Am I Going?* LP played next to the postman's ear. *Bloody ridiculous,* thought Reg. *Does the Scientist believe we're under surveillance by the KGB or something?* The answer came back to him: *Not the KGB, Reg... MoD2.* 'Okay, fair enough,' he mumbled under his breath.

Reg glanced at his watch. Side one of Dusty's LP concluded with an odd arrangement of Bobby Hebb's classic, *Sunny.* 'Could I hear side two, please?' the postman called to the shop assistant.

'It's Wednesday; we'll be closing soon,' answered the young woman. 'I'll play the first couple of songs.'

Close to You: birds suddenly appeared. Reg looked beneath the cut-off partition as a pair of shiny brown shoes entered listening-booth three. A hand appeared in front of the postman at eye level. He read the biro writing on the palm, *Sorry, traffic was crap.*

A pink carrier bag lowered to the floor, and one of the brown shoes nudged it under the partition. Having accomplished their assignment, the shoes left the building.

'Thank you,' Reg said to the shop girl, handing her the exact cash. He dropped Dusty into the pink carrier. 'Have a nice afternoon.'

When he arrived home from work, Reg placed the pink bag on the table and turned on the TV. Settling into his armchair with a cup of tea and a cigarette, he watched the scenes in Baker Street on the six o'clock news. Crowds of Beatles fans had descended upon the group's Apple boutique for the closing-down giveaway.

Following a Wednesday evening fry-up, Reg enjoyed the inaugural airing of *Dad's Army,* the first of eighty episodes.

Finally, at nine, he peered into the carrier bag. Next to the Dusty Springfield LP was a sealed white envelope.

'Cobblers,' muttered the postman, tossing the Scientist's letter aside. Eric's transmission had been a failure: the new machine did not work.

*

Julia returned to her bedroom and studied the cosmetics on her dressing table for the third time. Sensing movement at the far end of the garden, she hastened to the window and watched Eric wheel his bicycle in through the front entrance. He cycled towards the house in the bright August sunshine. Julia hurried along the top-floor corridor and down the stairs.

'Oh, hello,' smiled Eric. Pushing his keys into his pocket, he closed the front door. 'I thought you and Paul were going shopping today.'

'That was supposed to be two hours ago.' Julia appeared flustered. 'When I came home, Paul wasn't here. I've searched the house from top to bottom. Something's wrong, I know it.'

'Perhaps he's...' Eric's attempted consolation faltered. He could think of no good reason why Paul should be two hours late.

'He would have called, or left a note, or...' Julia sounded anxious, verging on panic. 'I'm going to the reservoir. Will you come with me?'

'Of course, but why would –?'

'Just humour me.'

Hurrying to the kitchen, Julia snatched her keys from the table and walked briskly back up the hallway. Neither spoke as they left the house. They strode side by side, their shoes crunching the gravel.

'This way.' Eric turned right on the walkway.

Sunlight reflected off the enormous empty reservoir.

Julia shaded her eyes, surveying the tangled woodland surrounding the orange-beige bowl. 'Oh God, he could be anywhere.'

'What makes you think Paul's here?' asked Eric.

'I'm not certain he is,' replied Julia. 'But I have my reasons. Come on then, let's work our way around the rim.'

Weaving among the bushes, Eric and Julia made slow progress as they searched along the northern end. A murder of crows took flight as Eric fought through the undergrowth, scratching his forearm in the process. Emerging from the thicket, he walked across the grass to the rim of the basin,

'Over here, quick!' Within seconds, Eric was down the metal ladder, crouching inside the brick-lined chamber.

Julia squeezed in next to him. Dropping to her knees, she leant over Paul's motionless, twisted body. Eric stared at the dishevelled blonde wig. The long yellow hair straggled Paul's heavily made-up face. His eyes were closed, the lids caked in blue shadow. Julia's Mary Quant minidress had crumpled up, revealing Paul's skimpy white panties and his smoothly shaven legs.

Julia drew the blonde strands from her son's glossy red lips. 'He's breathing! Ambulance, Eric. Run like the wind!'

It was early evening when Julia and Eric left King Edward's Hospital. The location had made the rescue difficult, and it was nearly two hours before Paul was wheeled into the emergency ward. An examination revealed a heavy concussion. The doctor insisted that Paul be admitted to the hospital, saying he would probably be discharged the next day.

Having delivered pyjamas and some fresh clothes to the hospital, Julia and Eric left with a bag containing the Mary Quant dress, a blonde wig, and a pair of white panties. The stiletto shoes that Paul had been wearing were nowhere to be found.

Julia sat beside Eric in the living room and removed the foil from a bottle of chardonnay. She sighed, 'It's been quite a day.'

Eric noticed her hands shaking. 'Are you okay?'

'Yes, all things considered. It could have been so much worse. When we first found Paul, I thought...'

'You were great,' said Eric. 'My brain had shut down.'

'You found him, and it was you who dialled 999.' Julia poured two large glasses of the dry white wine.

'Are you going to tell me now?' asked Eric.

'Tell you what?'

'How you knew that Paul would be at the reservoir.'

Julia sipped her drink. 'It was a guess, an educated guess. My makeup had been moved about, so I assumed he'd got himself dressed-up. Perhaps doing it in the house wasn't enough anymore. I thought of the reservoir. Where else could he go?'

'So you knew about it... The dressing-up?'

Julia hesitated. 'Kind of.'

'Go on,' Eric said quietly. He placed his wineglass on the coffee table and lit a cigarette.

Julia gazed out through the windows. The summer day was drawing to a close. Hazy yellow light lit the garden and the trees of Fox Wood. 'I've known, or at least suspected about Paul's... *fetish*, since the day we went to Chiswick. Remember when I thought I saw Pattie at my bedroom window?'

'Yeah. Then she walked in through the front door.'

'That's right,' said Julia. 'And there have been times when some of my clothes have gone missing and my makeup has been disturbed. I blamed those things on Pattie too, but in the back of my mind...'

Although they had been together all afternoon, this was the first time Paul's transvestitism had been mentioned. Julia seemed relieved to talk about it. Eric poured more wine, 'We all thought Tony had been making-up stories about seeing a blonde at the window.'

'Yes,' Julia said quietly. 'Eric, I need to ask you something, and please give me an honest answer. Sorry, I know you will.'

Eric heard Julia take a breath.

'Does Paul's dressing-up fetish bother you?'

'Not in the slightest.'

'Okay... Good. That's what I expected you to say.'

'I mean it,' said Eric.

'I know.' Julia sipped her wine. 'And what if... Just, *if*... What if it turns out that Paul is homosexual? Would you still want him as your friend?'

Eric stubbed his cigarette. 'Julia, Paul's my best friend. It would make no difference.'

Julia placed her hand on Eric's shoulder. He saw tears welling in her pretty green eyes.

Their embrace was warm and affectionate, the manifestation of a shared emotional experience. Julia and Eric were party to an intimate secret: a controversial predilection, the ramifications of which could be profound. Eric felt Julia tremble in his arms, and he knew she was close to tears.

Holding Eric's hand, Julia looked into his eyes. 'Eric, you and I have a way of looking at life which others don't. Not everyone could accept Paul for who he is.'

Eric nodded, 'You're thinking of Tony.'

'Yes, especially Tony. Paul may choose to divulge his secret. But until that happens...'

'Of course,' replied Eric. 'And when it feels right, that's exactly what I'll tell Paul when he comes home.'

'Can I have another hug, please?' Julia folded her arms around him.

Eric would never forget the long and tender kiss he shared with Julia. Golden evening sunlight filled the room as they locked together as one, temporarily oblivious to the world and its complications. In that timeless, transcendent moment, Eric knew perfect bliss.

25

This Was: Winter 1968

Bill and Mary were delighted by Eric's decision to stay on at school for the final year. For the sixteen-year-old, the prospect of A-Levels was daunting, but Paul had also made the grade and would be at his side to help him through. The disturbing image of his friend lying unconscious at the reservoir remained burned into Eric's memory. Paul occupied his thoughts when he arrived at the Ealing House on a dreary afternoon in September.

Mary Hopkin's *Those Were the Days* played quietly on the radio.

'Is he here?' Eric asked, dispensing with the customary greeting.

'Yes, he's upstairs in bed,' replied Julia. She rose from the sofa as Eric entered the living room.

The concussion had been more severe than initially thought, and X-rays revealed Paul had sustained a fracture to his right leg. Far from being discharged the day after the incident, Paul had remained in hospital for a week.

'Any other news?'

'About Paul? No, he's just glad to be home.' Julia walked to the window.

Eric sensed something was troubling her. 'But?'

'Oh, it's probably paranoia. But Tony's been very distant – more so than usual. I can't help wondering if he believed my story about Paul being set-upon on his way home from school.'

Eric considered Julia's suggestion. 'I suppose it's possible that Tony heard something from the crowd he hangs out with. Paul said his attackers were skinheads. Maybe there's a connection.'

'I thought of that, too,' said Julia. 'But Paul didn't recognise any of them.' She shrugged, 'What's done is done. And if Tony knows about Paul's secret, then he should understand why... why I lied to him.'

'That's true.'

Julia smiled ruefully, 'Why don't you go up and say hello to Paul. He'll be so pleased to see you.'

Passing Tony's bedroom, Eric glanced inside. Mickey's gloved metal hands pointed to ten-past-two. He heard the Casuals' *Jesamine* playing in the next room.

'Hello, my fine friend!' Paul said cheerfully. He lowered the volume on the radio at his bedside. 'Close the door if you would. There's a pesky gaggle of Jehovah's Witnesses roaming the corridors.'

Eric pushed the bedroom door shut. The hospital ward had not been an appropriate setting for the difficult discussion that both knew was coming.

'I'd have brought some grapes, but the cat got them.' Eric sat gently on the end of Paul's bed.

'Cats don't like grapes.'

'Must've been the parrot then.' Paul's long black hair appeared greasy and unkempt, his face gaunt and pale. 'How are you?'

'Fine. My leg hurts a bit, but my head's okay, and I've stopped aching. Sorry I messed-up our plans for the Isle of Wight Festival.'

'That's okay,' replied Eric. 'I didn't particularly want to see Jefferson Airplane, anyway. Is there anything you need? I know your mum's looking after you, but if there's anything I can get –'

'Since you ask,' Paul interrupted, 'could you open the wardrobe and fetch me my pink party dress and my mascara?'

Eric lowered his head and smiled, 'Have you been saving that one up?'

'I've been working on it for the past week.'

'Not bad.'

'Is it really not bad?' Paul asked quietly.

Eric looked at his friend, 'All that matters to me is that nothing changes between us. That's the line *I've* been working on.'

Paul nodded. Tears glistened in his eyes as he leaned to his side and raised the volume on the radio. Neither spoke as they listened to the current number-one single, *Hey Jude*. The Radio One disc jockey played the song in its entirety: all seven minutes and eleven seconds.

Hey Jude was followed by the flip-side, John Lennon's *Revolution*. *The BBC must have two copies,* thought Eric.

'That gives *Strawberry Fields* and *Penny Lane* serious competition as the best seven-inch piece of plastic they've ever put out,' Eric concluded.

'But the next observation you're about to make is that the visual imagery isn't as strong, so *Strawberry Fields/Penny Lane* is still the best.'

Eric smiled, 'You know me so well.'

'That was Mum's analysis,' admitted Paul. 'I know where you're coming from, but my brain isn't wired in the same way as yours and hers.' Paul scoffed, 'Apparently, it's wired quite differently.'

Eric noted Paul's self-deprecating sarcasm. A year or two ago, he would have let it pass, but experience had taught him that some issues needed to be addressed. The trick was knowing which, when, and how. 'I think all men have certain things that turn them on,' said Eric. 'I'm not so sure about women, but it's probably the same for them.'

Paul looked down at the paisley-patterned bedspread. 'Yeah. The thing is, I have the compulsive sex drive of a man... But I was born with the wrong body.'

Eric was beset by a feeling of emptiness. He longed to comfort his friend but knew straight away that he was out of his depth.

'It's okay,' said Paul. 'I can handle it.'

During Paul's extended hospital stay, Eric had finished the roll of film in his camera. Imagining himself reminiscing as an old man, he had photographed the Ealing House from both the front and rear. As he composed the second picture with the red swing in the foreground, Eric recalled Julia's paintings. *She must have painted them when she came to live here after the death of her parents.* Pattie's revelations about Julia's past added insight to Eric's perception of the house. The artwork he had chanced upon took on a new and intriguing significance. Very little about the property had changed, though on that September day in 1968, there was no mysterious figure peering out through the French windows.

Ten days later, Eric left the chemist shop on Northfield Avenue with the prints in his hand. *Best not to show Paul the photos I took at the reservoir.* Opening the yellow Kodak envelope, Eric stood outside the corner shop and sifted through the glossy colour photographs. The close-up of Pattie holding the daisy to her cheek was terrific. Eric thought of the girl in the Flake advert. The walkway shots had also come out well.

Pattie's black leather boots were a tad out of focus, but the fuzziness enhanced the motion effect. A red 55 bus whooshed past. Eric smiled as he scanned the prints. Pattie looked gorgeous in Julia's sky-blue minidress. It dawned on him that he held in his hands a Kodachrome memento of his landmark liaison. The next photo was a blurred picture of some bushes. There was no sign of Yogi Bear.

Eric became aware that someone was standing in front of him. 'Tony!' he exclaimed, closing the yellow envelope. 'Revisiting your old stomping ground?'

Standing stock-still, the shaven-headed fourteen-year-old glowered. Across the road, five skinheads observed the confrontation.

Eric glanced past Tony at the skinhead gang. 'What's going on?'

'What's going on?' Tony queried through gritted teeth. 'That's what *I* want to know.'

Eric's mind raced. He had not seen Tony since before the incident at the reservoir. This had to have something to do with Paul. 'What are you talking about?'

'I'll tell you what I'm talking about,' Tony retorted. 'The evening after Paul got duffed-up in the alleyway, I came home an' looked into the front room. You didn't see me cos you were too busy snogging my mum.'

Eric's scalp felt cold. There was nothing to be gained by denial, no room for manoeuvre. 'I...'

'You *what?*' snarled Tony. 'You've always fancied my mum. 'Ave you fucked 'er?'

Eric recoiled, 'No! No, of course not! We'd just got back from the hospital, and Paul was a mess. We were both upset and –'

Tony prodded Eric threateningly. 'If I ever find out you've been screwin' around with my mum...' There was a tense silence. The young skinhead stared at Eric, his expression a confusion of anger and hurt. Tony turned to the road, then looked back over his shoulder, 'Anyway, she's got a boyfriend now, so you've got no chance.'

Eric felt his legs trembling. As he walked home, one question dominated his thoughts: *Should I tell Julia?*

*

Bright up-lights lit Ealing Town Hall.

'The film was supposed to be entered at Cannes,' Paul said, as he and Eric left the ABC cinema.

'So why wasn't it?'

'Cannes was cancelled. Something to do with the Paris Uprising in May.'

Happiness Stan's anti-capitalism march, thought Eric. 'Marianne Faithful looked good as the girl on the motorcycle.'

'Looked good or was good?'

'Was good, considering some of the dodgy dialogue.'

'Your figure is like a Stradivarius in a plush-lined violin case.'

Eric laughed, 'Yeah. And it's a shame they cut the Mars Bar scene.'

When Paul opened the Ealing House's front door, he and Eric heard Pink Floyd's *Set the Controls for the Heart of the Sun* coming from inside. Firelight spilt through the front-room doorway flickering yellow in the dark hall. Hanging their coats and removing their footwear, the two teenagers entered the warm fire-lit room. In front of the flaming grate, Julia and Pattie sat cross-legged in long Indian dresses, their knees touching as they gazed into each other's eyes.

Scented candles burned on the mantelpiece, the aroma mingling with jasmine joss sticks and the musty smell ever-present in the old house. At once futuristic and pagan, Pink Floyd's psychedelic sci-fi mantra pounded hypnotically from the stereo. Silhouetted by the fire glow, the two hippie women swayed to the trance-inducing music.

Eric stood next to Paul behind the small sofa. *The girls haven't even noticed us.*

A figure emerged from the dark library area at the back of the room. Eric focused on the man's cowboy boots. Stan beckoned to Eric and Paul,

'How're you doin' guys?' Jim Morrison asked in an English accent.

The boys joined the tall hippie in the shadows.

'Great,' replied Paul. 'What's going on with Mum and Pattie? They look like they're halfway to Nirvana.'

Stan smiled, 'They are. I guess I am, too. I dropped two tabs before I got here to make sure it was okay.'

'LSD,' said Eric.

Stan nodded, 'Owsley acid – *California Sunshine,* man. A guy I know blew in from San Francisco with five-hundred hits sewn into the lining of his suitcase.' Stan extended his hand, 'I saved you a couple.'

Paul and Eric stared at the tiny yellow tablets on the man's palm. They looked like roughly hewn gold nuggets.

'Go ahead,' said Stan. 'This stuff's the best in the west. Don't worry; one hit won't launch you too far out into space.' He smiled, 'You'll be back by sunrise.'

Eric looked over at Julia and Pattie. Both women were on their feet, swaying from side to side, their upstretched arms entwining cobra-like in the now-familiar hippie dance.

Paul took one of the LSD tablets from the man's hand, studied it curiously, then swallowed it.

'Just think happy thoughts, space cadet,' smiled Stan.

'How long will it take to kick in?' asked Paul.

'Oh, half an hour, maybe. You'll know when it does.' Stan looked at Eric, 'This one has your name on it, brother.'

Eric raised the tablet to his mouth and swallowed. 'Thanks.' He looked up at the tall man. 'This'll be a first.'

'Have a great trip,' smiled Stan. He turned to watch the two spaced-out dancers by the fireplace.

Dislodging the LSD tablet from beneath his thumbnail, Eric slipped it into the small side pocket on his Levi's, pushing it down next to his plectrum.

The night was long. The customary conversation, to which Julia was usually central, had given way to introspection, punctuated by short verbal exchanges or incredulous exclamations. As darkness turned to light, Eric sat by the fireplace staring into the glowing embers. Beyond the high garden wall, the first rays of dawn lit the treetops of Fox Wood, its failing leaves brushed red, gold and brown by autumn's unfaltering hand.

Gazing out, Stan quoted a line from *Mr Tambourine Man*'s final verse, poetically describing the trees as haunted and frightened.

'That's beautiful,' said Julia.

That's Bob Dylan, thought Eric. Rainbow had picked up on the very same line. Eric stared at Stan's brown cowboy boots.

*

Keenly sensitive to his environment, Eric would, in future decades, envision 1968 as a return to the monochrome era of the early sixties. Black-and-white newsreel footage of Russian tanks, rioting anti-war and anti-capitalism protesters, Enoch Powell's immigration warnings; these stood in stark contrast to the psychedelic happenings of 1967. However, psychedelia was very much in evidence that October, with the release of Jimi Hendrix's double album, *Electric Ladyland*. On the cinema screen, Jane Fonda gave male sci-fi freaks a glamour goddess to drool over.

From his seat in the stalls, Eric watched eagerly as Barbarella floated above her interstellar bed and stripped out of her silver spacesuit. Later, Eric would wonder if Paul had also enjoyed the striptease or if he preferred Pygar, the handsome blind angel.

Paul dipped into his Butterkist, 'What did you think of the LSD?' There was no need to whisper; the Odeon was empty at the matinée screening.

'I couldn't tell you,' replied Eric. 'It's at the bottom of my wardrobe in my other pair of jeans.'

'You didn't take it? Why not?'

'I thought one of us should stay straight. If you'd had a bad trip, or Pattie, or your mum, I'd have been in a fit state to talk you down.'

'Stan had already tested the acid,' said Paul. 'He'd dropped two tabs before he brought it over.'

'Yeah, so he said.'

'You didn't believe him?'

Eric shrugged, 'I dunno.'

Paul and Eric watched Barbarella succumb to a vicious attack by flesh-eating dolls.

'You don't like Stan much, do you,' said Paul.

'I don't trust him,' Eric heard himself say.

Barbarella introduced her rescuer to Earth's method of having sex: exaltation transference pills and palm touching. Unimpressed, the spaceman opted for the traditional approach.

Paul turned to his friend, 'I honestly don't mind.'

'You don't mind what?' asked Eric.

'I don't mind that you fancy my mum.'

Eric felt claustrophobic. He pictured himself inside a big paper bag, punching frustratedly, unable to break out. He stared up at the screen and saw nothing. *First Pattie, then Tony, and now Paul. If they all know how I feel about her, Julia probably does too. Was I that obvious?*

*

A light covering of snow presaged the upcoming Christmas holiday. Leaving Julia alone at the house, Eric walked down the hill with his hands pushed deep into the pockets of his greatcoat. Ealing Broadway was busy that Friday evening. Taxis queued as commuters exited the station, mingling with office party groups and pub-goers. Across the street, students from Ealing Art College descended the steps to Tabby's disco, the tiny basement club that in a different guise had been instrumental to the careers of Eric Clapton, the Who and the Rolling Stones. Sid made a brief appearance in Eric's mind as he glanced over at the former blues club. He entered through the Feathers' side doorway and made his way down the narrow flight of stairs.

Eric pushed through the tightly packed bodies. The Cellar Bar was heaving. Jethro Tull's *My Sunday Feeling* played loudly. '*That Jethro Tull's a fantastic flautist*', Stan had remarked a few days earlier. Pattie saw the look on Eric's face. '*They haven't had sex*', she whispered. '*I asked her*'.

Eric saw an arm waving from the raised alcove at the back. The unruly mop of centre-parted wavy brown hair could only belong to one person.

'I saved you a seat,' grinned Phil. He moved his folded coat from the cushioned bench. 'That pint of lager's yours.'

Eric squeezed into the corner of the crowded alcove. 'Thanks, Phil.' He smiled, raising his glass, 'And thanks for introducing me to this cellarful of hippies!'

'I can't believe you live just up the road, and you didn't know about the Cellar Bar,' said Phil. 'All the Ealing freaks hang out here.'

'So I see.' Eric looked around at the packed bohemian crowd. 'I'll let you into a secret, Phil; I've never drunk in a pub before.'

Phil smiled his wide hobbit smile, 'Then I'm honoured to buy you your first pint. It's a bloody shame Cream split up.'

'Devastating,' agreed Eric. 'I never saw them live, but I bet they were the best ever.'

'Sometimes,' said Phil. 'Depending on the dope.'

'Pot, you mean?'

'Yeah,' replied Phil. 'Marijuana can send musicians either way. It can make them paranoid and boring as hell, or lead them into unchartered territory that – if they're genuinely gifted – may totally blow your mind.

If you'd seen Cream or Hendrix a few times, you'd know that. You pay your money and take your chances.'

Eric nodded, 'I can relate to that; I've been there. I'm not sure I'd risk smoking a joint before playing for an audience, though.'

Phil shrugged, 'It's the spirit of the times, man. If you want to transcend the norm, you've got to be prepared to fall flat on your face once in a while. Did you hear that John Lennon divorced his wife?'

'Cynthia, yeah. Do you remember the girl getting her clothes cut-off at the Technicolor Dream? That was Yoko Ono's concept.'

Phil sniffed, 'Yeah, man. Ally Pally's a little hazy, but I couldn't forget *that*. I bought John and Yoko's LP, *Two Virgins*. Trust me, it's what it says on the cover – bollocks.'

'Avant-garde?'

'Avant gotta clue.'

The Stones' *Sympathy for the Devil* segued into Fleetwood Mac's *Albatross*. *They must have a tape recorder behind the bar*, thought Eric. *I'd love one of those.* Above the hairy heads, a fog of swirling smoke clung to the low beamed ceiling. Eric detected the unmistakable smell of marijuana. 'They let you smoke pot down here?'

'Not officially,' replied Phil. 'But they turn a blind eye. If an iffy-looking bloke with short hair comes in, the joints go out. It's easy to spot the cops.'

'I'd have brought some if I'd known.'

'Got it covered, man.' Phil reached into his coat pocket, 'Just be subtle about it.'

Eric nodded. 'Harry would do good business down here.'

Phil lit the joint, inhaled deeply, then passed it to Eric behind the table. 'Harry is one of the reasons I phoned you.'

'Has he been busted?'

'Worse than that, I'm afraid.'

Eric took a second drag, then passed the joint back to Phil and waited.

'Harry got into speed,' began Phil. 'He was doing all kinds of drugs, but speed was the big one. He was dealing it, of course, but most of it went up his nose.'

'I know his girlfriend left him.'

'Crystal, yeah. That's ironic,' Phil murmured. 'The thing is, too much speed doesn't just make your teeth fall out; it makes you psychotic. Harry had become paranoid. He thought there were people after him. Maybe there were, I don't know. One night he went down to that Esso garage in Acton and paid for a quid's worth of four-star. Then he poured it over his head and lit a match.'

'Oh, God.'

'Yeah, a human torch – a horrible way to go.'

Eric stared down at the table. An overhead light reflected on the polished wood, and he heard Harry's screams.

'It's a lesson for the learning,' said Phil. 'Stay away from white powders.'

'Definitely. I didn't know Harry very well, but...'

'Yeah,' said Phil. 'But he'll be back.'

'He'll be back? You mean Harry's still alive?'

'No, I mean he'll be back in another life.'

Dear Prudence was up next. They were playing the Beatles' *White Album.*

'You believe in reincarnation?'

'Yeah, I think so,' said Phil. 'The way I see it, it kind of *has* to exist.'

'I'm intrigued,' said Eric. 'I'd always had you down as a sensible type. Well, more or less.'

Phil smiled, 'Okay, I'll tell you my *theory of everything,* then you can decide if I'm crackers.'

It occurred to Eric that he had been stoned for the past five or ten minutes.

'Right,' began Phil. 'The hardest part to get your head around is *eternity:* time without a beginning or an end. We're used to beginnings and endings, so that's a weird one.'

'But there must have been a beginning,' said Eric.

'I don't think so. How can you get something from nothing? Whatever it is that forms energy and matter must have always existed... So it follows that it always will.'

Eric nodded. 'Okay, I'll buy that. Nothing could pop into existence without a cause, so *something* must have always been there.'

'That's exactly right,' said Phil.

'But how does that prove reincarnation?'

Phil was becoming excited, speaking like a keen student teacher. 'So hold on to the concept: limitless time; no beginning and no end.'

'Okay.'

'Now, *because* you exist, that means you *can* exist.'

'Er, yeah...'

'So put those two things together. Given limitless time, everything that *can* exist *will* exist – over and over again, forever. And that includes you, me, and Harry.'

Phil leaned forward on the table, 'I think on a conscious level, we're *always* here. You wouldn't be aware of time passing between lives, cos you wouldn't exist. But as far as you're *aware*, as soon as your eyes close for the last time in this life, you'll open them again in your next one.'

'But what if I come back as a ferret?'

Phil shrugged, 'Build a dam.'

'You're thinking of beavers.'

'Oh… Yeah. By the way, how's Pattie?'

'Fine. Pretty.'

Shaking his mop of curly brown hair, Phil smiled broadly and pulled out another joint. 'Hold on tight, we're movin' to the right.'

'Huh?'

Eric turned up his collar. The fog reminded him of his childhood. The murky grey vapour grew thicker as he walked up the hill, and he was glad of his greatcoat. Paul and Tony would be late home, and Eric looked forward to sharing Phil's *theory of everything* with Julia. The third joint in the Cellar Bar had deposited him in dreamland, but he felt sure he would be able to recount Phil's speculative concept. It would be enough to fuel a late-night discussion.

Closing the gate behind him, Eric walked up the foggy gravel path. The old house was in darkness, except for a sliver of fuzzy yellow light between the drawn living-room curtains. Picturing Julia sitting next to a blazing fire, Eric smiled. Despite its large rooms, the Ealing House had a cosiness about it that would be especially welcome on this chilly winter night.

Reaching the porch steps, Eric heard laughter from inside. He edged past the tall plants and peeped through the chink in the curtains. The living room was in semidarkness, lit only by the firelight and a single candle on the coffee table. Bathed in the soft yellow glow, Julia sat on the big sofa facing the windows, engrossed in a magazine. Eric stared at her white blouse and her black pleated miniskirt. His tummy turned over. She had been dressed in exactly the same clothes when she had teased him following his first meeting with Rainbow. He knew that the magazine Julia was reading had been borrowed from Paul's wardrobe. Eric had once removed an erotic tennis skirt picture from the glossy mag. Paul had used it to see himself as a woman. Julia's lips were moving.

Inching to his left, Eric peered through the opening in the curtains. Stan sat on the adjacent sofa. The handsome hippie leant over the coffee table and passed a lit joint to Julia.

Reading the magazine, Julia seductively crossed and uncrossed her legs in front of her boyfriend. She lowered the dirty mag, and Eric drew back from the window. He watched from the shadows as Julia slowly parted her knees.

Stan adjusted his position, settling himself like a lecherous voyeur in the front row of a striptease club.

Julia opened and closed her legs.

Looking over his shoulder, Eric surveyed the dark garden. Fog shrouded the snow-topped foliage. Fox Wood loomed tall and silent beyond the high walls. Turning back to the gap in the curtains, Eric unbuttoned his greatcoat. The night air felt cold on his forehead. Stan unbuttoned his jeans. Eric moved back, obscuring the man from his view. His senses intensified by Phil's potent marijuana, Eric's breathing quickened, his heightening arousal masking lurking emotions of jealousy and guilt. Julia's green eyes were set in a glassy stare. They regarded the man on the adjacent sofa. Her long black hair fell forward. Julia's demeanour had changed, her fixed expression reminding Eric of the girl on the swing.

Resigned to his voyeurism, Eric peered between the curtains. His gaze settled on Julia's panties as she rudely gyrated her hips. *Lara smiled, 'One flash of her white knickers, and you're hooked. Have you noticed she always wears virginal white knickers?'*

Eric saw Julia speaking but could not make out the words. He glanced up at her glazed green eyes, seeing them widen as she watched Stan on the opposite sofa.

Tossing the magazine to the floor, Julia laid back. She slipped her hand inside her panties, and her pleated miniskirt began to jiggle.

Letting himself into the dark hallway, Eric quietly closed the front door. He silently removed his coat and shoes. Standing next to the front-room doorway with his back to the wall, Eric composed himself. Then he walked into the living room,

'Hi, I didn't – Oh, sorry!'

Reaching to her ankles, Julia quickly pulled up her panties. Stan faced the curtains, hastily buttoning his jeans.

Eric hurried out of the room. Moments later, he was upstairs on the first floor, sitting on his bed in the dark. He heard the front gate open. Peering down through the fog, Eric saw Stan disappear into the walkway. The gate closed behind him.

Julia entered the bedroom without knocking and crossed the unlit room. She glanced down at the garden below. 'He's gone,' she said coldly. Roughly drawing the curtains, Julia turned to face the bed.

Eric felt like a little boy about to be scolded by his mother. He was glad of the darkness. 'Julia, I'm so sorry I walked in on you just now, I didn't —'

'Liar.' Julia stood stiffly in front of the curtains with her arms tightly folded.

Eric looked up and waited.

'You walked in on purpose.'

'Why do you think that?' Eric asked, stalling.

'Because...' Julia faltered. She twisted to one side then the other. 'Why don't you like Stan?'

'Oh, I...'

'Don't *think* about it, Eric!' snapped Julia. 'Just tell me the *truth*, that's all.'

Eric knew that it was his turn to speak. 'Julia, it's complicated.'

'I've got all night.'

'Okay.' Eric gathered his thoughts. 'There are things I've noticed about Stan that make me suspicious.'

'Like what, Eric?' Julia looked as if she was about to start tapping her foot.

'Like... brown cowboy boots and *Mr Tambourine Man*.'

Julia waited, her arms still folded rigidly across her chest.

Eric heard her steady breathing. 'I think Stan and Rainbow might know one another.'

Julia rose up a gear, 'Cowboy boots and a Bob Dylan song? That's pathetic, Eric! Just because things didn't work out between you and your redheaded fairy queen —'

'It's not that,' interjected Eric. 'Rainbow — well, never mind her — I just don't want you to become involved in —'

'*Me?*' Julia was seething. 'I don't care what *you* want!'

'Please try to understand.' Eric stood up, joining Julia by the window. 'Things are happening...' He looked down at their bare feet.

'Things are happening that I can't tell you about, and I think Stan and Rainbow are part of it.'

'Things you can't *tell* me about?' Julia sounded exasperated.

Eric attempted to divert the argument, 'If you think I'm jealous, I probably am.'

Julia stared. There was a hardness about her face. 'Don't fall in love with me, Eric.'

Eric looked into Julia's green eyes, 'How could I not love you?'

26

The Midnight Lamp

'Don't leave it under the Christmas tree,' whispered Bill.

'I'd forgotten I'd asked for it,' said Eric. 'And I didn't know about the cover at the time.'

'I believe you,' replied his father. 'Thousands wouldn't.'

Eric disappeared into the front room and slipped Electric Ladyland behind dayglow-orange Disraeli Gears. The yellow-coated smuggler looked down at him from the mantelpiece. Eric stood up to leave, then changed his mind. Sliding his Christmas present back out from behind the psychedelic Cream cover, he played *All Along the Watchtower.* Jimi Hendrix's double album was currently top of the playlist at the Ealing House, or had been a week ago when Eric was last there.

That morning, Paul had telephoned with a cheery *Merry Christmas* message and invited Eric over for dinner the following day. Eric had conjured an excuse.

Christmas Day passed in a blur of swashbuckling pirates, a seasonal Z-Cars episode, and Cilla Black inviting viewers to *Step Inside Love* to join her, Shari Lewis, Michael Crawford and Scott Walker. The BBC news included a report on the Apollo space mission. A crew member of the moon-orbiting spacecraft read from Genesis.

'They're ahead in the space race, but in some ways, America's still half a century behind,' Mary observed, folding her knitting and tucking it into her basket.

'I hope they find something on another planet to replace all the resources they've used in getting there,' Bill added sarcastically.

Eric smiled. Perhaps his parents' views were not so far removed from those of Julia and the hippie generation.

Late that Christmas night, Eric smoked a joint in the back garden. It was cold outside, and a dusting of snow preserved his footsteps. Multi-coloured fairy lights twinkled in the rear window. A white-laced spider web hung heavy with frost between the downpipe and the fence. *And so ends another Christmas,* thought Eric. He extinguished the reefer and dropped the stub into his pocket.

In the darkness of his bedroom, scattered pictures blew through Eric's mind. Switching on his bedside lamp, he dispelled the images, but not the implications.

*

When he first heard *I Saw Her Standing There*, Eric had imagined himself at the same age as the girl in the song, though back in 1963, his seventeenth year seemed far away indeed. Having spent most of his birthday in the front room at his parents' house, Eric stepped out into the pale yellow twilight and began to walk.

The glacial weather had relented, becoming milder on that final day of 1968. On a green bench in a deserted Walpole Park, Eric huddled in his greatcoat, listening to the steady patter of drops falling from the thawing branches. He knew that the gates would be locked by now, and he would have to climb over the fence into Mattock Lane. On the long pond, the ducks had settled for the night on the two narrow islands.

Crossing Haven Green, Eric admitted to himself that his birthday walk had always been destined to end at the Ealing House.

In the dark walkway on the crest of Hanger Hill, he wondered how he would explain his two-week absence. *Tell the truth.* Well, some of it. *They know anyway.* Reaching the green wooden gate, he felt for his keys, then pictured them where he had left them, on the arm of the chair in the front room. Inserting his hand into the letterbox, he pushed the intercom button. A series of further presses went unanswered. Retracing his steps, Eric scrambled over the chain-link fence. He teetered on the disintegrating brickwork, then jumped down into the overrun garden. On this winter night, there was no sliver of welcoming light between the curtains. Repeated knocking confirmed that there was no one home.

Turning up his coat collar, Eric sat on the cold porch steps and stared up the path into the blackness. Within five minutes, he had relapsed to the dark, depressing days of Christmas. He reached into the side pocket on his Levi's and slid out his plectrum. Pushing his forefinger into the studded denim pocket, Eric retrieved the little gold nugget that had been there for over two months. Allowing himself no time to reconsider, he swallowed the tablet.

Paul and his mother found Eric slumped against the front door. Julia crouched down and kissed his cold cheek. 'Happy birthday, Eric.'

Eric opened his eyes, 'Thank you. I've taken LSD.'

'How long ago?' Paul helped his friend to his feet.

'I dunno, but it isn't doing anything.'

Julia opened the front door, 'Do you feel okay?'

'I'm fine,' replied Eric. The hallway shot away from him, stretching at least thirty-yards.

'Good.' Removing her black leather boots, Julia entered the living room.

'Just think happy thoughts, space cadet,' Paul said, reiterating Stan's advice. 'Oh, sorry, I didn't –'

'Bloody 'ell!' snapped Eric. 'Don't think you can't say his name!'

Paul hugged his friend, 'I'm so glad you're here. I meant what I said at the Odeon. I really don't care that you fancy my mum. Everybody does.'

Eric looked apologetically at his friend, 'I'm sorry, I don't know what came... Paul, the hallway looks like a tube station.'

'Right.' Paul guided Eric into the living room. 'Let's roll a joint before our train comes.'

Julia looked down at the full grate. Satisfied that the kindling had taken, she turned and walked to the door, 'My tobacco tin is by the sofa. I'm going up to change.'

'Thanks, Mum,' called Paul.

When Julia returned wearing an orange Indian dress, Eric's birthday joint was waiting on the coffee table. She approached her son and held out her hand. 'I thought we might keep Eric company.'

'Good idea, Mum,' Paul said, accepting one of the LSD tablets.

Flitting from room to room, rummaging through cupboards and drawers, Julia collected seventeen candles. A short time later, the living room looked like a Spanish Catholic church. A fire crackled in the hearth, warming the large room. Jasmine scented the air.

'Many happy returns, Eric,' Julia said, raising her wineglass.

'My best and dearest friend,' accorded Paul.

'Thank you.' Eric wrested his eyes from the folds in the green velvet curtains. He almost stood up, then thought better of it. Last time, the floor had felt like a water-filled lilo. 'Here's to the Ealing Hippies,' he said with a smile. 'Where in the world would I be without you two!'

Julia and Paul joined Eric on the big sofa. As they folded their arms around him, he vaguely wondered why he had never been able to read their minds before.

Soon all three were tripping intensely on the powerful Owsley acid.

'Set and setting,' Julia said, looking around the candlelit room. 'That's what Professor Leary says is important. I must say, I think we have things right in both respects.'

'Seventeen candles,' noted Paul. 'Perfect. One more would be one too many.'

Eric nodded, 'Yeah, please don't light another. I wouldn't want to miss 1969.'

'It'll be here in a few hours,' smiled Julia.

Eric felt like he was upside-down. He knew that he had it within his power to right himself but allowed the illusion to persist.

'How does it feel, turning seventeen?' Julia asked as Paul left the room.

Breaking the upside-down spell, Eric considered her question. He was experiencing a lull, the acid granting him a temporary respite. 'Sometimes, I feel like I'm twelve-years-old. And at other times, it seems like I've lived a hundred years.'

'Yes,' said Julia. 'Sometimes I feel that way, too.'

Upstairs on the second-floor corridor, Paul pulled a shiny new key from his pocket. Glancing back down the hallway, he unlocked Jack's bedroom and went inside.

'Oh, I'm going again,' murmured Eric. He blinked as a galaxy of tiny Ginger Baker's swam before his eyes.

'I've just been whizzing around inside a marble pinball machine,' revealed Julia. 'Shall I put on side three?'

'That would be great. If you can manage the journey to the record player.'

Her long orange dress radiated yellow beams as Julia walked up the near-vertical slope to the side of the room. Slipping the second LP from the gatefold sleeve, she peered at the label in the candlelight, then flipped the disc between her palms. Eric admired the way Julia delicately handled the record. She placed *Electric Ladyland* on the turntable and lowered the stylus gently onto the lead-in edge. Eric flashed back to the front room at the Ramsey's last house. He saw Julia hunched over the radiogram, cuing-up *Freewheeling*. There were green velvet curtains in that room, too. When Julia returned to the seating area, her orange dress still glowed, but the floor was no longer slanted.

Eric tapped into his internal philosopher; *What's the meaning of life?* he pondered, gazing up at the French clock.

'You have to find your own meaning,' the clock replied in a Maurice Chevalier voice. 'In your case, Eric, you should look to the arts.'

Julia glanced over the back of the sofa as Paul entered the room, 'You're just in time.'

Rainy Day, Dream Away entered the segue section that linked it to the next track. When Paul appeared on the opposite side of the coffee table, Eric immediately recognised the sky-blue minidress. Pattie had borrowed it from Julia's wardrobe for his photoshoot. The blonde wig had been restored; sleek straw-coloured hair hung long over Paul's bare shoulders; blusher highlighted his high cheekbones. Heavy dark eye-makeup and bright red lipstick completed the transformation. Eric looked at Paul's shaved legs and remembered the fuss he had made when Julia presented him with the cut-off Levi's. Eric was shocked by the sexual attraction he felt towards his friend.

Hiking up her long orange dress, Julia drew her legs up and snuggled next to her son. The signature guitar motif from *1983 (A Merman I Should Turn to Be)* scythed through the air, manifesting to Eric as a shimmering blue sword passing majestically overhead. Jimi's apocalyptic sci-fi extravaganza seemed attuned to the night-tripper, the thirteen-minute piece evoking one mind-blowing hallucination after another. Mitch Mitchell's hi-hat panned from side to side, laughing at Eric through a wide golden grin. Sprouting fins and a tail, Jimi returned to the ocean, the birthplace of life.

Eric looked over at his two best friends: Paul the transvestite and Julia the exhibitionist. It all seemed perfectly normal.

It was the first of January 1969. The cold winter air felt crisp and invigorating when Eric opened the front door. He picked up his plectrum from the sparkling porch step. Joining Paul in the ballroom, Eric strapped on his red guitar.

27

The Lulu Show

1969

A cloud of marijuana smoke hung above the two sofas in the living room. *Happening for Lulu* had started on BBC1, and Eric and Paul were looking forward to the Jimi Hendrix Experience.

'Do you think it'll be live?' asked Paul.

'Bound to be,' replied Eric. 'Lulu doesn't have people miming on her show. Jimi'll be plugged in, I'm sure.'

'Have I missed him?' Julia sat beside her son and reached for her Old Holborn tin.

One muted down-stroke from Jimi's wah-wah guitar was enough to identify *Voodoo Chile*. A typo modifying the song's title had been intentionally left in, though Electric *Landlady* reverted to its original name. Following a few words from Lulu, the band played their first single, *Hey Joe* – or some of it. Scuppering a planned duet with the Scottish hostess, Jimi stopped the song and dedicated an instrumental rendition of *Sunshine of Your Love* to the recently disbanded Cream. As was the case with most of the BBC's bans, the ensuing edict did the artiste's career no harm whatsoever; if anything, the reverse.

The spontaneous applause erupting from the sofas was interrupted by the ringing telephone. Julia handed the joint to Paul and went out to the hall.

'Stan or Pattie?' Paul inquired when she returned.

'Stan,' replied Julia. 'He's had a bust-up with his housemate. I agreed to have him stay here tonight.'

'I'll tidy my things in the spare bedroom,' said Eric. 'I was planning on heading home, so –'

'Oh, there's no need,' insisted Julia.

Eric felt prickles run up his neck. He resolved to show no signs of jealousy.

'Stan can have the sofa in the ballroom,' said Julia. 'He'll be perfectly comfortable in there.'

Shortly after nine o'clock, Stan walked up the dark gravel path with a suitcase.

I suppose a van will arrive tomorrow with the rest, thought Eric.

The living room had, at Julia's instigation, become a forum for late-night debate. Topics discussed that evening included: Richard Nixon's attitude towards the Vietnam War, the burning of the American flag at the Albert Hall by Keith Emerson of the Nice, Women's Liberation versus the Miss America Pageant, the manslaughter conviction of eleven-year-old Mary Bell, and the feasibility of a universal basic income.

'Paying everyone a living wage would give people the option to spend less time working,' enthused Julia. 'It would allow more free time for creative pursuits or for just walking in the park. It's not a new idea; Bertrand Russell suggested it as far back as 1918.'

'It's even older than that,' said Stan. 'Thomas Paine propositioned a *social dividend* in the eighteenth century. I wonder what society would be like now if it had happened.'

'*Happier,* I should think,' replied Julia. 'Less money-orientated and far more relaxed.'

'Sounds like the kind of world *I'd* like to live in,' Paul said, pulling three Rizlas from an orange pack.

'Me too,' agreed Eric. 'We should add it to our hippie wish-list.'

'You have a list?' Stan smiled, 'Far out, man. I'd like to see that.'

Making a rare appearance in the front room, Keith buzzed the seating area sending Paul's three Rizla's fluttering to the floor.

'Not a physical list,' Eric explained, looking over at Stan. 'Just a dream one.'

'What do you have on it?' asked the handsome hippie.

'Giant-sized Rizlas,' Paul said, picking up the scattered papers and glancing warily at the doorway.

At 2am, Julia went upstairs to her bedroom, returning with blankets and a pillow. 'I've put you in the ballroom tonight,' she told Stan. 'I suggest you close the door, or you may wake-up to find Keith standing on your head.'

The house was quiet. Alone in her room on the second floor, Julia opened her wardrobe and slipped her red Japanese robe from its hanger. The silky garment felt soft against her skin. She lit the single-paper joint she had rolled earlier. Seating herself at the dressing table, Julia leisurely brushed her long black hair then touched-up her makeup. She took her time; there was no need to hurry. By now, Paul and Eric would be tucked up in their beds on the floor below. At the far end of the long room, nine suspended marionettes hung motionless around the gold spiral staircase. Julia studied her reflection in the dresser mirror, then she reached under her robe and took off her panties. Taking a final puff, she stubbed the reefer in the ashtray and left the room.

Darkness filled the corridors. Creeping silently past the first-floor landing, Julia made her way down to the foot of the stairs. She adjusted the oriental robe, then quietly opened the ballroom door. The large room was dark, save for a streak of moonlight shining between the curtains. Julia peered around the door. Stan sat cross-legged on the floor, facing the far end of the room, where Tony's drums stood in front of the fireplace. Julia saw that Stan was wearing headphones and holding a microphone. Two round dials glowed amber on a small radio transmitter in front of him.

'Julia Ramsey – the *commie* – yes,' Stan said in a clear, hushed voice. 'She rules the roost. Yes… That's right, and there's no doubt she's a major influence on Grimes.'

Julia gripped the edge of the door as she listened in disbelief to Stan's covert communication. His speech was refined, the ultra-cool hippie vernacular supplanted by an upper-class Oxbridge accent.

Stan adjusted the frequency control on the transmitter, 'Yes, sexual guilt issues pertaining to her deceased uncle. I haven't got to the bottom of it yet.' There was a pause in the conversation. 'I have them with me,' Stan replied to his contact. 'I'll plant one in the living room and another in the kitchen; they talk a lot in there. Tomorrow, I'll get a third into Grimes' room.'

Julia stepped silently into the dark ballroom.

'I'll be here a few days,' said Stan. 'I'll advise of any developments.'

The ballroom light clicked on. 'You've got five minutes to get out, or I'm calling the police.'

Stan was gone in two.

The hallway tiles felt cold on Julia's bare feet. She climbed the dark stairway, gathering her muddled thoughts.

Eric stood in a meadow of crimson grass, watching Julia approach him over an arched Japanese bridge. She placed her hand lightly on his shoulder, softly speaking his name, 'Eric, wake up.'

Eric focused blearily on Julia's oriental robe, its vibrant colours muted by the darkness. The blankets fell away from his chest as he sat up, blinking and rubbing his eyes. Julia sat on the edge of his bed, so close he could feel her warmth.

'He's gone,' Julia said quietly.

Eric flashed back to the last time Julia had come to his bedroom. Looking out of the window, she had spoken the very same words. He said nothing.

'And this time, he won't be back.'

Eric wondered if she had read his thoughts. 'Stan?'

'Yes.'

'Why? What happened?'

Julia looked towards the drawn curtains. 'I went to his room.'

Uh-huh, thought Eric.

'Stan had a radio – a transmitter. I overheard him talking. You were right to distrust him, Eric. He had come here to spy on us.' Julia turned back to face him, 'And now I want to know why.'

Eric knew that in the light of his prior accusations, he had to offer an explanation. 'I think they're some sort of right-wing political group,' he said cautiously. 'I don't know exactly what they're... Maybe they think the revolution is being planned here at the house.'

Julia nodded, 'It sounds crazy, but after what I heard downstairs... Why didn't you tell me about this before?'

'I tri – As you said, *it sounds crazy*.'

'Yes.' Julia seemed uncertain.

'Stan and Rainbow,' continued Eric. 'I knew there was something fake about them. Stan had done his homework, but Rainbow gave the game away from the start. I just didn't want to believe... She was really pretty.'

Julia smiled weakly, 'Mata Hari in a fairy dress.'

'Yeah. I'm sorry,' said Eric. 'This is all my fault.'

'Oh no!' Julia wrapped her arms around Eric, hugging him tenderly. 'It's not your fault at all. I'm so sorry I doubted you.'

It is *my fault,* Eric thought, cuddling Julia in the darkness. *But maybe they'll leave you alone now. It's me they want.*

Leaning back on her hands, Julia moved her knee up onto the bed. 'That foggy night before Christmas when you interrupted Stan and me in the living room...'

Lowering his gaze, Eric swallowed heavily. 'Yeah, I'm sorry, I –'

'I saw you peeping at the window.' Julia studied Eric's face. 'I knew you were watching through the gap in the curtains.'

28

The Beginning of the End

On the 30th of January 1969, the Beatles performed in public for the last time. The stage they chose for their swan song was the Apple building roof in London's Savile Row. Earlier that month, Led Zeppelin had released their debut album, and at the beginning of February, *Goodbye Cream* appeared in the shops.

Paul sat next to the front-room fireplace and picked up his bass. 'Have you worked out the guitar bridge on *Badge* yet?'

'More or less,' replied Eric. 'The bit that's got me stumped is the twiddly hammer-on thingy he does at the end of *Sitting on Top of the World*. It's my favourite on *Goodbye*.' Eric leaned forward. 'For me, *Sitting on Top of the World* justifies the concept of the live recording,' he said earnestly. 'I reckon it's some of Clapton's best playing: melodic, bursts of speed, and expressive, wrenching notes that cry with the passion of the blues. And the other two blokes are pretty good, too.'

Paul kept a straight face, 'So you like it, then.'

'I'd rate it alongside *All Along the Watchtower* as the best guitar ever. Apart from the Bonzo's *Canyons of Your Mind*, of course.'

'Goes without saying.'

Craning his neck, Eric peered through the front window. 'Were you expecting a visit from the Dalai Lama?'

'Not till next Tuesday,' replied Paul. 'He's bringing a new prayer wheel for the front porch.'

'Well, he's a couple of days early,' said Eric. 'And he's brought one of his mates with him. They're both looking very orange.'

Before Paul could get to the door, Julia passed by in the hallway.

'Hare Krishna,' said the shorter of the bald-headed devotees. The chubby man smiled broadly, holding up a picture of George Harrison.

Julia recognised the print as part of the photoset included with the *White Album*. 'Would one of you mind closing the gate, please.'

'It was open when we –'

'Yes,' interrupted Julia. 'My youngest son was born in a barn.'

The orange-robed man grinned, 'Perhaps he's the –'

'No, there was no star in the east.'

'Can I borrow that?' asked the other man.

'Be my guest.'

'He's nicked my bike!' exclaimed Paul. He watched through the window with Eric as the taller of the two Hare Krishners cycled down the path to the open garden gate.

Paul gave his mother a sideways look when she entered the living room, followed by the two orange-robed men.

'Your home is most welcoming,' smiled the shorter man, savouring the sandalwood incense burning on the hearth.

Eric detected an American twang in his cosmopolitan accent.

'Thank you,' replied Julia. 'Please, have a seat.'

The round-faced man sat on the sofa facing the fireplace while his companion assumed a lotus position on the carpet. Julia, Paul and Eric then spent ten minutes listening to a well-rehearsed discourse extolling the virtues of Vaishnavism, the Bhagavad Gita, and the founding principles of the Hindu faith. The mood lightened when Julia opened her tobacco tin and rolled a long reefer.

Elated by the marijuana, the missionaries began to sing. Picking up on the simple song, Paul and Eric were soon jigging around the room behind the two shaven-headed men, waving their arms and chanting the Maha Mantra; *'Hare Krishna, Hare Krishna, Krishna Krishna, Hare Hare. Hare Krishna...'*

The smaller man grinned, slapping his thighs as he sat, 'Would you care to join us at one of our meetings?'

'I was quite taken with your philosophy,' said Julia. 'Especially the part about selfless deeds. Hinduism has always struck me as one of the gentler, less judgemental religions.'

'Yes, yes,' enthused the man.

'And I expect some of the myths carry sound moral messages.'

'Myths?'

Julia nodded. 'Regarding the theistic aspect, I suppose it depends on what you value most: truth or consolation. When it comes to getting through life, I believe truth – as best we can find it – is our most useful tool. I think that's what we should be worshipping.'

'What I've told you is *our* truth.'

Julia shook her head, 'The only reason to accept something as true is good empirical evidence. We live in a democracy, in a world facing tough challenges. We need people to be thinking straight and making logical, evidence-based decisions. Unfortunately, religion teaches the opposite.'

'If you're so certain of your convictions, why did you invite us in?' the man asked, lapsing into a broad New York accent.

'For the same reason you came here in the first place,' replied Julia. 'I'm hoping to persuade you to look at religion in a different light. You're not the only ones with a mission; mine's saving humanity from itself.'

*

'*Hold on tight, we're movin' to the right*. What kind of a crap slogan is that?'

Reg nodded, 'Yeah, it's shit.' The postman steered the Zodiac around a pothole in the Scientist's driveway. 'But it's catchy, and the catchy ones catch on.'

'It caught on with my friend Phil,' said Eric. 'Though I don't think he knew what he was saying. He's about as right-wing as Clement Attlee's Scottish scullery maid.'

'I see you've been brushing up on your history.'

'Yeah. The terms right and left were coined during the French Revolution. The king's people sat to his right, and the revolutionaries on his left.'

'I never knew that,' said Reg. 'Where did you read about it?'

'Julia told me.'

'Mm, Julia again. Is she pretty?'

'Yeah, very.'

'Do you think she'd be interested in a semiretired postman?'

'Probably not.'

'Worth a shot.'

'Yeah.'

Eric looked around the study at the groaning mahogany bookshelves. Paperwork lay strewn across a desk that faced out from the corner.

There was a cosiness about the room of the kind that comes from long years of habitation.

'It's good to see you again,' said the old scientist. He seated himself opposite Eric and polished his spectacles with his dressing gown. The elderly man's bush of grey hair stood flat above one ear, giving a good indication of which side he had slept on. 'Reg tells me you've had some suspicious visitors.'

'Straight to the point, then.' The postman scratched his nose, 'I'll make the tea.'

Omitting the see-through dress and Julia's steamy exhibitionism, Eric related the events involving Rainbow and Happiness Stan in some detail. He told the Scientist about the meetings at Kensington Market and in the car park behind Northfield Odeon; though Stan's provision of the high-grade LSD was limited to, *he brought drugs into the house.* When he had finished his lengthy account, Eric sat back and waited.

'Igor's been busy up in Hartlepool,' said the Scientist. 'It's a pity we don't have more staff.'

'More staff?'

'I'm afraid we've been distracted by the goings-on in the north-east when we should have been paying more attention to developments here in the south.'

'So you think I'm right about Rainbow and Stan?'

The Scientist nodded. 'It seems MoD2 have had you on their radar. Your appearance at Sidney's funeral no doubt sparked their interest, and I suspect it hasn't helped matters that you've taken up with a group of politically attuned hippies.'

'It's just Julia, really,' clarified Eric. 'She's the one with strong views. She wants to save the world.'

The Scientist smiled wryly, 'Then we share a common goal.'

Holding a digestive over his tea plate, Reg looked thoughtfully at Eric, 'How much does she know?'

Eric considered his reply. 'Julia knows about the spies. But she doesn't know who they are or what they're about. Once or twice she mentioned the *Capitalist Machine*, but she doesn't know that it actually exists.'

The Scientist shifted awkwardly in his chair, 'And it's best we keep it that way, for her sake as well as ours.'

Eric nodded.

The old man cleared his throat. 'I'm not overly concerned about the two intruders. They may indeed have been spies working on behalf of MoD2, but there's nothing untoward going on at the house, so I suspect their interest in you will drop off. Look at it this way, Eric, you haven't done anything! No one apart from us knows about the broadcast you made when you were eleven-years-old, and the transmission we attempted from here last year was a dud.'

Eric considered the Scientist's words. The old man's reassurances had a hollow ring. 'What about the broadcast in Skegness?' *Blue eyes win the prize.*

'If I remember correctly, Sidney did that one over the telephone. Besides, it was a localised broadcast heard only by a few hundred people. We've nothing to worry about on that score.'

Eric stared at the bookshelves. He wanted to believe the Scientist. 'I hope you're right.'

'Trust me,' said the old man, 'they were being cautious. I don't suppose you'll hear from them again.'

Having munched his way through an entire packet of biscuits, Reg lit a cigarette. 'Any joy with the new transmitter?'

'I'm afraid not,' replied the Scientist. 'But on a positive note, Igor has confirmed that the jamming mechanism we put in place is working. MoD2 can still send their propaganda out countrywide, but their plan to disseminate messages around the globe is being thwarted. The MkII listening device has proved useful. Igor has been eavesdropping from a nearby bedsit, and he tells me their boffins are tearing their hair out.'

'Do you think you'll get the new machine working?' Reg flicked his cigarette, missing the ashtray by a good four inches.

The Scientist shook his head. 'I'll keep trying, but I don't hold out much hope. So much depends on locating the correct frequency and zeroing-in on the sweet spot. The original transmitter hit it every time.'

'Still does,' said Reg.

The Scientist allowed himself a smile, then became serious. 'The problem, Reg, is that I used electrical components from the nineteen-thirties and forties that I could never procure in this day and age. We may have to come up with another plan, I'm afraid.'

Eric did not like the sound of a *Plan B*. 'How did you come to invent the transmitter in the first place?' he asked, hoping to ignite a spark of inspiration.

'You have to remember, this was during wartime,' began the old man, clearly pleased to revisit his halcyon days. 'We heard the music the Germans broadcast late at night. It sounded too clean and clear to be coming from a record; none of the pops and crackles that were always present on the recordings of that time: shellac 78s. We realised that unless they had an orchestra playing in the studio in the middle of the night, they must have invented a new method of recording and playing back sound. This turned out to be magnetic tape, though we didn't know that at the time. So we started experimenting with recording techniques. The army got wind of it and latched on to our work. They thought they may be able to use sound as a weapon – a frightening concept. We tried all kinds of hare-brained ideas.' The old man shrugged, 'The transmitter came about by accident, really.'

It had started to rain when Eric and Reg stepped into the porch. The Scientist placed his hand on the postman's shoulder, allowing Eric to walk ahead. 'Stay on your toes, Reg.'

*

Concord took off in March 1969. It would be the first aircraft to propel paying passengers through the sound barrier. Two days later, Jim Morrison of the Doors was arrested on stage for indecent exposure. Ronnie and Reggie Cray were both found guilty of murder and locked up for life. The Who released *Pinball Wizard*. Paul McCartney married Linda Eastman, and John married Yoko. Staging a honeymoon *Bed-In* at an Amsterdam hotel, the Lennon's used the wedding as a publicity stunt for peace.

April arrived, showing far more promise than it had twelve months earlier. With the departure of Happiness Stan, balance at the Ealing House was restored, and a welcome breath of spring air blew into the old residence.

Pattie knelt on the front-room carpet and opened Julia's tobacco tin. She placed a pack of papers on the coffee table, 'Have either of you heard about the *People's Park*?'

Eric shook his head.

'Sounds like a hippie happening,' said Paul.

'It is,' replied the blonde. 'In Berkeley, California, the authorities had earmarked a plot of land for a car park. But the local hippies decided they'd prefer a *people park*, so they commandeered the land and built one.'

'And the townspeople helped.' Julia entered the living room with a red ring box in her hand. 'They planted trees, put down grass... And there are masses of flowers, of course.'

When Eric saw Julia's yellow sundress, he pictured her on the swing in the snow. Closing his camera, Eric wound-on a new roll of film. 'You look gorgeous, darling,' he said, pointing the Pentax at Pattie.

The model held her palm towards the lens, 'No druggy pics.'

'Just a close-up of your lovely smile.' Eric's smarmy photographer lingo was beginning to sound Italian.

Pattie pulled a face and resumed her rolling.

The living-room windows had been thrown wide open, and in the rambling front garden, a multitude of seasonal flowers raised their faces to the sun. Eric and Pattie watched Paul and his mother waltz around the room to Peter Sarstedt's *Where Do You Go To (My Lovely)?* Springtime had arrived with a flourish, lightening hearts and lifting spirits.

'So Mother, what's in the mysterious ring box?' asked Paul. 'A mysterious ring?' He sat next to Eric. Fleetwood Mac's *Man of the World* came on the radio.

Everyone watched as Julia flipped open the red box. Inside on a shiny purple cushion were two yellow LSD tablets.

'This is all that's left,' said Julia. 'I nearly flushed them down the toilet. I won't be taking any more LSD in future, but I hid these away with a sunny day in mind.'

'For the four of us,' said Pattie.

Julia nodded, 'Yes, for the Ealing Hippies. There's half a tab for each of us, if everyone wants some.'

Paul elbowed Eric, 'My mum just offered us LSD.'

Pattie looked out at the blue sky above Fox Wood. 'We should go somewhere nice. I'll roll a couple more.'

Mindful of Eric's intention to photograph their outing, the two young women spent a few minutes at Julia's dressing-table. Availing themselves of her black eyeliner, Paul and Eric joined the makeup session then changed into their favourite hippie clothes. Having taken the LSD and shared the first of Pattie's pantyful of joints, the four set out along the shaded public footpath.

Pattie caressed Eric's bottom through his jeans, 'You're looking good.'

'You too,' grinned Eric. Admiring the pretty blonde in Julia's sky-blue minidress, he wondered if he should reciprocate.

Julia and Paul made a U-turn into Hanger Hill Park. To Eric, Julia's yellow dress and Paul's crimson shirt appeared exceptionally colourful that day, set against the fresh green grass and vivid blue sky. He was surprised to see that the rolling park was dotted with grazing sheep. At the base of the converging hills, the wooden shelter was full of the white woolly animals. Above the trees to their left, the observation turret was visible on the Ealing House roof. Sunlight glinted off the mounted brass telescope.

As they followed Julia and Paul down the gently sloping hill, Pattie took Eric's hand. 'What will you do when you leave school?'

'The same as you did,' replied Eric. 'Art college. I'm hoping that Ealing does a photography course.'

'You haven't bothered to find out?'

'Er, no.'

'I didn't either.'

Eric raised Pattie's hand, examining her immaculately manicured blue fingernails. 'Did I ever tell you that you're *Little Wing?*'

'Is this a line?'

'Mm, could be.' Eric relaxed her arm. 'In my head, you're the girl in the song.'

Pattie smiled, 'Oh, that's nice!'

'Whenever I hear it, I picture you walking up there among the clouds.'

'*Ahh,*' Pattie purred. 'Honestly?'

'Yeah.'

'Every time?'

'Yeah. You're her.'

Pattie looked at Eric, 'I hope you're still playing *Little Wing* when you're sixty-four.'

'I will be.'

The couple approached the shelter, and Eric noticed that the sheep had moved away.

Paul grinned, 'We've got the park's one and only shelter to our-selves.'

Sitting on the shaded bench seat with her feet up, Julia was grinning too. Eric was struck by the likeness between the mother and son. Paul's eyeliner and long black hair bolstered the resemblance.

Pattie joined the others in the shelter, 'I can't imagine life after the sixties.'

'Only eight months left,' said Paul.

'I can't imagine it either,' said Julia. 'Perhaps we shouldn't try.'

Eric thought this sounded very unlike Julia; it was more the kind of carefree comment he would expect from Pattie. A white polythene football bobbled down the hill towards them. Eric stood up and kicked it back. A rainbow arc trailed behind the ball, colourfully plotting its trajectory against the sky. The rainbow shimmered and turned to sparkling pink dust, then faded in the sunlight. Eric remembered they had taken LSD.

'Cheers,' called a boy on the grassy slope.

'The playground's empty,' Pattie observed, passing Julia a joint.

Eric photographed the others in various poses on the rocking horse, the seesaw and the witches' hat. Positioning the Pentax on the roundabout, he set the timer and joined his three friends. Julia and Pattie laughed together on adjacent swings while Eric and Paul pushed gently from behind. In later years, this would become Eric's most precious photo.

Pattie accompanied Eric when he retrieved his camera. 'Is this the roundabout?' whispered the blonde.

Eric smiled, 'Yeah, this is the one.'

'Do you want a picture? Show me where I was standing.' The blonde stepped forward, then hesitated. 'No, too weird!'

Eric laughed, 'Pattie, you're so wonderfully uncomplicated.'

'Thank you... I think.'

They sat together on the roundabout, watching some children play.

Standing by the swings, Paul waved, then pointed to the gate at the top of the rise.

'Okay, we'll be right behind you,' called Pattie. 'Let's not leave quite yet,' she whispered to Eric.

When Julia rose from the swing, Eric saw a faraway look in her eyes. He watched two sheep follow Paul and his mother up the hill. Laying back next to Pattie, Eric noticed that the sky was full of fluffy white animals.

Twenty minutes later, they left the sunny park with their arms around one another.

'Got any more panty pot?' Eric asked, opening the front door of the Ealing House.

Pattie smiled, 'Yeah, I have two more stashed away.'

'Great, it takes the edge off the acid.'

'Mm, LSD Alka-Seltzer. I wasn't expecting much from half a tab, but it's –'

'It's powerful stuff,' Eric said in his best Irish accent.

'Indeed, Andy,' agreed Pattie.

'Andy?'

'Andy Stewart.'

'It was supposed to be Irish.'

'Sorry – Val, then. Maybe you should leave the accents to Paul.'

Eric took off his shoes and looked into the living room, 'They're not in here.'

'Kitchen?' Pattie walked barefoot down the hallway. 'Helloo?'

Eric went into the ballroom. Walking to the French windows, he checked the back garden. He made a mental note to suggest to Paul that they clear the new growth creeping towards the house.

Pattie stood listening at the foot of the stairs. 'Come on, they're having their own party up there. Let's go up and gate-crash.'

When Eric reached the stairway, the blonde was already nearing the first floor. 'Hang on a minute.'

Peggy Lee's *Fever* had stopped playing before Pattie made the upper corridor.

Eric took the blonde's arm, holding her back. 'Maybe we shouldn't.'

'Oh, come on.' Pattie looked inquiringly at Eric, 'What's wrong?'

Orange sunshine beamed through the big round window that dominated the end of the corridor, the lattice throwing crisscrossed shadows along the deep-red carpet. On the left side, Julia's bedroom door was shut. The door opposite stood wide open.

'That's Jack's room!' whispered Pattie. 'What's going on?' she asked suspiciously. 'Why did you try to stop me from coming up here?'

'I didn't,' answered Eric. 'Well... I don't know, just a feeling.'

'Male intuition?'

'Something like that.'

Walking to the end of the passage, Pattie tapped lightly on Julia's bedroom door. 'Hello? Anybody home?' She knocked again.

Eric peered into the opposite bedroom. To the left stood a large dressing table. Behind it, tightly drawn curtains shut out the light from the front window. Ahead of Eric, a little to his left, a dark-wood four-poster bed backed on to the facing wall. Sturdy and ornate, the bed was the masculine equivalent of the one in which Julia slept.

'I've never seen inside Uncle Jack's room before,' whispered Pattie. 'It feels like we're trespassing.'

'Yeah,' replied Eric. 'Let's go back downstairs.'

Pattie brushed past, entering the long shadowy room, 'Look at all this stuff! It's a treasure trove!'

Eric reluctantly followed her in. 'I don't think we should –'

'Who do you think all this belongs to?' asked Pattie. She regarded the untidy collection of wigs, shoes, hats, costume jewellery, and dresses, some of which had been draped over a black-panelled oriental screen halfway down the lengthy room. Eric looked back across the four-poster bed towards the curtained front window. A thick layer of dust on the dressing-table had been brushed away at the centre, where an assortment of brightly coloured makeup revealed signs of recent use.

'Maybe Uncle Jack was into dressing-up,' mused Pattie. She stroked the long black wig on the chair by the screen. 'Or perhaps this stuff belongs to Julia.' Pattie pondered her question, then whispered to Eric, 'But neither of those would explain the blonde in the window.'

You may be uncomplicated, but you're sharp as a pin, Eric thought, walking back to the foot of the bed. He turned around to leave the room. 'Shit!' Eric recoiled from his reflection. A huge full-length mirror hung on the wall next to the doorway.

'That'll teach you to go sneaking about in other people's bedrooms,' Pattie said, breezing past Eric into the corridor.

No sheep were present in any of the photographs.

29

The Summer of '69

Providing an overture to the beginning of summer, the eponymous debut album from Crosby, Stills & Nash played frequently at the Ealing House, interspersed by the perennial sounds of Bob Dylan, the Beatles, Jimi Hendrix and Cream. Joni Mitchell's *Clouds* LP offered a lightweight alternative to the guitar pyrotechnics beloved by Eric and Paul. The Who's conceptual double-album, *Tommy,* emerged as an enigmatic opus for everyone to discuss and decipher.

In bed for a second stint, John and Yoko took up temporary residence at the Queen Elizabeth Hotel in Montreal, where they were joined by Timothy Leary and some likeminded others to record *Give Peace a Chance.* Bed Peace, Hair Peace, read the signs taped to the hotel window. To the press and to the public majority, the anti-war crusade appeared crazy. To Julia, Pattie, Paul and Eric, it made perfect sense. Paul spent the entire summer trying to coax Keith to say, *Parrot Peace.* Although he listened intently, the old bird stubbornly refused to participate in the hippie campaign, preferring to stick with established standards like, *Hello, Show us your knickers,* and *Fuck off.*

The crowded tube carriage smelled of food and patchouli oil.

'Name one British war, apart from the Hitler one, that was morally justifiable,' Eric said, as the red Central Line train approached Marble Arch.

Paul thought for a moment, 'Er, what was World War One about? Baltic land, alliances, and blank cheques?'

'I dunno. Playing football in the mud at Christmas,' replied Eric. 'People say it would have been over quickly if we'd stayed out. I asked my dad what he thought about wars, and he said we need them to keep the population down.'

'There must be nicer ways,' said Paul. 'Mum reckons wars are started by politicians and fought by the working classes. Things are changing, though. I expect in ten years there'll *be* no more wars.'

Eric agreed, 'The word's spreading. People are waking up. I bet religion will fade away, too.'

'Bound to... *Eric Lennon.*'

The underground platform was teeming with brightly dressed young people filing toward the exits. Tie-dyed T-shirts and jeans flared with scraps of material were *de rigueur* that day, though fashions were varied and individual. A busker strummed a beaten-up acoustic guitar; *Eve of Destruction* echoed through the warren-like tunnels.

'The station smells of over-ripe fruit,' observed Paul.

Eric clutched his camera case, 'We should've brought a picnic.'

Emerging into hot summer sunshine, the two longhaired lads followed the hippie throng across Hyde Park.

Eric looked back at the nineteenth-century landmark that stood at the juncture of Oxford Street and Park Lane, 'Funny place to leave an arch.'

'Marble Arch used to be a police station,' Paul said informatively. 'And before that, it was the entranceway to Buckingham Palace.'

'Bloody 'ell, how do you move something like that?'

'Grab an end each and lift on three.'

'And remember to bend your knees when you put it down.' Eric pulled his Pentax out of its case.

Paul wiped his brow with his forearm. 'Any idea where we're going?'

'Last summer's Pink Floyd/Jethro Tull concert was in a big grassy hollow by the Serpentine.'

'Sounds nice.'

'Yeah. With any luck, whoever's at the front of this procession knows where they're headed.'

'Blind faith, then.'

Eric smiled, 'Yeah.'

Making their debut at the free concert that day was a new band for whom someone in the music press had coined the term *Supergroup*. Following Cream's demise, Eric Clapton had teamed up with ex-Spenser Davis and Traffic man Steve Winwood. Clinging to Clapton's coattails, Cream drummer Ginger Baker elbowed his way into the line-up, along with ex-Family bassist Ric Grech. Recoiling at the hyperbolic *Supergroup* tag, Clapton had sarcastically named the band Blind Faith.

Standing beneath the trees on the Cockpit rim, Eric and Paul looked down at the large audience seated in front of a small roofless stage. Behind it, the Serpentine sparkled in the early afternoon sunlight. Eric watched rowing boats glide across the diamond-sprinkled water. He tasted cheese-and-tomato sandwiches and pictured himself sitting on the bank with Julia. 'Where's the safest place to smoke a joint?'

Paul surveyed the steadily widening audience. 'Down there at the front, I should think.'

The gathering was already much larger than the Pot Rally they had attended in 1967. The underground movement was merging with the mainstream as more people grew their hair and found themselves drawn to music and musicianship. Eric hoped the counterculture's poetry, art and politics would not become diluted in the process.

Paul led the way, followed closely by his friend. Endeavouring not to step on anyone, they tiptoed through the hippie bodies, making for the stage. To Eric's surprise, he found himself sitting on the grass next to Paul, no more than twelve feet from the WEM PA speakers. Tubular metal barriers formed a small press enclosure in front of the low platform. Seated amid other longhaired pot smokers, Eric and Paul shared a joint.

Eric heard one of the technicians say *400 watts* and wondered if he referred to the PA's output. The speaker setup looked small for such a big concert.

The first performance began at 2:30 with the Third Ear Band, who provided a pleasant opening to the free outdoor show with their blend of folky/Indian influenced music. Eric looked back at the audience. The grassy bowl was now packed with upwards of a hundred-thousand people, with more in the trees. A smoky blue haze hung in the still air. The vast crowd filled Eric's vision, blurring in the summer heat like celluloid cinema film.

Three-piece hippie rock trio, the Edgar Broughton Band came on next, cranking up their Marshalls and treating the audience to a series of original counterculture classics, including *Apache Drop Out* and *Death of an Electric Citizen*. Dressed in flowing psychedelic robes and sporting permed hair reminiscent of *Disraeli Gears*, two male Idiot Dancers stood among the cross-legged hippies, twisting and writhing in the yellow afternoon light. Eric thought if he lived through a million of Phil's universes, he could never do that, but he was glad that there were people who would. *Out Demons Out* had the crowd on their feet. They clapped and chanted as wild-haired Edgar exorcised the park of mischievous establishment spirits that may have crawled out of the Serpentine to pull out jack plugs and loosen strings.

Jamming like a black Pete Townshend on his acoustic guitar, Richie Havens previewed his upcoming Woodstock appearance with a version of *Motherless Child,* augmenting the old spiritual with a clarion call for *Freedom.* Paul traded half a joint for a cheese and cucumber sandwich, which he shared with Eric.

Donovan came on wearing a white shirt and jacket, and Eric flashed back to the clifftop at West Bay. The folkie sang *'Yellow is the colour of my true love's teeth',* and *There Was an Old Lady Who Swallowed a Fly,* but few of his hits. It felt surreal to be seated so close to the man, whose voice and poetry Eric and Paul had heard in the front rooms of their Ealing homes. It was like meeting an old friend for the first time. Eric pictured the folk singer stepping out of the radiogram.

There was a feeling of anticipation in the crowd; a deluge of hype had preceded the unveiling of the world's first *Supergroup,* Blind Faith. A burgundy Gibson Les Paul leaning against one of the Marshall stacks grabbed Eric's attention. Clapton had favoured Gibson guitars throughout his tenure with Cream.

When Blind Faith appeared on the stage, a hundred-thousand people moved forward. Clutching his camera, Eric squeezed through a widening gap in the barriers, and he and Paul found themselves sitting inside the press enclosure. Close up, the band sounded fantastic. Sitting at the feet of his favourite guitarist, Eric Clapton, it occurred to Eric that – probably for the only time in his life – he was occupying the most happening space on the planet.

About halfway through the first song, Buddy Holly's *Well All right,* it began to dawn on everyone that the new band was not set up to be a reincarnated Cream. Ginger Baker's lengthy drum solo in *Do What You Like* was as close as it came. Nonetheless, the gentle melodic music suited the summer day, and it was received well.

The yellow afternoon sunlight turned golden-orange as Blind Faith finished their set. The early evening was warm, the audience calm and relaxed. A casual onstage discussion among the four musicians preceded the encore, *Had to Cry Today,* then Blind Faith left the park.

Eric and Paul followed some exiting music fans around the back of the stage. A line of hippies traced the Serpentine's curve towards the tube stations and London's West End. Eric photographed the backs of the tattered Marshall speaker cabinets on which CREAM had been stencilled in white. Beneath a Star Trek orange sky, there were rowing boats on the placid lake. Eric and Paul joined the path, passing a line of colourful easel-mounted paintings.

*

Eric staggered into a deco-era house in North Ealing carrying a large bag of plaster. 'Where do you want it, Dad?'

'Upstairs in the front bedroom,' directed Bill. 'I've shifted the furniture and laid out the dustsheets.'

Eric looked up at the hole in the bedroom ceiling. 'What happened?' he asked, as his father came in with a paint-spattered stepladder.

'The Major had managed to clamber up into the loft,' explained Bill. 'Mrs Pertwee told me he was up there searching for his cricket bat, and he stepped between the joists. The lady of the house was in bed reading... She got a face-full of plaster, and a carpet slipper hit her on the head.'

'He's a bit old to be playing cricket,' observed Eric.

'Moles,' said Bill. 'There are hills all over the lawn out the back. The Major planned to entice them out with a tin of sardines, then bash them for six when they appeared. He never found his bat, though.'

'Good,' said Eric.

'Maybe not,' replied Bill. 'Now he's talking about dropping hand grenades into the tunnels.'

Carrying the plaster bag upstairs and fetching a bucket of water was the sum total of Eric's work that day. Bill had invited his son along to teach him the art of plastering, a skill that his father believed would stand Eric in good stead should his career in photography fail to materialise.

'Just out of interest,' Bill said, judiciously adding water to the mixture, 'your mum told me she saw you sitting in the postman's Ford Zodiac. It made me think. Reg has telephoned you at the house over the years.'

'Yeah.'

'Well, it seems a little odd for a teenage lad to socialise with a middle-aged postman. I mean, you're not even a football fan.'

'Reg would be happy to hear you calling him *middle-aged*,' said Eric. 'He's due to retire soon.'

'Are you avoiding my question?'

'Not at all,' Eric answered untruthfully. 'Reg is heavily into jazz. He likes a lot of music – Dusty Springfield, Tom Jones – but especially jazz. I've been to his house a few times. Don't you trust him?'

'Oh, I'd trust Reg with my life and my wife,' replied Bill.

Eric shrugged, 'So what's the problem? Just cos he laughed at your yellow hubcaps.'

Bill chuckled, 'You have a good memory, Eric. That must've been ten years ago.'

'About time you got over it then, Dad.'

Later that afternoon, the Major and his wife looked up at their freshly plastered bedroom ceiling.

'Another fine job,' the old man said, leaning heavily on his stick.

Turning to her husband, Mrs Pertwee smiled. 'Bill Grimes can fix anything.'

*

At the beginning of June 1969, guitarist Brian Jones left the Rolling Stones at the band's request. On the third of July, he was found floating face down in his swimming pool. Shortly before his death, the drug-addled Jones had told friends that he would soon be joining the Beatles.

Eric placed his camera in his rucksack alongside a pair of opera glasses that Paul had found in the attic. The picnic Julia had prepared for Hyde Park had already been packed. 'Are you sure it's still on?'

Paul nodded, 'They confirmed it last night on the news. The Stones are turning the concert into a tribute for Brian.'

'It was on the radio this morning,' said Pattie. 'They're expecting over two hundred thousand at this one.'

Julia gazed out of the living room window, 'They chose a lovely day for it.' The sun-drenched front garden was a mass of wild colour.

The free concert was to take place at *the Cockpit*, the same location Blind Faith had selected for their debut. The previous evening, mourners had arrived at the park carrying candles in memory of Brian Jones. Hundreds of fans slept in front of the six-foot-high stage that

July night, undisturbed by the central London police. When the four Ealing hippies reached the site, the crowd was already enormous.

Paul scanned the huge assembly, 'We won't be sitting at the front this time. I thought the Blind Faith concert was big, but it looks like half the country has turned up for this one.'

'Yeah, bigger crowd, bigger stage, bigger PA,' observed Eric. 'And big Hells Angels in German helmets.'

'The Stones hired the big Angels as security,' explained Pattie. 'I think it might be time for a big joint. Everyone gather in close while I unbutton my jeans.'

Julia glanced over her shoulder as they huddled around the blonde. 'The Serpentine looks so beautiful. Perhaps we could take a boat out later?'

In future years, Eric would recall little of the Third Ear Band, Screw, Family, and Roy Harper performances. Roy had only played one song, anyway. For the Ealing hippies, sitting near the massive audience's outer edge, the music assumed a secondary role to the occasion. Charlie Watkins had assembled a 1,500 watt PA – a monstrous sound system by the standards of the time – but the performers appeared as tiny ants on the faraway stage. The collective memory for Julia, Pattie, Paul and Eric, would take the form of a sunny watercolour montage, depicting the momentous gathering as a series of indistinct, overlapping images. A string of heavily loaded marijuana cigarettes enhanced the effect.

Among Eric's scant recollections of the music that day was King Crimson's use of a Mellotron on *Court of the Crimson King*. The taped string sounds within the keyboard instrument drifted across the park, impressively combining with Greg Lake's clear, well-pitched vocals to create an atmosphere of medieval mystery sprinkled with a smattering of Lewis Carroll. The song heralded the dawning of the *Prog Rock* era that was to follow.

Those *in the know* envisaged Alexis Corner's inclusion on the bill as an appreciative nod from the Stones. The blues aficionado had founded the Ealing Club where Mick and Keith had met Brian Jones earlier in the decade.

Eric would associate the Battered Ornaments' set with the picnic the four hippies shared. Battered ornaments tasted of brown bread, cream cheese, and sun-warmed fairy cakes.

Mick Jagger appeared on the stage wearing white loon pants. Some reports suggested that his matching frilly dress had been made for Sammy Davis Junior, while others identified the garment as belonging to Marianne Faithful.

Appealing for quiet, Jagger told the crowd that he wanted to say something for Brian. He opened a blue poetry book, *'Peace. Peace! He is not dead; he doth not sleep. He hath awakened from the dream of life...'*

'Adonais,' Julia whispered.

Mick concluded his reading to warm applause, and thousands of white butterflies flew from the stage. A girl sitting beside Paul had one land on her nose.

Julia's green eyes glistened in the late-afternoon sunlight. 'Shelley wrote that for John Keats. It was a lovely choice.'

Eric smiled. *How could I not love you?*

A wave of expectancy enveloped the natural amphitheatre. The Rolling Stones opened with a song that Eric had never heard before, then launched into *Jumpin' Jack Flash*. Jagger cavorted and pouted, working the crowd, but Eric only had eyes for Julia.

Mercy Mercy, Down Home Girl, Stray Cat Blues.

'They're a bit out of tune.' Paul handed the opera glasses to his friend.

'And they could have done with a few more rehearsals,' added Eric. Training the binoculars on the band's new guitarist, he wished he had the money to buy a Gibson SG. 'Mick Taylor's good, though.'

No Expectations, I'm Free, Loving Cup, Love in Vain.

'The Who are playing across the water at the Albert Hall tonight,' Pattie said, passing a joint to Paul. 'And Chuck Berry's supporting. If there are any mods and rockers left in London, it sounds like a sure-fire recipe for a punch-up.'

(I Can't Get No) Satisfaction, Honky Tonk Women, Midnight Rambler, Street Fighting Man.

Affixing his wide-angle lens, Eric took a series of photographs of his companions with the enormous audience and the Rolling Stones in the background.

'Let me take one of you,' Pattie said, holding her hand out for the camera. 'Jules, give Eric a hug.'

Julia wrapped her arms around him, smiling prettily and pulling in close as they posed for the picture.

Pattie handed the Pentax back to Eric with a sly wink. 'That'll be five bob,' she whispered.

Ginger Johnson's African Drummers joined the Stones for their final song, *Sympathy for the Devil.*

'Do either of you two strapping chaps feel up to rowing us girls around the Serpentine?' asked Julia. 'If we go now, we'll get a head-start on the crowd.'

Ten minutes later, after a short wait at the hut on the lakeside, the four hippies found themselves in a wooden rowing boat with Eric manning the oars. The air felt cool and fresh as they joined the flotilla on Hyde Park's recreational lagoon. The music was clearly audible from the water.

A full seventeen minutes into the closing song, Jagger announced that it was time to go.

'I have to go, too.' Pattie checked her watch, 'In about an hour.'

'Business or pleasure?' enquired Julia.

'A little of both, hopefully,' replied the blonde. 'Dinner at the Dorchester, then whatever. It's just over there on Park Lane.'

Eric smiled to himself. Despite his special relationship with the pretty model, he felt no jealousy. While others spoke of freedom, Pattie lived it. Eric could never imagine her settling down in suburbia with a banker husband and two-point-five children. Pattie was *Little Wing,* walking among the clouds.

'I've got one more joint tucked away,' said Pattie. 'Eric, if you could get us out to the middle of the lake...'

His mission accomplished, Eric rested the oars in the rowlocks. He watched Pattie unbuttoning her jeans as she slid down into the wooden hull.

Paul studied the long line of concertgoers shuffling slowly along the bank. 'Could you pass me your backpack, please, Eric.' Removing the opera glasses from the canvas bag, he scanned the shoreline.

'Have you seen someone you know?' Julia asked, skimming her fingers across the water.

'I'm not sure, maybe,' replied Paul. 'I think she's hiding.'

'*Hiding?*' Pattie lit the joint. 'It's not your mother, is it? Oh no, she's here next to me.'

'Who is it?' asked Eric.

'I think...' replied Paul. 'I *think* it's Cathy McGowan. I mean, not *Cathy McGowan.* It's the Cathy McGowan girl we met at Kensington

Market, and she was watching us. It looked like she had a walkie-talkie or something.'

'Are you sure?' Eric glanced back at Julia.

'No, but it's either her or her double.' Paul stood up and raised the opera glasses.

'Be careful, Paul,' warned Julia. 'You –'

Paul stumbled against the seat. 'Uh!' He slipped and fell sideways, his forehead glancing the hull as he tumbled overboard, splashing into the lake.

'Paul!' Julia shouted, dropping the joint in the water.

Eric reached down, grasping his friend's arm. 'I've got him!' He looked back, 'Move to the other side!'

Julia and Pattie leaned out, counterbalancing the craft as Eric hauled Paul back into the boat. Blood streamed from a wound above his eye.

'Oh, not again,' muttered Julia.

Rowing for all his worth, Eric powered the boat towards the bank.

Julia cradled her son, holding his head to her chest. Blood poured from his brow, matting his mother's long hair.

Pattie held Paul's hand. 'He still has the opera glasses.'

Alert to the perils of hippies in boats, the attendant had summoned a St John's Ambulance crew. When the four reached the shore, a stretcher was waiting to transfer Paul into the emergency vehicle.

Pattie turned to Eric, 'You were like fucking Superman when you pulled him out of the water,' she said, climbing into the ambulance.

'Sorry, son.' The uniformed man leant down, placing a hand on Eric's shoulder. 'We can't take any more passengers. Sorry.'

'Go back to Ealing, Eric,' Julia called from inside the vehicle. 'I'll phone you from the hospital.'

The double doors slammed closed, and they were gone.

Finding himself adrift in a sea of hippies, Eric shouldered his backpack and headed for Marble Arch tube station.

Music fans filed into the Royal Albert Hall. Across the road near the Albert Memorial, Rainbow lowered her walkie-talkie and entered a phonebox. A short time later, at the Ealing House, Stan scrambled over the perimeter wall and dropped into the front garden.

Pink and purple streaks painted the evening sky. Concerned that he might miss Julia's call, Eric hurried down the path and let himself into the house. As was the norm on a Saturday, Tony was not at home and would most likely not turn up until the following evening.

Eric left his backpack beside the coat rack. He took off his shoes and went into the living room. The house smelled musty, as it often did on hot summer days. Eric felt small and alone in the big house. He stared at the television but had no inclination to turn it on. His mind a confusion of jumbled images, he reran the moments preceding the mishap on the lake. The Cathy McGowan girl. Why should she be spying on them in Hyde Park? Paul thought he had seen her using a walkie-talkie. Who was she speaking to, and what information could she be relaying that would be of interest to anyone? Maybe she wanted to get them busted. Maybe it wasn't her.

Eric heard a tinkling that he knew was coming from the kitchen. *There'll be another any moment.* Sure enough, the sound was followed by a second, then a third metallic ringing, then a smash of breaking glass.

'Crap!' Eric exclaimed to the living room.

Hastening to the hallway, he slipped on his shoes and reached the kitchen in time to prevent Keith from tossing a second glass tumbler off the draining board. Knives, forks and teaspoons lay scattered across the flagstone floor amid the shattered glass. Standing on the edge of the counter, the old grey parrot leaned down, eyeing his mess. He glanced up at Eric, then flew back to his perch by the door.

'Thanks a lot, Keith.' Eric looked around for a dustpan and brush and found one in the cupboard beneath the sink.

Having picked up the cutlery and disposed of the glass, Eric crouched in front of the low cupboard. Replacing the dustpan next to the sink pipe, he hesitated, listening. He peered into the dark recess, and behind the U-bend, he discovered the source of the ticking. Tony's Mickey Mouse clock had been pushed to the back of the cupboard. Two wires were attached to the alarm mechanism: one to the metal hammer and the other to one of the two bells. A fragment of cardboard prevented a connection. Eric shifted a packet of Daz to one side, revealing a small metal box taped to what appeared to be a brick-sized slab of putty. The alarm on Tony's clock had been set for 2am.

Eric rose slowly and moved back. He held his forearm towards the parrot. 'Come on, Keith, we're out of here.' Keith stepped on.

'It looks like a bomb!' Eric spoke softly into the telephone, as if the explosive might hear him and self-detonate. 'I didn't call the police, because if it was planted by MoD2 –'

'Okay, yeah. You did the right thing,' said Reg. 'Where is it?'

'Under the kitchen sink.' Eric fiddled nervously with the aspidistra.

'And where are you?' asked the postman.

'By the stairs, outside the kitchen door.'

'Is there anyone else in the house?'

'No, just me and Keith... Keith's a parrot.'

'Right,' said Reg. 'You and Keith go down to the far end of the front garden and wait by the gate. And stay there! Got it?'

'Yes, but –'

'Don't let anyone go into the house. Help is on the way. Okay?'

'Okay,' said Eric.

'Good. Now grab Keith and go!'

There was a click, and the line went dead. With Keith on his shoulder, Eric walked briskly through the shadowed front garden and stood by the gate.

Time passed slowly. Eric stared along the pathway, wondering how he would explain everything to Julia if the house blew up. The alarm had been set for two o'clock in the morning, he told himself, almost five hours away. And help was coming.

Keith stood on one foot, preening his grey and red feathers.

'Did you know about the bomb?' Eric asked the bird on his shoulder. The old parrot repositioned himself, and Eric felt a warm wetness creep down the back of his T-shirt. 'Oh, thanks! Well, since you probably saved all our lives, I'll forgive you.'

The darkening sky had turned deep red, eerily silhouetting the tall house. Eric stared through the open front door into the gloomy hallway. If Julia rang now, would he run inside and answer the phone? And if he did, what would he say to her? *Sorry, can't talk for long; there's a bomb in the kitchen.*

After what seemed like an eternity, Eric heard footsteps in the walkway.

'Eric?'

Recognising the postman's voice, Eric breathed a sigh of relief and opened the gate.

'Hello young man,' the Scientist said, shuffling into the garden. 'My, what lovely flowers! I always think they look so much nicer when left to grow in a natural setting.'

Reg edged past the old man. 'Did you notice if the alarm was set?'

'Yeah, for two in the morning,' answered Eric.

'If that's the time, it'll be just fine,' an American voice replied from the walkway.

Eric saw the brown fedora first, then the pearly white smile.

'Hi kid, long time no see,' grinned Sidney Mars, DJ to the Stars.

When Eric stepped forward to hug his old friend, Keith dived off his shoulder, flying to the nearest high point: the top of Reg's head.

'You look rather good,' said the Scientist to the postman. 'There's a marked resemblance if you don't mind me saying.'

'Wh... where have you been?' Tears rimmed Eric's eyes.

'Oh, here and there, more there than here,' replied Sid. 'I guess you know me now as Igor.'

Eric nodded.

Sid pulled out a handkerchief and wiped parrot poo from his hand.

'Erm, there's the somewhat pressing matter of the bomb under the sink,' said the Scientist. 'Are you expecting anyone home, Eric?'

'No, Julia's going to be telephoning soon.'

'No time to lose, I'll go in and defuse,' rhymed Sid. Saluting the Scientist, he strode towards the house. 'Thunderbirds are Go!'

'It's in the kitchen,' Eric called. 'Straight down the hall and –'

Sid waved over his shoulder, 'I know the layout. Igor's been keepin' an eye on things.'

'Does he know what he's doing?' Eric asked as Sid disappeared into the house.

'Don't worry,' replied Reg. 'Sid had some experience with bombs during the war. Have you heard of the guns of Navarone?'

'Yes?'

'We saw the film together.'

'Oh... good,' Eric said hesitantly.

'You can come in now,' Sid called from the front doorway.

Eric and Reg walked slowly, keeping pace with the old scientist. Jumping off the postman's head, Keith fluttered back onto Eric's shoulder.

Sid took a flash photograph of the cupboard under the sink. 'Mind if I make some coffee?' he asked, lighting the stove as the others joined him in the kitchen.

'Good idea.' Eric switched on the kitchen light. 'It didn't take you long to disarm the bomb.'

'Nah,' Sid replied, lining-up four mugs. 'I just pulled the wires off.'

The Scientist slid out a chair and examined the Mickey Mouse clock on the kitchen table. 'Where is the explosive?'

'Jammed behind the pipe,' replied Sid. 'I'll get it out in a minute.'

'I think we owe you an explanation, Eric,' said Reg.

'It's okay,' replied Eric. 'Actually, I'm really happy about everything. Apart from finding a bomb under the sink.'

The postman half-closed the kitchen door and stood next to Keith. 'We cooked up a plan to fake Sid's death so he could work undercover and infiltrate Hartlepool.'

'And keep half-an-eye on the Ealing hippies,' Sid added, stirring the coffees.

Reg scratched his nose. 'Sorry about the deception, Eric. Only me and the Scientist knew Sid was alive. We were going to tell you earlier, but Sid suspected that something was wrong at the house.'

Eric sat next to the Scientist at the kitchen table. 'So you've been spying on the spies... Igor.'

Sid pulled a floppy rubber mask out of his jacket pocket. 'There's been eyes on you guys. Almost made a boo-boo tonight, though.'

Eric looked at the Yogi Bear mask, then up at Sid. The American ex-pat looked well: particularly so, in light of the gravestone bearing his name in Hanwell Cemetery. Eric turned to the Scientist, 'There was a bomb under the sink. What's to stop them trying it again?'

A hush fell over the kitchen.

'We've not been idle these past six years,' began the Scientist. 'With my gadgetry, Reg's inside work, and Sid's surveillance and photography skills, we've accumulated a mountain of evidence. Rest assured, we are not working alone, and that evidence is in reliable hands. It is now time to inform MoD2 of this insurance policy. We shall remain anonymous, of course, but you and your friends will be safe.'

Once again, Eric found himself wanting to believe the old man, but his uneasy feeling had resurfaced.

'Should MoD2 fail to comply,' continued the Scientist, 'envelopes like the one I have here in my pocket will find their way onto desktops in Whitehall and Fleet Street, the Pentagon, and the New York Times. MoD2 would be utterly exposed. In short, Eric, we have the insurance to safeguard ourselves.'

Reg spoke up, 'Me and Sid have seen the Scientist's evidence, Eric. We've reached a stalemate with Hartlepool... But it means we're safe.'

Eric trusted the postman, and his endorsement of the old man's precautions was reassuring, if not entirely convincing.

'Unfortunately, we cannot prevent MoD2 from sending out their subliminal transmissions,' the Scientist added with an air of irritation. 'The effectiveness of the broadcasts would be impossible to prove in a court of law.'

Eric sipped his coffee and glanced sideways at the old man. The Scientist was gearing up for his *grand finale*.

'If world leaders and industry moguls continue to foster greed and neglect, our species will become unsustainable. Our poisoning and plundering of the planet will result in rising temperatures, floods, and famine, eventually leading to wars being fought over arable land and dwindling resources. The planet will recover, but humanity may not. It is within our power to change this apocalyptic version of the future, and with Eric's invaluable help, we will.'

Keith cocked his head to one side, 'Show us yer knickers.'

Eric opened the kitchen door in time to see Julia disappearing up the stairs.

Hurriedly disposing of their coffee cups, Reg and Sid each took an arm and sped the Scientist along the hallway. Eric waved out at the dark garden and quietly closed the front door.

Ambling back down the hallway, Eric was wondering what he should say to Julia, when she stepped out from behind the aspidistra.

'Hello Eric.' Julia rested her arm on the stair rail. 'Paul's okay, but the hospital is keeping him in overnight. By the way, I've been home for about ten minutes.'

Eric met Julia's eyes. 'Paul's okay?'

'Yes.'

'And you're alone?'

'Yes.'

'How much did you overhear?'

'Oh, nothing much really,' Julia replied casually. 'I heard about an organisation in Hartlepool called MoD2, spies, bombs, subliminal propaganda... And apparently, there's some sort of *doomsday machine*. Oh, and it seems that you, Eric, hold the key to the future of the planet.' Julia paused. 'I'm sorry I didn't phone; I got straight into a cab.'

There was a long silence.

'It's not exactly a doomsday machine,' began Eric.

30

The Isle of Wight

Eric's disclosure had been accompanied by an overwhelming feeling of relief. Once he had begun, his words spilt out like a swollen river bursting its banks. He told Julia everything he knew about the Scientist, MoD2, and the transmitter's unique capability, even about Sid's faked death and the Yogi Bear mask. He accepted Julia's response with stoic resignation: *'I believe that* you *believe it, Eric'.*

Dusty Springfield looked down from Reg's mantelpiece.

'I had the shock of my life when Sid walked through the garden gate.'

'Yes,' smiled Reg. 'Taking Sid out of the picture enabled him to work undercover. But as you know, Eric, Sid had other reasons for wanting to disappear. He'd already gone into hiding before the Scientist returned.'

Eric recalled the Soho club and Sid's paranoid glances in the Minx's rear-view mirror.

The postman lit a Senior Service. 'So Julia overheard everything?'

'Yeah.'

Reg settled back in his armchair, staring at the cigarette in his hand. 'What was her reaction?'

'She's not sure whether to believe any of it, and she's worried about another bomb.'

'Fair enough,' said Reg. 'But I can tell you that the Scientist acted straight away. MoD2 can't touch us now.'

'Are you sure?'

'As eggs is eggs. You can assure Julia that the house is safe.'

'Mm.'

'Eric, I'm guessing the Scientist will want to talk to Julia. Do you think she'd be okay with that?'

'I'd guess that Julia would like to talk to the *Scientist*,' replied Eric. 'But I'd have to ask her.'

'And in the meantime, you're certain she understands the need for secrecy?'

'The bomb convinced her that something serious is going on,' Eric said, not intending to sound sarcastic. 'Don't worry, Reg. Julia's cool.'

'Okay.' The postman flicked his cigarette with his thumbnail. 'What about the plastic explosive? Is it still under the sink?'

'No, I put it in a carrier bag and handed it in at Ealing Police Station. I told them I'd found it on the town hall steps.'

Reg raised an eyebrow, 'Did the police take your name?'

'No, the desk sergeant went out the back for something, and I left.'

'Good,' said Reg. 'As long as you didn't blow up the cop shop. My turn to make the tea.'

'Can I have coffee, please?' asked Eric. 'White, no sugar.'

*

John Lennon's *Give Peace a Chance* and Thunderclap Newman's revolutionary reveille *Something in the Air* were the singles of the summer for Eric. Many songwriters had turned away from the subject of teenage romance, electing to utilise their craft to promote political and social change. Bohemianism had become global, at least to the extent of a general awareness of the lifestyle. Many dipped a toe in the water, while some embraced the concept wholeheartedly.

On the twentieth of July 1969, the Ealing hippies were joined by Tony and around 700 million others to watch the Apollo 11 moon-landing live on television.

'It should have been, *one small step for* A *man*,' Paul pointed out, as Neil Armstrong embarked upon his lumbering lunar walkabout.

'Perhaps they'll dub it in later,' said Eric.

Up in the observation room, Tony aimed the telescope at the moon.

Julia was unusually quiet that night; she had been deep in thought for days. Lifting off on a *Space Oddity* of his own, Eric smoked a lot of marijuana and managed to partially switch off.

*

Dressed to kill, Eric thought, when Julia entered the living room. She had exchanged her T-shirt for a crisp white blouse, and her jeans for her black pleated miniskirt. The last time Eric had seen her in the sexy short skirt had been on the night she had worn it to seduce Stan. It occurred to him that Julia's feminine wiles were an integral weapon in her armoury.

'Ready?' Julia brushed her blazer sleeve briskly. 'Do I look all right?'

'Fabulous,' replied Eric.

Reg was waiting in the Zodiac when Eric and Julia emerged from the walkway. The postman caught himself ogling the attractive dark-haired woman. He was disappointed when she opened a rear door and Eric slid onto the front passenger seat.

'Hi Reg, this is Julia.'

'Pleased to meet you.' Reg shook Julia's hand over the seatback.

'You too, Reg,' said Julia. 'Thanks for picking us up.'

Reg nodded, 'I'm glad we're having this meeting.'

'Me too,' Julia replied flatly.

The day's objective having been broached, the subject was dropped.

Reg followed the Uxbridge Road through West Ealing and Hanwell, turning left at the Iron Bridge towards Gillette Corner and the Great West Road. By this time, the conversation was firmly rooted in jazz. To Eric's delight, Julia was able to hold her own with the aficionado. The car radio played quietly: *My Cherie Amour*, Stevie Wonder, *Oh, Happy Day*, the Edwin Hawkins Singers.

Jethro Tull were *Living in the Past* when Reg drove up the tree-lined driveway. 'Sid's coming later.' The postman pulled up on the forecourt and turned off the radio. 'Let's hope the old man's awake.'

Answering the door dressed in his customary yellow pyjamas and dark-blue robe, the scientist ushered in his guests, greeting Julia with a polite *'Thank you for coming'*. Eric thought the aged eccentric looked younger, almost sprightly.

'Go on through to the back.' The Scientist indicated the way with his stick, 'Reg, Sidney's not here –'

'I'll make the tea,' smiled the postman. 'And some coffee.'

'Thank you, Reg. I stocked-up the digestives.'

Eric and Julia looked out at the chalk man on the hillside.

'The locals call him Big Ted.'

'He's probably some sort of fertility god,' said Julia. 'This is a lovely house.'

'Thank you,' the Scientist said, joining them in the laboratory.

'May I?' Eric leaned across the bench and picked up the Mk1 listening device.

'Be my guest,' smiled the Scientist.

'*Bah*,' said a sheep, from fully four hundred yards away.

'It's all very *James Bond*, isn't it,' remarked Julia.

'Necessity is the mother of invention,' said the Scientist.

Julia smiled, 'I'm not sure that eavesdropping on sheep was quite what Plato had in mind.'

'This is my latest project.' The man patted the top of a television. 'It's similar to the listening device, but the camera attachment is designed to film at long distances.'

'Isn't that what a normal TV camera does?' queried Eric.

'Yes,' said the Scientist. 'But not through walls.'

'Does it work?'

'Not yet,' admitted the inventor. 'But quite by accident, I picked up Australian television on it the other day.' The Scientist shrugged, 'That's how it goes sometimes. You set out to find a cure for something and end up formulating Coca-Cola.'

'Two teas and two coffees,' Reg announced, entering the laboratory with four cups and a packet of biscuits on a silver tray.

'Ms Ramsey, would you care to join me in my study?' the Scientist enquired courteously.

'Lead the way.' Julia took a tea and a coffee from the tray. 'Thanks, Reg.'

'You're welcome,' replied the postman. Placing the tray on one of the benchtops, he opened the biscuits.

Admiring the sizeable book-lined study, Julia waited while the old man closed the door and shuffled across the room.

The Scientist motioned to the leather wingback chair in front of his desk, 'Please, have a seat, Julia.'

Julia placed the tea on the desk and sat down. Cupping her coffee, she looked up at the books behind the Scientist, many of which bore titles requiring dictionary definitions. The man settled into his chair and opened his mouth to speak.

'Eric has told me a rather fantastical story,' said Julia.

'Yes,' replied the Scientist.

'Is it true?'

'Yes.'

'They tried to blow up my house,' Julia said nonchalantly.

The Scientist opened a drawer and pulled out a leather-bound folder. 'As you are already versed in the background, Julia, permit me to begin at the end.'

Meanwhile in the laboratory, Reg helped himself to another biscuit. 'Australia? That's the other side of the world.'

'Yeah.' Eric slowly turned the washing-machine dial on the side of the TV. The static cleared.

'A Spanish version of Criss Cross Quiz!' exclaimed Reg.

'Sounds Spanish.' Eric checked the dial. 'It's one notch past Cold Wash. Shall I write it down?'

Leaning forward on the leather chair, Julia placed her empty cup on the desk, 'I can't call you *Mister Scientist*.'

'Jack,' the Scientist said affably. 'But not in front of the others, if you'd be so kind. I'll admit, I've grown quite fond of the title they gave me.'

'Thank you, Jack.' Julia folded her arms. 'Before I came here today, I was undecided, but tending towards believing Eric's story. Despite being absolutely preposterous, it made sense of several things that have happened at the house.'

'And now that you have seen the evidence?' The Scientist returned the folder to the desk drawer.

Julia drew a breath. 'If I am to be complicit in this... *espionage*,' she said, parting her knees, 'I would like to be shown what you intend to broadcast – *before* any of your subliminal messages go out to the world.'

'Agreed,' the old man said, glancing under Julia's skirt.

'What are your views on communism?' asked Julia.

'Too extreme,' the Scientist replied dismissively. 'No one has ever successfully accomplished it, and I doubt that anyone ever will. We are not radicals, Julia, quite the opposite. We simply believe that unregulated capitalism poses an escalating threat to humanity: to its temperament and ultimately to its continued existence.'

Julia stood up and walked slowly along the bookshelves perusing the extravagant titles. 'That's exactly what I believe, Jack.'

'I know, Julia.'

Julia looked back, smiling. 'Yes, of course you do... Jack.'

'My apologies,' said the Scientist.

'No, *I'm* sorry,' said Julia. 'It's just a little shocking to discover that someone has been observing your private world. Stan, too, of course. He was at the point of moving in.'

'Yes, we were aware of that,' the Scientist replied, polishing his glasses with his gown. 'Stan left rather abruptly one night, never to return. At least, not in his former role.'

'You *have* been doing your reconnaissance, Jack.' Julia walked back across the study and reseated herself in front of the Scientist's desk. 'I suppose being in the spy business, you must be privy to all sorts of personal goings-on.'

'It was never my intention to enter the *spy business*, as you call it, Julia.' The old man adjusted his robe.

'Oh, it's okay, Jack.' Julia smiled prettily, deliberately exposing her panties. 'I wonder if you would have any objections if I were to help Eric compose some of the counter messages?'

'Objections?' the Scientist mumbled, fumbling under his desk.

'There are a few ideas I'd like to put forward.' Relaxing into the leather chair, Julia turned her head to the side.

The Scientist stared up her miniskirt. 'Ideas?'

Julia gazed up at the bookshelves, 'Oh, it's nothing major, Jack, I know you have the crisis in hand. But if you're going to pull it off, I'm sure I can help. You don't have any objections to that, do you?'

'No, I...' The old man's face reddened. His chair squeaked. He grunted twice, then sighed. 'No, no objections at all. I –'

'Thank you, Jack.' Julia stood up and straightened her clothes.

The Scientist leaned forward over his desk, 'Julia, I've been thinking of hiring a private secretary.'

As the visitors said their goodbyes to the beaming scientist, Sid pulled up on the forecourt in the old man's Bentley Continental. Reg and the Scientist spoke at the front doorway while Eric introduced Julia to his recently resurrected friend.

'Thank you for keeping an eye on the house,' Julia said, admiring the big black car.

'No probs,' replied Sid. 'Sorry I didn't cut-in sooner. No one was expecting the MoD's to leave a present under your sink.'

'So I gather,' said Julia. 'I was wondering, Sid. Did you use the Scientist's *James Bond* listening device at the Ealing House?'

'The MkII? Uh, only when that Stan guy showed up on the scene.' Sid quickly changed the subject, 'I used to drive a cute little pink-and-white Hillman Minx.' He stood back, eyeing the Bentley's elegant lines. 'This baby handles the asphalt a whole lot smoother.'

'I'm sure it does,' said Julia. 'No doubt the new X-ray vision camera came in useful, too.'

'He showed you that?' exclaimed Sid. 'The camera's still on his top-secret list. Your meetin' musta gone good.'

'The Scientist was satisfied by the upshot,' smiled Julia. 'I'm glad to have met you, Sid.'

'Likewise.' The tall American beamed. He waved as Julia opened the Zodiac's passenger door and slid in beside the postman.

The Beatles' *Get Back* played on the dashboard radio as Reg and the two hippies cruised through the English countryside.

Sliding down the red upholstery, Julia gazed out at the passing fields, 'Reg, do you happen to know the Scientist's real name?'

'Oh... Yeah, it's Richard,' replied the postman.

*

On the 8th of August, Paul McCartney slipped off his shoes for the camera, and the Beatles were photographed traversing a zebra crossing for the cover of *Abbey Road*. The LP marked the last time the group would record together.

The following evening in California, disciples of Charles Manson embarked upon the first of their *Helter Skelter* killing sprees. Five people died at the Los Angeles home of film director Roman Polanski, including his pregnant wife, actress Sharon Tate. The next night, two more were murdered by the deranged cult. Manson claimed the Beatles had been sending him coded messages in their songs.

Mid-month, the Woodstock Festival took place in upstate New York. Half a million people enjoyed performances by a host of well-known musical acts, including Jimi Hendrix, the Who, Crosby Stills and Nash, Joe Cocker, and Janis Joplin. The festival represented the pinnacle of the hippie movement's tenure: the culmination of the peace and love crusade that had flowered throughout the latter half of the decade. Central to Hendrix's performance was his rendition of *The Star-Spangled Banner*. As his wailing white Stratocaster screamed and dived, you could hear the bombs and bullets of the south Asian war. No one would ever play the anthem in quite the same manner again. No one could.

*

Early on the final Friday in August, Julia, Pattie, Paul and Eric set off for the Isle of Wight. Renowned for its quaint villages and seaside towns, annual regattas, and dinosaur fossils, the diamond-shaped island off England's south coast was hosting its second pop music festival. The Who were headlining on the Saturday night, and topping the bill on Sunday was Ealing House favourite, Bob Dylan.

Dismissing the festival as *hippie shit*, fifteen-year-old Tony had made arrangements to stay with a friend in South Ealing.

Later that morning, the Ealing hippies stood on the ferryboat's upper deck, looking out over the sun-kissed waters of the Solent. Pattie had entwined coloured beads in her tressed blonde hair. Seagulls circled overhead, hoping to share in the passengers' packed lunches.

'It's such a shame,' said Julia, her long black hair billowing in the breeze. 'Tony might have enjoyed this little holiday.'

'Maybe,' Paul said doubtfully. 'He would have loved to see the Who. Sometimes he's too bloody-minded for his own good.'

The crossing was completed in under an hour. When the boat commenced its docking procedure, the four hippies made their way down to the lower deck. Eric sat in the passenger seat of Pattie's purple Volkswagen and unfolded an Esso map. Driving off the ferry, Pattie made for the south side of the island, heading for the coastal ravine known as *Blackgang Chine*.

When they stopped for an English cream tea in the picturesque village of Godshill, Eric noticed the locals were staring.

'You'd think they'd never seen hippie mainlanders before,' Paul whispered, slapping a dollop of clotted cream on his scone.

Eric guessed that the looks they were getting, predominantly from the male villagers, had more to do with the two pretty women.

Completing their run across the island, Pattie stopped on a clifftop overlooking the English Channel. She pointed down the winding coastal road, 'Blackgang's up ahead. Time to break out the stash!'

Opening the purple Beetle's bonnet, Pattie delved into Eric's backpack and pulled out four joints. 'One each,' she grinned, holding up the reefers. 'A psychotropic perspective is highly recommended for the next couple of hours.'

Eric struck a match. Shielding the flame with his hand, he lit Pattie's joint, then his own. They strolled towards the cliff edge. 'When did you first come here?'

'When I was a little girl,' replied Pattie. 'My parents loved the Isle of Wight.'

'So did Queen Victoria,' said Julia. 'Vicky enjoyed a smoke, by all accounts. I expect she got stoned here, too. She and Albert were very into art.'

Sitting cross-legged among the daises, Eric gazed out over the calm blue sea. He was transported back to the holiday at West Bay, and Donovan sang in his head. On that occasion, he had been wandering alone. *Thank you for sending me these wonderful friends*, he thought, beaming the mental message to Neptune or Poseidon, or whichever thalassic god happened to be looking after the seas at that time. A sleek white yacht sailed across the gleaming reflection of the afternoon sun.

The clifftop pleasure ground, the oldest theme park in the country, shared its name with Blackgang Chine. The colourful group followed one of the narrow pathways past a giant sun-bleached whale skeleton. Trees, bushes and landscaped gardens bordered the winding walkways that snaked the fractured chalk cliff.

'The park's been here since the mid-nineteenth century,' said Pattie. 'Whoever's been adding to it over the years must've been eccentric.'

'Lewis Carroll?' Eric suggested as they passed a singing toadstool.

Soon they were all lost in the maze.

'This must be new.' Pattie clung to a wooden handrail as the four friends stumbled through the Crooked House. 'I'm sure it wasn't here in the fifties.'

From their hiding places in the shrubbery, concrete dinosaurs watched the hippies pass, smiling and giggling in the sunshine.

Slender flower girls raised their petalled heads in greeting.

'The Weather Wizard!' Eric murmured, encountering a Merlinesque automaton figure. He knew the name but could not recall where or when he had heard it. Perhaps his parents had once visited Blackgang Chine.

Tracing the coast, the purple VW passed through Shanklin and Sandown before turning north towards Ryde. Enchanted by the island's rustic beauty, everyone was in high spirits when they arrived at

Woodside Bay. A fence ringed the festival arena. Adjacent fields served as temporary campgrounds.

Paul looked around at the village of coloured tents, 'How about on top of the hill?'

'Good idea,' said Julia. 'If it rains, we won't get flooded out.'

Pattie aimed the car towards an open farm gate.

Paul had borrowed an old four-person tent from the scouts. With his expert knowledge and with everyone's help, it was up in no time. The heavy canvas *Baden Powell Special*, as Paul called it, looked out of place on the orange-and-blue hill. Some of the temporary residents employed large cardboard boxes or slept alfresco.

Eric was the last to roll out his sleeping bag. A space had been left between Pattie and Julia. It occurred to him that Paul may have positioned his bedding on one side to put him at ease. Eric smiled. Although he was still unsure of his friend's orientation, homosexuality was not an issue.

Paul was the first to experience the joys of pop festival toilets. 'It's a long stinky trench with bedsheets hung round it.' He wrinkled his nose, 'If it smells that bad now, God knows what it'll be like by Monday morning.'

The night was drawing in as the four friends looked out across the tranquil Solent. Lights twinkled on the mainland shore. Groups of longhaired music fans roamed the beach; some gathered around small fires strumming acoustic guitars. Dylan's *Lay Lady Lay* played on a transistor radio. Finding a stick, Paul wrote *The Ealing Hippies Were Here* in the sand. The four strolled leisurely along the lapping waters' edge, each with their recollections of the diminishing day.

'I'm so glad we came a day early,' said Julia. '*Blackgang* was a trip, and it was lovely to see some of the island.'

'I thought you'd like it,' smiled Pattie. 'It's like going back in time, don't you think? The amber screens they have in the shop windows to protect the merchandise from the sun... It's like whizzing back twenty or thirty years.'

'The land time forgot,' said Eric.

'Yes,' agreed Julia. 'North Wales has the same timeless quality.'

'But with more sheep,' said Paul.

'And more Welsh people,' added Eric.

'And more castles,' said Pattie.

'And more dragons,' Julia said as they headed up the foot-worn path.

'I haven't seen any dragons,' said Pattie. 'Are you sure they have them this far south?'

'Certain,' Julia replied, gazing up at the starlit sky. 'Look, there's one flying across the moon!'

The batteries in the heavy-duty torch were all but exhausted.

'It must've been *on* in the car,' said Paul. 'We'll use it sparingly.'

A round of squashy homemade sandwiches followed by a couple of joints finished off the day. By midnight, the campsite was quiet and still, save for the occasional wandering hippie.

Borrowing the weak torch, Eric went into the tent on all fours. It smelled of damp grass and old canvas. He fashioned a makeshift pillow using the spare clothes he had brought with him for the long weekend.

'Don't waste the batteries,' the resident Boy Scout advised from outside.

Eric switched off the torch. It was pitch black.

The flap opened, and Pattie crawled in, followed by Julia and Paul. When Paul secured the entrance, the interior of the tent was again plunged into blackness. Eric knelt between the two women. On either side of him, Julia and Pattie were undressing.

Removing his jeans and T-shirt, Eric slipped into his sleeping bag. Pattie lay on his right side, their bare arms brushing. They heard the low sound of an engine from somewhere behind the tent, then car headlights passed slowly across the canvas. Pattie was on her sleeping bag, wearing a red T-shirt and white underwear. Eric's eyes shot to Julia on his left. She was on her knees facing him and the light from the car. Julia was naked except for her panties. The slender woman remained upright, her arms hanging loosely by her sides. The headlights passed across the tent, and darkness returned.

The outstanding musical highlight on the first day came courtesy of the Who. Singer Roger Daltrey swung his microphone, his fringed jacket flailing beneath curly blond locks. Lanky Pete Townshend thrashed his Gibson guitar, dressed in a white boiler suit and red Dr Martens boots. John was impassive John, and Keith, *Moon the Loon. I Can't Explain, Pinball Wizard,* and *My Generation* were the only singles performed by the Who that evening, the band electing to devote most of their set to the recently released rock opera, *Tommy*. Earlier in the day, a pretty female dancer had been stopped by a member of the event's security staff. 'Why can't they let me be what I am?' complained the naked girl. 'I just wanted to be free.' A giant inflatable penis spurted gallons of soapy foam over the crowd. Artistes sharing the bill that Saturday included the Moody Blues, Joe Cocker, the Bonzo Dog Do-Dah Band, and Free.

Paul had selected a relatively flat piece of ground on which to pitch the tent. By the second night, having already slept once on the same spot, Eric relaxed in his sleeping bag, feeling almost comfortable. Before he went to sleep, he made a mental note to investigate Free's back catalogue. The band, and in particular their guitarist, Paul Kossoff, had made a strong impression on him that day. Laying in the dark tent, Eric felt Julia's breath on his shoulder.

An eerie pink-tinged mist filled the wood-panelled hallway. When the door swung open in front of him, Eric saw that the Ealing House's living room was full of dancing skinheads. *Long Shot Kick the Bucket* played on the stereo. The skins wore red Dr Martens boots. There were no girls. Julia and Pattie drifted past Eric from the hall. He tried to speak but could make no sound. As the two women entered the crowded room, the skinheads moved aside, creating a space in the library area. Encircled by the leering teens, Julia and Pattie danced deliriously, lost in the Bluebeat music. They, too, wore heavy Dr Martens, the big red boots looking oddly out of place with their short psychedelic dresses. The music was loud; pounding bass vibrated the room. A dozen or more erect penises pointed stiffly at the two girls from the boundary of the inner circle. Pink mist filtered through from the hallway, curling tendrils creeping across the carpet, enshrouding Eric's feet. He tried again to warn the dancing women, but the sound died in his throat. The ring began to close in, sweat glistening on the cropped heads. The two hippie women danced provocatively, taunting the skinheads, teasing the advancing pack. The circle closed, enveloping Julia and Pattie.

'All right... It's all right, Eric.' Pattie's voice sounded far away as if echoing down a long tunnel.

Eric felt a hand on his wet chest, and he opened his eyes, staring up into the darkness.

'You had a bad dream,' Julia whispered. 'It's over now.'

Inside the arena, the Ealing hippies chose a spot near the edge of the 100,000-strong crowd. Sunday's line-up was less rock orientated, featuring lightweight acts such as Julie Felix, Pentangle, and folk singer Tom Paxton. The laidback music was graciously appreciated by the audience, and, as on the previous day, there was little or no trouble. Preceded by his backing group, the Band, Bob Dylan took the stage later than scheduled at 11pm. The Ealing House hero began his set with *She Belongs to Me*. Dylan's hour-long performance included *Maggie's Farm, It Ain't Me Babe, Mr Tambourine Man, Like a Rolling Stone, I'll Be Your Baby Tonight, Quinn the Eskimo,* and *Rainy Day Women # 12 & 35.* Unbeknown to Eric and his friends, Eric Clapton was at the concert to see Bob, along with three Beatles.

Eric slept soundly that night, recalling none of his dreams. When he awoke on Monday morning, Pattie and Paul were outside the tent preparing for the journey home. Turning onto his side, Eric watched Julia sleeping.

31

No Cakes Please

On Friday nights, the Cellar Bar in the Broadway was always buzzing. For Paul and Eric, the smoky basement meeting place had become a regular haunt. Pattie's occasional appearances at the hippie hangout turned heads in their direction, ingratiating them to the local in-crowd of beautiful people. Eric divided his attention between this exclusive club and the other hippie patrons, many of whom were acquaintances from his Ealing Art College classes.

Intrigued by Phil's preoccupation with astral travel, reincarnation, and the eternal cycle of regenerated universes, Paul became enamoured with the guitarist. When Pattie spoke to Phil, he became dumbstruck, managing only mundane utterances like, '*Would you like a drink?*' and '*I had one of those but the wheels fell off*'.

Having undergone structural repairs, the ex-hotel on Eel Pie Island had reopened under the new name, *Colonel Barefoot's Rock Garden*. While the old building was now less prone to collapse, it looked much the same. Eric and Paul saw many up-and-coming bands at the historic music venue, including Mott the Hoople, Deep Purple, and Black Sabbath. Phil earned the dubious distinction of being one of the first heavy metal head-bangers. For the trio of music fans, the most memorable evening of the Colonel Barefoot era was provided by a pre-*All Right Now* Free, supported by the relatively unknown Genesis. Peter Gabriel stood on a chair and sang. The old hotel ballroom was packed to capacity that night.

By the autumn of 1969, Eric had virtually moved into the Ealing House. A psychedelic Jimi Hendrix poster was pinned to the spare bedroom wall, which everyone referred to as *Eric's room*. Julia had refused to accept rent, so the money Eric earned with his father was his to spend as he pleased. His contributions to the pantry were gracefully accepted. Everyone, including Pattie, was by now wholly vegetarian, except Tony, who subsisted almost entirely upon meat, and frequently took the piss. Aside from the occasional instance of mischief, such as the phallic graffiti on Paul's Easy Rider poster, Tony had become less cantankerous, channelling his angst into his explosive drumming. Julia had been right about that.

October 1969 was notable for Monty Python's Flying Circus and the Beatles' Abbey Road LP. Released near the end of September, Abbey Road was musically pleasing and sonically appealing. Predictably, it was the album of the month at the Ealing House. The *Monty Python* team were the comedy equivalent of the leading creative writers, filmmakers, and musicians of the decade, propelling humour into previously unchartered territories and changing it forever.

*

Eric was not surprised by Julia's reticence following their meeting with the Scientist. He knew that she was considering the information she had been given, reluctant to commit to an opinion pending further thought. Early in November, she was finally ready to talk.

The first discussion between Eric and Julia took place in the living room. As would be the case with each of these meetings, Julia chose the time and place, ensuring that the two of them were alone.

'It's only a temporary job,' explained Julia. Lifting one leg onto the sofa, she toyed with the frayed knee on her jeans. 'If we hadn't left it so late to apply, Paul would be at university now.'

Eric shook his head, 'Yeah, but gardening? And in November?'

Julia shrugged, 'The council were advertising, so they must need someone. Between you and me, Eric, I hope Paul doesn't get it. I'd rather he were here at home.' Julia relaxed on the sofa. 'Have you heard anything from our friend the Scientist?'

Here we go, thought Eric. *It's about time.* 'No, not a peep. After all that hoo-ha, everything's gone quiet. Nothing from Reg or Sid either.'

Julia nodded, 'I've been giving it a lot of thought.'

'I guessed you had.'

Julia leant forward, clasping her hands. 'Well, Eric, I'm still not convinced about this magical transmitter, but I've concluded we have nothing to lose.'

'What do you mean, *we?*'

Julia paused. 'At my meeting with the Scientist, I told him I intended to work with you on some of the messages.'

'Oh. And what did he say?'

'He agreed.'

This was one of the scenarios that Eric had anticipated. 'The idea is to counter the messages that MoD2 have already broadcast. Don't you think the wording would be better left to the Scientist? He's the expert. I'm sure we can trust –'

'If this transmitter is all it's cracked up to be,' interrupted Julia, 'we should be doing more with it than counteracting what's already been sent out.'

'I don't know,' Eric said doubtfully. 'Doesn't that make us as bad as them?'

'Not if we send out the right messages,' insisted Julia. 'Have you heard that new song, *Melting Pot* by Blue Mink? Integration is key, and it's one of the toughest obstacles to overcome. The lyricist is right; it'll probably take a hundred years to...' Julia's voice trailed off. 'Oh, Paul's back,' she said, looking out at the grey front garden.

*

Four chairs had been arranged in a semicircle facing the Scientist's desk. Placing the silver tray with five cups next to the inkstand, Reg sat at the end of the row. Next to him, Sid was studying a street map of Hartlepool and glancing at Julia. Eric sat quietly, staring straight ahead.

The Scientist shuffled into the study and sat behind his desk, 'We meet again,' the wiry-haired inventor said cheerfully. Removing his spectacles, he rubbed them on his sleeve. 'As always, I thank you all for coming. I have something of great importance to discuss with you today.'

Eric shifted. He had an uneasy feeling about what was to follow.

'How 'bout if I start and upset the cart?' Sid rhymed, refolding the map.

'Oh, very well,' the Scientist mumbled with a hint of irritation.

'Listen up, here comes the rub,' began Sid, not caring that he was stealing the old man's thunder or that his rhyme was below his usual standard. 'In the last few weeks, I bin spendin' some time in my favourite little town up there in the north-east.'

'Hartlepool,' interjected the Scientist.

394

'Yeah,' said Sid. 'An' with the help of the good Scientist's *James Bond* gizmos...' he glanced sideways at Julia, 'I found out a few facts.'

'Yes, thank you, Sidney. I'll take it from here.' The Scientist settled himself. 'As you are all aware, I have been blocking MoD2's attempts to broadcast their messages worldwide.'

'And now they've found a way to unblock them,' said Reg.

The Scientist looked surprised, 'You knew?'

'An educated guess.'

'What does that mean, exactly?' asked Julia. 'Are they sending global messages out now, as we speak?'

'Not yet,' the Scientist said gravely. 'But judging by Sidney's intel, they'll soon have it cracked.'

Eric frowned, 'And there's nothing you can do about it?'

The Scientist shook his head. 'I'm afraid not. There's always the possibility of a flash of inspiration, but –'

'But don't hold your breath,' said Sid.

'Bollocks,' muttered the postman.

'Quite,' said the old man.

'Plan B, then,' sighed Reg.

Julia sipped her coffee. 'And what does Plan B entail?'

'We had hoped to transmit our counter-messages from here,' the Scientist explained, looking at Julia. 'I built a new transmitter, but –'

'The man's done what he can, but the shit's hit the fan,' interrupted Sid. 'The new machine don't work.'

'Oh, I see,' said Julia.

'Bringing us back to Plan B,' said Reg. 'Which means breaking into the office in West Ealing and doing the broadcast using the original machine.'

Julia thought for a moment. 'You work there, don't you, Reg? Do you have a key to the office, or can you get hold of one?'

The postman shook his head, 'Not a chance.' He paused. 'But there's a way in. It just takes a bit of climbing and a screwdriver. I've already done it once.'

'Then you could do it again?' suggested Julia.

'I could,' said Reg. 'But it's a little more complicated.'

This is getting worse by the second, thought Eric. He flicked the handle of his cup, making little pinging noises.

The Scientist took a breath, 'For the broadcast from West Ealing to remain undetected, adjustments need to be made to the equipment in

Hartlepool. These things must be done simultaneously. And the task in Hartlepool will require two people.'

Silence filled the room.

'So,' Eric said quietly. 'You want *me* to break-in to the office in West Ealing, while Reg and Sid break-in at the place in Hartlepool. And both break-ins have to happen at the same time.'

'Yes,' said the Scientist. 'That's Plan B.'

*

To his dismay, Paul had sailed through the job interview and been hired on the spot. So it was that Paul spent the daylight hours of his eighteenth birthday sitting in a cold shed in Walpole Park, reading the previous week's edition of Melody Maker from front to back.

That evening, Tony joined the Ealing hippies on a trip to London's West End to take in a performance of the anti-Vietnam War musical *Hair*. Made possible by the abolition of theatre censorship the previous year, the production featured profanity, drug use, and nudity. In deference to Paul's younger brother, the hippies abstained from their usual intake of marijuana, though later that night, Tony had his first smoke. The giggle-filled session in Paul's bedroom laid a foundation upon which the future unity of Clockwork Mouse was to be built. Now it really felt like a band.

Paul's landmark birthday was enjoyed by all. Eric even managed to shake off the feeling of foreboding that had plagued him since the Scientist's meeting, albeit temporarily. It was a good night.

*

On the 25th of November, John Lennon returned his MBE, explaining that he had done it as a protest against British involvement with Biafra and the Vietnam War.

Early that gloomy Tuesday afternoon, with Paul at work and Tony at school, Julia instigated the second discussion. When she breezed into the fire-lit living room wearing her short black skirt, Eric deduced that the lady of the house was determined to have her way. Julia could be extremely persuasive when she set her mind on something, and it seemed the alluring tactic she had employed to coax the Scientist was again to be put into practice. Or so Eric optimistically surmised. The unlit joint in her hand reinforced his suspicion.

'Pattie and I are going to the Broadway later.' Julia sat on the big sofa next to the fire. A log fell sparking, flaming as it settled in the grate. She looked at Eric and smiled. The young woman appeared ghostlike in the subdued winter light, her face partially shadowed by her long black hair. Orange firelight played on Julia's bare legs and feet. She held up the unlit reefer, 'Pattie left me some excellent grass, and I wondered if you fancied a joint?'

'Of course, lovely!' Eric made himself comfortable on the adjoining sofa. 'It's always a treat when some nice grass comes along.'

Julia's white blouse looked pale-grey. The tailored cotton shirt hugged her chest, and, as usual, she was braless. If the revealing clothes were designed to disarm, either she underestimated Eric's awareness of her ways or did not care.

'We're smoking more than we used to,' said Eric. 'Most days, really. Do you think that's too much?'

'Probably,' replied Julia. 'I'd defend it on the grounds that pot enables one to look at things from two different perspectives – and both of them are *you*. That comes in especially handy in creative situations, including evaluating your work. And we're all creative in our own ways, aren't we?'

'I'd like to think so.'

'Of course, you have to balance that against the health issues,' she continued. 'But we're all responsible for our own choices. And that's how it *should* be: *our* choice, not the government's.'

Eric noticed Julia pause, visibly changing tack.

'That's why people have to learn to think for themselves. But if their minds are subjected to coercion by big businesses and...'

Julia's voice fluttered away like the wingbeats of a departing bird. In the past, Eric had hung on her every word, agreeing with her liberalistic opinions and ideas, but the last thing he wanted to do now was discuss her plans to save the world. He understood the adverse effects that capitalism was having on people; the hippies were saying the same. And he believed she was right about humanity's greed-driven threat to its own existence: the callous consumption, the pollution of the planet, the burgeoning population. But the Scientist's machine; the subliminal transmitter. There were moral considerations, and Eric was at the very epicentre of the quaking dilemma. Today he wanted to escape, to lose himself in another dream, to blast-off to a different planet.

'...and if the population continues to grow at its present rate, there'll be *triple* the number of people in the world in thirty years.' Julia held out the depleted joint, 'There you go. There are a couple of puffs left.'

Reaching across the coffee table, Eric accepted the reefer from Julia's outstretched hand. She was right about the grass. Julia had been talking, but he had heard almost nothing she had said. 'Great gear,' he murmured. 'I'm flying.'

'Me too.' Julia nudged the ashtray. 'I've been working on a few ideas, Eric, you know, for the broadcast. I'm sure you'll like them.'

Julia's knees parted. Eric returned instantly from his escapist head trip. *Oh God, she's doing it!*

Julia gazed out at the heavy November clouds, and her leg began to sway. 'You know, Eric, perhaps it's our *duty* to say something about what we're doing to our planet.'

'Perhaps,' Eric answered, staring brazenly up Julia's miniskirt.

'I'm glad you think so,' Julia replied, still looking out at the sky. 'It's so important that we all do what we can.' Her legs slowly widened.

Eric caught his breath. 'I'm not sure...' he said ponderously. He became aware that Julia was now facing him, though in his stoned, dreamlike state, it was as if it was happening to somebody else. Eric's heartbeat quickened. He had told himself that if she caught him peeping, this time, he would not look away.

Raising the stakes, Julia fixed on Eric's eyes, but he continued to stare, a willing participant in her sexual game.

Julia became quiet. Dancing orange firelight flickered on her skin. The French clock ticked on the mantelpiece. Eric glanced up at Julia's faraway eyes, wondering if it was him she saw before her.

Julia slid slowly down the sofa. Resting her palms on her hips, she extended her fingers. Her miniskirt rose slowly, inching up her slender thighs.

Eric jumped as the intercom buzzed.

Julia sat bolt upright. Bowing her head, she stared down at the carpet, her swaying black hair almost brushing her knees.

The intercom sounded again. *Karma*, thought Eric.

Julia flattened her skirt, covering herself. She leant across the sofa arm and pressed the button, 'Hello?'

'I'm here,' said Pattie. 'Sorry, my house keys are on your dresser.'

'Yes... Yes, wait there, Pats, I'll be... two ticks.'

'Are you okay?' asked the thin female voice from the intercom.

'Hang on one minute.' Without so much as a glance at Eric, Julia hurried out of the living room.

Eric sat back, his mind racing.

Julia returned shortly, stopping outside in the hallway. She had changed into her blue jeans. 'Eric, there's some grass in my tobacco tin,' she said breathlessly from the doorway. 'It's in the trunk at the foot of my bed. Do help yourself.'

Eric heard the front door close and went to the window. He watched Julia slip her coat on as she walked briskly down the garden path, then glimpsed Pattie's blonde mane as the garden gate opened and closed. He turned around, finding himself once again alone in the house.

Entering Julia's bedroom, Eric saw her discarded miniskirt on the cover of her four-poster bed. A large manila envelope lay next to the sexy black skirt. Kneeling on the carpet, he raised the lid of the monogrammed trunk. Julia buried the Old Holborn tin somewhere near the bottom, though she was aware that Tony knew it was there. Rummaging among the photo albums and paperwork, Eric uncovered an envelope marked *Birth Certificates*. He placed it to one side and took out the tobacco tin. A look inside revealed a plastic bag crammed full of grass.

Closing the lid of the trunk, Eric sat on the floor and opened the envelope. He read the first certificate,

Name: Anthony Earl Ramsey

Sex: Male

Birth Date: 5.1.1954

Father: James E. Ramsey

Mother: Julia Ramsey

Eric smiled. Tony's middle name was Earl. He had kept it a secret all these years. It was a good name but unusual enough to use as ammunition. He looked at the second certificate,

Name: Paul Russell

Sex: Male

Birth Date: 20.11.1951

Father: John Russell

Mother: Julia Stewart

Eric stared at the second certificate. The 20th of November was Paul *Ramsey's* birthday. The Paul on the document – Paul Russell – had been born on the same day in the same year.

Eric puzzled over the names. There must have been a mistake. But no one made errors on birth certificates, did they?

The initials on Julia's trunk: J.S.… Julia Stewart. Of course! *Stewart* had been Julia's maiden name. Paul had been born before Julia was married and christened *Russell*. They had changed it later to Ramsey.

Sitting on the floor, Eric leaned back against Julia's bed, watching the clouds drift by the high window. *Does Paul know?* he wondered. *So who was his real father, the man with the same surname? Who was John Russ –?*

'Jack!' Eric exclaimed to the room.

He looked through the open doorway at the locked bedroom across the corridor. 'Uncle Jack was Paul's dad!' At some point, Julia had entered into a relationship with her foster-uncle, her mother's brother. Paul had been the result. Little wonder then, that Julia was reluctant to talk about her past.

Replacing the certificates where he had found them, Eric closed the trunk and began rolling a single-paper joint on the lid. The question kept repeating: *Does Paul know that Uncle Jack was his father?*

That'll teach you not to go snooping through other people's things, said a schizophrenic voice in Eric's head. He opened the bedroom window and lit the small joint. The chilly winter air felt fresh on his face. As he looked out over the skeletal trees of Fox Wood, the potent marijuana began to work its magic. Julia had put on his favourite miniskirt, the shortest one she owned. Stan and the Scientist had both been seduced by Julia's sexy skirt, and both had succumbed to her charms. *Who wouldn't?* He took another drag, inhaling deeply. Fact gave way to fantasy as he imagined what may have transpired had Pattie arrived just a few minutes later.

Eric's head felt suddenly cold. *It really fucking happened!* His entire body tingled. *Drug-shock*, he thought, at the same time relishing the onrushing reality of what had just taken place downstairs.

Flicking the spent reefer into the garden below, Eric lowered the sash window then sat on Julia's bed. He picked up the manila envelope that was laying there and tossed it to one side. Three glossy colour photographs slid out of the open end, revealing a stockinged foot. Eric grabbed the envelope and slipped out the photos.

There were six pictures in all. The first four were marketing shots: close-ups of Julia's stockinged legs, perhaps intended for use on the product's packaging. Eric perused them slowly, lingering on the fourth print in which Julia's panties were visible at the top of the photo. *'One flash of her white knickers, and you're hooked. Have you noticed she always wears virginal white knickers?'* Eric's pulse raced when he saw the next picture. Apparently from the same session, this was a full-length shot. Julia posed provocatively, seated on a peacock fan chair. The stockings lay discarded next to her bare feet. Wearing her black miniskirt, she gazed alluringly at the camera with her legs parted.

There was one last print in the set. As he laid back on her bed, it seemed to Eric that he could smell Julia's scent on the pillow. Holding up the photograph with his free hand, Eric stared between Julia's open legs. As in the previous picture, she had on her sexy black miniskirt. But for this photograph, Julia had taken off her panties.

In the days that followed, Julia mentioned nothing to Eric about her plans for the broadcast. Nor did she enquire about the photograph that had gone missing from the envelope she had left on her bed.

*

The beginning of December brought with it cold, cloudy weather and every day, a fire burned in the Ealing House's front room. On the first Saturday of the month, Eric sat in front of the stereo listening to Fairport Convention's *Meet on the Ledge*. He imagined himself fifty years on, remembering the days with his friends at the big old house on the edge of Fox Wood. *Reverse nostalgia* offered a different perspective, one that he believed enhanced his appreciation of the here and now.

Mingling with the Christmas shoppers, Julia and Pattie were in Ealing Broadway, waiting to cross the Uxbridge Road.

'A bomb fell right there during the war,' Julia said, looking back at the shoe shop.

'Where?' Pattie asked, seeking a gap in the slow-moving traffic.

'Lilly and Skinner's,' replied Julia. 'The staff and customers were sheltering in the basement when the building collapsed. They survived the blast, but it ruptured a water main, and everyone drowned.'

'Oh, that's horrible!' Pattie stepped into the road manoeuvring her carrier bag between two stationary vehicles. 'Those poor people. Do you remember it happening?'

Julia followed her friend in the direction of Bentalls' red, green and gold Christmas windows. 'I may be a couple of years older than you, Pats, but not that many!' Piped carols played from the churchyard on the opposite corner. 'Anyway, that was then,' said Julia. 'I don't suppose war will happen again here.'

'I wish I had your confidence,' Pattie said, turning to her friend. 'The sixties are nearly over now. People might not want peace and love anymore.'

'Time is a human concept,' said Julia.

'It's humans I'm talking about,' replied Pattie. 'We divide our lives into time-boxes: the grey fifties, the psychedelic sixties. And the sixties time-box is almost full. That's the one with the little rainbows and stuff in it.'

They walked up the incline towards Haven Green. 'I want rainbows and stuff, too,' said Julia. 'So it's up to us to keep the spirit of the sixties alive.'

'And how are we going to do that?'

'Maybe there is a way,' Julia said, mostly to herself.

The two women moved aside, making way for a Silver Cross pram with a wobbly rear wheel.

'Like what?' asked Pattie.

'Uh!' exclaimed the mother as the big pram wheel parted company with its axle and went rolling down the hill.

Julia supported the pram with both hands.

Dropping her shopping bag, Pattie ran down the one-way street after the runaway wheel.

'Who's going to fix it?' the mother sighed, parking the three-wheeled pram against one of Bentalls' side windows.

'Bill Grimes can fix anything,' said a passing pensioner.

'That's what they say,' Julia replied automatically.

Pattie held up the spoked wheel, 'It rolled out into the road, but a nice taxi driver stopped for me.' She re-joined Julia, the mother, and the baby, who had slept through the averted accident.

'Penny for 'em,' said Pattie, as she and Julia followed the pathway across Haven Green.

'Oh, it's nothing,' Julia replied evasively. She pulled her car keys from her coat pocket. *Bill Grimes can fix anything.*

When the Twins arrived at the house, they heard the unison guitar and bass passage from *Hey Joe* playing loudly from the ballroom. Leaving their shopping bags in the hall, Julia and Pattie walked down the wood-panelled corridor to the kitchen. 'Hello,' Keith said, bobbing and raising his foot. The kettle was soon on.

Paul came in, followed by his guitarist and drummer.

'You sounded great,' grinned Pattie, holding her coffee cup to her chest with both hands. 'Isn't it about time you played somewhere?'

'We're playing at the Boathouse next Friday,' joked Tony.

Everyone knew the reputation of the skinhead hangout next to Kew Bridge.

'Pattie's mourning the end of the sixties,' Julia said, pouring out three more coffees. 'Unless you can fit your first gig in over Christmas, Clockwork Mouse is going to be a seventies band.'

'That's right.' Pattie checked the Barbarella calendar by the door. 'Only twenty-five days, then the sixties will be nothing but a memory.'

'Thanks,' said Eric, taking a coffee from the draining board.

'You're welcome,' replied Julia. 'By the way, remind me, what's your dad's first name?'

'William... Bill.'

Pattie looked across at Julia, 'I met Bill in the record department at Bensteds when you were buying the stereo.' She smiled, 'He's lovely.'

'Bill Grimes can fix anything,' smiled Paul, unaware that the widely used phrase really did refer to his friend's father.

'P'raps he could fix your face,' quipped Tony.

Julia glanced sideways at Eric, who had turned towards the window. 'I know!' Julia exclaimed, addressing the kitchen. 'We could have a New Year's Eve party – to celebrate the sixties and Eric's eighteenth birthday. And Clockwork Mouse can play their first gig!'

'I can borrow a PA from the scouts,' Paul said, already two steps ahead.

'We'll have to do *Midnight Hour*,' said Eric.

'Can I sing it with you?' asked Pattie.

'Of course!' replied Paul.

'Tony?' Julia smiled at her youngest son.

Tony screwed up his face, 'I'll never live it down if me mates find out I spent New Year's Eve playin' to an 'ouseful of 'ippies.'

Julia interpreted this as Tony's way of reassuring everyone that he would not be giving invitations to his friends.

Eric hoped his face had returned to its natural colour. 'I love the party idea, but can we make it more sixties and less birthday? I'd feel silly playing my guitar as the *birthday boy*.'

'Got it,' replied Julia. 'You have to be *Guitar Guy* in your head.'

Eric nodded, 'Yeah.'

'I went skiing once,' said Pattie. 'I'd had no lessons or anything, so I struck a *skier pose* and pretended I knew how to do it. It worked a treat. I went like the wind – really fast. It ended in the most horrific wipe-out. But my point is, I zoomed all the way down the hill – top to bottom – by becoming *Ski Woman*.'

Paul grinned, 'Guitar Guy and Ski Woman... Cool! *Midnight Hour*, Pattie. I haven't forgotten.'

'There's only one problem,' said Julia. 'To have a party, we need guests.'

'I'm sure I can drum up a few interesting people,' offered Pattie.

'There are some pretty cool students in my year at college,' said Eric.

'Oh, don't worry about numbers, Mum,' said Paul. 'If Eric and I spread the word at the Cellar Bar, the place will be heaving.'

Julia smiled cautiously, 'That's fine, Paul, but perhaps you could be a little selective about who you invite?'

'Of course,' replied Paul. 'Only the *crème de la crème* of the drugged-up hippie dropouts.'

'It's settled then,' laughed Julia. 'We're having a party!' She turned to Eric, 'To celebrate the sixties at the turning of the decade. Everyone who matters will know it's your birthday. No cakes?'

Eric smiled and shook his head, 'No cakes, please.'

32

Ten to Midnight

On a cold, wet afternoon in mid-December, Eric and Reg sat together in the Zodiac, going over every detail of Plan B. It had been the postman's idea to meet in the car park behind Northfield Odeon.

'...and I'll disable the alarm system before I head up to Hartlepool with Sid, so don't worry about that.'

Eric gazed out through the rain-spattered windscreen, 'We first met Happiness Stan in this car park.'

'Stan, the spy?'

Eric nodded. 'He saved us from a gang of skinheads. Or that's how it was *supposed* to look.'

'A setup?'

'Had to be,' replied Eric. 'I thought it felt dodgy at the time.'

Reg sniffed. 'Okay, in case we don't see each other before the night, are you clear on everything, Eric?'

'*The night?* Shouldn't it have a codename or something?'

'It's *Plan B*,' Reg said patiently.

'Yeah. And yeah, I know the plan... Over the gate, up through the window, do the broadcast, go home.'

'Perfect.'

Eric squeaked a forefinger across the misted passenger window, 'The Scientist's timing could have been better. Julia's having a party.'

'Yeah, sorry about that,' said Reg. 'It's all about reaching the maximum number of people.'

'I understand,' sighed Eric. 'But it's bloody inconvenient.'

'Yeah.'

Eric pushed the Scientist's two-page script down into his backpack. The embroidered Sgt Pepper drum patch still looked bright. 'Reg, it's pissing down. Would you mind dropping me at the Ealing House?'

The postman was pensive on the drive to Ealing Broadway. Cruising up Mount Park Road, he glanced at his passenger, 'It's for the best, Eric.'

Eric closed his eyes and nodded, 'I'll be there.'

The rain had stopped.

As Eric stepped out of the Zodiac by Hangar Hill Park, Reg smiled confidently and raised his thumb, 'Ten minutes to midnight.'

'Ten to midnight,' Eric replied, shouldering his rucksack. 'Good luck in Hartlepool, Reg.'

*

Snow fell on the 17th. Partway through the band's rehearsal warm-up number, Eric gazed out through the French windows. Watching the red swing turning white, he mentally named the improvised twelve-bar *Blues for Julia.*

The eight-minute jam concluded with a raucous concert ending.

'Played with feeling, my friend,' smiled Paul.

'Thanks,' replied Eric. 'I must've been inspired by the weather.'

'*Jingle Bollocks* next, then,' said Tony. 'I'll get me sleigh bells.'

'Oh bloody 'ell, no Christmas songs,' groaned Paul. 'What's first on the agenda?'

Eric consulted his scribbled setlist, 'The Temptations, *Get Ready.* Maybe Pattie could sing this one, too?'

*

Much as he would have liked to spend Christmas Day with his friends, Eric adhered to his resolution. Bill and Mary seemed genuinely pleased with the percolator and the selection of exotic coffees that their son had bought for them. Eric recalled his mother savouring the enticing aroma as they walked by the specialist coffee shop in the Broadway. Perhaps the thoughtful gift went some way towards making up for the plastic-framed photograph of the Beatles he had presented to his dad on Christmas morning, 1963. Multi-coloured fairy lights twinkled on the imitation tree by the frosty dining-room window. There was something comforting about the annual appearance of the paper-chains, baubles and bells.

Bill relaxed on the sofa with festive editions of both the Radio and TV Times on his lap. 'This is the first Christmas with full-colour on all three channels. Perhaps this time next year, we'll have a colour telly of our own.'

Mary stroked her husband's forearm, 'Maybe we'll have it in time for Wimbledon, hint, hint?'

Eric smiled. His parents seemed happy and contented.

Later that evening, the family laughed as one at the first Morecambe and Wise Christmas Special. Ernie began the show dressed as a hippie.

Before they went up to bed, Eric turned to his parents. 'I love you both,' he heard himself say.

Bill and Mary smiled warmly. Eric knew that his declaration had taken them by surprise. The L-word being reserved for romantic novels and the like, it had come as a shock to him, too.

*

Early in the afternoon on New Year's Eve, Eric went upstairs to his room on the Ealing House's first floor. Engulfed in purple smoke, Jimi looked down from the wall. Eric closed the bedroom door. He slipped Julia's neatly written page of messages into his rucksack next to the script the Scientist had prepared for the broadcast.

There was a knock on the door. Eric pushed his backpack under the bed, 'Come in; it's open.'

Pattie smiled, spreading her arms wide, 'Happy birthday!'

'Thanks,' Eric said, hugging the gorgeous blonde.

'I have something for you.' Squeezing him to her, Pattie kissed Eric lovingly on the lips.

Eric looked into her pretty blue eyes and smiled, 'Best birthday present I ever had!'

'That wasn't what I meant, silly!' Pattie reached into the back pocket of her jeans.

Eric examined the small red package. 'You got me a box of matches!' Removing the wrapping paper, he was surprised to find that it was indeed a matchbox.

'Open it the right way up,' warned Pattie.

Eric smiled when he saw the contents.

'It's sinsemilla,' said Pattie. 'The pokiest grass on the planet!'

'Thank you!' Eric sniffed the refined marijuana like a love-struck girl presented with a posy. 'Should we partake of a joint?'

'Already sorted.' Pattie unbuttoned her skin-tight jeans.

Five minutes later, they sat giggling together on the unmade bed, high as metaphorical kites.

Julia appeared at the bedroom doorway with her sewing box and a slip of paper, 'Ah, you're up here, Eric. Your bandmates are looking for you.'

'Right, thanks,' Eric replied, grinning slightly stupidly.

Pattie eyed the sewing box. 'It's about time you came up to darn these curtains, Jules. And while you're here, would you mind putting a few stitches in my knicker elastic? I'm falling apart at the seams.'

'Perhaps you should stop using your knickers as a handbag, Pats. Actually,' said Julia, 'I'm marking the room keys with coloured cottons.' She held up the sheet of paper. 'The codes are written here. Blue cotton for Paul's room, red for Tony...'

'Ingenious,' said Pattie. 'Any particular reason?'

'I'm locking the doors to the upstairs rooms tonight; I'm not having anyone throwing-up in the beds. If either of you need to get in up here, the keys will be on my dressing table. I'll keep my room key with me.'

'Good idea,' said Pattie.

'Past experience,' replied Julia. 'New Year's Eve brings out the boozer in people. Besides, we don't want any moochers nosing about.'

'What colour am I?' asked Eric. 'In case I need to come up and feed my goldfish.'

Julia checked her list, 'You're purple, Eric. I'll do your key now.' Kneeling on the floor, she opened the sewing box. 'The upstairs doors will be locked before the guests are due.'

'Okay, purple,' repeated Eric. 'If I forget, Jimi'll remind me.'

'He'll be locked away in here,' said Pattie. 'Where's your goldfish, by the way?'

'West Ealing,' replied Eric. 'He's renting a top hat and tails for tonight.' *From Burton's,* he thought, feeling a little less jovial.

Preparations for the party had been underway for the past few days. A long table stacked with drinks stood against the back wall in the ballroom. At the opposite end of the large room was a portable stage that Paul had borrowed from the Scouts and the Vox PA system the troupe used for public events and jamborees. Balloons and streamers filled the room. Julia had paid particular attention to the atmospheric lighting, scouring the house for suitable lamps, which she fitted with coloured bulbs, mostly red.

The Cellar Bar was virtually empty that night.

A light fog hung over the snow-covered front garden of the Ealing House. Phil was the first guest to arrive.

'Brass monkey's tonight,' the hobbit man grinned, rubbing his hands. His wavy brown hair bounced off his shoulders as he walked down the hallway with Eric and Paul. Phil looked around at the wood-panelled corridor, 'Crikey, this is some place! It looks like a Hammer Horror house!'

'Here's one of the resident vampires,' said Eric.

Pattie came down the red-carpeted stairway wearing her psychedelic minidress and knee-high black boots. She was jingling with enough costume jewellery to equip a bordello.

'Hello, Phil! I'm so glad you could come,' chimed Pattie. She threw her arms around the blushing man leaving bright-red lipstick lips on his hot cheek.

'Wouldn't have missed it,' Phil replied huskily, then clammed up.

Guests arrived in a steady stream. By 8:30, the party was swinging.

'There must be half of Ealing here!' Julia shouted over Amen Corner's *(If Paradise Is) Half as Nice*. She poured a ladleful of pink punch into a paper cup.

'There's enough room.' Paul stood on his toes, peering over the hairy heads. 'They're dancing in front of the stage.'

'*Just about* enough room,' smiled Eric. 'If any more people turn up, they'll be spilling into the hall.' He looked at Julia. She was wearing a long green Indian dress and had plastered her eyes with heavy dark makeup, Dusty style. She looked stunning.

'Which one of you made this punch?' Julia asked, raising her cup. 'It's delicious!'

Pattie looked surprised. 'It wasn't you? There are bowls of the stuff all around the room.'

Paul shrugged, 'I dunno, but I'm having a top-up before we go on.'

Eric checked his watch, 'Blimey, it's gone nine. We'd better get up there and start the first set. Where's Tony?'

Right on cue, a booming percussive barrage thundered from the stage, drowning-out Andy Fairweather Low and co. Eric peered over the party guests. Sitting behind his drums, Tony was dressed in his best skinhead attire, his yellow-and-white-striped Ben Sherman shirt complemented by a pair of bright-red braces.

'It's the boots, you know,' Eric said dryly. 'Gives him that extra bit of wallop that sets him apart from the rest.'

'Break both legs!' beamed Phil. He flashed Eric his wide hobbit grin as the young guitarist stepped up in front of an audience for the first time in his life. Eric strapped on his red Rapier guitar and felt the nervousness he had been experiencing fall away. Gulping down his punch, he scrunched the paper cup and playfully aimed it at Tony's shiny shaven head. The drummer batted the crumpled ball with his sticks, sending it spinning through the air towards his brother. Paul caught the crushed cup and tossed it over his shoulder into the fireplace behind the stage. Smatterings of laughter and applause broke out. Clockwork Mouse were off to a good start, and they had not yet played a note.

Stepping on his Fuzz Face distortion pedal, Eric turned towards his amplifier and cranked up his guitar. He hit the harmonics at the twelfth fret. Feedback howled across the packed ballroom as he shook the red Rapier, fluctuating the pitch.

'It's small, but it's bloody loud!' Phil shouted joyfully from the front.

Tony clicked his sticks four times, and Clockwork Mouse plunged into the main riff from *Get Ready*. Three became four as Pattie walked on from the side of the stage. Applause and appreciative whoops broke out among the crowd. Grabbing the central mic, Pattie launched into the Motown song, her singing punctuated by Eric and Paul's backing vocals.

'Yes!' shouted Julia, spontaneously throwing her arms in the air and raining pink punch on the people behind. The band sounded great, and Pattie was their secret weapon. Having rehearsed with CM regularly over the past week, the sexy blonde would be singing lead vocals on more than half the songs. Pattie's soft voice was surprisingly strong, and her pitching confident. The male audience members wanted her, and the women wanted to *be* her. The band was an instant hit.

Eric watched Julia dancing in the front of the stage, her long black hair flying wildly. In her green ankle-length Indian dress, she was the archetypal hippie woman.

Paul sang *Jumpin' Jack Flash* with Pattie sharing Eric's mic for the choruses.

'We hope you're gonna stick with us all the way tonight...' Pattie petitioned.

'Yeah!' came the unanimous reply from the crowd.

'...all the way through to the *Midnight Hour!*'

Tony held back the tempo; the band had never nailed the groove on the Wilson Pickett song as well as they did that night. Eric pulled off the brass middle section perfectly, utilising double-stops. *Having a great audience really helps,* he thought.

Seven songs later, *the Mouse* prepared to wind-up their first set. Pattie stepped up to the mic, 'I'm gonna leave you in the capable hands of these three guys, then we'll see you again after a short break.'

Having played the instrumental many times at Tony's insistence, *Wipe Out* was a walk in the park for Eric. As fantastic as their debut set had been, he was relieved it was nearly over. During the last few songs, he had been feeling decidedly strange. The audience had adopted an odd ghostly appearance, as if the bones of their skulls were becoming visible through their skin.

Sticks flying, Tony commenced the first of his extended drum breaks.

Pattie approached Julia with a white envelope in her hand, 'I found this beneath one of the punch bowls. It has your name on it.'

Julia opened the envelope and read the handwritten note:

Dear Julia, Hope you like the acid. Have fun prick-teasing your little hippie friends. Love, Stan x

'Stan,' Julia said flatly. She handed Pattie the note. 'That solves the mystery of the pink punch. Stan spiked it with LSD and had it sneaked in somehow.'

'Shit!' exclaimed Pattie. 'That explains the weird visuals. I thought I was having flashbacks.' She sighed. 'What do we do?'

Julia thought for a moment. 'We'll have to warn everyone. There's punch left in some of the bowls and –'

'Yeah, point taken,' said Pattie. 'Okay, I'll do it.'

Applause erupted as Pattie stepped back onto the stage. The band played on. Looking back over her shoulder, the blonde motioned to the musicians to stop. The music fell apart, and there was silence. Pattie looked down at the upturned faces,

'I, uh, have to make an announcement,' she began. 'This has nothing to do with us – the organisers of the party – but as you'll have seen, there are bowls of pink punch around the room. If you've drunk any, hold on to your hat... It's been laced with LSD.'

For a few seconds, it would have been possible to hear a pin drop, then the room filled with murmuring voices.

'Look, don't worry if you've had the punch,' Pattie told the crowd. 'We're all together, and if we *stay* together, we'll be fine. Has anyone here had acid before?'

About a quarter of the room answered affirmatively; some raised their hands.

'Okay, so the party goes on,' said Pattie. 'And if you happen to feel a little... *different*, you'll know why. So don't worry about it... *and have fun!*'

A cheer went up from a small section of the crowd. Eric estimated that about a third of the guests were actually pleased to have been dosed-up with the mind-expanding drug. Others were bemused, and a significant number left the party immediately.

Paul put the music back on. His selection of *Lucy in the Sky with Diamonds* was met with mixed reactions.

The ballroom was soon half-empty. Someone had found a football in the garden and had brought it into the house. Before long, a soccer match was taking place in front of the stage with Tony at the centre.

'This isn't good,' said Julia. 'And the acid's really coming on.'

'Yeah, for me too,' Pattie replied, lighting a joint. 'Here,' she said, offering the reefer to Julia. 'This'll take the edge off.'

Pattie stepped back onto the stage, a big smile lighting her face. 'Come on, get your coats, everyone,' she shouted enthusiastically. 'Let's play football in the park!'

Somebody booted the football into the hall, and the crowd gave chase.

'I'm in goal!' Phil grinned at Pattie as they ran down the hallway among the chemically elated pack.

Taking advantage of the chaos, Eric ducked beneath the stairs. He crouched in the shadows behind the sprawling aspidistra. A handful of stragglers followed the crowd into the foggy front garden. Eric recognised Tony's voice,

'Is anyone still 'ere?' the skinhead drummer shouted back down the hallway.

Eric heard the front door bang closed, and the house fell silent. He squinted at his wristwatch, trying not to move in case there were others still inside. It was just before ten. There were more than two hours until midnight. He had plenty of time.

'Hello,' said Keith, startling Eric as he entered the kitchen. The old parrot's eyes grew larger, becoming giant yellow saucers. When Keith fluffed-out his tatty grey feathers, clouds of sparkling red and purple dust billowed into the air, dissipating like exploding fireworks in a night sky.

A magic parrot, Eric thought, leaving the kitchen and entering the ballroom. *Every home should have one.* The big room was empty. Eric saw his red guitar resting against his amp where he had left it. The low stage seemed very far away. Walking to the end of the room, he stepped up onto the platform and switched off the amplifiers. Music echoed in his head as he looked across the empty floor, hazy images of the crowded party flashing through his mind. There were five punchbowls around three sides of the room, some still containing noxious dregs of the pink hallucinogenic liquid. His thoughts returned to the task that lay ahead: a challenge he would now have to meet while under the disorienting influence of LSD.

When Eric left the ballroom, the front door at the end of the hall shot away. *Oo, stretchy hall*, he thought, trying to make light of the dark feeling of apprehension that was rising unstoppably within him. He had seen it all before, he told himself. Last time, the long tiled hallway had transformed into a tube station. No speeding underground trains had assailed him then, and illusion was not to be feared. Still, he could not quiet his beating heart. The house felt empty, a sensation he had become accustomed to, though now there was something else: an entity not human, yet still very alive. Somewhere in his subconscious mind, Eric knew that the presence of which he was about to become fully aware was that of the house itself.

Focusing on the mission ahead, he climbed the red stairs to the first floor. *Feeling better now.* Breathing steadily, he turned into the corridor and concentrated on the round window in front of him. The passage tilted, skewing to the left. Recalling the Crooked House at Blackgang Chine, Eric groped along the wood-panelled wall. Reaching his room, he twisted the doorknob. It was locked. *Purple cotton.* 'Fuck!' The keys were on Julia's dressing table. Her door was probably locked too, but he had to try.

Steeling himself, Eric returned swiftly along the first-floor corridor, then up the next flight of stairs, taking them two at a time. *Don't think, just go!* The unnerving presence was disturbingly palpable here at the top of the old house, aware of him, observing his every move. *Go on, get on with it!* The voice in his head was alarmingly real, but Eric made no attempt to dispel it. There were others waiting to talk.

Eric watched himself walk down the passageway. At the far end of the corridor, Julia's bedroom door was closed. The one opposite stood ajar.

Unwilling to turn his back on the half-open door, he reached behind him and tried the knob. As he had expected, Julia's room was locked.

Eric crossed the corridor and tentatively pushed open the door to Jack's bedroom. There was no light inside, save for that spilling in from the passage. He saw the large four-poster bed in front of him, backed against the far wall, a little to his left. 'Julia? Hello?'

Eric stepped towards the bed and peered to his right into the gloom. He could make out the Japanese figures on the black oriental screen halfway down the long bedroom. Feminine apparel and accessories were draped over the panels. Dresses, tops and skirts lay strewn about the floor. Turning around to face the door, Eric switched on the light, then flicked it off in horror as his reflection stared back at him from the enormous full-length mirror on the wall. Unable to avert his eyes, he backed into the room, bumping against the foot of the four-poster bed. He held a corner post with both hands and squinted into the darkness. Standing in front of the oriental screen was Eric Grimes, an expression of abject terror etched on his tortured face.

Eric's knees buckled. He toppled onto the large bed and crawled disoriented across the cover. Rolling onto his back, he closed his eyes, but the horrific image remained. Slowly it began to change, becoming Christ on the cross, then a fat laughing Buddha.

The familiar sound of finger snaps and a double bass crept into Eric's consciousness. Was the music real or just another of the mischievous drug's cognitive tricks? He dully acknowledged the song, associating it with the room he was in and the bed on which he lay. *Fever.* When he opened his eyes, the vision persisted, hovering in the near-darkness above the foot of the bed. Beyond the morphing hallucination, a haloed yellow flame threw flittering light across the darkened room. Reality crossed swords with illusion. In the jaundiced light, the atmosphere in the bedroom felt thick and heavy, the walls breathing gently with a life-force of their own. The music played on; *Fever.* Eric gathered his wits. The room seemed darker now. The door had been closed, excluding the light from the corridor. Standing there was a barefooted woman dressed in white, holding a burning candle. As she passed by the foot of the bed, the flame grew tall, and Eric saw her reflection traverse the floor-length mirror. His eyes fell upon her short white tennis skirt, and Eric saw his mother walking before him.

Placing the candle on the dressing table, the woman turned her head and spoke soothingly,

'Hello Jack, I've come to make you better.'

Eric watched mesmerised as the feminine apparition appeared to glide across the blood-red carpet towards him, leaving in its wake a ghostly white trail. He shuddered, unnerved by the faraway look in her eyes as Julia approached the bed, stopping within touching distance of where he lay. Shrouded by an eerie white aura, she stood with her feet apart and her arms akimbo, staring blankly down at him. Beneath her fitted white blouse, Julia's nipples stood hard and erect, projecting little pink points in the thin material. Slowly, sexually, she swivelled her hips in time with the music; *You give me fever.*

Her shoulders dipping and rising, Julia's shiny black hair fell cascading to one side then the other, her green eyes staring wildly through the tousled black strands. A smile touched the corners of her mouth as twisting and writhing, she reached down with both hands, grasping the zig-zagged hem of her short pleated tennis skirt. Eric's eyes dropped to Julia's legs as she gyrated provocatively, her pleated miniskirt rising and falling, revealing tantalising glimpses of her white cotton panties. Laying back on the four-poster bed, Eric felt a tingling surge of sexual excitement. The dancer bent over him, moving in close. 'Are you looking at me, Jack?' Julia whispered coyly. 'Are you looking at my legs, you naughty man?'

Eric lay prostrate on the bed, his libido fired and yearning for release. The LSD hallucination had evaporated, banished by the erotic intensity of Julia's miniskirt tease. Her sexy short skirts had played a central role in Eric's most private dreams, and it was Julia who had nurtured his fixation, knowingly encouraging his furtive glances. It made no difference that she addressed herself to her deceased uncle; in Eric's mind, she danced for him.

Adopting the persona of a striptease artiste, Julia slowly unbuttoned her blouse, revealing a narrow strip of pale pink flesh down the length of her chest. She leaned over Eric, placing her hands on the pillow on either side of his head. He looked at her small breasts inside her open top. He felt Julia's body heat, sensed her arousal. Long black hair brushed his cheek. In a conspiratorial tone, Julia whispered, 'You're a naughty man, Jack. I know what you do under the bedcovers when I dance for you.'

Behind the Japanese screen, Paul watched in rapt anticipation. He had spied on his mother before from this concealed place, witnessed her trancelike voodoo dance. But tonight was different. This time she was unaware that he was watching. And this time, she was not alone. Paul's raven-black wig hung long over the green-and-orange Mary Quant dress that he was wearing: his favourite, though the hemline stopped short below his waist. Leaning towards the back of the screen, Paul sidled to the edge of his chair. The enlarged gap that Julia had fashioned between two of the hinged panels afforded a clear view of the room.

The music stopped. There was a series of quiet clicks as the record-player arm returned to its starting position, then lowered back down, crackling on the spinning vinyl. *Finger snaps and stand-up bass.*

Laying back, his head pressing the pillow, Eric unbuttoned his jeans. He knew that Julia was watching him, and he knew what she desired.

His heart pounding, Paul leaned forward on his chair, peering through the gap between the panels. Lowering his silky white panties, he stared eagerly towards his father's bed.

Sweat beaded on Eric's brow. He pleasured himself as Julia moved closer, teasingly raising her pleated skirt and bumping and grinding like a burlesque dancer. Slowly and seductively, she lowered her panties, leaving them stretched taut between her parted thighs. Saliva dripped from her fingers. Julia's body jerked, then her knees sagged, and her short pleated tennis skirt danced to the rhythm of her hand.

Behind the black screen, Paul felt himself floating. His father lay on the bed, the old man's hips rising and falling in unison with Eric.

Peggy crooned drowsily, then went to sleep. The open white blouse fell from Julia's shoulders, and she crawled onto her uncle's bed.

Their bodies entwined, Eric and Julia kissed passionately as lovers for the first time.

'I know what you like,' Julia whispered breathlessly. 'I'll keep my skirt on, Eric.'

Dressing next to the big bed, Eric looked down at Julia. There was no need to wake her; he had already checked, and her bedroom door was open. Strapping on his watch, he noted the time. It would be tight, but forty minutes would be long enough for him to cycle to West Ealing and break into the office above Burton's. The hallucinogenic effects of the LSD had diminished. Still, the trip was far from over, and he knew from experience that the mind-altering drug was capable of returning with a vengeance at any time.

Closing the door quietly behind him, Eric crossed the corridor and found the key with the purple cotton among the others on Julia's dressing table. There were last-minute preparations to make before he set off. Turning back to the dresser, he picked up the door key tagged with red cotton.

Alone on her uncle's bed, Julia gazed absently at the wavering candle on the dressing table. The liaison with Eric had been inevitable, and there would be no regrets. This time, she recalled more than just fragmentary images. This time, she remembered every moment. Naked except for her tennis skirt, she looked down at her glistening chest.

Startled, Julia jerked her head to the side as Paul emerged from behind the screen wearing her Mary Quant minidress. In his long black wig, he bore a striking resemblance to his mother.

'Hello Mum,' Paul said sheepishly.

Julia closed her eyes and sighed, 'Did you like the show, Paul?'

'Very much.'

When Julia opened her eyes, her son was standing at the bedside, 'That dress is much too short on you, Paul.'

Eric checked his watch. It had taken longer than he had anticipated to assemble everything he would need. Now he would have to hurry. And to make matters worse, when Eric went to his room to collect his backpack, he noticed it was snowing again. Scampering downstairs, he turned into the hallway.

'Hello, Eric,' said Julia. Her keys dangled from her fingers. 'I'm glad I caught you. I've borrowed your RAF coat. I hope that's okay?'

Eric would have preferred to tackle his mission alone, but there was no time to argue. He grabbed his old grey duffle coat from the rack.

'How did you know?' Eric asked as they hastened along the dark public walkway.

*

'Two and two,' replied Julia. 'It's New Year's Eve; most of the country will be within earshot of a television or radio around midnight. Besides, I can read you like a book.'

Snowflakes filled the air on Hillcrest Road. They heard distant voices in the park.

'Are you sure you're okay to drive?'

'No. Are you sure you could ride a bike?'

'Not really.'

'Okay then, shut up and get in.'

Avoiding the Uxbridge Road and, she hoped, any watchful police patrol cars, Julia sped the Mini through the snowy backways as fast as she dared. Shimmering rainbow trails streamed from the amber street lights reminding Eric that the LSD was still at work in his brain.

Julia glanced at her passenger, 'You look worried, Eric.'

Eric gazed into the flurrying snow. 'I love art, but that doesn't mean mine is any good. I have opinions, but I know they're not always right.'

'You have to believe in yourself.'

'Oh, I do... But no one has a monopoly on wisdom.' Eric turned, 'If you could change one thing about humanity, what would it be?'

Julia considered the question. 'I just want people to be friends and fix the world together. A united planet is the only way we're going to achieve what's required.'

Eric nodded. 'Do you feel okay?'

'Yes... Yes, I feel fine.'

Eric understood. Julia had inherited the house, but she had paid a heavy price. He flashed back to the bedroom, wondering how many times she had re-enacted the terminal scene. *I'll keep my skirt on, Eric*. The spell had been broken. The part Julia had played in her uncle's fatal heart attack was something she must now learn to live with. *If Jack could have chosen, it's how he would have wanted to go.*

They passed only three pedestrians and four cars on the journey to West Ealing.

Julia parked on the deserted high street next to Woolworths. 'Do you have the screwdriver?'

'Yeah, I've got it.' Eric turned, grabbing his rucksack from the back seat.

'What else do you have in there, a couple of house bricks?'

'I brought sandwiches.'

'And my notes?'

'Yeah, I've got everything.' Eric rested his fingers on the door handle, 'Will you be okay?'

'I'm coming with you,' said Julia. 'I'm your lookout.'

'No you're not!'

'There's an alleyway opposite the shop; I'll hide down there. If the police turn up, I'll ring the office phone twice. Two rings, and you head straight back out of the window. Okay?'

'But how did –?'

'The Scientist was kind enough to provide me with the office number.'

'Of course he was.'

'And there's a phonebox on the corner.'

Eric looked at Julia, a smile of resignation crossing his face, 'You've thought of everything.'

'I've done my homework. Now let's get going – it's a quarter to twelve.'

The snow fell heavily, white flakes settling on Julia's black hair and across the greatcoat's shoulders. Crossing the empty high street, Eric and Julia hurried arm-in-arm to the corner of Canberra Road.

'Two rings, and you're out of there!' Julia reminded her accomplice. She kissed him quickly, then ducked into the alley at the end of the side street next to Burton's.

And all because the lady loves Milk Tray, Eric thought, hauling himself and his backpack over the wooden gate. Dropping into the yard behind the tailoring shop, he clambered up onto the annexe's flat roof. The windowsill was thick with snow. Eric took out the screwdriver. *I hope you sorted the alarm, Reg. Either way, I'm about to find out.* As the postman had promised, the sash window opened easily. No alarm bells rang.

Finding himself in the room at the back of the office, Eric stared at the grey transmitter. Childhood memories often distort reality, making things larger than they actually are, but in this instance, the machine appeared as big and imposing as he remembered. He threw the power switch. There was a low thud, and the exposed rows of glass valves glowed yellow-orange. Seating himself at the desk, Eric pulled a torch from his backpack and examined the microphone. He spread the three pages of messages on the desktop. *Here goes nothing.* Eric pressed the button marked SEND.

'Julia? Julia! Where are you?' There was panic in Eric's voice. He ran to the end of the dark alley where she had been hiding. A cat scrambled away over the fence. Turning back to the road, Eric saw Julia standing in the falling snow, orange in the glow of the sodium streetlight. Racing back to the pavement, he grabbed her by the arm, pulling her in the direction of the parked car.

'Someone came out of the house,' began Julia. 'I –'

'Never mind,' snapped Eric. 'Come on, we need to go – now!'

'There's nobody about,' protested Julia. 'But it'll be less suspicious if we –'

Halfway across the high street, Eric glanced at his watch, 'Quick, get over to Woolworths!'

The pair huddled together in the recessed shop doorway.

'Did you broadcast the messages?' asked Julia.

'Most of them,' Eric replied distractedly. 'My contribution was to take the role of editor.'

Julia nodded. 'That's fair enough, Eric. After all, you –'

On the desk in front of the big transmitter, Mickey's hands clicked together, pointing to midnight. A bright orange flash was accompanied by a thunderous explosion. The ground shook as the office windows above Burton's blew out, raining glass over West Ealing high street. Eric enfolded Julia in his arms as they watched from the safety of the doorway, experiencing the blast in glorious psychedelic slow-motion. Flames leapt from the empty window frames, bathing the shopfronts in flickering yellow light. A singed Sgt Pepper patch lay in the snow at their feet.

Eric looked down at the tiny lines on Julia's face; he had never noticed them before. Turning back towards the burning office, he sighed, 'All's well that ends well.'

'That's what they say,' replied Julia, her green eyes gleaming in the light from the fire. She took Eric's arm, 'Let's go home now.'

'Yeah. Now the future is in the hands of the people. I hope they get it right.'

DAVID GALE

Acknowledgements

My richest resource when researching the background information for this book was the works of Barry Miles. *Hippie* and *London Calling* remained on my desk throughout. Like me, *Miles* was there, though unlike me, he was smack in the middle of Underground Central. (I was nine miles west in the suburbs, though that had its happenings, too.) For detailed first-hand info on London's sixties hippie scene, check-out Barry Miles' books.

Reading Donovan's autobiography *The Hurdy Gurdy Man* gave me the idea for the beatniks at St Ives.

Those familiar with Richard Dawkins may have detected his presence here and there.

Lots of BBC documentaries: see David Attenborough's films on overpopulation and climate change.

For Edward Bernays, and for more on the psychological propaganda topics raised in this book, see *The Century of the Self* by filmmaker Adam Curtis. It was available on YouTube the last time I looked.

Finally, I should mention the Beatles. I was that spellbound kid in British Home Stores.

*

For Polly and for Malcolm, who, struggling through the early drafts, unflaggingly supported and encouraged me along the way.

For John, with whom I shared the experiences at Eel Pie Island, Hyde Park, and the Ealing and London scenes, and who kick-started my music career.

And for Chris. We talked in tongues and laughed ourselves silly.

Printed in Great Britain
by Amazon